Other titles by Emma Whittaker

Chalk Hearts

Lipstick and Lullabies

Emma Whittaker

SRL PUBLISHING

SRL Publishing Ltd
London

www.srlpublishing.co.uk

First published worldwide by SRL Publishing in 2026

SRL PUBLISHING
THINKING DIFFERENTLY, DELIVERING CHANGE

ISBN: 978-1915-073-57-0

1 3 5 7 9 10 8 6 4 2

A CIP catalogue record for this book is available from the British Library.

SRL Publishing is a climate positive publisher, offsetting more carbon emissions than it emits.

This is for Margaret, the most inspirational and wonderful mother in the world.

And in loving memory of Christina, always in our hearts x

One

In the blink of an eye, mascara was a memory, flushed away with the figure-hugging dresses and glossy red lips of the past. These days it was an accomplishment if Leah managed face cream before her daughter's tantrums reached the pitch that could send social services to the door.

She abandoned the dressing table once again, throwing on a tattered hoodie and wiping her tears with the cuffs.

'It's OK…' she sniffed, reaching for Kiki as she thrashed and howled on the floor. 'I've got you.'

She fastened her into the car seat, and even that was a chore. Arms and legs smacking into her face and her back arching in protest as she wrestled with the straps.

'You think I want to go, either?' Leah shouted, reversing off the drive and eyeing Kiki's shrivelled face in the rearview mirror. 'I can't do a thing anymore. Can't take you anywhere because you never stop!'

She slammed on the brakes just in time, as a car slowed in front of her.

'See? I can't even drive properly now.' She sobbed. 'It's me that needs a healthcare check, not you!'

Sucking in a slow breath, she moved forward and

tried to stay calm, hating herself for being so angry when Kiki was tiny and defenceless. But life was impossibly hard.

No struggling mother should suffer in silence. It was the golden rule of every parenting handbook. But the only thing lonelier than being stuck at home with a screaming baby was taking her out in public. Routine health checks like this one were the worst, forcing her into a community where she didn't belong. Delayed appointments and prolonged waiting time with Kiki bawling her eyes out in a room of quiet strangers. And they were usually other parents with more-than-perfect offspring.

Leah approached the entrance of the building, but the *Welcome* sign made her want to back away. There it was again, that logo of a woman with sunshine all around her as she cradled a tiny child.

She searched the sky, watching the pearl succumb to grey like a giant crochet throw. Her chapped fingers stung in the wind as she clenched the buggy. Pushing down with all her weight, she tilted Kiki backwards, only just managing to steer her safely into Dankton Family Centre.

Wedging the wheels into a crevice of the crowded porch, she flung a rucksack over her back. Kiki gazed up with her rounded hazel eyes and dribble oozing over her bright pink cheeks. Then her brows stiffened and Leah winced as the grizzly cry started to pierce the air.

'Shhhh…' she whispered tensely. 'You're coming out now.'

She hauled Kiki onto her hip, trying to steady her daughter's feet as they flailed madly in their frilly ankle socks.

'Oh dear!' called a chirpy voice from the reception desk. 'Are we a bit tired today?'

Leah tried to avoid eye contact.

'Kiki Frost. Here for her check.'

'Perhaps she's hungry?'

'She had porridge for breakfast and she napped on the way here. This is just what she's like.'

'Oh, she's a sassy one, is she?' The woman tickled Kiki's hand. 'There are some toys and books in the waiting area. That'll cheer her up.'

Leah gritted her teeth and pretended to appreciate the advice. 'I'll try those, then. Thank you.'

Her grateful expression sank away as soon as she turned her back. And as the growing wail of nursery rhymes chimed along the corridor, she almost thought she preferred the sound of Kiki's constant whining. It was Wednesday morning. Baby Rhyme Time taking centre stage in the other half of the waiting room. Just what people needed while they were anxiously waiting for health checks.

Leah took a seat on the quieter side where the chairs were set out for appointments, observing the ring of ecstatic parents and the oblivious babies being jiggled on their laps. She watched them moving like puppets, their hands being made to clap. *Tiny* babies, who were too young to even know what a nursery rhyme was.

She perused the cliquey mums with their dungarees, effortless bobs and happy lack of makeup, knowing their carefree world was one she could never be part of. Yes, she too had no time for cosmetics, for hours on hairstyles or dressing to impress. But the difference was, *their* babies were blissfully unaware little blobs, who probably gurgled tunefully in their highchairs and slept from the moment they were put down, whereas Kiki had always been a screamer, no matter what Leah tried to do.

This room was the same place where she had brought Kiki as a three-month-old. Where she had thought she might have fitted in when she'd tried out the baby groups. Instead, she had sat in a corner on her own, holding a dummy in Kiki's screeching mouth, while the others had thrown her the odd pitiful stare as they'd chatted about weaning and those miraculous first words.

Then there was the *Little Suckers* breastfeeding club when Kiki had gone through a latching issue. Leah had felt sure she would meet new friends who were all in the same boat. But in a room filled with mothers roaming hands-free while their babies were clamped on with slings, she had never felt more of an outsider.

'Keep her strapped to you at all times,' the founding member had instructed as she'd handed out a six-metre-long perplexity of fabric. 'You get your life back and she won't cry.'

So, that was having your life back these days. A baby bandaged to your body. Leah had left the building feeling worse than before she'd arrived. Since then, she had only returned to this place for obligatory weigh-ins and appointments.

'Alfie Kemp?'

A lively health visitor called over to a couple sitting a few seats away. They stood their son up and held his hands, but he toddled ahead unaided.

Leah looked down at the bundle in her arms. Kiki was lying almost flat across her knees and frowning back in response, the endless threat of another outburst etched over her face. If only her beauty could be matched by a calm disposition. She had astonishingly glowing olive skin and her full head of dark hair had been admired since her birth. Her two perfect hands rubbed her teddy over her eyes. Perhaps she was tired, after all.

'Kiki Frost.'

It was Janet, another health visitor, who had checked Kiki many times before. Leah heaved Kiki up her body while she balanced the bag on her back.

'So, how are we getting on?' asked Janet, beaming straight at the tot.

'Fine.' Leah feared her expression would betray her.

'Eating well? Sleeping?'

'Yes, that's all OK.'

'Good for you, Kiki!' Janet praised. 'Have you got her health record?'

Delving into the rucksack, Leah pulled out the all-important book. The one with the fluctuating weight charts that had made her feel like a failure in the early days of feeding.

'So, she's eleven months and five days now, isn't she?' Janet leafed through the pages. 'How is the crawling going?'

'Well… it isn't.'

Janet laughed. 'Still a bit wobbly, is she? Bashes into things while she's getting around. Don't worry, that's all normal.'

'No, I mean, she isn't mobile at all.'

'Right.' Janet's face fogged with doubt. 'That is a little concerning. She should definitely be on the move by now. Pop her on the couch and let's look at her.'

Leah placed Kiki down on her back and stepped away while Janet leaned in. Almost immediately, she began the jagged wriggling, with hands screwed up into two thrashing fists. Her nose reddened as the deafening sound rang out from the tunnel of her mouth.

'Oh, she is a grumpy girl!' Janet sounded surprised as she prodded at Kiki's thighs and rotated her legs in a cycling movement. Then, working her way to the shins, she stopped as she reached the feet. 'I must say, she's very flexible in the ankles. Look how far I can turn them!'

Feeling sure Janet would snap a bone, Leah flinched as the screams multiplied and she could no longer hear a word of the comments. Unbearable as it always was to deal with the grating noise, nothing was worse than watching Kiki being bent and yanked in all directions.

'All done now,' shouted Janet, so Leah grabbed Kiki and tried to calm her down.

'I'm going to refer her for physio at the hospital. She's clearly not meeting her milestones, so we'll need to get that checked out.'

'Hospital? You mean there's something wrong?'

'Not necessarily.' Janet typed some updates. 'They get there in their own time, but we need to be on the safe side.'

Leah stood Kiki up on her knees as if trying to make her bear weight, but instead she flopped down and cried even louder, kicking out hard in the air.

'But how likely is it that something isn't right?'

'I can't say… I'm sorry. This is one of those things I don't often come across.'

'How often?' Leah tried to swallow but her throat had dried out. 'How many times have you seen this before?'

Janet jotted a note in the book and clicked the top of her pen.

'In all honestly, I haven't. That's why I'm getting a second opinion.' Her expression softened. 'Please don't worry at the moment, Mrs Frost. She's in the best hands now.'

'Do you think this is why she cries all the time? She just never seems to stop.'

'What kind of crying? As if she's in some sort of pain?'

'No… but it's constant. She starts up all over again if I dare to put her down.'

Janet shot Leah a knowing look. 'Then I'm afraid you just have a very clingy baby. It's all about entertaining her.'

'Oh, I do! Every minute of every day… but it's just never good enough. I can't ever get on with anything else.'

'Well… what else is there?' Janet looked confused.

'Cooking, shopping, and sorting out the house. It's never going to get done if I don't have a chance to…'

But Janet was already shaking her head. 'That's not your responsibility anymore. You're a mother now, remember?'

'Of course, but I'm at home all day. I need to be getting other things done. I *want* to. I want to be able to at least move from room to room without being screamed at for trying.'

'Traditionally, when a woman had a baby, the family rallied round to do all the mundane tasks. The mother's only duty was to be exactly that. What you need to do is forget about everything else. Just nurture your precious daughter and let others take care of the rest.'

'It's not just housework. I can barely get ready in the mornings. Have a shower, do my makeup—'

'*Makeup?*' Janet interrupted with a patronising laugh. 'That's hardly a priority with a little cherub who depends on you.'

'I feel better with it on. You know, more on top of things when I've freshened up a bit. I know I look like I've been dragged through a hedge right now, but that's all I get time for. It's like I'm… not myself anymore.'

'And that's part and parcel of being a parent. You can't have these early years back again and the sooner you get used to that, the less pressure you'll put on yourself and the happier you will be.'

'But self-care is a basic need!'

Janet pursed her lips. 'There is always the possibility that Kiki is picking up on your resentment. You wouldn't want to be the root cause of her misery… would you?'

Leah stared in response as the guilt flooded in. She squeezed Kiki tighter, exacerbating the whimpers.

'No, of course not. I just thought life would be back to normal by now.'

'Kiss goodbye to normal and say hello to motherhood,' Janet said matter-of-factly as she shut down Kiki's file. 'Keep an eye out for the physio date. At least you'll get some answers about what's going on with her mobility.'

Leah nodded slowly as she stood up to leave. 'I'll wait to hear then. Thank you.'

'And just remember, Mrs Frost…' Janet winked. 'Let yourself go.'

The door closed with a parting bang and the corridor smudged to water. Tasting salt on her lips, Leah dabbed her eyes with the hand that clutched Kiki and rushed along the stepping-stone tiles, trying to mask the shrieking from the body pressed against hers.

Every forced vowel of the nursery rhymes came to an abrupt standstill as she slunk past the open archway of the waiting room. The permed leader's open mouth matched the pose of her hand-stuffed crocodile. Each fuzzily unbrushed head and shoved-up bun all turned to face her, covering their babies' ears as if to protect them from this ghastly noise that had wrecked their jolly session.

Leah plunged Kiki back into the pushchair, frantically untangling the seatbelt straps. Where the hell was her dummy? Forcing open the drawstring of the backpack, she felt her way through folded nappies, plastic spoons, and crinkly toys, desperately grappling for the elusive little soother.

'Sorry, but do you think you could take her outside?' The receptionist met her with an overstated cringe, her lanyard swinging as she bent across the desk. 'We don't want to disturb Baby Rhyme Time, do we?'

'No worries,' Leah answered, smacking the exit button. 'I was just leaving.'

The wind lashed out as she thumped the wheels down the ramp, fighting against gravity as the pushchair gained momentum. When her feet found the flat concrete, she slumped over the handlebars, allowing her sight to climb away into the bitter mist above. A tarry bleakness stirred its way through the fluff, like food dye tainting the freshness of a cake mix.

At the bus stop, more mums queued up in the shelter, their toddlers wide-eyed in coats and wellies, pointing to the raindrops that painted the murky glass. Their giggles echoed behind her like a sound she had never heard. The essence and ease of daily life when you had a contented child.

Clicking Kiki into the car seat, Leah folded the pushchair away and watched in the mirror as she turned on the ignition. Like magic, Kiki's eyes fluttered closed as she nestled into her bear. Leah drove slowly home through the downpour, wishing she lived further away than the five-minute trip it would take.

Skirting around the bump in the driveway, she brought the car to a halt. Perhaps she could get Kiki indoors without a sound. But the handbrake screeched much louder than she'd intended, and Kiki's yowl sounded out like a choir of fighting foxes.

Two

At lunchtime, a homemade vegetable bake was squished like playdough and slathered over the highchair. Leah wiped Kiki down and offered an apricot yoghurt, which was duly gobbled up in one precious minute of silence.

Aware of her own tearstained face, Leah remembered Janet's words about Kiki picking up on her demeanour. She handed the tot some juice and tried a funny song.

'This little piggy went to market, and this little piggy stayed at home…' she chanted, squeezing every pea-sized toe.

Kiki's forehead sprung back to perfection, the wet eyelashes spiking up as she fixed her gaze on the actions. Butterflies filled Leah's stomach as she watched her daughter listening. The mouth was curving now. Was that actually a smile? It widened… then froze. And in the next second, Kiki was screaming again while Leah's hair got soaked in apple squash.

They moved into the living room as the drink dried stickily on her head. Securing Kiki in her arms on the sofa, she powered up the TV, hoping for the respite of CBeebies. And, at last, as the colourful creatures bounced across the screen, Kiki's breathing deepened, and she fell fast asleep.

Leah sat deathly still, just calculating how many paces it would take to get Kiki into her cot. She practiced in her mind, lifting Sleeping Beauty up in her arms, navigating the creaking floorboards, fitting seamlessly through the doorway, and tucking her into bed, all without one single jerk that might obliterate the peace.

She took a breath and began, one excruciating step every thirty seconds, each movement followed by a pause to avoid the chance of Kiki stirring. It was almost surreal when she released her onto the mattress and joy rippled through as she pulled the blanket to her shoulders.

This rare freedom was exhilarating. She filled the kettle and clicked it on to boil. The bubbling was melodious in comparison with what she was used to. The light tinkle of the spoon in the mug. The plop of the teabag and the swirl of water as it stroked the leaves into a deep infusion. When milk hit the darkness like a foamy wave on sand, she inhaled the steam as the clock ticked audibly for the first time in forever.

She stared, almost in disbelief at having made a complete cup of tea. Then, fuelled with accomplishment, she seized the handle of the snack cupboard. There stood the shiny packet of unopened custard creams. If she could just pick it up without the rustling. Actually manage to tear the dotted seal and take a bite of even one, she would feel on top of the world.

Swooping in, she pinched the corner of the wrapper. It hovered back and forth in her grip, brushing precariously against the threat of tin cracker boxes and scrunching crisp multipacks. She watched with childlike hope, as if she had slotted her last coin into a toy-grabbing machine. Rejoicing in the gentle thud as she landed it on the worktop, she prepared herself for transporting both the tea and biscuits to the living room.

A tray would be the answer, so she slid it out from

the side of the microwave, but the rim hooked onto a chopping board and sent it whacking to the ground. Her heart plummeted as she watched the baby monitor, knowing the short distance between the kitchen floor and Kiki's room at the top of the stairs. The purple screen flickered. Leah waited with dread, processing the cooling tea and wondering if she'd ever get to drink it.

Exhaling as the hush crept on, she kicked off her slippers and edged her way to the sofa with the silent footsteps of her socks. More oversized critters in fur suits sang a shrill tune through the TV screen. She zapped them away with the remote, feeling triumphant at the news programme in all its blissful boringness.

A good ten minutes had passed now, and Kiki was on a world record. Leah turned her attention to the tray, pinning the custard creams down like a predator to its catch. The sandwiched sweetness revealed itself as vanilla dusted her nostrils. She plucked the first oblong from the stack and dunked it into the bath of tea, before sliding it between her lips where it melted like heaven on her tongue.

She had another. Then a third. *Three* biscuits, all devoured in a haze of uninterrupted glory. Each slurp of tea eddied away like a calming stream down her throat. She sank back and closed her eyes as if she were on a spa day.

'And in other news, the actor Gideon Knight has taken the stand at his defamation case against…'

'No….!' Leah hissed as the sound boomed out. Diving onto her side, she grabbed the TV remote from underneath her thigh, where she had inadvertently pressed it at the precise point of the volume control.

Drilling a finger on *Mute*, she knew it was too late. Flashes of purple lit up the monitor and gurgling peppered the speaker. Leah checked the video screen to see Kiki babbling to her toys. Not even fifteen minutes of nap time. But this was happy cooing because Kiki was distracted. Only catching sight of Leah would set her off crying again.

All the drive to finish her tea was quickly going down the pan. Leah sighed glumly at the liquid as it sloshed like soup in the lower half of her mug. Yes, Kiki was awake, but now it would be even harder to relax, knowing the slightest noise would definitely be heard.

For a few moments, she stayed glued to the sofa, unable to move for fear of Kiki hearing a sound. But the chatty decibels continued to sail from the monitor, and Leah slowly got to her feet in a bid to start some chores.

There was an empty laundry basket in the utility room, just beyond the kitchen. Leah went to fetch it, imagining the achievement of getting one load of washing done. Even Eric's face might light up at the thought that there was a proper wife somewhere deep inside her. That this was the start of a marital home which would match the impeccability of his mother's.

Leah took a glimpse up the staircase and eyed the half-open doorway of Kiki's room. She had to make this move with utmost precision and get herself past the gap without a shadow of attention. Then she could pounce on the overflowing clothes, spilling from the wicker boxes just inside the bathroom.

She dropped to her knees, pushing the basket ahead of her up the stairs. Thanks to the carpet, it sailed along like a boat, and she made it to the landing in one piece. She stayed on all-fours and stopped at Kiki's room, where the warbling voice rang out at its loudest into the hallway. The solid end of the cot was covering Leah from view, so she boldly shuffled forward, but something stabbed her leg. Trying with all her strength not to yelp out in pain, she retrieved the small wooden train and placed it down into the soft lap of a ragdoll.

A couple more slithers and Leah made it past the doorway, her sight now focused on the laundry stash in the bathroom. As the fuzzy towels crept closer into view, Leah neared the end of her mission. Finally leaning on the cold porcelain wall, she bent gleefully over the washing pile.

Then the phone blasted out from Leah's bedside table.

It was like her world had turned upside down. That her wondrous snippet of normal life had been stolen away by a ringtone. Should she even answer it and let Kiki hear her voice? Then again, if it rang for much longer, the object of doing that would be defeated.

Leah leapt across the hallway, collapsing onto the bed as she took the call.

'Hello…' she mumbled.

'There you are!' said her mother, Cheryl. 'Been ringing your mobile non-stop!'

'Sorry, I'm… just upstairs.'

'Nothing to worry about, anyway. Just to say that I've bought this gorgeous little frock for Kiki. It's the most fabulous pastel blue. I got it in a bigger size so she can grow into it. Can't wait to see it on her!'

'Thanks Mum, sounds lovely.' Leah closed the bedroom door with a toe.

'Are you OK? You sound a bit quiet.'

'Yes, fine.'

'What is it then?'

'Nothing.'

'I can hear it in your voice. You're all distant… Leah, what's going on?'

'It's just, I'm trying not to disturb…'

'Kiki!' Cheryl gasped. 'Oh, darling, she's asleep, isn't she? I'm so sorry.'

'Not exactly,' whispered Leah. 'I just don't want her to hear me or she'll…'

A whine floated out from the direction of Kiki's room.

'Oh, please, no.' Leah almost dropped the phone as she tossed herself onto her pillows. More tears burned her eyes, and she held her breath to suppress them.

'What is happening?' rasped Cheryl's voice from Leah's outstretched wrist. 'Leah… talk to me.'

The room blurred like it was spinning as Kiki's roar swept in. And Leah drowned in the flood of it all as the turbulence took hold. She forgot about Cheryl on the other end of the line. The washing basket that she hadn't even filled with so much as a single bra. Instead, she stumbled to her feet and faced the full brunt of the racket head on.

She pushed open Kiki's door and looked over the cot bars. There she was, all red-faced with her shock of chocolate hair, having wriggled out of the blanket. Clocking Leah coming towards her, she kicked the wooden railings and screamed all the more.

'It's OK, I'm here.' Leah put on a smile as she lifted her out of the cuddly toy chaos and took her over to the window. 'Is that better?'

But Kiki slammed her body around and headbutted Leah's chin, whimpering furiously and refusing to calm down.

'Hey, Kiki-Koo, look!' sniffed Leah, blotting her eyes. 'What's that? It's a squirrel!'

For a split second, Kiki listened as Leah tapped the glass. But as the squirrel danced away out of sight, the cries returned with an even stronger vengeance. Leah's arms were getting bruised from Kiki's flinging, so she slid a playmat into the middle of the carpet and placed her gently on top of it.

'Tell you what we'll do...' Leah fought to make her voice sound animated as she turned to the shelf and gripped a handful of books. 'Let's have a read!'

She sprawled out on the floor next to her daughter and opened *Bunty Bunny and the Curious Carrot*.

Deep in the veggie patch
What can Bunty see?
A big purple beetroot
And crunchy green peas...

Kiki batted the page with her hand over and over again. Then she took hold of the paper and ripped it in a rage.

'Now, that's not very good, is it?' scolded Leah as she tried to salvage the picture. 'No, Kiki... Nice story.'

Leah was determined to distract her with the words.

Tomatoes, red and juicy
The sweetcorn, gold and tall
But the yummy orange carrot
Is the best one of all...

Kiki smacked the book shut on Leah's fingers. Letting out an agonising squeal, she doubled over as the pain throbbed through. Kiki flopped down flat on her back, taking hold of a plastic toy and hurling it over the room.

'Get on with it, then.' snapped Leah. 'You don't want to sleep. You don't want to play or read books or... or anything.'

Leaving Kiki on her mat, Leah clicked the baby gate shut. Then she stormed back to the bathroom, insistent she would at least get the whites ready to shove in the washing machine.

Rifling through the endless clothes, she battled to concentrate on the simple task in hand while Kiki's unrelenting screams continued their attack on her eardrums. In went a flannel and various pairs of socks. Six of Eric's trunks and two or three of his work shirts. But for every white item she pulled out of the pile, something brightly coloured fell into the basket, until Leah finally lost the plot and broke down in a barrage of tears.

Dragging herself out of the bathroom, she was hit by another blast of howling as Kiki shrieked through the doorway of the nursery.

'Kiki, please!' Leah choked out the words as she crawled like a beaten animal in the opposite direction. 'I can't take this anymore… please… please…'

But it was no use. Kiki just wailed at an earth-shattering pitch and there was nothing Leah could do to block out the noise.

With a last shred of strength, she inched into her bedroom, digging her nails in the duvet as she slowly lost control. The recurring buzz of the phone bleeped in vain from its quilted burial place and an ache seared her forehead as she reached out for the wardrobe. She pushed the hinge open at the corner nearest the carpet, falling inside the confines of the dark closet walls. Then, hunching up in the space below the dresses she used to wear, she turned away from the outside world as the door clicked shut.

Three

'Eric, it's Cheryl…' The familiar voice met Leah's ears in fragments. 'I'm round at yours. I think you need to come home.'

Leah blinked until Cheryl's figure solidified, her mauve jacket swishing as she jiggled Kiki on her hip.

'No, Kiki's fine,' she continued. 'But it's Leah. She's not right at all… I've found her here in a terrible state.'

There was now a pillow behind Leah's head and her feet poked out of the open wardrobe door, resting on piled-up cushions.

'Blacked out, I think. Or maybe just a very deep sleep…. No, she's awake now,' Cheryl eyed her as she slowly came around. 'Just about.'

'Mum… what are you doing here?' murmured Leah, sitting upright.

Cheryl motioned for her to lie back down.

'I don't *know* yet, Eric. But she needs you.'

'No, it's OK.' Leah waved drowsily. 'I'm fine. I'll be… fine.'

'How long is your meeting, then? Can't you get out of it?' Cheryl asked curtly, perching on the bed. 'I see…' She nodded. 'Well, I'll stay with her until you're home. Just get a move on as soon as you can.'

Cheryl hung up and raced over to the wardrobe.

'My poor darling, are you OK?'

Leah nodded carefully, feeling dizzy each time she did so.

'Do you need me to call an ambulance?'

'No… nothing like that.'

'Right. Stay there and don't move.' Cheryl directed. 'I'm putting Kiki in her BouncyBop chair and then we'll get you more comfortable.'

Fifteen minutes later, Leah was lying on the sofa all plumped up with pillows and the fleece throw keeping her warm. Kiki was occupied with a soggy chunk of rusk and Cheryl brought in a hot water bottle with a sugary malted drink.

'Thank goodness I came round.' She pressed a cool hand against Leah's face. 'I knew something wasn't right.'

'I fell asleep, Mum, that's all. It's just been a tiring day.'

But Cheryl was already shaking her head. 'Don't brush this off. There's more to it than that.'

'Honestly, Kiki's just a bit grouchy and—'

'You were crashed out in the wardrobe, for heaven's sake!'

Leah was too groggy to argue any longer. 'She wouldn't stop crying and I just…'

'Couldn't take anymore?'

Sighing in defeat, Leah covered her face with her hands.

'No one could blame you. We all know what she's like! I've had three, remember, and none of you were quite as dramatic as Miss Moody Pants here.'

'I tried everything, but she wasn't interested. I'm just no good at this, Mum.'

'Rubbish! Of course you are,' soothed Cheryl. 'In fact, you were probably a bit too good at first, and that's why she always plays up when you're around.'

'What do you mean?'

'Well, you wouldn't put her down for the first few weeks as a newborn. All that co-sleeping and clinging to her night and day. She's used to having you at her beck and call.' Cheryl leaned backwards to check on Kiki, who was whingeing intermittently. Then she turned to Leah and took hold of her hand. 'What you need is a break.'

'Not much chance of that,' Leah replied with a yawn. 'I've got a long wait until pre-school.'

'No,' Cheryl responded firmly. 'You need to do something now. Something that would get you away from all this, at least on a regular basis.'

'I can't exactly take myself off on holiday. Or, you know, leave home.'

Cheryl gazed with meaningful eyes, tucking a strand of hair behind her daughter's ear. 'You could get a job.'

Leah recoiled like the suggestion had wounded her.

'Oh, what's that look for? You know it makes sense.'

'I can't go back to work, Mum. They wouldn't give me part-time hours.'

'Who says you have to do journalism?' Cheryl asked. 'What *I'm* talking about is an easy little shop role. Anything to get you out of the house.'

'But she needs me here. That's the whole point of being a parent, right?'

'And you still can be! Just a couple of days a week won't make any difference to Kiki.'

'Who's going to look after her?'

'Me, of course. Alan and I can have her on weekdays and if you find a Saturday job, she'll just be at home with Eric, won't she?'

Leah hugged her hot water bottle and glanced guiltily at Kiki, feeling her heart melt at the rare image of cuteness. Her eyes shone peridot in their dreamlike stance as she rubbed the mushy snack over her tongue. For Leah to abandon her now would be the glaring proof that she had screwed up as a mother. It was unimaginable to think of dumping her on others when it had been *her* who had brought this child into the world. To prioritise anything else over that was plain selfish and no matter how difficult Kiki was to deal with, it would be criminal to make that someone else's problem.

'I know it's a lot to take in right now, but just think about it.' Cheryl stepped next door into the kitchen. 'I'll get some dinner on.'

There was a stock of Cheryl's homemade pasties in the freezer and plenty of baked beans to go round. As the comforting smell of pastry puffed into her lungs, Leah closed her eyes, wishing she always had the company. Just the simplicity of adult conversation and help on hand without even having to ask, made all the difference in these torturous times.

'And here he is now,' called Cheryl with a flap of the blinds. 'He's just trying to park without knocking over next door's wheelie bin.'

Eric's keys turned in the lock and he put down his bag in the hallway.

'I know when you're around,' he gave Cheryl a kiss. 'Dinner would never be this organised normally!'

Leah heard Cheryl tut at the comment.

'She's in there.' Then her voice lowered to a whisper. 'I found her in the *wardrobe*, Eric.'

'Hey…' he said gently, coming into the room. 'What happened to you?'

'Just a bit of a bad day, I guess.' Leah nodded her head towards Kiki.

'Playing up again, is she?' He mock scowled at his daughter. 'What have you been doing, Pickle?'

Kiki giggled for the first time that day and bounced

excitedly at Eric's words.

'She seems OK now. Might just be another tooth coming through.'

'No, Eric. She was beyond cranky.' Leah felt annoyed at Kiki's convenient transformation. 'Non-stop crying and it just got too much.'

'Maybe it's the way you handle it. She knows how to press your buttons.'

'Why is it always *my* fault? You try having her for a day when she's got a bee in her bonnet.'

'I don't mean that you're to blame. But you do need a coping mechanism.'

'That's exactly what I've been saying.' Cheryl placed a tray of food in each of their laps and took a bowl over to feed Kiki in her chair. 'She can't keep this up, Eric. You have to admit, you have a little live wire here.'

Eric cleared his throat. 'Look, I know where this is going. You think I should cut my hours and be around for Kiki… I just don't think I'd get much done. Not if she's kicking off all the time.'

Leah expected nothing less from Eric. As the Director of a media design company, he was literally married to his office.

'No one is asking you to do that,' replied Cheryl. 'You'd only make things worse if you were moaning about the disturbance. No…' she winked at Leah. 'We've had a much better idea.'

'Mum, I never said—'

'Leah is going to look for a job. Have a break for a few hours a week.'

Eric's eyes widened and Leah waved dismissively.

'We've been through this already. I don't want to be a part-time parent, at least not when Kiki is so young.'

'Hang on a minute,' Eric set his plate aside and stepped across to Leah, perching on the arm of the sofa just behind her head. 'It could be just what you need.'

'I need to stay at home. I *have* to do this for Kiki.' A tone of exasperation sounded in Leah's voice. 'I just want to have a happy kid, like everyone else.'

'You wouldn't be letting her down,' soothed Eric, squeezing her shoulder. 'In fact, it might be good for her to spend some time with her Nana.'

'And her dad, if it happens to be on a weekend.' Cheryl chipped in.

Eric glanced at Kiki, nodding in agreement.

'I can't leave her now!' Leah almost shouted. 'There's… something wrong with her.'

Eric shuffled to her side. She welled up again, blinking Cheryl's worried expression into view.

'Wrong? What do you mean?'

'The routine check today…'

'Oh, sorry!' Eric clapped a hand over his face. 'Forgot to ask how it went. Manic day with staff training.'

'She's been referred to the hospital because she isn't mobile. The health visitor was looking at her legs… saying she is too flexible.' Leah began to sob. 'What if she can't ever walk?'

'Not necessarily.' Eric put an arm around her. 'Pete at work said both his were late. Lucas was nearly two before he even took a step. They all do it differently, remember?'

'But Janet said this is a first. She has never seen another baby like this.'

'Doesn't say much for her experience, then!' Cheryl piped up. 'Just because *she's* never seen it, that doesn't mean there's definitely something wrong.'

'I wouldn't even worry until we've spoken to a specialist,' said Eric. 'Right now, this is only an initial flagging up.'

'Exactly. Even more reason to go and find a job. The perfect way to take your mind off things.' Cheryl spooned Kiki the last scrape of food and started to collect the plates. 'Just give it some thought.'

Leah said nothing. There was no more energy to protest, and she was far too overwrought and emotional to continue the conversation.

'Anyway, I'd better get back to Alan if that's OK. We've got to get those plants ready for the church sale on Friday.'

'Come on then, Twinkle Toes!' Eric dived at Kiki and lifted her out of the chair. 'Let's get you in that bath before you start your antics again.'

'Thanks for everything, Mum.' Leah kissed Cheryl lazily.

'That's what I'm here for,' she answered with a grin. 'Now, put your feet up and let Eric see to Kiki. You'll feel much better after a good rest.'

Eric and Kiki saw Cheryl out of the door and Leah was left to relax on the sofa while the bedtime routine was taken care of. She dozed sporadically, only half conscious of Eric warming milk as he carried Kiki around in her yellow chick sleepsuit. The bedtime stories merged into each other without Leah even hearing they had ended.

A nudge woke her, and she peeled her cheek from the sofa, squinting through the darkness.

'She's off,' whispered Eric, with an open shirt and arms finally free of Kiki. 'Come on you.'

He pulled her to her feet and gathered the pillows to take back upstairs. Leah threw on her saggy pyjamas and sank so deep into bed, it almost felt like a swamp. Her lids drooped magnetically over her eyes and she breathed away the day, the world, and every waking moment of endurance.

The duvet lifted behind her and Eric's hand brushed through her hair, lingering at the top of her neck.

'Feel better for a break this evening?'

His words jerked her awake and her tight, tear-stained skin would only allow a muffle in response.

'Don't ever say you're a failure,' he continued, resting on her shoulder. 'You're doing just fine.'

She nuzzled the pillows in a bid to get some sleep. But Eric's arm slipped around her waist, and he kissed the nape of her neck. She tensed her stomach, as always, to disguise the baby weight as he ran his hand along the front of her. The light was off, but that didn't change her snotty face and the dry slick of apple juice, still clinging to her hair. Or the fact that she hadn't shaved her legs for literally weeks. Instinctively, she covered her chest with an elbow, shielding the unflattering shape that her body now made in a lying position.

This was the way she responded now at the slightest hint of intimacy. Because having a baby had not just interfered with the practicalities of a quick shower. She was physically ravaged. An emotional wreck. And she no longer knew the skin she was living in.

Her textbook pregnancy had ended in a traumatic forty-hour labour, stalled by Leah's impossibly slow dilation. Throughout the ordeal, she had stood her ground, refusing epidurals and endless offers of pain relief, until Kiki had arrived with forceps via a surgical cut reaching the top of Leah's thigh. A cut that had made her unable to move for the first three weeks, and that even her GP had gasped at during her postnatal assessment.

In the almost year since the birth, everything had healed in time. Except the feeling that she was nothing more than a machine. The carrier and grower. The milk factory. The comforter through tiredness, bugs, and boredom. The earpiece for the hours of constant crying. And the prospect of adding 'pleasurer' to that list from the moment each day was done, only served to make Leah feel even more of a utility.

Stiffening as Eric nestled further into her back, she exaggerated heavy breaths to make him think she was asleep. Then her limbs flopped like jelly as he finally rolled away and the starlight through the window turned to dust in the blinks of her tears.

Four

Leah woke to a strange sense of calmness. The autumn wind played with the half-open curtains and apart from the intermittent chirping of sparrows, this was the only sound creeping into her ears. It was bizarre, this feeling that she had slept for as long as she'd needed. Like the world had gently waited until she was ready to face it again.

She stretched to check the time on her phone, unable to believe it was nine-thirty already. There was also a message from Cheryl, so she squinted blearily at the words:

Hope you had a good night's sleep. Eric didn't want to disturb you, but he's brought Kiki to me for the day just to give you some space. All fine here. Eaten well and she's got the toys out. Will walk her around the lake soon and Eric is picking her up after work. Do something nice! Love you.

x

It was tempting to collapse back into bed while she could. But Leah knew she should use the time wisely to make the most of the freedom.

The sheer joy of cereal flakes that were

uninterruptedly crunchy, and warm coffee at the bottom of a cup, felt like an entirely new experience. She lingered at the table in her dressing gown, reading the news on her laptop. As she scrolled through the headlines, various adverts kept popping up in the way. Clothes store discounts for twenty-somethings. Shiny new cars she would wreck in five minutes with sprays of baby juice and half-open packets of cheesy puffs. Job websites.

She clicked the crosses in the corners of each ad, determined not to waste the day searching through the vacancies. But even breakfast in total peace was just too therapeutic to ignore. There was only one way to reclaim this independence, at least on a weekly basis. What harm could it do, just to look?

Visiting the next job site that flashed up on her screen, Leah filtered a search. The magazine editorial work she had done since leaving university was clearly not an option, as the only vacancies available were all full-time. Keeping an open mind, she cleared the box that specified a job title and instead opted for anything which would fit in with her life.

There was plenty on offer at supermarkets, but Leah had been there before. She thought of her stint at Wilbury's as an evening job in her Sixth Form years. The injuries she'd suffered from the over-laden cages and their defective wheels. The pungent smell of smashed pickle jars that festered for hours after a breakage.

Caring and cleaning jobs were abundant in the search results, but still for too many days a week. Evening bar staff were in demand, but then Leah would never see Eric. Every role working from home was full-time, which would be a non-starter with Kiki around. Cold calling? No chance. Selling double glazing? Think again.

It was the same old story on every site she tried, but at least she could tell Eric and Cheryl that she'd searched with no luck.

A chime sounded from her phone, distracting her from the thought.

Everything OK? Hope you got my message. x

Remembering she hadn't replied to Cheryl, Leah keyed out a response.

Sorry Mum! Slept for ages and just had breakfast. Checked for jobs but there's nothing. Thanks so much for looking after Kiki. Hope she is behaving. x

Keep searching! You never know what might be available. x

But after an hour of trawling, Leah was fed up. Instead, it was time for a decent shower and, at long last, the chance to wash yesterday's juice out of her hair.

As she lathered shampoo over her scalp, the sensual notes of sage and rhubarb mingled with the bergamot base. The matching conditioner made each strand feel like velvet and the body wash caressed her skin with ginger and pink grapefruit.

This was the reason she had waited to use the gift set. It had no place in a two-minute wash with the company of a wailing baby. For the first time in months, she was transported back to the days when she'd had proper time for a pamper. And as the sweet simplicity of a long shower took hold, it made her realise just what she had been missing. How much of herself she had given up in order to prioritise other people.

Finding the fluffiest towel on the rack, she enrobed her body in its warm cocoon and her cares seemed to drift away. This was how babies felt. Wrapped up in a blanket and someone's arms, their every need being met.

Then they would emerge into a frantic world of rules and responsibility, where their carefree spirits must bow down to the restriction and sacrifice of adult life.

She stood in front of the mirror and let the towel fall to the ground, inspecting her new physique, each part of it marred by motherhood. The several months of 'breast is best' that had left them less than perky. The 'bun in the oven' tummy that had never quite snapped back. The scar where she had not widened enough to give birth without being butchered. And the fine lines that stress and neglect had etched on her forehead in the aftermath.

Leah followed her outline until she was staring directly at her toes and the sharp chill of ceramic tiling felt cold against her feet. Stepping into the bedroom where the fuzzy carpet met her, she was faced with yet more evidence of the person she had left behind. Slowly, she perused her belongings, feeling like a ghost visiting its past.

The feeble swish of florals and chiffons caught her eye through the closet door. Each blouse and smart dress relegated to the back since the last day she had dressed for the office. Scarves, overcoats, and high-heeled shoes. They all belonged in a bin bag, ready to throw in the clothes bank. And the handbags in their patent rows, with decorative clasps and chain straps. These days, her purse and phone were tossed into a unicorn backpack, stuffed with nappies and muslin cloths.

Her dressing table was pristine. Because nothing ever got used. The makeup brushes were coated in dust, not the pink dip of blush from times gone by. In the drawer, her eyeshadow palettes were still in their packaging, yet to be blended and brought to life. The perfume bottles, just a squirt or two short of being full, stood aimlessly like ornaments. What good was gardenia and sandalwood when it was masked by mucky hands and sour milk burps?

As the remnants of her former self continued to flood her vision, she found some clothes from the heap on the ottoman and blasted her hair dry in two minutes. Although there was more than enough time, at last, to plaster herself in cosmetics, she couldn't spend any longer here in the melancholy realm of reality.

She closed the front door, not sure where she was going. A blizzard of leaves pinged from the windscreen as she drove along the tarmac, struggling to keep her eyes on the road when the sky wound over her in tentacles of ink.

Nearing the end of the roundabout queue that led in three different directions, she took a left turn and headed for Ropeshore-By-Sea.

As the traffic stalled on the bridge, Leah gazed out across Coombe River, watching the surface crinkle as the tide came in. Small planes dived and soared from the airfield that lay just over to the west. She followed with her eyes as their wings scored the rainclouds and showery droplets flecked the ground as if they had been sliced from a packet.

She parked outside the library and ambled through the cemetery of the fifteenth-century church. The Ropeshore Square shopfronts were concealed by the flapping market stall covers. Paper bags rustled as the sellers twisted them closed and their voices yelled of breads and chutneys, and fresh catches of the day via the harbour just ahead.

The last time Leah had even set foot in *MochaBlock*, a two-month-old Kiki was so minuscule, her head had only reached halfway up her pram. Managing to lull her down to a distant grizzle, Leah had seated herself cautiously in the corner, waiting for the tendrils of heat to diminish on her cappuccino. Just seeing if the feat of a sip could turn into finishing a whole cupful, and she could finally feel like other mothers did. Mothers with babies who snoozed at the drop of a hat and whose peaceful coffees were a normal way of life.

But no. Her lips had barely brushed the foam when Kiki had started the writhing. Then the screaming had persisted until Leah pulled the scrunched-up infant into her arms, trying to bob her up and down while fending off the tuts and frowns, and the crockery being clattered in annoyance around the room. Shaking heads, whispers, earphones being plugged in and even customers leaving. And away Leah had skulked with Kiki on her shoulder while she'd steered the empty pram, the steam fading flatly into her abandoned drink.

Today, though, was different. The nutty aroma of roasting beans welcomed her in like open arms, and the layered wafts of patisserie treats were surpassing the outdoor fish stench. There was the corner where she had sat all those months ago, and now she would settle in the same spot again, as if to undo the memories of that last stressful day.

Boats swayed in the smoky water as the breeze jolted them on the mooring line. Through a large window bejewelled with rain, Leah watched the seagulls defying the weather in their quest to scavenge for scraps outside the fish and chip shop. She ripped the end from her croissant, savouring the icing sugar and almonds on her tongue, and the airy spoons of coffee froth blitzing on the roof of her mouth. She felt almost naked as she sat there, with two free hands and not a pushchair handle or squishy toy in sight.

Her phone started ringing, so she pulled it from her pocket.

'Hey, it's me,' Eric's voice was low. 'Can't be long. Got a webinar in a minute. Just making sure you're alright.'

'I'm fine. Tired but I'll live.'

'Well at least she's off your hands for a bit.'

Leah looked at her watch. How could it be midday already? A few more hours and that would be the end of it.

'Anyway, I said I'd meet Pete later to watch *Temper Alley 2*. There's a showing at seven. You'll manage putting Kiki to bed, won't you?'

There was silence.

In an instant, all the lightness and freedom slipped away. Leah stared at the trickling water, dripping in a slither off the kerb and into the drain. If only this break could have truly lasted all day, right up until she would flop into bed. She had hoped that Eric would be seeing to Kiki this evening, letting Leah charge up with energy for a full-on day tomorrow.

A microwave meal. Music in the bath. Morning to bedtime in complete and utter peace so she could really make the most of the time completely uninterrupted. But now, the day was racing by, and it would come to an abrupt end from the minute Eric got home with Kiki and handed her straight over to Leah. His day out of the house at work would continue conveniently until late at night when Kiki would be fast asleep by the time he rolled in.

'Right, OK.'

'What's the matter? I don't have to go if you'd rather...'

But at the same time, the guilt was rearing its head again. She would love to be assertive right now and extend her free time the way she craved. Yet the thought of ruining Eric's night was enough to make her back down. He worked so hard and deserved the break just as much as she did, but if only he could get inside her head and know how desperately she needed it too. If only he had the initiative to see things from her point of view.

'No, you go.' Leah sighed inwardly. 'I'll have had a breather all day. It's only bedtime.'

'I'll be straight home afterwards. Promise.'

'I said it's fine, really.'

'Great. Best be off anyway. See you later.'

'Bye.'

She waited for him to hang up before opening her social media apps and checked for anything interesting.

There was a notification she had been tagged in a post by her cousin, Nicole. Opening the link, her heart stopped as her eyes fell on an old photo of the two of them on a night out a good ten years ago:

Leah Frost *OMG look at us! This was such a good night. Remember when you were so drunk, you tried to open the door of the taxi with your keys?! Those were the days. Shame we're mums and can't have a laugh like this anymore. All boring from now on! X*

She gazed at the picture. At the image of herself she had forgotten had ever existed. Her hair was glossy and full of volume because she'd spent hours styling it. Her eyes looked huge, lids heavily caked in glittery eyeshadow, thick liner, and a double coating of dramatic mascara. The care she had taken over contouring had sculpted her cheekbones and there had been time and effort put into her lips, with pencil, brushed on lipstick, and even a layer of gloss.

In a second, something clicked. There had to be some way of saving herself before she hit rock bottom of this downward spiral. Perhaps a job really would be the solution, and she had simply searched in the wrong place earlier. Maybe she needed to find a role where she absolutely *had* to look good. Something that would reignite her long-lost love of beauty and cosmetics.

Loading up an online search, she began to find company websites, checking each one she came across for vacancies in her area. Some were too far away, and others were too technical to even understand. She racked her brains, thinking of all the brands she had ever used or tried. Finding a list of the bestsellers, she worked through the alphabet and found nothing from A to the start of the E's.

Reaching EdenCore, she almost gave up. If the other companies had nothing suitable, then this one definitely wouldn't. Classy, iconic, and all naturally sourced, it was very unlikely they would have any vacancies to fill. Nevertheless, she scrolled her way down to the jobs section at the very bottom of the page, fixing her sight on one particular description:

Creative Consultant
Glovers department store, Starlingford

Do you have a passion(fruit) for skincare? Would you be glad(iolus) to work for a pioneer of the industry? Could you suc(seed) in making our products shine? Do you want (syca)more out of life? Then we are (root)ing for you!

In this dynamic and exciting role, you will make our ranges stand out from the crowd with your wealth of knowledge, eye for detail, and love of natural ingredients. You will be a team player who is impeccably presented, with artistic flair, a fighting spirit, and an irresistible way with words!

Leah's eyes drifted over the write-up as she tossed more croissant shreds into her mouth. As if *she* could ever do something like that. But as she read the details again and again, and she saw that the hours would fit in with childcare, it slowly became more possible.

After all, she wasn't just a tired, lonely, suffering parent. She had also been a journalist with nearly ten years of experience under her belt. Although she hadn't specialised in anything to do with beauty, she knew how to make even the dullest products come to life.

She sent the application form there and then, as a sliver of hope took hold. Then she polished off her coffee, thrilled that she'd managed to finish it this time.

Five

It felt strange to drive the car wearing a thin pair of tights and her court shoes teetering on the pedals. As air wafted from the heater and mingled with her wrists, a wave of her jasmine and cedarwood fragrance hit the undertones of a half-eaten Bolognese squeezy pouch.

But Kiki's seat was empty today and Leah arrived outside the house with only her handbag to carry. The neighbours were chatting across the road and they stared back as they clocked her. Then June nudged Bill and they both smiled widely when they realised she was waving.

'I get it,' she whispered, too far away to be heard. 'You didn't think I owned anything other than jeans and trainers.'

For once, it was good to attract attention without the reason being a screaming child. And with any luck, Cheryl would have dropped Kiki back to Eric and there'd be something tasty waiting in the oven.

'Honey, I'm home!' Leah announced theatrically as she opened the front door, feeling for a moment how Eric did every day.

'At last.' He hitched Kiki up with his back turned and wiped the worktop. 'She just can't be put down for a second. I could hardly nip to the bathroom or even check my emails. Every time I stepped away, she started up all over again.'

'Welcome to my life.'

'It's hard for me too, you know…' Eric jerked around in annoyance, then stopped as his eyes fell on her. 'Wow!'

'What?'

But Leah knew exactly what. It was an outfit she had bought literally years ago but life had never let her wear. A fitted navy shift dress and a pearl-grey bolero that buttoned chicly over to one side. She was still getting used to the feel of mascara, weighing heavily on her lashes when she blinked, and the usual mousy ponytail had been swept up in a clip, leaving neat strands gently dusting her jawline.

'You look nice.'

Leah registered the compliment. 'Obviously not my usual style of daywear.'

'How did it go, anyway?'

'Well, nothing went drastically wrong, but who knows?'

'Surely you've got an inkling.'

'They seemed to like me, so if that's anything to go by, I'd say there's a chance.'

'Did they grill you with awkward questions?'

'Not at all. They just showed me pictures of the products and filled me in about the job. It does sound amazing!'

'See what I said? You'll love getting stuck into all that. Who did the interview?'

'The EdenCore manager, Rhona, and the Glovers boss, Dawn.'

'They were alright, were they?'

'Yes… *they* were.'

'Ugh, here we go.' Eric tutted yet smiled fondly at his wife. 'Did you blow it or something?'

'No!' Leah scowled. 'Nothing like that. It's just… well… the description in the advert isn't exactly accurate.'

'Too technical? I wouldn't worry. They'll train you on the job.'

'I wouldn't describe it as creative, Eric. I'd basically be on the counter with a sales target.'

'Come on, Leah, it's not computer parts or windows that you're flogging. You love all this beauty stuff, so you can pass that onto the customers.'

'Listen to you!' she smirked back. 'Anyone would think you wanted me out of the house.'

'And I do… but not like that! I just know you'll be happier with something else in your life.' He waggled Kiki's hand as he spoke. 'And if she misses you for a few hours, she might just start behaving.'

'That'll be the day.' Leah carried her shoes upstairs as she went off to get changed. 'Anyway, let's not jump the gun. I haven't even got the offer yet!'

She hung her jacket back up in the wardrobe and reluctantly unzipped the dress, already missing the feel of the skirt hugging her hips to perfection.

It had been hard to tell what they'd been thinking while she had sat there in the meeting room, back rigid against a classic green Glovers chair.

Rhona had been immaculately turned out. Black liner penned like a signature along her lashes and a sharp, asymmetrical crop that could have been sheared into her hair by a topiarist. She had listened and nodded to Leah's words, flicking the longer side off her jaw and sitting in a stiff pose as if to assert her role as the counter boss.

In comparison, Dawn, the Glovers store manager, was chatty and laid back. Leah had observed the way she slipped both shoes off under the table. Her style of makeup was colourful, with bottle-green mascara to match the uniform blouse, and a vivid salmon gloss on her lips. The wink she'd given at the end of the interview had been a big hint that Leah was in luck.

Now, back in the bedroom, Leah released the butterfly clips from her delicate pear-drop earrings. She watched each silver swirl disappear into the bottom of the trinket box, hoping it wouldn't be too long before she opened the lid again.

***

Nearly a week later, it was back to business. Leah forcing clothes over her soaking wet skin while Kiki screamed the house down. Leah scraping her damp hair into another dead ponytail while tiny feet battered against the floor.

'Shhh, it's OK. Won't be long now. Just give me a second.'

She searched the dressing table for her small pot of moisturiser, the persistent cries stamping out any ability to concentrate. Getting down on hands and knees, Leah stretched to the back of the furniture, exasperation boiling over as she collected up old kirby grips and a few used cotton buds, yet she couldn't for the life of her seem to locate the jar she was looking for.

'Oh, dear!' Leah bent over Kiki press-up style, and tried to turn the frustration into fun. 'What did Mummy do with her face cream? Has she gone mad?'

Widening her eyes, she clamped her teeth into a smile and started to play peek-a-boo with a tissue. But there was no let-up. Instead, Kiki's cheeks gave way to the gaping circumference of her mouth.

'Here… what about this?' Grabbing the nearby changing bag, Leah waded with her hands through the contents, finally pulling out a giraffe toy with an extendable neck. 'Want to play with Flexy Lexie?'

But she flinched as another yowl hit every wall.

'Oh, whatever!' Leah's rage reached breaking point, and she hurled the plastic creature across the room, smashing it at a chest of drawers and sending it straight into the bin. 'Why do I even bother trying?'

She gritted her teeth as she seized Kiki's nappy cream from the pit of the bag and smeared it over her face.

'I guess this will have to do, won't it, Kiki?' Leah squared up to the screaming tot, her cheeks smattered with the thick ointment. 'Everything in my bloody life will just have to do.'

With the cream just about rubbed in, she stashed the supplies back into the bag hoisting it, along with Kiki, over her shoulder. Then, squashing her feet into her trainers without even being able to see them, she set off in the car on the short drive to the hospital.

As usual, the car journey calmed Kiki down and by the time they entered the Terrapin Unit for children, her outburst had diminished to a grumpy whinge. As usual, Leah was being stared at and she knew exactly why. How could she be in this much of a state over nothing more than a grouchy youngster?

'Kiki!'

Leah looked up at a young woman with large glasses and a sleek black ponytail. A purple jacket lifted her outfit, and her flat pumps squeaked over the tiles as she led them to a door. A desk was tucked over to the side while the floor space was covered in footprint patterns, with a low table and a toy box against the wall.

'I'm Zara.' She smiled at them both. 'This must be Kiki.'

'That's right.' Leah could see from Zara's badge that she was a physiotherapist.

'So, your health visitor tells us Kiki hasn't been reaching her milestones. Is that right?'

'Well, she turns one in a couple of weeks and there's no sitting up or crawling yet.'

'No shuffling or anything like that?'

Leah shook her head. 'She just lies flat when I put her on the floor. And she can sit in her chair, but not unaided.'

'I see.'

'Most babies are moving about by her age… aren't they?'

'Not necessarily,' Zara stopped typing. 'Of course, they should be bearing weight at least partially by now and getting themselves around that way.'

Leah nodded, feeling the despair creeping in.

'But some just get there earlier than others. There's still a good chance that she's just taking her time.' Zara flashed a grin at Kiki. 'Shall we check her out then? Just put her on the rug.'

Placing Kiki gently on her back, Leah stepped away leaving Zara to examine her. As she gently squeezed her leg muscles and pushed against her feet, Kiki began to grizzle.

'Ooh, yes. I know…' Zara spoke in an animated tone. 'But we have to get to the bottom of this and find out what's going on!' She wrapped each of Kiki's hands around her index fingers and tried to encourage her to pull herself upwards.

'Go on, Kiki!' Leah praised. 'Up you come.'

But her daughter's eyes scrunched up tight and the piercing sound of her scream froze Zara's smile.

'I'll tell you what we'll do, then,' said Zara, reaching into the toy box. She lifted a colourful cube onto her lap and began to wind a lever to the side, starting up some circus music which clanged tinnily from within. 'Meet Ringo the Ringmaster! Everyone loves him. There's never been a single child who hasn't cheered up when they've seen him.'

Leah watched Kiki as the tune tinkled on, holding her breath in the hope she would be distracted.

'Get ready…' Zara said with glee. 'Three, two, one…'

The lid shot upwards and out sprung a bear with a top hat and a smart red coat, stunning Kiki to silence for a momentary second. Then she bawled and kicked in a heap of chaos, with Leah unable to hear Zara's voice.

'Sorry, Kiki! I didn't mean to…' Her lips kept moving as she gestured to Leah, but every word drowned in the tantrum of tears. 'You'd better pick her up now. Perhaps she needs a cuddle.'

Back at Zara's desk, Leah tried to soothe Kiki, dabbing her eyes with a tissue.

'I think…' Zara tried again, 'the best thing to do is…'

But she stopped talking. The high-pitched shriek was unbearable as it bounced relentlessly off all four walls. Zara clenched her teeth, clearly taken aback and trying to remain calm.

'The best thing to do is go,' shouted Leah. 'I mean, what's the point?'

'You don't need to do that. But maybe if you sit in the quiet room, she might snap out of it.'

'Well…' Leah answered wearily, fighting to control her lower lip each time she opened her mouth. 'I think that's unlikely.'

There was a flash of sympathy behind Zara's glasses as she noted Leah's growing distress.

'Just try. It's only around the corner. I'll see the next patient and then we'll check how she's getting…'

Kiki's lips widened and her cries rocketed up an octave or more.

'OK.' Leah hung her head as she skulked over to the door. 'Sorry about all this.'

But instead of making her way to the area Zara had

suggested, she hurried out of the double doors and clipped Kiki into her car seat. Then she sped away from the hospital as her tears blinded the signposts.

'Can't take you anywhere, can I?' She clutched the steering wheel, raising her voice while Kiki lulled in the motion. 'That's right, you can listen to *me* being loud now for a change. See how it bloody feels!'

Leah put her foot down, nearly knocking a cyclist over, and hurtling through a zebra crossing as people stepped out into the road.

'I can't have this anymore, Kiki. I can't live a normal life. You won't let me do anything!'

She dozed in response. Leah then slowed at a shelter, where a bus was just pulling out of the space and an elderly couple waited for the next one. They peered adoringly at Kiki through the window, then gazed at Leah as if she should be proud.

'Looks perfect, doesn't she?' she shrieked, the hardship etched on her face. 'Well, you don't know the half of it. How she is every day. If this is motherhood, then sod it!'

She drove off in a whirlwind, leaving the couple frozen in position at the kerb while she raced to get home as quickly as possible in the desperate hope of putting Kiki down for a nap.

But no chance. As she heaved Kiki through the front door, the unexpected pounding of Led Zeppelin filled the hallway and Leah followed it all the way to Eric's study.

'What are you doing here? It's only one-fifteen.'

'Power cut in the office, so we're all working from home.' Eric leaned over, pausing the track. Then he looked up and registered the state of Leah. 'Not again. Was it the physio? What happened this time?'

'Wouldn't stop crying.' Leah thumped Kiki on his lap. 'She could barely even look at her. From the minute she started checking her legs, off she went with the screaming.'

Eric rested his eyes on the tot, suppressing a smile as she gurgled back.

'Are you naughty?' he asked Kiki as she tugged at his jumper, and he couldn't help smirking at her seemingly-instant contentment.

'It's not funny, Eric,' Leah retorted. 'You get to sit behind your desk while I have to lug her to all these places and face the humiliation when she kicks off.'

'I'll go next time,' he answered, bobbing Kiki up and down. 'When is it booked for?'

'The sixteenth.'

'Well, I can do that...' Eric scrolled through the calendar on his phone. 'No, I can't. We're axe throwing?'

'You're what?'

'Team building day. Then burgers afterwards.'

'Of course.' Leah got up to leave the room. She would hit the roof if Eric gave Kiki back.

'Wait a minute.'

'Eric, please. I'm exhausted. Just hang onto her while I have a wash or something, will you?'

'Are you listening?' he answered sternly. 'Stop talking and maybe you'll do yourself a favour.'

'You don't need to speak to me like that, thanks. I've had enough for one—'

'That Rhona from EdenCore has been trying to ring you. Maybe you've had your phone turned off at the hospital or something.'

Animation lit up inside her. 'What did she say?'

'Sounded really nice.'

'Yes, but did she leave a message?'

'Just said to ring her back.'

Leah was already running to the kitchen.

'Make us a cuppa while you're at it,' he called after

her.

Tempted to top his mug up with Kiki's powdered milk, Leah clicked the kettle on, resting the phone against her tired face. Then she strained to hear through the boiling bubbles, trying not to miss a word as she listened to Rhona's voicemail.

Six

Stepping onto the escalator in her patent high heels, Leah grabbed the handrail as she travelled down to the beauty floor. Immaculate in the renowned magenta blazer and matching knee-length skirt, she checked her low bun as she glided past the mirrored wall and made sure that not a single hair had fallen out of place.

Then she walked onto solid ground as fragrance hit her nostrils and the department was like a sweetshop of cosmetics from every major brand. From Chimie, with their lab coats and bold silver logo, to the classic black of fashion houses Poirier and Auclair. The retro KittyPie stand stood out in a curve on the centre of the floor and just beyond it, a flick of Rhona's fringe caught Leah's eye as she smoothed something over a customer's hand. She was drenched in the same bright pink uniform, looking like a model in a hair advert. Leah made her way over and Rhona smiled as she approached.

'Hi there!' She twisted from her place at the makeup rack, juggling cotton wool pads and a cleanser bottle while tending to the woman she was serving. 'Be with you in a minute. Just grab that tablet under the till and type your name at the top of the first page. Feel free to look around and try stuff out, too.'

'Nice to see you again,' Leah smiled. 'Will do.'

She stepped behind the counter and entered her new employee password, tapping her name and registering where Rhona had directed. Then she turned around to inspect the display shelves which wrapped around the sweeping window, where the pavement outside cascaded downhill and the feet of passing shoppers became whole bodies as they walked by. Promotional posters lined the glass and could not be missed by anyone, while the giant white brand name stood out on magenta frames.

Every transparent sliver of shelf was bedecked in white packaging, with each name and description stamped in bold pink print. A jewellery box of testers glinted temptingly at the side of the till like an iceberg scattered with the shafts of a rainbow. Here was the treasure within all the shells. The bottles and tubes unleashed from their cardboard cocoons.

She glanced over the skincare pots, arranged in age order. For teens and the twenties, there was *The Hit*, a zesty collection in bright citrus tubes. A step up from this was *The Boost*, in its bronze-topped jars, ideal for those of thirty and above. *The Lift* was the forties range with its firming qualities beneath its silver lids. And there at the top of the display, was the most expensive. *The Afterlife*, for the over-fifties, was extravagant, luxurious and finished in gleaming gold.

'You'll be an expert on that by the time we've finished with you!' Rhona swanned past her as she led the customer to the till. Packing two items into a shiny branded bag, she added a sample sachet of foundation and beamed at the woman until she'd walked away. 'Did you manage to have a look at it all?'

'Some of it.' Leah grinned with glee. 'Can't wait to start using everything.'

'Come on,' said Rhona, marching her towards the

containers, filled with magic ingredients. 'I'll show you all the bestsellers.'

Being careful not to knock anything out of its slot, she leaned over the bottle tops and grabbed a white tube.

'There are three things you can literally sell to any customers. Doesn't matter what their skin type is or how old they are. This is one of them.' She tilted it towards Leah who read the title against the white. *Palm Oil*.

'*Palm Oil*? Does it actually contain…'

But Rhona was already shaking her head. Clearly, she had answered that question for many confused customers.

'I can assure you, we wouldn't use anything like that!'

'OK, so why…'

'We like to have fun with the names. Gets people curious about our products. Then you're straight into a nice little chat and bingo, they want to buy it.'

'Oh, I see!' Leah smiled, allowing an ivory blob to be squeezed onto her fingers.

'This, my dear, is the only hand cream you will ever need.' Rhona's Glaswegian accent became more pronounced as she stressed each word through thin cerise lips that were doll-like against her freckled skin. 'Dates are the main ingredient here. Smoothing, hydrating properties and just one or two applications last all day.'

'Wow, it feels amazing.'

'Like velvet, isn't it? Same as it's always been and get this… even the royals use it.'

'Seriously?'

Rhona winked. 'We're supposed to keep it a secret, but they have it on tap in every boudoir at the palace.'

'I'm not surprised.' Leah held up her other hand to compare. 'I can see a difference already!'

'Same with our *Cream of Tomato Soap*, but we'll come

to that later.'

Leah followed Rhona to three glass bottles, all of the same large sphere shape, but each one a different colour.

'The second guaranteed sellable items are our fragrances.' She popped the lid off the orange one. *Peach to their Own* has exactly that as the top note, but there's also a standout quality in it that no other perfume can claim.'

'I'm intrigued,' said Leah, eyeing the liquid swirling around inside.

'It makes a totally different scent on every single person, meaning that no two will ever get the same result.'

'Spray away!' She raised a wrist in anticipation. 'I wonder what mine will be like.'

Rhona tapped the nozzle with her fingertip and the fruity mist puffed into the air. It was slightly too sweet for Leah's taste, but she reserved judgement until it settled on her skin. Admittedly, it did improve the more it mingled and dried, but she had always preferred something floral if given the choice.

'Yes, it's quite nice,' she nodded appreciatively.

'Now, moving on…' Next was the purple bottle and Rhona used a paper strip for this one. '*HeartBeet*. You might think it's unusual to have beetroot in a fragrance but wait until you get a whiff of this.'

Leah was apprehensive. She was not going to like it. If something as harmless as peach had failed to float her boat, it was highly unlikely she would enjoy the pong of an earthy vegetable. With masked reluctance, she leaned in and inhaled the spattered stick.

She almost slipped on her stiletto heel. It was so much better than the first one. A far cry from the muddiness she'd been expecting and much more reminiscent of a field after a rainstorm.

'This is gorgeous,' she mused, breathing in the aftermath of what smelled like aniseed mixed with a hint of lavender. 'I did not expect that at all!'

'It is designed especially for the chest area, hence the name,' Rhona continued proudly. 'The skin there is different to anywhere else and it brings out the depths of this particular fragrance.'

'Well, in that case, I'll give it a go…' Leah was about to add a dash to her collarbone, but Rhona held out a hand to stop her.

'Just a second.' She grinned smugly, eyes twinkling as she gazed at the top of the stand. 'You're probably going to forget all about that once you've had a burst of the best.'

There, in the centre of the three, was clearly the frontrunner. A truly striking elixir in the classic EdenCore magenta. Leah moved closer, reading the words etched on the glass.

'*T-Radish-ional.* As in, traditional?'

'You got it!' Rhona seized it from the rack and held it in her hands as if she were selling it on QVC. 'Our original, iconic fragrance, totally unchanged since we first launched it.'

'Sounds good.' Leah's eyes widened, imagining how perfect it would look on her dressing table.

'Oh, I know it might sound crazy to think of radish working in a perfume, but believe me…'

'Not at all,' replied Leah adamantly. She was already convinced. If beetroot could smell as captivating as they had made it, then radish would clearly steal the crown. Eagerly, she seized the strip and let every waft penetrate her nose and throat.

'Don't tell me… you love it, right? They all do.'

Leah's smile froze on her face. It was possibly the vilest stench she had ever come across. Fighting to hide the sensation that she was being strangled, she pretended desperately to seem impressed.

'I mean, that is…' She clamped her mouth shut before more of the putrid stink could envelope her again. 'It's something else!'

'Sure is!'

Flapping the stick frantically, in the hope that something miraculous would evolve once it set, Leah allowed herself another sniff. As Rhona's eyes remained hooked on hers, Leah nearly gagged as the bitter pinch attacked her senses for a second time.

'I can definitely get the radish,' she spluttered. Because it was literally the only thing she could smell. Peppery and vinegary with the base notes of someone's armpit. She wrestled with the instinct to shield her face. 'What else is in it?'

'A touch of hibiscus and clove, but it's deliberately very minimal so the star of the show comes through. Want some on?'

Rhona offered her the bottle, but she quickly shook her head. 'Actually… I think I'll go for the *HeartBeet*.'

'Help yourself.' She continued to clutch the *T-Radish-ional*. 'But this is the one you want to shout about. We make a point of introducing it to every customer.'

As Rhona cloaked herself in a dozen more puffs, Leah turned her head away and stepped subtly out of the suffocating trail.

'Hey, Kehlani!' A voice sailed towards them and heels clicked loudly against the marbled floor. 'I'm loving the Sorbet shower gel. Can I have some more samples?'

'Sure, hun,' replied a girl in a pastel pink KittyPie top. 'Want them now?'

'I'll grab a few later. Just coming off break.'

Leah saw the bun, heaped high like a bird's nest, before the rest of the body emerged and passed the

Browzilia Bar. The magenta-clad colleague had not a strand of black hair straying from the scraped-back lacquer. She was shorter than Leah, but the piled coiffure made up the rest of the inches. Her uniform fitted to perfection, and she strode up to the counter, gleaming a brighter-than-white smile.

'Hiya!'

'Hello, I'm…'

'Leah, yeah? I'm Tiffany.'

'Nice to meet you.'

'Tiff is quite new, too,' Rhona added, turning to her. 'What's it been… a couple of months now?'

'Yep. Two next week,' replied Tiffany, rubbing her perfectly manicured hands together. 'You must be so excited, Leah.'

'Oh, definitely.'

'I've just been showing her a few different products.' Rhona returned the fragrances to their stand and polished them with a tissue. 'We've done these and the hand cream.'

'Not got to the crème de la crème yet, then?'

'Well, I was working up to that one, but I don't think I can hold back any longer.'

'She's going to love it.'

'I know!' Rhona bounced excitedly on the spot.

'Go on… show her.'

Both faces gleaming, they parted shoulders to reveal a bottle under the shield of a glass dome. Leah had seen it in magazines and in the brochure at the interview. A tall, thin cylinder filled with green liquid, and a decorative gold leaf either side to make it look like a plant stalk.

'Introducing…' Rhona's voice leapt up an octave as she removed the glass cover, unleashing the product in all its glory.

'*SySTEM!*' Her voice blended with Tiffany's as they

both purred in unison.

'I've heard about this.' Leah was already nodding. 'It's one of the serums.'

'No, babes. It's *the* serum.'

'OK.' She glanced back at Tiffany in response. 'What does it do?'

'What doesn't it do, you mean.' Rhona's confidence was mesmerising. 'It does everything.'

She twisted the bottle around in her hands, showing there were two extra chambers at the back. One was glinting with a yellow concoction while the other looked as if it had run out.

'So, we have taken the three essential elements that a plant needs for growth – water, sunlight and oxygen – to create a serum that does the same things for the skin.'

'Sounds incredible!' Leah gushed. 'How is that even possible?'

'Well, at the front here, you have the water part.' Rhona's glossy nails tapped on the green shaft of the bottle. 'This is enriched with hydrating juices from kiwi, celery, artichoke, and gooseberry.'

In her well-versed selling style, she swivelled the container around once again.

'Then if you look at the back, this yellow section contains the sun bit – the illuminating, light-reflecting particles of sunflower, forsythia, saffron, and kumquat.'

'Looks like we've run out of the third one,' said Leah, eyeing the empty tube.

'No, that's the oxygen compartment,' chirped Tiffany. 'It's a mixture of gases extracted from hemp and plantain.'

'You forgot the fig and rosehip.' Rhona winked. 'And all three compartments pump out together. Watch this!'

As she gently pressed the gold disc, a blended smear of green and yellow landed in her palm, while a puff of air sprayed into it from the third invisible column.

'Just mix it together and warm it up.' She blended it in a circle with her fingers. 'Now, give me your hand.'

Leah's jaw dropped as the textural fusion kissed her skin. It was like nothing she had ever felt before. Too gloopy to be classed as fluid, yet watery enough that it wasn't a gel, the elements had combined into the heavenliest of formulas. For the first few seconds, it coated her palm, then it sank deeper down like a wave on wet sand, leaving it swathed in smoothness with a shimmering, healthy finish.

'Oh my word!'

'I know, I know…' Tiffany beamed. 'I remember my first time, too.'

The smell was equally as glorious. It positively pulsed with exquisiteness. Like melon and passionfruit erupting from depths of almond, geranium, and matcha.

'I'm actually speechless. No wonder it's all over those posters and everyone's talking about it. What skin type is it for? What age?'

'The whole lot, hun.' Tiffany brimmed with pride. 'Anyone can use it. And the best thing is, it's new and exclusive to us here at this branch of Glovers, so Parlour down the road doesn't even stock it. They're a cosmetics emporium with the only other EdenCore counter in the city.'

'She's right, it's universal. All ages, all skin types…' Rhona squeezed some out for Tiffany and slathered more on herself. 'Yes, we have other serums that work with each range, but this is better than the rest of them. There is not one person who could come up to this counter and wouldn't be able to use *SySTEM*.'

'And you don't just have to put it on your face. It conditions split ends, works well as a cuticle oil and is also a brilliant cellulite smoother.'

'Which reminds me…' Rhona cut in, hurrying around to the till and waving a padded envelope embossed with trademark magenta. 'This is your welcome pack. In here is our full catalogue of products for you to get familiar with. You're booked onto next week's training course at London HQ, so all your travel info is there, and whatever you do, don't lose the letter at the front. On there is your unique staff code and password, so you can go straight online and order your allocation.'

'My what?'

'Allocation, babes,' replied Tiffany excitedly. 'You get a choice of five free products every month.'

'Free?' Leah's eyes could have popped out of their sockets. 'I thought we'd just get a discount!'

Rhona shook her head with a grin. 'You need to be wearing as much as possible on counter, and anyway, we like to treat our staff for all their hard work.'

'Come on,' Tiffany beckoned, leading Leah back to the testers. 'Let's make a list of what you want to get. Then you can do your order at home tonight.'

As the two new colleagues acquainted her with the array of jars and squeezy tubes, Leah could not have felt more welcomed. With adult conversation igniting her soul amid the layers of invigorating skin soothers, this was the best first working day she'd probably ever had. She was not just a mother now. She was a woman again.

Seven

As the train pulsed with rush hour commotion, Leah sat hunched behind her luggage, trying to erase the vision of the platform sucking them away. Eric's proud smile, smacked into obscurity by the closing glass, and Kiki's cherry cheeks encased in her cream pompom hat as her tiny mittens sped into dots with the distant station streetlamps.

Three whole nights away from the demands and the screaming. The feeling of being an empty husk and a robot for everyone else. It was the kind of break she had dreamed about since Kiki plunged into the world. But as she tried to focus on the conveyor belt of trees, darkening by the minute as evening set in, a strange pull clamped on her heartstrings as she thought of the tiny tot she had just left behind.

Across the carriageway, a toddler was babbling to her mother as they played object-spotting games and giggled through a pop-up book. They gazed at each other with matching eyes, and the girl moved intermittently from the lap to her own two feet, watched on by the doting woman.

Leah looked down at herself and knew she had failed. A suitcase instead of her own little one. An escape route as the only solution. She'd envisaged a journey of freedom from the moment she stepped out in her striking magenta suit. She had been waiting to seize normal life again and to take off into the crowds. Instead, commuters poured in on each stop, shoving themselves into the spaces around her and talking so loudly, she could barely think.

And what about Eric? She might be on the road to respite, but it didn't seem fair to leave for so long while he had to deal with Kiki. Tears threatened to ruin her foundation, and she didn't need the attention from the throng of surrounding strangers, so she plugged in her earphones and turned up the volume, letting the music soothe her mind and make her feel more positive.

High heels and exposed legs were not the best choice for a trek across London, but she had been instructed to arrive in the full EdenCore uniform, so the cold wrists and unsteady feet had to be endured as she wheeled her baggage through the sea of people filing out into the tube lines.

Thirty minutes later, she climbed out of a taxi and made it through the revolving doors of the Brassington Hotel. She blinked crystal into her tired eyes as the decadent chandeliers led the way along a burgundy carpet to the check-in desk. Marble swirled from floor to ceiling, coating the hall in a mesmerising glaze and as she pushed the button for her allocated floor, a golden lift gracefully enclosed her.

Not getting her hopes up and expecting a basic room, she waited for the green flash and slowly turned the handle. Then the lights clicked on, and her jaw fell open at the sprawling space before her. The TV was bigger than the one in her living room. There was a coffee machine and a fridge, full to the brim with complimentary drinks. And there was even a sofa. She peered into the ensuite bathroom, complete with a jacuzzi and a shower that doubled up as a steam booth. There was more storage space and square metres of floor than she had ever seen in a hotel room, and then there was the bed. King size and luxuriously plumped with pristine sheets and cloud-like pillows.

Leah couldn't kick away her shoes fast enough. The plush carpet felt like bliss under her soles, massaging away the tension of her stiletto-spiked trudge. She leapt across the room and dived with a squeal into the middle of the mattress.

Rolling over, she opened the bedside drawer and took out the TV remote. It was like being in the comfiest cinema ever, with characters from drama shows in massive shapes on the screen. She turned up the volume as *MasterChef* started, revelling in the clarity of sound without the usual backdrop of a wailing toddler. How Eric would be moaning right now at having to endure a cookery programme. She tilted her head and squealed out loud. Then she pressed mute.

Eric. Caught up in her moment of selfish glee, she had forgotten to contact him on arrival as she'd promised. Quickly, she scrambled over to her bag and tapped out a message on her phone.

Got here safely. Hope all is OK. x

As contestants served their plates of food, dripped in an array of sauces, she thought of the chaos she had left him in right now. He'd be bouncing Kiki in one arm, trying to calm her down while he struggled to butter her toasted soldiers and lift her dippy egg from a hot pan of water. He wouldn't even have his own meal until her bedtime was done and dusted. Leah might be free of that for now, living it up in a room fit for a queen, but all the lavishness that had fallen in her lap could never give her a true release, knowing that at this moment, someone else was struggling in her place.

'I'm much more confident this time,' said a budding chef, just as the camera zoomed into a close-up of the judges cutting open a half-cooked pie.

The phone buzzed. Part of her didn't even want to look. Just a hint from Eric that havoc was on the cards and Leah would be in for a dreary night, too plagued by her conscience to make the most of her stay. She held her breath and glimpsed at the message.

All good here. We've shared pizza and choccy mousse. Got a bit narky when we couldn't find zebra blanket but it was under the pushchair, so fine now. She's tired and should go off nicely. Hope you're alright. x

Leah closed her eyes with relief and keyed out a reply.

As long as you are. x

Then Eric messaged again.

We're fine! Just make sure you enjoy the trip and come back soon. x

Followed by a second beep.

Proud of you Mummy. x

Next to the words was a picture of Kiki, cuddled up in the crook of Eric's arm. She wasn't smiling, but the tip of her tongue was showing goofily between her lips, and it made Leah melt. The football was on in the background, and everything seemed peaceful. Now she was safe in that knowledge, she could well and truly relax.

Love you both. x

With that, she put her phone to one side and headed to the bathroom, where she stayed under the shower for triple her usual time. She dried off in a bathrobe, the effects of the top-end shampoo and conditioner even visible while her hair was still damp.

Drawing the curtains across a sky snowing with stars, she turned to discover a thin white box adorned with magenta ribbon and *Leah Angelina Frost* etched in perfect calligraphy on the front. She opened it up on the table, unfolding the leaves of crisp white tissue paper and rose petals in the same unmistakable pink.

Inside was a glossy EdenCore catalogue, her new name badge, and an envelope at the front, embossed with the logo. She carefully took out the card inside and perched on the chaise longue to read it.

Dear Leah,

Welcome on the journey of your new life.

You are now a part of the EdenCore universe and we know you will never look back. Working for us is so much more than just a job and we can't wait to show you all the appreciation you deserve for choosing to come on board.

CLEANSE
Prepare for an experience where a fresh start is an understatement. Whatever your story might be, and no matter where you are joining us from, our products, our teams and our philosophy will transform your mind and body.

TONE

Get set to become an overnight expert with a training course like no other. Immerse yourself in the sublimity of our skincare and learn top techniques with our pioneering makeup range. Armed with the knowledge and passion to succeed, you will become a fully-fledged ambassador, ready to share us with the world.

MOISTURISE

Just as our creams quench the thirst of needy skin, you'll take pride in spreading joy to a wealth of different customers. You'll glow from within once your soul is alive with the treats in store, and you'll make every dream come true, working magic like the superstar that you are.

Thank you for joining us. We can't wait!

EdenCore HQ
20 Kennedy Square
London
W1G 2FU

(Please arrive in full uniform at 9.00am).

Leah glanced at her bright pink suit, hanging up ready on the clothes rail, and the polished black shoes that set it off to perfection. As comfy as she was in the towelling robe, she couldn't wait to put it all on again.

She glanced back down at the card and focused on the last paragraph.

AND RIGHT NOW…

What can we say? Enjoy your stay! The minibar is free and

your fridge is stacked with tasty snacks, so go ahead and help yourself. Fancy the gym and spa? It's on us, so use it at your leisure. And did we mention room service? You guessed it… tuck in!

Tossing the card in the box lid, she fluffed up her pillows and sighed as their marshmallow softness squished against her back. Too tempted by the delectable dishes being flaunted on the TV, she flipped open the hotel menu, ready to order a feast.

Within half an hour, her glass tray arrived and its contents were spectacular. She devoured the crabcakes with dill and cucumber salsa, followed by halibut in a curried broth. A pear and almond souffle was the perfect finish and she polished off two dark chocolate truffles with a cold glass of the finest pinot grigio.

She sat at her dressing table mirror to do the bedtime skincare routine that would soon be a thing of the past. The convenient three-in-one cleansing water and her toning lotion from a supermarket shelf. She skimmed the cotton pad over her cheeks, following with her usual budget pot of cream.

Then, slipping into her pyjamas with the widest grin on her face, she sprawled under a duvet as springy as dough and clicked off the light.

Eight

It had seemed like the longest twenty minutes she had ever walked, the balls of her feet grinding against the stiff arch of her shoe soles. Pain splitting her calves in two from the razor-sharp root of the heels.

But the moment she set eyes on 20 Kennedy Square, all that was a distant memory. The grimy backbone of London had been left far behind as the white palatial heights greeted her with their golden railings and pristine steps. Pillars like doormen stood proudly to attention as she approached.

She checked her reflection one last time in the mirrored panels of the doorway. Deliberately natural makeup in preparation for any extra she might apply. Hair swept off her face in a sleek French braid. Her nose was beginning to redden from her icy stint of walking, and she quickly warmed her blotchy wrists that were exposed to the cold by the cropped jacket sleeves.

As she gave her name through the intercom, the door glided open to reveal a hallway like the home of a film star. The glass droplets of rose-pink ceiling lamps glistened in the sheen of the black and white floor tiles, accented by magenta sofas and walls of bestselling products in poster-sized frames.

She checked in at the front desk, which housed the receptionists in its avant-garde sculpture, and followed the signs into a huge room where the other trainees were just getting seated around a long, U-shaped table. The space was spotless and minimalist, with the full product range in display racks at the back.

Leah put her handbag under her chair and glanced around the room. A couple of trainees had arrived bare faced, clearly in anticipation of applying the products. Another was impeccable, with just the right touches of base makeup. But many were a good deal younger than Leah, with inflated lips and trowelled-on foundation in shades of orange that clashed against their necks. One whipped out a compact mirror to reglue her wonky eyelashes and backcombed her brows to a caterpillar fuzz.

Then all at once, familiar music filled the air and cheers crowded in from the hallway with clapping in time to the beat. The door flew open and in marched three women, who stood in a line at the front of the room, gazing out across the table of new employees while they swayed and slapped their palms together throughout the song.

'*I will never let you down!*' They mouthed the lyrics of every chorus until the tune faded out.

'And I promise you everyone…' said the youngest of the three in the middle, 'EdenCore will never let *you* down!'

Then they all stepped forward to introduce themselves.

'I'm Elaine,' said the first one. 'Assistant Head of Training.'

'Hilary.' The eldest flipped her pristine bob and pressed a hand to her chest. 'Area Manager for the South East.'

'And I'm Kerry!' All eyes were fixed on the blonde in the centre, whose prettiness was effortless. 'I'll be your trainer for the next few days but first, my *gorgeous* colleagues are going to give you their top tips. So, over to you first, Hil.'

As Hilary made her way to the stand, the other two whistled as the music pumped back up. Then she cleared her throat and began a speech about how much she related to the new joiners, remembering being in their shoes many years ago.

Leah studied the perfection of her hair. It was lustrous, deep umber and literally looked like a shampoo commercial. But her face did not match, making the style appear wig-like. In stark contrast, her skin looked haggard and was only aged more by the plummy lipstick.

'You all seem so nervous, but don't be!' The slits of her eyes moved over the row of trainees. 'These products will sell themselves and do all the hard work for you. When I was starting out on the counter, I was terrified! Didn't help that it was at Langridge's which, in case you didn't know, has the second largest beauty department on Oxford Street. Talk about intimidating!'

'I wish!' whispered a girl to the person sitting beside Leah. 'We're lucky to get two people a day at our branch of Glovers.'

'But I needn't have spent a minute worrying,' continued Hilary, gesturing to the bottles and jars, layered over the back wall. 'From the very moment this little lot glides over someone's skin, they are sold. You darlings have just landed yourselves the easiest job ever. Just a dash or a spray and the customers come running.'

'Can I get a word in edgeways?' Elaine cut in, laughing at her own question. 'You see, this is the problem once you start working for EdenCore. You'll be waxing lyrical about every part of it, and no one can ever stop you! This one here could charm the hind legs off a donkey!'

'I'm sorry, my dear, am I boring you?' answered Hilary, winking at the crowd as if the dialogue was part of a script.

'Oh, I could listen to you all day!' giggled Elaine. 'Now, I must dash to the spa suite where a session is about to start for our amazing new salon staff, but I welcome each and every one of you to our family and we are all here for you, every perfectly pedicured step of the way.'

She left the room waving as Hilary handed over to Kerry with another burst of music. As Kerry shimmied vivaciously to the stand, Leah noted her captivating presence and could just tell that this woman was a more than decent dancer.

'As I said earlier, I'm Kerry, your trainer. To be honest with you, I haven't been with this wonderful company long.'

Hilary received the flash of her smile and wrinkled her nose to return it.

'In fact, my first love is acting. I've been performing in the West End since I left stage school.'

'Are you serious?' asked the girl with the eyelashes, which still weren't attached properly to the edges of her lids. 'Then why would you want to work somewhere normal like...'

'Oh, no... no!' Kerry shushed with her hands, looking almost pained by the words. 'This is no *normal* job. I just got tired of the late nights, so I snapped this up instead. Anyway...' she raised her voice a few pitches louder and her platinum ponytail swung from side to side. 'Are you ready to get started?'

Heads nodded from square magenta shoulders.

'OK, Hil... you hand out the kits and I'll grab the

trolley of delights!'

Hilary went around the room with packages containing towels, cotton wool pads, tissues, and flannel headbands while Kerry wheeled in a stack of testers. Then she picked up three bottles, each containing a different lotion, and held them so that their fronts were viewable by everyone in the room.

'So, here we go, my budding beauties! Please turn to page one in your catalogues. We are going to start with our Wake Up cereal cleansers. *Rice and Shine* for dry skin, *Oat Float* for oily, and *Barley Blend* for combination, which is also ideal for sensitive. They're all enriched with plant-based milk, so they're totally vegan too.'

Passing them all along the line, she instructed the trainees on the amount to use and to keep working it in for a full three minutes. Leah made a beeline for the rice one, which she knew would be the best for her type of skin. The smell was so subtle, and she adored the simplicity without any strong scents destroying it. Smoothing it on with her fingertips, the cool drizzle was instantly reviving. She could just imagine a slathering of this starting her morning routine off with a bang.

'Have we all had a try?' asked Kerry. 'OK, so now you can remove it with your pad and then just have a feel of how sublime your hand is.' She waited, then grinned as sounds of pleasure rang out around the room. 'I know, I know. And we haven't even got to the moisturisers yet!'

She pulled more bottles out of the tray and this time, all three were filled with liquids in shades of green.

'Moving onto the next step, we're following on with toner and these ones are to die for. Just sweep them on with your cotton wool and get a load of the herbs.'

Leah wasn't wild about *Turn Back Thyme* or the *Mint Condition* dead cert that promised to cut the grease. Instead, she waited patiently for *Chive In* to reach her, and yet again was lucky that the hydrating option was her favourite of the three.

As the day went on, so did the endless chain of jars and tubes. They covered all the age-specific ranges Leah had seen in the store, and she already knew which fragrances to spray like mad or avoid. There was exfoliating soil, vegetable peel masks, and a series of exotic fruit lip balms.

As they finished the first session, Leah was fully immersed in the brand and had surpassed herself on the knowledge tests that were done at the end of each section.

It was almost a wrench to tear herself away, setting off into the nippy evening air, but as she headed back towards the Brassington Hotel, another lavish night to herself wouldn't be going amiss.

***

By late afternoon on the final day, the extensive training had taken its toll. Leah was exhausted from an overload of role play and her exercise book was full to the brim with the gruelling tasks that were part of the programme.

She had been like a robot, reciting ingredients and learning sales techniques until she was blue in the face. There had been a whole day dedicated to the body range, with shower gels and suncreams coming into play. Then yesterday, the makeup had taken centre stage and Leah was now an expert with contour sets and primers.

It had been nothing short of amazing, but now she needed a breather. Time to let it all sink in while she stepped away from the deluge. Her train would be leaving for home in an hour and she could hardly wait to get back. She had missed Eric and Kiki, and it would feel so good to be with them tonight after a full-on but therapeutic week.

'I just want to say a huge well done to every single one of you!' said Kerry, who was lined up with Hilary and Elaine in just the same way as they'd begun. 'And congratulations are in order, because now you have all officially earned one of these.'

She called each trainee up one by one to receive their certificates. Then Hilary slipped out of the room and made several trips back and forth, armed with enough EdenCore bags for everyone on the course.

'Now, go off and treat yourselves for all that hard work,' Kerry smiled proudly. 'We'll call it research, but you all know really that it's one big pamper party! Thank you so much, everyone, and we cannot wait to see you in action.'

The trainers bid a noisy farewell as Leah and the others left the building. As a ticket had been booked in advance for the train, Leah had a guaranteed seat, and it could have been made of memory foam for the joy it felt to take the weight off her feet. The goody bag had been so heavy that she had looped the handles over the back of her suitcase to transport it. But now, with a little more time to kill, she opened it up and silently shrieked.

The entire contents had been tailored to her skin, based on forms she had filled during registration. Large bottles of the cleanser and toner were packed in next to the full range of *The Boost*, for the over-thirties. She picked up the box of *Sweet Potato Face Mash* and the *24 Carrot* night cream that sat on the top of the pile. And, delving deeper, she found there was even more. Body lotion, cellulite cream, bath foam, and her favourite massage oil, as well as lipstick, mascara, and the newly-launched concealer pen – all lying over the top of one last item. An extra-large *SySTEM* serum.

She looked out of the window, counting down the

stations. Willing the time to come when she would arrive at Dankton. How she would hug that little girl and the husband she had never gone this long without seeing.

And then, later on when she had kissed Kiki goodnight, it would be time to unleash the freebie bag for the facial of her dreams.

Nine

Her first thought the next morning was that it was an unusually bright sun for this time of year. Or perhaps it was just exhaustion from all the travelling and training. She tried once more to wake herself up, wondering if she had slept at an odd angle, with her pillow wedged into her face.

Then the panic set in. She really couldn't open her eyes.

Sitting upright, she tried to prise her lids apart and twisted groggily to the mirrored wardrobe, almost choking as she squinted into the glass. And as she slowly took back control of the movement in her eyes, they focused on a dappled rash, stinging in a goggle shape around them. She glanced downwards and couldn't see her chest for the two swollen balloons that had become her cheeks, and which burned every time she clenched them.

'Oh, God,' she whispered. 'Don't let it be the…'

Tears began to well and she grabbed a tissue from the bedside box, frantically dabbing them away. The salt would be a killer on top of all that. What the hell was she going to do?

'Tea for you.' Eric's voice swarmed as he placed a

mug down beside her. Then he got back into bed with his own. 'Did you sleep OK last night after all that London luxury?'

Leah kept her back turned but she nodded.

'Kiki's still asleep, I've just looked.'

She didn't respond. Just shrugged her shoulders.

'She missed you so much…' His arm curled around Leah's waist. 'And so did I.'

Tensing up, she did her best and squeezed his elbow with affection. 'Missed you, too.'

Gently, he ran a finger down a lock of hair and stroked it back from her face, then slowly guided her jaw so that she would turn around to face him.

'Eric!'

She wriggled out and threw on her dressing gown, still refusing to look his way.

'What's wrong?'

'Nothing, it's just…' Raising her wrist higher than usual, she checked the time on her watch over the puffy swells of skin. 'I have to get ready for work.'

'But… I thought you weren't in until eleven.'

'I'm not, it's… the traffic, and I've got to get Kiki ready for Mum.'

'I can do that! Leah…'

'Sorry.'

She stumbled along the hallway and locked herself in the bathroom, unable to let Eric see her in this state. Rifling through the medicine cabinet, she downed an antihistamine with water from the basin. Then she scoured the other cupboards, searching for cream to treat the inflammation. Shaving foam, handwash, but nothing remotely useful, until she started on the next shelf down and caught a tube before it fell out on the floor.

This was her only hope. She had stopped breastfeeding a good six months ago and had nearly used it all up, but there were no other options on offer right now and Leah had nothing to lose. Dabbing the nipple gel all around her eyes, she marvelled at the sensation as it slowly soothed the sore patches and within fifteen minutes, there was a visible improvement.

But with Kiki to sort out and road closures to detour around before she could get to work, it was going to be more of a mission to make her face suitable for counter service. Taking the lid off the new EdenCore cover-up stick she'd dabbed on the night before, she leaned towards the mirror. Then stopped. Was it this that had caused the bad reaction?

Or was it the eye cream? The toner or the mask? Everything had been fine on her hands when she'd tried it out during training. But clearly, it had a different effect once it absorbed into her face. She rummaged through the whole bag, reading the ingredients. Trying to think which of the umpteen products had made her flesh red raw. And then, another thought. What if it was *all* of them?

'Leah?' Eric called, banging on the door. 'Are you sure everything's alright?'

'Shhh!' she hissed, pressing her ear to the other side. 'You'll wake…'

In seconds, Kiki's cry pierced the air. Leah searched hysterically in the toiletry bag she had taken to London and dug out a few cosmetics she hoped would do the job. Quickly, she smeared on fingerfuls of her cheap drugstore options, until the rest of the rash was at least minimised. She patted on powder to reduce the shine of the nipple gel, and at last she felt slightly normal once again. Hurrying out of the bathroom, she bashed straight into Eric.

'I'd better get her up,' she said, diving past him in the doorway.

'I'm more worried about you!' Eric followed her into Kiki's room. 'Did something happen in London? Please… you're acting really strange.'

Leah gazed down at the whingeing tot and grinned with a patience replenished from the trip. Then she looked over at Eric with more confidence, now the disaster of her face was at least not so obvious.

'I'm fine, honestly. I just really don't want to be late on my first day after training. This is where the serious stuff really starts.'

'Is that all?' Eric looked relieved. 'You're going to smash it, I told you.'

'Well, I'm still nervous! It's early days.'

Leah squished Kiki's nose and lifted her out of the cot.

'Oh, look at her! She's glad Mummy's back.' Eric hugged them both and guilt shot through Leah, that she had given him the brush off in the bedroom.

'I've missed her, too.' Leah turned to him and managed a quick peck on the lips. 'And you.'

Kiki gurgled between them, giving Leah an excuse to pull away.

'Right then, you, breakfast time!' She carried Kiki across the room but turned to Eric in the doorway. 'Look, we'll do something nice tonight. Maybe watch a film when she's gone to bed.'

He nodded in response as he tidied up the cot. 'Sounds good. What's that Edwardian one you were going on about?'

'Thistlecross House.'

'I suppose I'll let you choose that, seeing as it's so nice to have you home…'

But Kiki's whinging began to drown him out, so once again, Leah scurried away from Eric and headed off to the kitchen.

***

'She's back!' yelled Tiffany, with the biggest smile, as Leah joined her at the counter. 'How did it go?'

'It was good. I really enjoyed it.'

Leah did her best not to look at her for too long. Although the swelling felt better than it had done earlier, the flaky red rash could still make itself known at any minute.

'Who did you have for the training? Was it Hilary?'

'She helped out, but it was mainly Kerry.'

'Oh, I know. The one who's been in shows and stuff.'

Leah nodded.

'Lucky you! I bet she was fun.' She lowered her voice. 'Hilary just seemed a bit… I don't know, smug?'

Her comment made Leah grin. 'We didn't have her much, but she did have this funny way of looking at us all.'

'Kind of patronising?'

'Maybe. I guess I didn't see enough of her to find out.'

'Well, she visits here every so often, being the Area Manager and all that. Maybe you need to get to know her better!' Tiffany winked sarcastically.

'Can't wait,' replied Leah, trying not to laugh and weaken her mask of foundation.

'And how was the hotel?'

'Amazing.'

'I know, right? I was literally chugging down champagne and posh food every night.'

'Don't remind me! You have no idea how hard it was, going back home to jacket potatoes.'

'Oh, bless. Was that hubby?'

'Sure was,' Leah smiled. 'Mind you, he was doing Kiki's dinner at the same time. That's my daughter.'

'You've got a little one! How old?'

'She's just coming up for one.'

'Awww, how adorable!'

'Sometimes,' Leah smirked comically.

'Come on, I bet you can't stand being away from her.'

There was silence for a while. Then Leah spoke.

'Actually… it's quite tough right now.'

Tiffany turned to her with total sympathy.

'She cries a lot.' Leah glanced at her colleague, who wrinkled her nose in an oblivious smile. 'I mean, a *lot*.'

'They do at that age, though. You know, when they can't talk much, so they scream at you instead. And, of course, there's the Terrible Two's, when they really start having tantrums.'

'It's hard.' A tear glistened in Leah's eye, and she fought to stop a salty streak from slicing into the hidden flare-up. 'Really, really hard.'

'Oh, Leah…' Tiffany frowned. 'You really are having a time of it.'

Leah blinked. 'That's why I'm here. I feel terrible for saying it. But… I was going crazy and I just needed some time.'

'Of course you do. I remember how it was with mine. Well, my eldest at least. He was way more demanding than his brother. Mind you, it's always a minefield with your first.'

'You've got kids?'

'Yeah.' Tiffany flashed an ice-white smile. 'Well, I wouldn't say kids now. Jayden's nineteen and Junior is just coming up for fifteen.'

Leah was almost too stunned to speak. 'You don't even look old enough! Sorry… I didn't mean that to sound rude.'

But Tiffany was already beaming. 'Actually, it's a compliment. I turned forty a couple of months ago.'

It took effort for Leah to clamp her mouth shut. Five years *older* than she was. There wasn't even a hint of a line on her face.

'So, are you single? Married?'

'Divorced.' Tiffany's expression soured. 'The bastard was having it away with his secretary and he tried to cheat me into giving him my life savings.'

'Seriously? How awful for you.'

'Water under the bridge, it seems like so long ago. Junior was only five when I walked out and took the boys with me. I'm only in touch with him now because he's their dad. Otherwise, I'd literally never have seen him again.'

'Sounds like you've been through so much,' Leah said, almost feeling guilty for complaining about her life when she at least had a husband who was loyal and dependable.

'It was tough when it happened,' replied Tiffany. 'But I'm so proud of my boys, or should I say, young men. And at least now they're older, I've got my life back and can think about me for a change instead!'

'Excuse me…' A woman interrupted them. 'I'm looking for a new night cream. And I've heard about this super serum you do…'

'*SySTEM*!' answered Tiffany with glee.

'That's the one.'

'You've come to the right place.'

As she walked the woman over to the seat, Leah marvelled at Tiffany's tiny figure and her lustrous hair, piled up high in its glossy bun on top of her head. It almost boosted her own confidence. If somebody could look like that after they had hit forty with two grown-up children, there was hope for anyone in Leah's shoes.

'Well, I'll have a gallon of the stuff if *that's* what it does for your skin…' The customer's eyes lit up as

Tiffany opened the lid of a jar and closed in on her to apply it. 'Is this the one you use? My goodness, you're stunning!'

'Actually, I use *The Lift* but the horse chestnut in this one here has the best firming qualities.'

They chatted on, so Leah took a cloth and began to clean the shelves. It was still hard to look straight down, and her cheeks stung every time she blinked. For a moment, she considered topping up the coverage with a smidge of foundation from the makeup stand, but it was too much of a gamble when any number of the products could have been the very cause.

'It's *natural?*' The woman's shriek caused Leah to jerk her head around. 'That is your actual hair?'

Tiffany nodded and rolled her eyes. 'Heard it a million times. People always think I've got extensions. Trouble is, it's just so thick I can't even wear it down.'

Leah glanced into the mirrored wall that lined the back of the shelves, her heart sinking at the baby-fine tresses, smoothed flat against her own scalp. Even her thin ponytail was an effort, with annoying little bumps of hair popping up the minute the elastic was secured.

'Go on then, I'll take two boxes of the *Conker It All,*' said the woman, as she inspected Tiffany's work on her face. 'Mind you, I'll need two serums as well in that case.'

'What size would you like?' asked Tiffany.

'The largest, thank you.'

Tiffany took the boxes from the shelf and placed them down on the counter.

'I'd better have the exfoliating soil as well. And what colour are you wearing on that perfect pout of yours?'

'Azalea Kiss from the *TuLIPS* set.'

'I'll take two palettes. One for me and one for my daughter… actually, three, because my niece's birthday is coming up.'

Taking some tissue paper from behind the counter, Tiffany sprayed it with fragrance before scrunching it softly into an EdenCore bag, just as she and Leah had been taught to do with every customer.

'Mmmm, I know that smell...' said the woman knowingly. 'It's the beetroot one, isn't it? I tried it the last time I was here.'

'Absolutely!' Tiffany continued to scan the products and loaded them inside.

'Grab me one of those, will you?'

'No problem. Again, there are two sizes...'

'Largest, please.'

In the bag it went, along with a selection of samples.

'Anything else for you?'

'No, I think that's about it.' The woman dug into her handbag, fishing out a packet of mints, some travel tissues, and an old, squashed tube of *Palm Oil* hand cream. 'You're not going to believe this, but I think I've come shopping without my purse.'

Leah took a glimpse at Tiffany and felt terrible for her that she was about to lose the sale. She saw the disappointment creep in on her face, but she expertly masked it all with her tone of voice.

'No worries, I can easily put everything aside for you.'

But the woman was already shrugging her shoulders. 'To be honest, it'll be a long time before I get the chance to come back again.'

'OK. That's such a shame.'

It was Glovers policy that items could only be held for twenty-four hours. There was nothing else that Tiffany could do.

'Oh, hang on...' The woman chuckled as she reached inside her coat and, at last, she pulled out her small leather purse. 'It was in here all the time!'

'That's a relief, then!' A smile broke out on Tiffany's

face and she brought the shopping to a total on the till. 'Right, where were we? That will be…'

'In fact…' said the woman, eyeing her flattened hand cream. 'As I won't be back for a while, I should probably stock up on that.'

'Of course.' Tiffany turned her back, skimming the shelf with her fingers. 'I assume you would like the large one?'

'Three, if you don't mind.'

'Last ones left, just for you!'

'Lovely. Better get out of here before the husband sees.' The customer lowered her voice. 'It's his credit card, after all!'

Tiffany grinned as she gave her the receipt, placing the string straps of the bag into her hand. As soon as the woman had left the store, she seized the tablet from behind the counter and flicked on the screen to the sales chart, typing in the generous figure under her name.

'That's my target done already!' Her beam was bright white and creaseless around the eyes.

'You can put your feet up now then,' joked Leah.

'Chance would be a fine thing.' Tiffany started to back away. 'I'm just going up to the stockroom to see if we've had a delivery. Are you OK on your own?'

'I'll be fine.'

'Just ring upstairs if you need me. The number is on the list by the phone.'

'Will do.'

Leah held her smile until Tiffany disappeared beyond the top of the escalator. Then she immediately ran to the mirror and made sure her makeup was intact where her skin was getting flaky underneath. Despite the glare of the ceiling lights showing up just about every fleck possible on her face, the signs of the reactive flesh were still surprisingly hidden.

Alone on the counter for the first time, Leah started to feel uneasy. She had been there for nearly two hours now and still hadn't sold a thing. Compared to the megabucks that Tiffany had just raked in, Leah knew she had a lot of catching up to do and she couldn't bear Rhona coming in tomorrow and seeing just how far she had missed the mark. She had to do something fast.

Thinking back to the training week, when they covered troubleshooting for empty counters, she remembered the suggestions for things she could try. She hated to admit it, but the vile, red perfume which had quickly become her nemesis might just be the item that would get her a sale.

She lifted the bottle from the top of the rack and stood with it over by the main entrance to the store.

'Morning!' she said cheerily to the first couple through the door. 'Have you tried our amazing signature fragrance?'

'Not today.' One of the women pushed her palm in Leah's face. 'In a hurry.'

Three teenage boys were next to enter.

'Why are we even in here, you knob?' asked the middle one, cracking open a can of cola and flicking the froth in his friend's face.

'Getting deodorant for you, mate, 'cos everyone knows you smell.'

They all laughed raucously, turning the head of the security guard. Leah pursed her lips, knowing that their grans would be more interested in EdenCore products than they could ever be. She waited for them to walk away and turned her attention back to the door.

More people shook their heads as she spoke while others deliberately looked the other way. Mothers with pushchairs were only after nappies and office workers on their lunchbreaks made a beeline for the sandwich chiller, already calling up the voucher codes on their phones.

Next one in and I'll have them, Leah promised herself.

In came a woman who couldn't be less than sixty, her bleached blonde hair scraped up as high as it would go. She wore skinny jeans and a clingy vest under a faux tiger fur jacket, with huge hoop earrings and patent knee-high boots.

'Hi there…' Leah greeted her, holding out the bottle. 'Can I interest you in *T-Radish-ional?*'

'Oh, I know it well, love. Got loads of it at home.'

'OK… have you tried the other two?'

'The peach is good.' She grimaced. 'But they've never got that beetroot one in stock.'

Leah frowned. 'Yes, we have. Definitely! Would you like to come over and I'll show you.'

The woman leaned in closer, her lips glinting as she slowed the chomps on her chewing gum. 'Where's your boss?'

Of course, Leah thought. She wanted to see Rhona. Probably one of those faithful customers who will only purchase from their favourite staff member.

'Sorry, she's not in today. She'll be back tomorrow, though.'

'That's alright then!' The woman winked. 'I'll just get my cod liver oil and then I'll be over.'

She scuttled off to the healthcare department, so Leah went to check the full stock of fragrance.

'Still no delivery!' Tiffany announced on her return. 'This is a joke. What are we going to do when we run out of serum?'

'Keep going the way you did earlier and we'll be just fine,' Leah said proudly. 'Anyway, I've got another customer coming over in a minute. Flagged her down at the door.'

'Well done, you! Where is she then?'

'Getting some vitamins over there.'

'Excellent. Go for it! And remember the number one rule: Five to invest, Two to test.'

'Got it,' Leah replied, remembering the training. Staff were not allowed to give out any free trial sizes unless a customer bought five items. Only then were they eligible for two complimentary samples.

'Hello?' A young woman was at the cosmetics stand. She had drawn three colour swatches on the inside of her wrist. 'I got given this voucher over there. Three for two lip liners. Will it work on EdenCore stuff?'

Leah shook her head. 'It's only for Capital G products I'm afraid. That's why they get handed out at all the tills in here, being the store's own brand.'

'Well, they could have told me that.' The woman looked irritated. 'These are gorgeous.'

'Which one do you like?'

'I don't know. All three are so nice.'

'You'd definitely know which one suits you best if we tried them on you.'

'No point now. Can't afford all three at these prices.'

'No… but neutral shades like these will work with any colour lipstick, so you only need one.'

The woman squinted. 'OK, I'll give it a go.'

'Just take a seat.' Leah smiled as she raised the chair to a decent height and laid out some cotton wool pads next to it. 'Now, the way to get the best effect is to cleanse the area first. How would you describe your skin?'

'Combination,' she replied without hesitation. 'Oily nose and chin but dry everywhere else.'

'No problem.' Leah reached for the appropriate bottle. 'This is *Barley Blend*, the combination cleanser from our Wake Up cereal range.' She smoothed it on gently, removing the excess with a pad before following with *Mint Condition* toner. Knowing that neither of these had been in her free gift bag from training, Leah recommended them with confidence, as they couldn't possibly have been responsible for the reaction on her own skin.

'I love how they feel…' the woman purred. 'And the smell is so soothing!'

'Sure is,' agreed Leah, screwing the caps back on the bottles. 'And if you like these, you're going to *love* our serum.'

Leah opted for a balancing type that went well with the combination cleansing range. As she patted a pump on her customer's face, she hoped with all her might there would be no bad reaction.

'And the final step of your skincare is, of course, moisturiser.' Leah looked into her eyes. 'Do you mind me asking how old you are? You see, each range is tailored to age.'

'I'm thirty-one.' The customer smiled, knowing she looked far younger. 'Still get ID'd every time I'm buying booze in the supermarket.'

She laughed, but Leah had a sinking feeling as she stepped over to the tester stand. She was going to have to demonstrate the *Sweet Potato Face Mash*. The over-thirties' day cream that could easily be another culprit. She had hoped the customer would be younger than this, and then at least she could have shown her the zingy range for teens to twenties. She reached for the jar but couldn't bring herself to take it.

'You know what?' she called over instead. 'You're only just in your thirties, so I'd be tempted to make sure that the younger range definitely doesn't work for you before going up to the next stage.'

'OK…'

'So, I'm going to try this instead.'

Leah came back over with a bright yellow pot. 'It's our *Lemon Meringue* moisturiser, infused with citrus in a whipped consistency that is ideal for youthful skin. Try this…'

The woman immediately sucked in a breath. 'Wow! Nothing like anything I've tried before.'

'Just let it melt in.' Leah was getting a real kick from her first ever consultation. 'Now, right before we do the lip liner, we have got the loveliest primer which will give you the best results once the colour goes on.' She squeezed a pea-sized amount from another small tube, applied it softly and then pressed on with the liners.

Starting with the lightest shade, she progressed to the medium nude and then the deepest reddish brown. The woman took pictures of each one on her lips and scrolled back and forth, trying to make her mind up.

'I think the *Birch* is too pale, but *Mahogany* isn't natural enough.'

'You're right.' Leah cocked her head and leaned back a little to examine her. '*Aspen* is the one for you. Absolutely made for your skin tone.'

'I'm definitely getting the whole lot. Everything you've shown me.'

'Amazing!' enthused Leah, hardly able to wait until she could start ruffling the tissue paper. 'So, that's cleanser, toner, moisturiser, primer, and your lip liner. And the best news is that when you buy five products, you get free samples.'

'How long is the offer on?'

'Oh, it's not an offer. It's a permanent thing we do.'

'Even better!' The woman took a picture of the products on her phone.

'I'll get everything together then and see you at the till when you're ready.'

'Oh, no… you see, my boyfriend's not here today.'

Leah was confused. 'Right.'

'I've taken a photo so he can get it for me online. That way, he can do it when there's a discount and get it all even cheaper.'

'Of course, they don't always do everything on the website that we have here.'

'If not, he can get it down the road at Parlour. They seem to have much better offers than the Glovers counters ever do.'

'Well…' Leah was becoming tongue-tied and as she glanced up, the woman she had met at the store entrance had arrived and was about to be greeted by Tiffany. 'My name's Leah anyway, and if you change your mind, please do come back and I'll be happy to help.'

'Thanks.' The woman stuffed the phone into her handbag. 'Where did you say the Capital G stand is?'

Leah pointed. 'It's over there, just past KittyPie.'

'I think I'll spend that voucher after all.'

She sped off, leaving Leah to clear up the consultation area just in time to see the other woman racing up to Tiffany and grabbing her in a hug.

'Mum!' Tiffany yelled as she nuzzled into the woman. 'Knew you'd be popping by.'

'I hear Rhona's not in today,' she said with a cunning wink. 'Perfect timing!'

'Come on, then.'

Tiffany whizzed to the drawers at the till while her mother followed as quick as a flash. Glancing over her shoulder, she opened up a carrier bag while Tiffany threw handfuls of samples inside. Leah watched open-mouthed as Tiffany continued adding to the stash, being sure to hurl in everything she herself wanted too.

'Ta, Tiff, that should do us.'

Tiffany's mother shoved the bag under her shopping and checked warily around the counter from the corner of her eye, catching sight of Leah as she did so.

'Hello again, sweetie!' She tottered over, smiling from ear to ear. 'We meet again.'

'Leah, this is my mum, Diane.'

'Hello, love.' She shook Leah's hand. 'My gal here was getting lonely working Sundays on her own. Nice you've got each other now.' She turned to Tiffany. 'She's adorable, ain't she darling?'

'Yeah, we've hit it off already, haven't we, babes?'

'It's actually weird,' said Leah. 'I feel like I've known you for ages, Tiff.'

'Same! We've got so much in common, Mum.'

'She's an absolute doll, bless her!' Diane cooed. 'She was talking to me about that beetroot perfume over there. Said you've got it back in stock.'

But Tiffany was already shaking her head. 'We've had it on order for months, Mum. I checked through the drawer just now too. Would have given you a load if we'd got it.'

Then it dawned on Leah. Of course, Diane wasn't wanting to buy it.

'That's what I meant when I said you were out of it.' She whispered into Leah's ear, splaying her garish nails. '*Samples.*'

'Got it,' Leah winked, knowing she would just have to go along with their antics. She was too new to start reporting staff members and if there was something she didn't need in her already stressful life, it was strained relationships as a result of getting someone into trouble.

'Be careful on your way out, Mum.' Tiffany warned. 'That security guard's got his eye on you.'

'Oh, has he now?' Diane grinned like the Cheshire Cat before sauntering seductively in his direction. 'Just leave him to me. He'll be sorry he stared once I've had my way with him.'

The pair giggled as she walked brazenly away and after flirting just a little too long until the brawny man was blushing, she swept past the window with the samples safely in her grip.

***

As late afternoon crept in and it was almost closing time, Leah took a seat behind the counter and added on the last couple of sales she had managed. Both customers had totally refused to even look at any other products. One had only bought some face wash for her husband while the other had purchased a single eyeshadow. Against Tiffany's lucky sale of multiple expensive items, Leah's row of single units looked less than impressive in comparison.

But before she could allow herself to worry too much, she decided to let it go. She was new to this, after all. It would take time and practice for the sales techniques to kick in and reach their full potential.

Tiffany was just pulling the boxes forward on the shelves, making everything tidy for when Rhona was back in the morning, when a woman in a long burgundy coat began to peruse the display.

'Hi there…' she stopped neatening up and stepped over to assist her. 'Can I help you at all?'

Leah closed her eyes in annoyance. If only she had been over the other side, she could have got in there and approached her first.

'Just looking, thanks.'

'At the sun care, I see.' Tiffany replied. 'Going away on holiday anywhere nice or are you just staying around—'

'I'm not buying anything.'

'No problem at all.' Although she was clearly taken

aback, Tiffany kept her manner polite. 'Feel free to have a look and I'll be over here if you need anything.'

Tiffany turned towards Leah, subtly rolling her eyes. Then she stepped away, leaving her to browse as she wished.

'You never have the shaving foam in stock, do you?'

Leah heard her, but didn't look up, assuming that she was speaking to Tiffany.

'I said...' The insistence in her voice caught Leah's attention, but the woman's back remained turned away, her ponytail straggly over her shoulder. 'You never have the men's shaving foam.'

Tiffany had ducked behind the counter, doing a final clean with her spray and rag, so Leah stepped in to respond.

'It's a popular one, to be honest. My husband is keen to give it a go, so I'm looking out for when it comes in. We can take your number, if you like, and let you know when it's delivered.'

'What about the sun cream? You're out of Factor 50.'

Hearing the way she snapped at Leah, Tiffany cut into the conversation. 'Again, we've got it on order. We don't get much in at a time, only one or two boxes.'

'Not very good, is it?'

'I can only apologise. Shouldn't really recommend a rival brand, but Chimie do a good shaving foam if the man in your life would be up for trying it.'

The woman let out a grating laugh. '*Man?*' She looked at Tiffany as if she were stupid. 'Not me, thanks.'

Leah detected a Brummie accent and glanced subtly over to see more of the woman's face. She was a similar height, and she didn't smile with her eyes.

'Have to say, I know what you mean!' said Tiffany. 'Husbands suck. I split up with mine years ago and haven't looked back. Me and my boys have always been better without him.'

'Can't say I've had a bad experience,' the woman replied. 'It's just that I hate *people*. I love my life too much. I'm forty-two, live on my own, always have, always will. I've got my little flat, my kale smoothies for breakfast, my bed all to myself and I never have to share. I would just loathe being married or having someone else I'd have to see every day.'

'Me too. Who wants to compromise everything they do because of having to take their other half into consideration?' Tiffany sneered.

'Exactly. I have no respect for anyone who is partnered up. It's so... *dependent*!' said the woman mockingly.

As they continued to exchange negative thoughts on the chores of coupled life, Leah felt slightly offended when they were both aware of her own marital status. To each their own, of course, but she couldn't fathom the need be so judgemental on a fairly common arrangement.

The woman then left without saying goodbye and Tiffany dashed off as she had to meet Junior and buy him a new pair of trainers.

Leah left the counter and drifted up the escalator, gazing back beneath her at the rapidly-emptying store. Eric would be picking Kiki up right at this moment from Cheryl, and she was looking forward to a proper dinner in for the first time in days. The single life had been fun for a week, but nothing could beat a foot massage and a bottle of wine for two.

Ten

'OK, birthday girl, are you ready?' Leah said excitedly to Kiki as she reached into the wardrobe. 'I have waited too long for you to wear this!'

Unhooking the hanger from the rail, she pulled out a pale pink dress with puffed sleeves and a diamante bow at the neckline. Frothy tiers poured out from the waist downwards, as if the skirt was made from reams of cotton candy.

Leah knelt down at the changing mat where Kiki was lying in a white romper vest. As she wiggled her feet, the lace around her socks hit the air like butterflies. Leah unbuttoned the back of the dress and opened it out to put on her.

'Where is she, then?' she called playfully into the hole where Kiki's head would poke through in the next minute. 'Hellooo, is there a princess in here?'

Leah eased each hand into the armholes.

'Well, I've found these. But where's the rest of you?'

She pulled the dress down over Kiki's body until her soft chestnut locks appeared at the top.

'Here she comes…'

As the cherubic face revealed itself, complete with pouting lips, Leah fastened the dress and leaned back to admire Kiki, supporting her while she sat.

'Oh, my word!' she almost whispered, her chirpy voice diminishing as awe took its place. 'Look at you, so gorgeous.'

Propping Kiki up against a pile of cushions, she reached across for her phone and took a few snapshots. Then she scooted back over to her daughter. She smoothed Kiki's cheeks and ran her fingers over each tiny toe, taking a deep breath.

'Sometimes… I forget how lucky I am. That I've got such a beautiful girl.'

As she spoke, Kiki uncrumpled her face and gazed into her eyes. She fiddled with handfuls of her dress hem, and didn't show the hint of a grizzle.

'I know you can't help it. And Mummy's sorry. She's sorry to get impatient and… sorry if it seems like she doesn't want you around. She does, Kiki. I do.'

Leah smiled, trying to control her tears.

'Sorry I'm a bad mother…'

'*What?*' Eric's voice startled her. 'You're not a bad mother.'

Leah looked around at him, quickly returning her gaze to Kiki.

'I just feel like it's my fault. I guess I need to hold it together better and not fly off the handle so quickly.'

Eric cleared some toys off the floor and neatened up the cot bed. 'Everyone knows she's hard work and *anyone* would struggle. I mean, I've not heard many other kids scream like her. She's a little monster! Aren't you, eh? You're a…'

Leah shuffled sideways so Eric could see Kiki in the floaty folds of her dress.

'Look at you! Who's Daddy's perfect girl?' He pulled her onto his lap. Kiki shoved her hands into her mouth and gurgled as he spoke. 'I take that back. You are definitely not a monster on your special day!'

'She does look lovely, doesn't she?' Leah beamed. 'There's just one thing missing.' She slid open the top drawer from the unit behind her and brought out a pastel pink flower on a clip. Parting Kiki's hair to the side, she secured it in place and smiled proudly at the tot in all her finery, just as the doorbell rang.

'That will be Aunty Flora and Uncle Glen.' Eric handed Kiki back to Leah. 'I'll shout up when everyone's here and you can bring her down then, OK?'

Leah nodded as he kissed the top of her head.

'Don't worry, she'll be fine. And no more talk of not being a good mum.' He turned before leaving the room. 'You're the best.'

Kiki tried to reach for her textured octopus toy, so Leah handed it over and laid her back down on her mat. Once Kiki was occupied, she closed the baby gate and slipped into the bathroom.

Her makeup looked smoother than it had in a fortnight, now that her skin was fully healed of the blistered mess from the EdenCore products. She still hadn't dared to use any of them since. Instead, she topped up her bronze Capital G eyeliner which complemented the garnet red of her blouse.

The doorbell went several times more and a growing throng of voices chattered away downstairs.

'That ivy needs cutting back, Eric.' Cheryl's voice chimed as she came into the house. 'You'll have no light in your living room if you let it get out of control. Alan will do it… won't you, Alan?'

Leah smiled to herself, knowing that her stepfather's face would look exactly as it always did when Cheryl roped him into things.

'Can we at least have a cup of tea first?' he boomed in his Northern-Irish twang.

'Yes, and you can make it.'

Leah put some earrings in and swept half her hair up so they could dangle freely. Then she reapplied some old pink lipstick, blotting it on a tissue.

'OK, Mummy!' Eric shouted upstairs. 'I think that's everyone.'

She stepped back into Kiki's room and smiled as the child looked up at her. And Leah just wanted to stay there forever, in this moment, where Kiki was actually happy. Those eyes, when they weren't screwed up and spluttering teardrops, were a thing of beauty. Leah could have stared into them for hours. Her neat little mouth was like a rosebud against glowing olive skin when it was not stretched out in its usual howl, turning her cheeks an infuriated claret.

'Come on, then. Let's show everyone what a darling you really are!'

Hoisting Kiki into her arms and finding her body under the mass of frills, she walked gently down the stairs, grinning as all eyes fell on the two of them. There were gleaming teeth, clapping hands, words of adoration and little whistles of delight. Leah whisked Kiki quickly around the crowd so she didn't have time to get crotchety after each chin tickle and every arm squeeze. Eric stood at the doorway and motioned for Leah to enter the lounge.

As the friends and relatives followed them through, Leah gasped at the huge pile of gifts that had formed in the middle of the room.

'Oh wow, thank you so much everyone, for all this!'

'Do you want me to hold her while you open them?' Cheryl asked. 'Or Alan will have her.'

'Oh, I don't know about that,' he joked.

Kiki jerked at Alan's voice and reached her arms out for him, whimpering until Leah passed her over. She wished he were a permanent resident in her home as he had always managed to calm her down. He was a bear of a man with a voice so soothing that even Leah could imagine falling asleep whenever she overheard him reading Kiki's bedtime stories.

The visitors settled into armchairs and perched on sofa ends, while Leah knelt beside the stack of surprises, all lovingly wrapped in unicorns, heart prints and fairies. Alan and Cheryl sat on the two closest chairs so that Kiki could see her new things being opened.

Leah started with a shiny lilac bag which held two small items taped up with tissue paper. In one was a red headband, embellished with a ladybird on a leaf, and in the other was a cloth character from a TV show.

'Look what your cousins got you, Kiki!' She placed it in her daughter's lap and gazed across the room at the children of Eric's brother. 'Thanks, both of you. She watches Poppy and Patch all the time.'

Kiki started chewing on the squishy head, then lost her grip and it fell to the floor. Her face instantly shrivelled, and Alan frantically rummaged beneath the seat with his free hand.

'It's there, Mum…' Leah pointed to a spot just behind their legs, willing someone to hand the toy back before Kiki got too worked up. Cheryl seized it, dancing it playfully back to Kiki's grasp where it was swiftly soaked in more dribble.

Next was a larger package from the neighbours across the road. It shimmered with seahorses, jellyfish, and mermaid tails. Leah tried to involve Kiki in ripping open the paper, but she thrusted her body the opposite way, nuzzling into Alan. Leah giggled and rolled her eyes, trying to make light of the disinterest, but she clenched every muscle in her limbs while the roomful of people watched on.

'Oh, she's going to love this!' she squealed as an interactive keyboard emerged from inside the wrapping. Leah took it out of the box straight away, now overwhelmingly eager to keep Kiki amused. She flicked the button and the noises sprang to life. Surely, this would be enough of a distraction. Placing it on Alan's lap, Leah pressed the coloured keys, each one featuring a different animal, so Kiki could see the lights and hear the automatic tune in a chorus of voices.

Can you sing a happy song?
Have a go and play along!

Kiki dropped the cloth toy and instantly listened to the words. Leah watched hopefully as her eyes widened and spreading her fingers out readily to try it. She started by pressing the highest notes, touching the mouse, then a flamingo and a lamb. Her cheeks began to lift as a smile crept in. She kept going and the sounds got deeper. A kangaroo, a dolphin. She pulled away. Her face tightened and Leah clenched her teeth.

'Come on…' Alan laughed. 'Don't stop halfway through!'

He guided her hand to where she had left off.

'Crocodile next, Kiki,' urged Cheryl.

Kiki pressed a few more keys, but the penultimate note was considerably deeper than the one before it. She started to whinge.

'Are you scared of the hippo?' said Alan, hugging her tightly. 'Well, that's a shame. I really wanted to hear the elephant at the end.'

'I'll help you with that…' Eric leaned over and winked at Kiki. 'Listen to what Daddy can do.'

He pushed the lowest key all the way down and held it there while a deep drone echoed out from the speaker.

Kiki started to thrash about, kicking her legs and pummelling the back of her head against Alan, but Eric continued to hold the note.

'OK...' Leah's mouth was clamped in a smile while she gestured at Eric to stop. 'Give it another go later.'

'Oh, what's up, you little pickle?' He smirked and tapped the same key again, upsetting Kiki all the more.

'Eric, that's enough.' Leah grabbed his arm, then hissed warily when her voice was out of earshot. 'She doesn't *like* it.' Then, she faced the neighbours with a reassuring grin. 'It's just new to her, that's all. I'm sure she'll love it with a bit of practice.'

But Eric pressed the main music button again in a last-ditch bid to snap Kiki out of it.

Can you sing a happy song?
Have a go and play a—

Kiki's deafening wail pierced the walls and she knotted her hands into fists, thumping them down on the keys and wriggling so wildly that even Alan fought to contain her. The keyboard flew off his knee and landed with a loud smack against the corner of the coffee table. A large chunk of plastic chipped off the side and the happy tune blurred into slow motion until it sounded like trolls in a horror movie.

The jolly demeanour around the room dropped to an awkward hush, the remainder of the chuckles purely from embarrassment. Leah stared at the carpet, hardly able to look up at her neighbours. When she did, Moira's face was one of woe.

'Of course, I could have taken it back, but now...' She shrugged her shoulders, which were patted from behind by her husband, Dennis.

'I'll fix it,' Eric said quickly. 'I'm sure it's nothing a

toolbox won't sort out.'

'Alan will do it,' Cheryl cut in. 'Won't you, Alan?'

Alan nodded doubtfully as he bounced Kiki up and down. No one else spoke. Leah breathed through pursed lips, trying her hardest not to cry. She saw Eric clock her.

'Right, next present!' He clapped his hands together, encouraging Leah to continue through his silent eye contact. 'Look at that massive one there!'

'Now, if you don't think it's right for her, please just say,' said Cheryl.

Leah gathered herself and pulled it over, wishing she was somewhere else. Kiki had paused from her outburst and had now reverted to chomping on her cloth character. With enthusiasm ebbing away from her by the minute, Leah pulled at the tape and tore away the stars and cats dotted over the wrapping.

She saw the wheels first, and then a pink frame. There was a baby doll strapped into a padded seat at the front and one thick handlebar running along the back. But this wasn't just a toy pushchair. It was a baby walker modelled into one.

'Mum… Alan, it's lovely, but…'

'I know, darling, you don't need to explain. I did say to Alan in the shop that it's a bit too old for her. You need things she can use right now. It's useless if it's serving no purpose.'

'No, that's not the problem.' Leah could feel her heart sinking. 'If she was definitely going to grow into it, I couldn't think of anything better. But… she might not ever walk, remember?'

'Not necessarily,' said Alan, firmly. 'You know what the physio says. She has to exercise those ankles. That's why your mother and I thought…'

Cheryl coughed deliberately.

'That's why *I* suggested that it might not be such a

bad idea.'

'It's brilliant,' Eric spoke up. 'Just what she needs.'

'A lovely thought, thank you. We'll see how she gets on,' agreed Leah.

'Go on…' said Eric to Alan. 'Stand her behind it at least. Let's see how she measures up.'

Fully supporting Kiki, Alan lifted her off his knee and Leah put her fingers gently on the handle. She was almost the right height. Just seeing her there on her own two feet, albeit with help all around her, nearly broke Leah in two when she thought of what could, but might never, be.

'What a big girl with her pushchair, just like Mummy!' Eric gushed against a backdrop of coos.

But Leah watched the agitation building in Kiki's expression. The face flushing rapidly like a volcano verging on eruption. Then came the downturned corners of her mouth and the snivelling began to mount.

'Let's not rush her.' Cheryl swooped in and lifted her out of the commotion. 'Come on, Kiki Koo, sit with Nana while we do the rest of the presents.'

Feeling like her soul was being sucked slowly out of herself, Leah carried on. There were fluffy bears and new books, finger paints and outfits, but Kiki rejected all of them, screaming even harder when each one was revealed. She kicked until her socks fell off. She mushed her hair until the clip popped out and got lost in the depths of the sofa. Then she arched her back with a thunderous wail and elbowed Cheryl in the neck.

'Oh my God, Mum, are you OK?' Leah gasped, dropping the last gift and shuffling over to see her.

'I'm fine…' Cheryl mumbled as Kiki was fished out of her arms.

'Maybe she's getting hungry,' shouted Eric above the chaos as Kiki continued to flail around in his hold. 'I think we should head into the other room and get started on the food.'

As the guests followed, he plonked Kiki down in her highchair and fixed her safely inside. Upon the extended dining table was a pretty cover patterned with rabbits having a tea party. Balloons were tied to the back of each chair and confetti number one shapes were scattered between the plates. Leah had spent a fortune making it look perfect and had put painstaking effort into the buffet all weekend. Sandwiches and sausage rolls, homemade quiche and vol-au-vents. She had copied Cheryl's recipe for coronation chicken and had even created her own dips, surrounded by an array of crudites.

When Eric had filled a plate for Kiki, the rest of the crowd helped themselves and Cheryl, having recovered from the blow, sat with Alan, coaxing Kiki with the snacks.

'I'll just get the drinks,' Leah said, walking over to the kitchen area. She pulled wine and lemonade out of the fridge and slapped them absently on the worktop, her sight blurring between the tiles where the grout had yellowed on the wall. The throng of chatter swarmed in her ears as if it were whooshing against her skull.

'Leah…' Eric's shout interrupted her quiet subsidence. 'What are you doing? Have something to eat.'

She clasped the bottles with her shaking hands and brought them over to the pile of paper cups. Sitting upright in her chair, she slowly collapsed inside.

With a forkful of potato salad pushed between her lips, she watched Kiki's hands slapping restlessly on the tray. The corn puff crisps swelling to double their size as she took large handfuls and stuffed them into her cup of juice. The tomato ketchup being daubed around like paint as she smeared it on her forehead and coated her dress in saucy red. The munched-up cucumber dripping from her mouth as its screaming hole widened like a cave full of moss.

As the platters started emptying, she got to her feet and collected them up, throwing them into a bin bag and tossing it across the kitchen. She thumped out new plates, not uttering a word while she peeled back clingfilm on delicate iced biscuits, profiteroles, an impressive raspberry jelly, and a vat of vanilla ice cream. Everyone else dug in, politely ignoring the gruelling howls, but Leah just watched Kiki, maddening by the second. She only saw the spoon once it launched from Kiki's hand, spattering chocolate sauce over the new cream window blinds.

'I think I... need some fresh air.'

Leah got up from the table and left the oblivious guests. She stepped out into the cloudy afternoon, gripping the patio door.

Within minutes, a hand covered hers. 'Leah...'

She didn't reply. Her whole body felt like elastic, just waiting to snap.

'I know, OK? I know.' Eric forced her to look him in the eyes. 'You can do this. You've just got to be strong.'

Leah looked away again, almost fighting for breath. Everything ahead of her melted into obscurity, like watercolours being rinsed from a brush. The petals trembling in their plant pots and the cobweb-covered watering can as it scraped over the paving slabs under the lashing breeze.

'It's almost over. Let's just get through this last bit, alright?'

She looked past his shoulder into the lounge, where the keyboard pieces were scattered on the rug amidst a crumpled mass of ripped up wrapping paper, and she gave the slightest nod.

'See you in there.' He kissed her forehead and dashed

away again.

No one noticed her slipping into the kitchen and peeling back the foil tent she had encased around the cake. A huge pink castle that had taken her hours to make. It had fondant towers and glittery turrets with clear sugar windows and marshmallow flowers over layer upon layer of pink sponge, buttercream, and jam. It was the final chance to make Kiki smile. All Leah's love had gone into that cake and now, all her hope did too.

She lit the candle in pride of place at the very centre of the frosted roof, and just managed to balance it all in her two quivering arms. Eric saw she was ready, and he roused the guests into the all-important singing.

Happy Birthday to you,
Happy Birthday to you…

Leah sucked in the avalanche of emotions as she sung the words to her daughter for the very first time.

Happy Birthday, dear Kiki,
Happy Birthday to you.

She set the cake down in front of Kiki, whose eyes widened in wonder at the enormously sweet treat.

'Did you do that all yourself? It's wonderful!' Cheryl exclaimed.

'Yes, I did,' Leah said in a hushed tone, almost terrified to disrupt Kiki's mesmerised reaction.

'She gets it from you.' Alan put his arm around Cheryl and winked.

'Look at that!' Eric froze as he spoke. 'She loves it, Leah!'

'Here you go…' said Leah, a trickle of relief daring to inch through her. She picked a pink wafer biscuit off the side, still fluffy with the icing, and held it out for Kiki, who took it between her fingers and rolled it over her tongue. 'Is that nice?'

Kiki blinked at her, and despite all the food slop, the flustered cheeks and the broken toys, in that split second, she was Leah's beautiful girl again. Because she wasn't crying. She was listening.

'Do you like it?'

Leah could feel her lips quaking as she watched Kiki's every move. And then, in the next moment, Kiki pulled the wafer away and her face began to crease. She crushed it in her hand, smashing her palm up and down on the tray until there was nothing left but a crumbly blob of goo.

'Oh, come on, Kiki,' said Eric. 'Mummy's worked very hard and...'

Kiki batted and writhed until her highchair toppled and Alan had to hold it still while she spiralled into a rage. She kicked out hard with both her feet, sending the cake straight over, where it squelched upside down in the middle of the table, catapulting buttercream all over Leah's face.

Releasing her whitened knuckles from the serving knife, Leah backed away from the table while everyone sat in silence.

'I'm done.'

'Leah...' Eric started to get up.

'No, I'm... I'm just done.'

'It's OK, Leah...' said Cheryl, watching her expression morph into madness. 'Leah, darling...'

'I said...' Leah panted, reaching behind her for her car keys. 'I'm done with it. I'm done... I'm just...'

Horror flooded into Eric's eyes when he heard the jangling from Leah's hand, yet he was trapped behind the table and sandwiched between the relatives. 'Don't do this. Please.' He tried to stay calm, but she had already opened the door latch and was racing down the front steps. 'Leah!'

She started the car as Cheryl shot out of the house to try and stop her. In the mirror, she could see Eric sprinting along the driveway. She slid into first gear and he dived into the back seat, just as she sped off down the road with no idea where she was going.

'Pull in, Leah!' he cried, but she ignored him, hammering down on the accelerator and screeching around each corner. 'You're going to have an accident! For God's sake, pull the bloody car in.'

She could barely see for the tears that were leaving tracks in the buttercream, tinging it with salt as it leaked down to her mouth. As she clasped the wheel with sugar-coated hands, she swerved left on the roundabout, then faster onto the main highway, eyes glazing over as they stared lifelessly ahead. Each monotonous lane marking sweeping away under the car in just the same way her conveyor-belt existence did.

Jam was splodged across the windscreen from her frenzied entry into the vehicle. It fused in a blaze with the traffic lights, and horns tooted wildly as she shot past the queue.

'God, Leah! It was red, for Christ's sake!'

But there wasn't so much as a glance Eric's way. Instead, she crossed the bridge where the river tossed below them, and she helter-skeltered the car around the flyover junction. From there, she took off down the first route to Ropeshore and swung into a side road that led sharply uphill.

'No… not the cliff!' Eric shouted. 'You're going to get us killed!'

The car laboured up the rocky pathway, flanked by irregular houses and ragged walls of weeds. But the track smoothed out again and she picked up speed over the towering viaduct, where the traffic whizzed beneath them, now reduced to a miniature scale.

'Look out!' Eric screamed at the top of his lungs as something small and dark appeared like a bullet at the headlights. He threw his whole body through the gap between the seats and brought the car to an almighty skid until the bonnet wedged itself into a bush, and leaves clouded everything from view.

Leah felt like she would explode under the weight of Eric's body. He wheezed over the top of her, still clutching hold of the steering wheel.

'Sorry…' She almost choked on the words. 'I'm so…'

'Out, Leah.' Eric shook, his face squashed tight against the control unit. 'Get out of the car.'

She felt for the door handle and managed to create a gap between the seat and the shrubbery. Then she slid out from beneath Eric's shoulders and crawled on all fours into the undergrowth, her palms prickled by brambles and slapping against the damp earth.

Clambering onto the grass verge, she turned until she was sitting upright with her back against the rear tyre. She folded her arms around herself, feeling the rips in her blouse, and with one last look at the sky, she threw her head back and sobbed. And everything she had stifled inside – the whole disaster of the day, and her life – poured out in a waterfall.

All she could do was rock back and forth, clenching her teeth with her eyes shut tight, wishing it was the last she would see of the world as she knew it right now.

The weary thud of the passenger door sounded to the side of her and Eric's two hands covered her knees, easing her into his arms. Awash with cake and mud, she collapsed in a heap, burying her face in his chest.

'Shhhh, it's OK,' he whispered, still catching his

breath. 'It's going to be alright.'

'I can't do it, Eric. Not anymore.'

'You know you can. It won't be like this forever.'

'How long do I have to put up with it though?' She sniffed helplessly. 'Years…?'

'No one can answer that.'

'Three months, that's what everyone said. It gets easier from then. She's bloody one year old now and nothing is ever good enough.'

'Look, it's shit, OK? We all know that. But she's getting the help she needs with her physio and that will work wonders with a bit of time.'

'Or maybe not, if she never ends up walking.'

'You'll see…' He squeezed her tighter. 'Once she's getting around and exploring, she won't just sit there being grumpy anymore. Then you'll have something to complain about. Chasing around after her while she sneaks off into places she shouldn't be!'

Leah blotted her tears on his shirt. 'I hear other mums moaning about that all the time. If only it was my problem, too.'

'Be careful what you wish for,' Eric smiled.

His phone started buzzing and he took too long to remove it from his pocket. It stopped before he could answer it.

'Your mum's frantic. Seventeen missed calls. I'd better ring her back.'

As he tapped away at his phone, Leah rested against him while the chilled grass blades wove around her numb wrists. She could hear Cheryl's panicked voice on the other end of the line, which Eric tried to placate.

'Yeah, it's OK, we're safe… no, stopped driving now and she's sitting with me on the road… I mean, no, not *actually* on the road!'

Cheryl continued to ask anxious questions.

'Where are we? Well… just outside Ropeshore… nowhere near the cliff, don't worry… yes, coming now. Is Kiki still at it?' He nodded and closed his eyes momentarily. 'I'm not surprised she's stopped now, probably got no energy left! Just plonk her in the bath and I'll put her to bed when I get in… OK, thanks for all this. See you soon.'

Eric shoved the phone away and stretched as he got to his feet.

'She's all done with crying. Falling asleep on Alan apparently.' He held his hands out to pull her up. 'Come on, it'll be nice and quiet once she's in bed.'

Leah gave her full weight as he lifted her off the kerb, but she stood there in silence instead of heading to the car.

'I'm such a screw up,' she whispered as more tears seeped hotly down her face.

'You are *not*.' Eric shook his head. 'This is just a hell of a phase and you'll come out of the other side.'

'I don't know what I was thinking, driving off like that… putting both our lives at risk. I'm sorry.' She whimpered as he guided her towards the car.

'Us and that… I don't know… cat? You almost ran it over. Lucky escape there.'

He clicked the passenger handle and a faint squeak sounded, just as Leah stretched the door open. Eric looked at her and frowned.

'What was that?'

Leah glanced around tiredly. 'What?'

Eric put a finger up, hushing her to silence. The shrillness echoed out again and he craned his neck further towards the hedge.

'That noise…'

'Don't know. Maybe the doors need some oil.'

But he shook his head dismissively. 'It's not that.

Just… get in and I'll have a look.'

He disappeared below the windows, using the torchlight on his phone. Branches contorted and thrashed over the car as he shuffled further under the hedges, trying to follow the urgent squeals.

Leah reclined in her seat, letting her eyelids fall shut and fully expecting not to wake again until Eric was walking her up their driveway. But a tap on the glass made her jump and she turned drowsily to see the fabric of his shirt, pressed up against the panel, with something obscure in the crook of his arm. She slid the window halfway down and froze when she saw black fur.

'Oh, please… no!' she wailed into her hands. 'Poor little cat, what have I done?'

'Don't jump to conclusions.'

'I was going too fast, of course it's my fault. Is anything broken? Is it even… alive?'

Eric climbed into the back seat as the driver's side was still stuck in the foliage.

'Firstly, it walked over to me and secondly…'

He held it out in front of him, parallel to the handbrake. Leah slowly turned her head and was stunned when she looked at its face.

'A dog!'

'Only a pup by the looks of it.'

'I didn't hit it, did I?' Shame ripped through her bones all over again. She had to look away from its bewildered eyes, a deep, glossy brown, like a teddy bear. 'Eric, I'll never forgive myself if I did.'

'You didn't,' Eric said with certainty. 'Missed it by a whisker, though. It ran out of sight just before we caught up with it.' He surveyed the area in the last light of dusk. 'There are only a few houses on this stretch of road. It must belong to one of them.'

Leah waited while he knocked on each door. She dug

her nails into the passenger seatbelt, peering out to check the demeanour of every person Eric spoke to. They only had to take one look at the car, half buried in hedging, to see that an idiot driver had endangered their beloved pet.

But as evening clung to the unlit hilltop, and the meagre security lights glimmered to life, just covering the garden gates, Eric emerged through the mist, still clutching the lost little soul.

'No luck?' Leah asked, climbing back out of the car.

'They think he's a stray. Either that or he's escaped from further afield. We'll have to go to the vet and see if they can help. Here… just take him for a sec. I think there's a box in the boot.'

'*Him?*'

Eric nodded, placing the pup in her arms. His tiny body shivered as he nuzzled into her elbow. She pulled him close, and her heart felt inexplicable. A satisfying fullness that she wasn't used to knowing.

'This will have to do,' said Eric, stuffing the box with an old blanket of Kiki's. 'Pop him in here and have it on your lap. I think it's my turn to drive.'

He managed to back the car safely out of the ditch, and soon they were heading down the main road to Dankton, where they would carry on past the turn-off for home and go straight to Orchard Inn veterinary hospital. There, they would drop the pup off in the hope that a microchip would reunite him with his owners.

As wafers of moonlight spun in through the glass, Leah's sleepy vision met with those two trusting eyes and the soft swipe of his tongue every time she stroked his ears. And as she wrapped the blanket tighter, ensuring he was warm, she only wished that Kiki would take a leaf out of his book with the gratitude.

Eleven

'Hey… are you OK?' Rhona raised an eyebrow as Leah raced to the counter the following Tuesday.

'So sorry I'm late,' she replied breathlessly, seizing the tablet to sign herself in.

'What, three… no, just about four minutes? And you've got a little one to sort out too. Give yourself a break!'

'It was thanks to those roadworks along the seafront.'

'I know,' Tiffany rolled her eyes. 'I've just got here myself.'

'They never put any warnings up,' Rhona added. 'You just find yourself stuck in a massive queue with no chance of turning around.' She nodded at the empty KittyPie stand. 'Kehlani hasn't turned up yet and Taeng is usually there on Poirier by now, so you did well to get here this early.'

'You really reckon they're both stuck in traffic? Way too much of a coincidence.'

'They're up to something?' Rhona's eyes widened. 'How can you not have filled me in?'

'I know nothing,' said Tiffany with a grin. 'But they were banging on about a big night out yesterday.'

'I predict a couple of hangovers this morning, then!'

Tiffany nodded. 'Wouldn't be surprised. Kehlani sure knows how to knock them back!'

'Kehlani, *what?*'

Kehlani walked over with her hands on her hips, tossing the ebony mane of hair that spilled down her back. Her KittyPie shirt was tied up at the waist, showing just a flash of her coffee-smooth midriff.

'You're cutting it fine! Caught in the roadworks, were we?' Tiffany grinned. 'Or was it because you rolled out of bed late after partying with your bestie?'

'Shhh, keep it down!' Kehlani shot a smile over at Taeng, who had just arrived in her all-black uniform and a neat braid woven with tiny coral flowers. 'Not only that, but Dawn cornered me at my locker. Gave me even more Capital G vouchers to hand out at the till literally every time someone spends a tenner. I mean, I know she's the Glovers boss and all that, but aren't we supposed to be selling our own brands?'

'I see your point,' said Rhona. 'But at least it entices people back into the store and then it's up to you to show them how much better your stuff is!'

Kehlani's eyes lit up. 'Speaking of which...' She nipped across to the KittyPie counter and came back, holding some small cases. 'We've got a load of these freebies left over. Have one, all of you.'

'Thanks so much!' said Leah, inspecting three eyeshadow strips in a shimmery cream, a delicate pink and a rich brown. 'What have we got here?'

'A promotional Neapolitan Ice Cream palette.' Kehlani opened the lid on a spare one and held it up to Leah's face, encasing it in her turquoise acrylic nails. 'You know, you'd look amazing in any of these.'

'Very kind of you,' Rhona remarked, snapping her own box shut and springing into manager mode. 'We'll try them outside of work. You know the rules. Us three must strictly wear EdenCore only.'

She glided off to the far side of the counter, where she had already started changing the window display.

'Rather you than me,' Kehlani grimaced.

'What do you mean?' asked Tiffany.

'Seriously, eight shades of foundation when every other counter here has at least double the amount? You guys have some catching up to do!'

Leah observed Kehlani as she bantered away with Tiffany. The dewy BB cream fused effortlessly with her complexion and the ultra-slick gel shaped her brows into perfect arches. The candied glaze of *Soda Kiss* lacquer popped like bubblegum over her naturally pillowy lips. There was no escaping the superior quality of her brand's makeup.

'And anyway…' Her tiny nose stud twinkled as she raised her chin with a flash of defiance. 'You only make one type.'

'That's true.' Leah stared back at her knowingly. Several customers had left empty-handed, finding the EdenCore foundation to be too thick.

'I did mention it in training and Hilary was quite dismissive,' said Tiffany.

'But they're working on it.' Rhona had overheard and was now leaning over the counter. 'There'll be a whole new collection coming our way soon.'

'Hey, no worries,' Kehlani waved her bangled wrist. 'It's not like you girls make the decisions.' A customer arrived at KittyPie so she turned to leave, throwing a cheeky grin at her colleagues. 'Anyway, I'll be getting back to the *decent* stuff now.'

'Would you girls mind doing a wee bit of marketing magic?' Rhona asked them once Kehlani had stepped away. 'I need you to grab whatever you think would work on an autumn display, going by the ingredients. I've got dried leaves and lichen over there to sit it all on and I'm just off to ask Taeng if we can borrow her little table.'

'We'll do our best!' said Leah.

'Yep,' added Tiffany. 'Although, I think Leah will have the edge on that. She's way more artistic than me.'

'That's why we're a good team. You can teach me the hard sell and I'll bring out your creativity,' Leah winked.

'I'll prepare for something mind-blowing then!' Rhona walked off to the Poirier counter while Leah and Tiffany went straight over to the EdenCore shelves.

'I know what will be brilliant.'

'Fire away,' said Tiffany. 'We'll go with whatever you think.'

'Definitely the night syrups. They're tree-based, aren't they? So, that gives an autumnal vibe straight away.'

She took some small boxes off the top shelf and placed each one into Tiffany's outstretched hands.

'Right, I'm going to try and remember this without even looking. Maple is for dry skin, Walnut is the oily one, and Sycamore is for anti-ageing.'

'Oh, very good, Tiff!'

'Not bad, considering they're some of our lesser-known products.'

'All the more reason to push them, I guess.' Leah led her over to the bag of dry foliage which was ready to be spread out on the table. 'We'd better check Rhona's happy with it and then we'll set it up.'

'She'll be a while,' Tiffany nodded. 'Poirier have got a whole new bunch of nail polish out today. Look, Taeng is showing her.'

Leah grinned and began to relieve Tiffany of the boxes she was still holding.

'How did your weekend away go? Now that we've got a minute.'

'Well, me and Mum had a nice time but the boys

were a bit bored. I guess a country cottage in the middle of nowhere wasn't really their scene. Junior just wanted to go and buy trainers, but he was never going to get far with one tiny village shop!'

'No,' said Leah jokingly. 'A teenager's worst nightmare!'

'Did I miss much on Sunday, then?'

'I had a few good sales. I just… was quite shattered from the day before.'

'Of course, Kiki's birthday!' Tiffany smiled, then her face straightened. 'Oh, don't say she kicked off again.'

Leah nodded. 'I kind of lost it by teatime. Got in the car and just didn't even know where I was going.'

'It must have been so hard.' Tiffany squeezed Leah's arm. 'What happened in the end? Did you just calm down? I bet hubby was frantic.'

'Actually, he was in the car,' said Leah, cringing into her hands. 'But I still carried on. I didn't stop until… I nearly ran over a puppy.'

'No way!' Tiffany looked horrified. 'Oh, I can't deal with this. I love animals so much. Was it OK?'

Leah nodded. 'He had a lucky escape, but the vet is checking him over, just to be safe. Hopefully they'll find the owner soon.'

'I couldn't stand it if anything happened to my Crystal and Quartz.'

'You have dogs?'

Tiffany beamed. 'A Shih-Tzu and a Papillon. My pride and joy. Now the boys are older I hardly see them, steaming in and out with their mates, so I needed the company.'

Leah glanced up and down at Tiffany as she spoke, the envy creeping further in with every glimpse of her toned body and the tiny uniform that must be a good few sizes smaller than her own. Apart from the chest area, that was. Unsurprisingly, many customers struggled to maintain eye contact with Tiffany. Her bust seemed to enter a room before she did, defying her years and the slim contrast of her waistline.

This was exactly why it was better to have children early. Your body sprung back into its twenty-something shape and you were young enough to live your life to the full again once the kids grew up. Now Tiffany could do as she pleased, hitting the gym most nights a week and eating her own selfish salads instead of yet another round of cheesy beans on toast. She had the precious gift of *time*. Now, she could swan around the clothes shops for as long as she wanted or lie on her back in a spa all day being slathered in beauty treatments. She had mornings to herself for perfecting her elaborate hairstyles and blending her makeup seamlessly over a canvas of pampered skin.

Leah caught sight of herself in the line of the sunlit window and sucked her midriff in just a little more than was comfortable.

'Hello there, dears,' said a voice behind her. She turned to see a small woman in a beige, belted coat and butterscotch streaks through her hair. 'Wonder if you can help with a mature anti-ageing range. I usually go for Auclair, but they've changed something in their serum and I can't get on with it.'

'Oh, really?' Leah swerved the *SySTEM* bottle, still unsure if it had caused her inflammation, and instead reached for the pistachio-infused option from the *AfterLife* collection, which happened to be from the highest-priced range, as well as the most appropriate. 'Well, this won't ever be messed with. It's one of our absolute classics for a reason.' She squeezed a pea-sized droplet into her palm. 'If we dared to change it, there'd be two hundred and fifty people per second who would never forgive us. That's how often it's sold.'

'Interesting…' said the woman, as Leah warmed it with her fingers. 'I just don't know why these companies always have to discontinue or ruin perfectly good products.'

'We know how disappointing it is for customers.' Leah gently took the woman's wrist and pressed the serum on the back of her hand. 'Now you'll see why we're sticking with this one.'

'Oh, it smells superb!' She examined it in the light and sighed again as she smoothed her fingertips over the silken patch of skin. 'I don't suppose I could try it on properly?'

'Of course. Just make yourself comfortable.' Leah smiled, leading her to the chair. Using two large hair clips, she pinned back some loose tendrils off the woman's face. 'The right cleanser will make it work even better. If you're happy for me to have a closer look, I'll make sure we use the best one for you.'

'Go ahead.' The woman closed her eyes and continued to speak. 'I'm sixty-three next month but still get quite oily on the nose and chin. Normal everywhere else.'

Leah carried out the tests she had learned during training, touching the moist areas and lifting the upper cheekbones for signs of dehydration. There were a few creases as Leah applied the pressure, but then again, the same thing happened with literally everyone she had tried this on. Sometimes even the healthiest faces ever would be dehydrated according to the EdenCore methods of detection.

'It'll be the *Oat Float* cleanser for you then. And the *Turn Back Thyme* toner matches perfectly with that.' She filled both arms with testers from the stand and swept the products across the woman's contours, finishing with a cooling press of serum, before handing her a mirror. 'How is it feeling?'

'Like my skin is being kissed!' she marvelled, inspecting herself in the glass.

'You do look beautifully fresh,' Leah nodded. 'But I'm just going to finish off with the moisturiser from the same range.'

The nutty notes poured upwards out of the jar as she released the lid and delved a disposable applicator deep into the mixture. In the background, Rhona had returned to the counter and was subtly observing Leah at work.

'It feels incredible.' The woman enthused as the ingredients sank magically in. 'What on earth is it?'

'It's our *Brazillionaire* butter day cream. Brazil nuts are amazing for restoring your skin, and they have natural lifting and firming properties, too.'

'Not to mention a gorgeous smell. You can just tell there are no chemicals in this.'

'Of course, the serum is fine on its own, but it is designed to work together with the other products in the collection, so you'll get the best results that way.'

'You're right,' agreed the woman, reaching down for her handbag. 'I'll take one serum then, and a pot of *Brazillionaire.*'

'Absolutely. I'll get those packed up for you. Just come over to the till when you're ready.'

She made her way to the shelves and took both items to the payment point where the woman soon joined her.

'Actually, what cleansers did you use? I'll go for those as well.'

'Oh, I'm really sorry,' Leah said as she glanced up at her customer. 'I didn't take your clips out!'

The woman laughed while Leah reached over and pinched the grippers from each side of her face, letting her fine strands fall back around her cheekbones.

'I think I preferred it well out of the way. Unfortunately, it's not thick and luxurious like your colleague's here!' She gestured towards Tiffany. 'Is it all your own, dear?'

Tiffany was already nodding like it was the thousandth time she had been asked.

'Sure is.' She patted the shimmering coil of hair, pristinely pinned to the top of her head. 'But it costs me a fortune in shampoo!'

'I'd rather that than the endless trips to the hairdresser to sort mine out!' The woman then noticed the leafy presentation of facial syrups that Tiffany and Rhona were arranging. 'Nice display you're doing there, ladies.'

'Good idea about using these, Leah' Rhona jiggled a box in her hand. 'They'll work perfectly.'

'I was also going to suggest adding this.'

Leah held out a *Conker It All* and Rhona's eyes lit up as she eagerly seized it, placing it down in the middle of the stand.

'In fact, that's the night cream from the same range as your other items, if you're interested,' she said to the woman.

'Yes, please. I might as well buy one straight away. I know I'm going to love it.'

Leah scanned the box and added it to the bag along with the cleansing products that she had also requested.

'I've put some samples in for you, too. Exfoliating soil and our *Palm Oil* hand cream.'

'Palm Oil?' The woman raised a horrified eyebrow.

'Don't worry, it doesn't contain any palm oil,' explained Leah. 'It's actually date extract.'

'That's alright then! Sounded a bit worrying for a minute.'

'Just the name.' Leah put the receipt in the bag and

handed it to her customer. 'Enjoy your new skincare routine. I can book you in for an appointment if you'd like to come back in a few weeks' time.'

'I'd love to, but I'll need to give you a ring later. The battery's gone on my phone so I can't see my calendar right now.'

'Absolutely fine,' replied Leah, slipping her a card. 'Here is our number. I'm Leah, so just ask for me and we'll get that arranged.'

'Thank you for everything, Leah, you've been so helpful.' The woman smiled gratefully and turned as she left the counter. 'See you again soon.'

'Well done, you!' Rhona beamed, once they were alone again. '*And* she commented on your service.'

'Done your target for today, I reckon!' agreed Tiffany with a wink. 'Anyway, off for my break, so see you in a bit.'

'Actually, Tiff, before you go, there's a little trolley of stock by the lift. Can you just grab it for me?'

'Yep, no problem.'

She returned seconds later and wheeled it over to Rhona before disappearing away up the escalator to the staff area.

'Do you need me to put that out?' asked Leah, nodding at the shallow cardboard trays in the trolley.

Rhona shook her head as she peeled back a layer of paper and film. 'It's not for the shelves. These are our free travel sizes to give out with the promotion that's starting next week. You get three when you buy two normal items and we're going to give them out in these adorable little washbags. Aren't they ideal for Christmas? I'd take it on a night out, never mind keep it in my bathroom.'

'Yes, so pretty!' Leah gazed at the black velvet pouches, embellished with glittery magenta sprigs. 'I'll definitely be asking Eric for one of those.'

'No need.' Rhona unzipped one of the bags and held it open for Leah. 'Go on. You've done so well here in the last few days and you were brilliant just now. Choose the three you fancy.'

'Are you sure?'

Leah's gratitude was peppered with the fear that any of the travel-sized treats could bring her out in blisters.

'You've more than earned it.'

She observed the glint in Rhona's eyes and the warm smile that glowed in her cheeks, enhancing the dusted freckles that suited her so much. Leah felt lucky to be under her wing.

'Thank you, that's so lovely!'

The tubes and bottles all looked the same in their pure white packaging and pink-lettered descriptions. As Leah rummaged through them all, she tried to think of the products that she definitely hadn't used. Nothing she'd have ordered in her first allocation or received in the bag of training goodies.

'I'll give these a go,' she said, picking up a *WaterMellow* serum and a *MandaRinse* hydrating lotion, both from the *Crush On You* collection for dry skin.

'And another,' Rhona smiled.

Leah decided to try the matching face mask and Rhona enclosed all three items before placing the bag into her hands.

'I can't wait to try them,' said Leah, already planning to use them that night, so she would have four days for her skin to recover before she'd need to be back on the counter. 'Thanks again, Rhona.'

As the next few hours passed, Leah helped a steady flow of customers, resulting in more sales and further praise from Rhona. Leah watched her manager at the times she was doing the serving. Her warm but knowledgeable presence as she listened to concerns, and her nurturing hands as they tended to each and every skin. Leah felt so fortunate to be around her, and to bounce off the bubbliness of Tiffany, too, all in a day's work.

'How's it going, my lovelies?' Dawn appeared with a clipboard and summoned the three of them towards her, eyes looking extra bright with their green rim of pencil liner that matched the stone in her gold pendant. 'I've just been going over the figures upstairs and EdenCore is our bestselling counter for the third month in a row. Well done girls!'

'Nice one, lassies!' Rhona clapped excitedly. 'This is down to you, so keep it up.'

'And you,' said Tiffany. 'Best boss ever.'

'Exactly,' agreed Leah. 'I second that.'

'Obviously, with my Glovers hat on, I'd rather it was Capital G leading the way, but I didn't just say that!' Dawn joked.

'We'll pretend we didn't hear.' Rhona's eyelashes fluttered as she patted Dawn's wrist.

'Anyway, I need a picture of you all for the noticeboard. Let's do it over by your new display.'

Dawn slid a phone from her skirt pocket and marched over to the autumnal décor, spilling from the table they had worked on earlier. Then, with Rhona in the centre, the three held their grins while Dawn took some snapshots.

'Love it,' she said, scrolling through the pictures. 'I'll send these to you all later too. Well done again. Some of these others could learn a thing or two from you.'

She breezed past the KittyPie stand as Kehlani looked unamused.

'Let's do dinner!' Rhona suggested. 'About time we got together outside this place. What are you two up to the week after next?'

'Quite a lot, to be honest.' Even Tiffany's tense expression didn't raise a line on her forehead. 'But I'm free on the Friday.'

'I can do that,' Leah said, knowing Eric could stay in then with Kiki.

'Brilliant. I'll book somewhere then. What about that *Sundara* place?'

'Sounds good. It's meant to be really nice.'

'Our first EdenCore night out!' chimed Tiffany.

'Sorted then. I'll let you know the time in the next couple of days.' Rhona checked her watch. 'Right, I'm off. Tiff, don't forget your appointment. You'd better get going now.'

'Oh, I know,' groaned Tiffany. 'I just hope there's no fillings or anything. I hate the dentist.'

'Me too. Good luck with that!' Leah waved a hand as the pair left the counter, their heads of glossy hair disappearing into the colours of the beauty hall.

The next few hours were quiet and as much as Leah had enjoyed the company, it was also a relief to be alone. In the absence of the others, she could be the sole face of the counter in confidence, without feeling inadequate whenever she stood next to her colleagues.

All around her, the huge window brought the outside world indoors. The pigeons flapping in the grey city sky that matched the colour of their feathers. Leah polished the shelves, her eyes chasing litter as it blew downhill over the paving stones. Across the road, cafes and shops were closing for the evening, while *Bap Starz* was still buzzing with people stopping by for burgers.

Soon, the Glovers staff began locking up the doors, so Leah walked away through the hall as the bright ceiling lights clicked off one by one. It was even darker upstairs in the corridor, which led to the locker room right at the other end. She creaked open the door and flung her shoes under her peg, sliding her feet into much comfier boots. Pulling her coat over her shoulders, she caught sight of a tiny object glimmering on the floor, just below Tiffany's peg.

Leah picked it up between her fingertips. Tiffany had dropped an earring. She had definitely been wearing it on the counter that day, as Leah instantly recognised the pretty shell-shaped pearl.

At first, she considered keeping hold of it, with the intention of returning it to Tiffany next Sunday, but she would hate to forget what could be a precious item. She tried the door of Tiffany's locker, but it was shut tight.

Leah turned around again where Tiffany's EdenCore jacket was hanging on the wall. Carefully, she opened the inner pocket, slipping her hand deep inside to ensure that she dropped the earring into safety. But she screamed out loud, thudding backwards against the locker unit, reeling from the furry sensation that had crawled around her fingers.

There was some kind of creature in there. A mouse or… even worse, a rat. Squinting through the dimness, she could see the tip of a tail hanging out of the pocket, and as she tried to steady her breath, she waited for it to move.

As the moments whizzed to minutes, Leah realised that there were no signs of life. So, she edged ever closer, hoping no one else would enter the room and cause whatever it was to spring out at her in shock. Grabbing her phone and flicking on the torch, she beamed the ray over the pocket, stopping suddenly as a plastic tip caught the light.

Leah winced as she took hold of the end and slowly pulled the whole length out, until the long, thick hair extension was dangling between her fingers. The same shining black that adorned Tiffany's head.

Without hesitating for a second longer, she stuffed it back out of sight and left the building with a mind full of thoughts.

Twelve

Leah stepped out of the shower and the steam felt velvety against her healed skin, which had thankfully not reacted to the new travel-sized products she had dared to try the night before.

While Eric was on the phone and spooning Kiki her Weetabix, Leah scurried back to the bedroom to dress as quickly as possible. Sitting at her mirror with her hair in a towel, she smoothed on a luminous pink squeeze of the serum, smelling the subtle watermelon as she applied it for a second time. The mandarin lotion worked equally as well, and she revelled in the knowledge that she was safe to use them both.

The sound of Kiki's rattling highchair echoed up the stairs, so Leah headed to the kitchen with no chance of a blow-dry.

'Hey…' She just managed to dodge a flying blob of mush. 'What's all this about?'

Taking over from Eric, allowing him to have his call in peace, she smiled goofily at Kiki as she continued to feed her breakfast.

'That's brilliant news,' said Eric down the receiver. 'So glad he's OK. Honestly, my wife would never have done that on purpose. We'd have hated anything to have happened.'

'Go on,' Leah whispered to her daughter. 'Try some more… just a little bit left now.'

'So, no one has come forward yet then? What will you do if they never…'

Kiki started banging her feet on the table, so Leah moved her seat out of its reach.

'Well, actually… perhaps we might be able to… I mean, she's…' Eric glanced at Leah. '*We're* the ones who should be responsible. What would we need to do?'

'Shhh!' ordered Leah, putting a finger over her own lips as Kiki screwed her face up and shouted some garbled vowels. 'Want milky?'

The tot took the cup and began to glug in a moment of respite. Leah's heart had the hint of a flutter as the little gulpy noises filled the air and Kiki stared over the spout with her perfect hazel eyes.

'I don't see why not,' continued Eric. 'One of us is around most of the time. We've already got gates on the stairs and…' He paused. 'Yes, a daughter. She's only one but… she's quite easy-going.'

He made eye contact with Leah, whose mouth was gaping at the inaccuracy of his last statement.

'Yes, high fences in the garden. And actually, we're right on the border of Dankton Clump. Plenty of countryside for walks.'

Kiki smashed her cup down and the lid sprung off, shooting milk in a jet at Eric's glasses. He ducked out of the way and stepped into the living room to finish the conversation.

'Home check? No problem. I can be here today at say, four-ish?'

Leah mopped the patch on the floor, craning her neck over Kiki's yelling so she could hear what Eric was saying.

'We're Lupin Crescent, right on top of the hill. About two doors past the red post box. Brilliant… See you then and thanks for everything.'

He hung up.

'I take it that was the rescue centre,' she asked, flinging the wipe into the bin.

Eric nodded, coming back in the kitchen. 'The pup is fine, so the vet has handed him over to them.'

'Thank goodness for that. I don't know what I'd have done if I'd hurt him.'

'He's been checked over, had some jabs… they think he's around four months old. Greyhound or lurcher type, they said.'

'No sign of the owner yet, then?'

Eric shook his head and Leah folded her arms, waiting for him to elaborate.

'And the rest…'

'What?' Eric feigned confusion.

'Oh, come on. Kiki's lungs might rival a fire engine siren, but I could still hear you. You've told them we'll have the dog.'

'Fostering, Leah.'

She rolled her eyes and covered them with a hand. Eric moved in front of her and gently took hold of her wrists.

'Just until they find him a new home. It won't be for long.'

'Eric, no. Not at a time like this.'

He looked over Leah's shoulder and gestured at Kiki. 'She'll love it. You never know, she might even like having him around.'

'Are you actually kidding?' Leah let out a sarcastic laugh. 'Nothing ever makes her happy. Do you hear me? *Nothing.* And you think adding a dog into the mix is going to make things easier?'

'Yes, you know what? I do. I always had dogs growing up. When we got married you said you'd consider it.'

'That was before we had a kid like this one.'

Kiki started howling, so Leah huffily unstrapped her, hoisting her up on a hip.

'See?' Her eyes widened as she laid into Eric. 'This is what I have to contend with and now I've got to have my shoes chewed up while I'm crawling around on my hands and knees cleaning dog poo off the carpet. Sorry, Eric, but puppies and babies do not mix!'

'You won't know until you've tried it.'

'I've had cats. That's similar enough.'

Eric flung his arms around in frustration. 'They're crap… well, not exactly… but they're not the same! They scratch furniture, throw up furballs everywhere and they hate screamy children.'

'Right, and you think a little puppy isn't going to be scared to death of all the constant crying?'

'They're more resilient than you realise,' Eric replied firmly. 'And you never know… maybe it'll give Kiki something else to think about. She might like watching him play. It's better than a stuffed teddy bear.'

'Oh, so now you think it's a toy?'

'No!' Eric ran his hands through his hair, revealing the waviness that he always tried to suppress with gel. 'Leah, it's only for a week or two. Just until they rehome him.'

She shook her head adamantly.

'It's the least you can do.'

'*Me?*' Leah shot back. 'Why is it up to…'

'Because you nearly killed him!'

The room went quiet and even Kiki nibbled silently on her fist, hushed momentarily by her father's raised voice.

'If you hadn't been driving like a maniac, none of this would have happened.'

Leah had nowhere else to direct her sight than down at the ground on her faded violet slippers.

'And my God, Leah…' said Eric, his tone lowering with emotion, 'Even if you hadn't destroyed the poor thing, imagine the damage you could have done…'

'Alright.' She closed her eyes as abruptly as she had spoken, hardly able to believe that she was going along with this. 'I get it… and I know how stupid I was. How… terrified he must have been.'

'You don't even have to do anything. I'll be here to help out.'

'Yes, you will.' Leah stormed upstairs with Eric following behind her. 'You're in charge of the training, the clearing up, the walks…' She perched on the side of the bath squeezing fruity paste onto Kiki's toothbrush. 'You can do the whole lot.'

'There you go!' said Eric merrily as Kiki whinged through the scrubbing. 'I knew Mummy would come round. And you're going to love your new puppy pal, my princess.'

'She'll probably go off on one the minute he licks her face.'

'Well, we'll cross that bridge when we come to it, and it might not even happen.'

Leah shrugged with resignation. 'If that little dog keeps her happy for five minutes, we're getting ten of them.'

'Fine by me.' He kissed Leah's lips and planted a peck on Kiki's cheek. 'Got to hurry to the office. Ring me after the physio session.'

Gathering up the essentials in a changing bag, Leah did the poppers up on Kiki's puffy coat. It was like her mind was so cluttered with chaos that she might as well just forget about being rational when it came to further commitments. Like life was already in such a spin that it was beyond becoming worsened by the addition of further demands.

Today's appointment was not at a good time. The last one had been earlier in the morning and Leah had got Kiki home just in time for her half-nap. But scheduling for ten-thirty meant that Kiki was now doubly as tired, paving the way for crankiness instead of making progress. She was already grumpy by the time Leah entered the hospital, hoping the waiting time wouldn't be too long.

'Hello, you two!' greeted Zara after five minutes. 'Come on in.'

Leah sat on the chair nearest the desk feeling exhausted before the day was even halfway through. She dreaded times like these when she would clench every bone in her body, willing Kiki not to kick off when someone was trying to communicate with her.

'So, how's everything going?'

'Not much to report, I'm afraid,' replied Leah weakly.

'No worries,' Zara reassured her. 'Have you been doing the exercises?'

'Every day. Sometimes it seems like she kind of… pushes with her ankles more strongly against my hands, but she mainly just flops, so maybe I'm imagining it.'

'Stay hopeful, Leah! That sounds promising. The first signs will be those pushes. Tiny little bursts of more pressure in the ankles than before.'

'OK.' Leah let out a heavy sigh. 'Sorry, it's just not easy when she hates doing it so much.'

'Up we get then, little lady. Kneel on the rug please, Mum, and sit her on your lap.'

Leah did as instructed, allowing Kiki to lean back on her while she propped her up, ready to support her. Zara pulled a parrot toy out, directing Kiki's sight above her shoulders and encouraging her to lift herself upwards.

'Who's this, Kiki? That's right... watch Pandora. Here she goes!'

Leah craned her neck to check Kiki's expression. She was gazing up in wonder and reaching as high as she could with outstretched hands.

'Good girl, that's it. Now... keep looking,' said Zara, clicking a button underneath, which spread the wings out in a kaleidoscopic canopy. 'What colours can you see?'

She floated the parrot gently in different directions, almost teasingly close so that Kiki would respond with her body.

'Red for rubies and green for grass,' continued Zara.

Kiki was mesmerised and she started to babble excitedly in response.

'Or purple for plums... orange for orangutan.'

Leah's heart pumped unstoppably in complete contrast to her stiffened limbs. Kiki shuffled forwards and bounced on her lap with more resistance than she had ever seen.

'Go on, Kiki, higher!' she coaxed, widening her arms to give her daughter even more freedom. She was almost sitting up unaided now.

'If you can *really* try and stroke her, she might just give you a hug!' Zara glided the bird slightly lower and Kiki's kicking stopped as she slid to the bottom of Leah's knees and planted her feet on the floor. 'Yes, brilliant! Now, just push up... push...'

But the pressure on her ankles made Kiki buckle and she tumbled backwards into Leah's arms. In minutes, the screaming pierced every corner of the room.

'Oh, and you were doing so well.' Zara's look of sympathy made Leah cave in, despite the efforts to hide her despair. 'Here...' she said, folding the parrot's wings away and passing it over to Kiki. 'You definitely deserve that cuddle.'

Kiki arched her back, banging her shoulders against Leah's chest, and booted the bird straight back at Zara, knocking her glasses off her nose and poking feathers straight in her eyes.

'Kiki, no!' Leah yelled, the fuse of humiliation well and truly blown. 'I'm so sorry.'

'It's no problem, Leah. Honestly, these things happen.'

'That's kind of you, but let's face it…' Leah smiled tightly as everything around her started to drown. 'Not many of your patients are as bad as this, right?'

'I have to admit that most are a bit easier to please, and even when they're not, I can usually distract them or calm them down enough to cooperate with me.'

Kiki smushed her gunky face across Leah's jacket and reduced her pitch to a threatening whinge. Reaching to the side of her chair, Leah felt for the handle of her changing bag.

'Right. Probably best to abandon this for today, then.'

'Are you sure? There's twenty minutes left.' Zara swung around in her seat. 'Maybe we could try the activity table or perhaps she'd respond better to a fluffier puppet.'

'I know her too well. Sorry to have wasted your time.'

Leah started to get up, but Zara put a hand on her arm.

'Please listen,' she ordered gently. 'When I said that most of these physio kids are easier to please, I didn't mean *all* of them.'

'But none are quite as bad as Kiki,' replied Leah with a resigned nod.

'Yes, actually, they have been.' Zara's eyes reached out and a tear fell down Leah's cheek. 'I've seen this before.'

At Zara's words, Leah sank back into her chair and she clutched Kiki, urging her to stay quiet just long enough for Zara to finish speaking.

'It's all frustration, these tantrums and meltdowns. She sees you and your husband moving around everywhere and because she can't do the same, her only answer is to get in a state.'

'But *why?*'

'Most likely mild hypermobility. It's an over-flexibility of the joints. In her case, the ankles.'

'I knew it.' Leah could no longer mask the panic. 'I knew there was something going on with her. This explains everything.' She swallowed and looked straight at Zara. 'She's never going to walk, is she?'

Slumping her forehead against Kiki's back, Leah creased her eyes up and began to sob.

'You don't understand.' Zara passed her a tissue from the desk. 'There's every chance that she will.'

Leah dabbed her face for a moment, then found sudden solace in the smile awaiting her.

'Not long ago, I was seeing another little girl her age with exactly the same thing. Her mum was just like you… at her wits' end with all the screaming.'

'Exactly. It never ends…'

'It did.'

Zara's words stopped Leah from burying her face back into the tissue.

'*How?*' she whispered.

'Persistence, for a start.'

Leah gave a defeated shrug.

'Total dedication with the exercises - and I mean, not even missing a day,' Zara said. 'It sounds harsh, but you have to just go for it and not allow her hissy fits to stop you strengthening those muscles.'

'And it really worked for this other girl?'

'Absolutely. That and a special pair of magic boots.' With a click of her fingers, Zara turned to her laptop screen and loaded up the online medical catalogue. 'In fact, that's exactly what I'm going to order for Kiki. Now, little lady, what colour would you like?'

Trying to ignore her puffy face in the lenses of Zara's glasses, Leah glanced at the pictures as the array of ankle boots scrolled past her vision.

'What do you think, Kiki?' She sniffed, pointing at the different styles in animal prints and flowery patterns. 'New shoes?'

Momentarily distracted by the moving images before her, Kiki blinked and waved her hand outwards, stopping at a pair in plain pastel pink and pressing her palm against them.

'Good choice!' Zara beamed, selecting them with Leah's consent and tapping in the code. 'They should be here for one of your next appointments.' She sent off the order, then sat back again, facing them at the desk. 'Now, let's just leave it there for today while the going's good. Get yourself home, have a nice hot drink and if she starts up again, please know that this is a phase.'

'Thank you for all your help,' said Leah as she walked towards the exit. 'Sorry about everything.'

'Do not apologise!' Zara started typing up the appointment notes. 'And remember, you will get through this.'

'Zara…' Leah stopped with the door ajar. 'What happened to that little girl in the end?'

'She was walking unaided by eighteen months. Didn't even need her boots anymore.'

The words filled Leah with a glimmer of lightness, and she smiled weakly until she had stepped out onto the walkway.

'And remember,' Zara called out after her, 'they're called baby steps for a reason.'

Acknowledging her advice, Leah clicked Kiki back into her pushchair and trudged through the reception area, where every other tiny toddler seemed to be dashing around without a care in the world. Then, as the doors banged open, it was as if she were being forcefully ejected as the wind hit her face.

Once through the parking barrier, she drove through the surrounding town of Chatsworth, looking out on an alien world from the glass case of the car. The prams and buggies of happy mothers, chirping at their babies and walking around in peace. Women reading magazines in beauty salons with time on their hands for the hours of highlights and thick enough hair to look good at the end of it. Joggers freely keeping in shape while the glistening sea lacing the promenade was the source of the air in their lungs.

Leah stopped at a pedestrian crossing and glanced behind her at Kiki, who only scowled back at her mother's teary smile. Her finger hovered over the indicator, where she would usually take a left turn back home to the north of Dankton. Instead, she continued forwards, alongside the waves as they wrinkled and thrashed, until she pulled up at the large house, just metres beyond the recreation green.

Cheryl was out on the driveway before Leah even reached the porch.

'Come on, my girl, it's OK,' she soothed as her daughter fell into her embrace. 'Another shocker of a physio session, was it?' She tilted her head towards Kiki, who was still in the back of the car. 'What did madam get up to?'

'The usual, Mum, you know… just screeching to the point of no return.' Leah stiffened in frustration. 'I really thought she was getting somewhere. She was looking at this parrot thing, really into it, pushing herself up to reach it…'

'Well, that's good!'

Leah shook her head. 'Then she started screaming and there was no calming her down.'

'Has she had her nap?'

'No, thanks to the appointment time. I guess I'd better get her home to bed.'

'Put her down here in the spare room. Then you can have a nice, sweet cuppa and I'll make you something to eat.'

Leah smiled in agreement and turned back to the car.

'Alan will get her in…' Cheryl called through the front door. 'Alan! Here a minute.'

He appeared within seconds and kissed Leah on both cheeks.

'Bring Kiki in, will you? Leah's had a time of it at physio again.'

Immediately, he reached into the back seat and lifted her into his arms. She let out a squeal and slapped him playfully on the face.

'There, there…' he chuckled. 'Behave yourself! I know what mischief you've been causing.'

'The cot's out upstairs,' Cheryl said as they all came into the house. 'Do her a quick story and pop her in while I get started on the sandwiches.'

Alan disappeared with Kiki, already lying flat in his arms, while the others went into the kitchen which looked out peacefully onto the garden and the two ponds that rippled in the breeze.

'Tuna mayo for you, am I right?'

'Sounds good. I'm starving.'

'You really must remember to eat well and get plenty of sleep. No one can look after another person if they don't take care of themselves.'

Leah gave her mother a slightly annoyed glance.

'Yes, I know…' said Cheryl, waving the butter knife. 'It's not easy and you hardly get the chance, but you must put yourself first sometimes.'

'Couldn't keep her eyes open!' Alan joined them at the worktop. 'No wonder she was crabby.'

Leah sighed as she turned to put the kettle on.

'Alan will do that,' Cheryl insisted as she sliced into a cucumber. 'You go and make yourself comfortable, and not at the table either. Get on the sofa with a blanket. We'll bring you a tray.'

Gazing at Cheryl with exhaustion, Leah smiled gratefully and kicked off her shoes in the hallway before snuggling up under a large, fleecy throw. Right now, she wanted nothing more than to stay like this forever, being looked after and doted on by the people who loved her the most. But she knew that later on, she would have to get up again and take Kiki home for an evening of more outbursts.

She could have drifted off to sleep there and then, but Cheryl was soon sliding the sandwiches onto her lap with a creamy hot chocolate, a chopped apple, and a generous slice of homemade treacle tart.

'I don't know what I'd do without you,' said Leah, tracing the print of the marigolds on the tray.

'It's being a parent. You'll be doing the same for Kiki one day.'

'God help her if she ever has a child with the same temper.'

'So, how did things end with the session today?'

Leah swallowed a mouthful of warm chocolate. 'Before or after she knocked Zara's glasses off?'

Cheryl bit her lip and glanced at Alan, as if trying to bolster her sympathy with his.

'Well, she ordered her some special walking boots, but I've just got to keep going with the exercises, and not back down when Kiki kicks up a fuss.'

'That's why they say, be cruel to be kind,' Alan added, tossing a bread crust into his mouth. 'Just like your mother, putting cucumber into these sandwiches.'

'Salad is good for you,' said Cheryl with a triumphant smile. 'Now, Leah, you have to use some kind of mantra. Something you chant in your head that will keep you strong whenever you reach the last shred of sanity. Even at Kiki's age, you do have to be firm and show her who's boss…'

The drink oozed lazily through Leah's body, her cold hands defrosting on the steamy porcelain, and her tired head beginning to droop. Cheryl and Alan cleared the plates and left her to rest while Kiki slept, but Leah was not even aware they'd tiptoed away.

Her eyelids became curtains over the colours of the living room, and everything blanked out. She leaned backwards into a fuzz of softness, the hard tray giving way to the gentle squish of warmth and wool. There were no more words. Just the deep swirls of her own breath, punctuated by clock ticks lulling away from somewhere on the mantlepiece.

'Good girl. You can do it!'

She blinked upwards at Cheryl, then sideways at the kitchen drawers which were suddenly level with her height. Her feet were bare and tiny enough to fit on just one floor tile. Cheryl crouched in her white knitted top, the one she had made herself that was studded with pastel bobbles. Leah was always fiddling with them, entranced by the dots of mint and lemon, sky blue and candyfloss pink.

Her mother smiled, her eyes glittering with their Irish green over tanned cheekbones, all framed by her honey-blonde strands of hair, and Leah focused on her whole world.

'You can do it.'

Watching Cheryl open her arms, she stared into the safest place she could ever imagine being. There were strawberries shimmering from the chopping board and her favourite golden teddy bear sitting to the side. But nothing could distract her from Cheryl's lilting voice and the need to follow each word with another trusting footstep.

The room wobbled as she lurched forwards, then paused on the spot and somehow regained her balance. Garbled decibels rolled off her tongue and made Cheryl's grin all the wider when they reached her. The cushions of her soles held her sturdy legs in their place on the ground, and she stamped forwards another two steps, then a third, where her dimpled hands were almost touching Cheryl's fingertips.

'That's right... nearly there!'

In the next moment, she dived into the cashmere haze of Cheryl's clutches, and the foamy sink sponge, the half-sliced crusty bread and the crayoned pictures on the fridge all blurred into one as she squealed with joy to be spun around, high above the room.

'Good girl! Good girl!'

Then all was suddenly motionless. She jerked at the strange sense of stillness, her cheek hot against the leather sofa, where her head had slipped off a pillow that hadn't been there earlier. There were voices coming from beyond, muffled by the closed living room door.

Leah wriggled out from under the blankets, stretching as she stepped into the hallway.

'Well done. You can do it!'

With the turn of the door handle, she peered into the main sitting area to see Cheryl and Alan kneeling behind

Kiki as she held onto the new baby walker pushchair she had received for her birthday. While Alan's two hands supported her around the back, Cheryl was placing each foot on the ground and Kiki looked like a different child. Her brows were tense with concentration, but with each push forward, she was smiling.

'OK, I think she's stable…' Cheryl gestured to Alan. 'Now, slowly let her go, just an inch.'

Leah watched Alan release Kiki, his arms ready to catch her if she toppled, and their mouths widening as she continued to balance unaided.

'Yes! You're doing it!' whispered Cheryl in delight.

'That's our girl!' Alan could barely contain the triumph.

'Kiki…' Leah shot out of the doorway into the middle of the room. 'I can't believe…'

At Leah's voice, Kiki turned her head and immediately collapsed into the safety of Alan's body. The wondrous gaze scrunched away in a reddened fog of bawling.

'Of course.' Leah slammed herself down on Cheryl's large sewing box that doubled up as a stool. '*I've* come along and spoiled it. This is all because of me.'

'You took her by surprise, that's all. Don't give yourself such a hard time.'

'She was fine until the second she saw me.' Leah dragged her skin as she wiped away her tears. 'Then she takes one look at me and off she goes again.'

'Listen to yourself, will you?' said Alan. 'Spending so much time getting all wound up that you're not even thinking about the positives.'

'There aren't any,' Leah mumbled, waving a dismissive hand.

'She very nearly stood up!' Cheryl couldn't help raising her voice.

Silence overcame Leah for a moment.

'But she didn't really…'

'Yes, she did.' Alan scooped Kiki up, jiggling on the spot to calm the crying.

'You saw her, Leah,' said Cheryl, draping an arm around her shoulder. 'For a few seconds there, that little girl was almost on her feet.' She coaxed Leah into eye contact. 'Your thin ray of hope just became an inferno.'

'Well, I wouldn't go that far.' Leah shrugged, 'But I guess it's something.'

'Here you go…' chimed Alan, passing Kiki to her. 'Have a congratulations hug from your mummy.'

'Good work, Kiki Koo.' Leah kissed her dark curls and she grizzled in response. 'But, the question is, are you going to do it for me when we try again at home?'

'Just keep going,' urged Cheryl, in the steadfast way that she had always done. 'You can do it.'

Thirteen

Time was running out, and Leah still hadn't found her blusher brush. She checked her storage pots again before hurrying down the stairs, where the upbeat music from the bedroom was quickly overtaken by the TV in the lounge.

The Cupcake Family was blaring out in the background. Over Eric's shoulder, in a baking scene, Papa Pecan and Mummy Sugar Plum watched in horror as Baby Sprinkles drenched Brother Banoffee in a sticky splash of batter.

As Leah checked around the side of the sofa, she saw the pup's jaw clenched firmly onto her missing makeup tool.

'Oh, not again!' Leah sighed, kneeling down and reaching towards his mouth.

Staring determinedly back at her with his two glossy eyes, he gnawed even faster, his teeth grating against the plastic handle.

'What's he got?' Eric asked, as he and Kiki continued to be engrossed in the chaotic cartoon kitchen.

'My brush,' said Leah, heading for the dog treat jar, out of which she chose a bone-shaped biscuit. 'Now, drop!'

She held it out near his nose, but he carried on nibbling regardless, covering the bristled end with his little black paw.

'Now… whatever your name is… do as you are told.'

'You need to toss it over there a bit,' said Eric, finally turning his attention to her. 'Then grab the brush when he lets go of it and he's distracted.'

Leah did as Eric suggested, and the pup immediately dropped it, scrambling across the rug to sniff out his treat, so Leah pounced and picked up the brush.

'Have they found him anywhere permanent yet?' she asked wearily, cleaning it with one of Kiki's baby wipes. 'We've lost slippers, TV remotes, and now he's starting on my entire makeup bag.'

'Actually…' Eric said slowly. 'I was going to ask you about that.' He turned around to face her while ensuring that Kiki was still able to see the screen. 'What about us?'

For a moment, Leah just stared back.

'You're joking, right?'

'He's settling in so well and Kiki seems to love him. It's good exercise doing the walks, and… I don't know… maybe it's not fair to let him get so used to it around here and then pack him off again.'

'Look, I can't talk about this right now. I've got to be out of the door in the next twenty minutes. Kiki is hard enough work as it is, without a puppy to think about.'

'Yes, but she's happy to have him here. It's something else for her to focus on. He's a baby just like her.'

'I can't even begin to…'

'Think about it, will you?' Eric pleaded. 'Just at least say that.'

Leah started to rub her hand tiredly across her face, then thought better of it when she realised she might smudge her foundation.

'I was looking forward to this dinner tonight. Now I'm just going to sit there in two minds about what to do.'

'OK, so I picked a bad time, I'm sorry. But look at him!'

The little dog had trotted over to Leah where he was now sitting at her feet wagging his tail and gazing up longingly into her eyes.

'I know, I know…' She bent down to stroke him. 'He's gorgeous. That's why we can't get too attached. It isn't the right time, Eric. Maybe if things with Kiki ever improve, then we'll think about getting a dog.'

'Please, Leah…'

'Eric, I can't do this right now.'

She swept out of the room and started to climb the stairs.

'Can't do what?' he called behind her. 'Talk about it or keep him?'

'Both!' Her voice snapped at top volume as she reached the landing and sat down at her dressing table.

Adding a trail of liquid liner to her green-foiled eyelids, she caught sight of the carpet in the bottom of the mirror, where the squeaky sausage toy and a selection of tennis balls were strewn amongst Kiki's numbered building blocks. The pup wasn't even allowed upstairs, but already, that rule was sailing out of the window.

Eric's long morning walks, combined with a wholesome breakfast, were admittedly setting their furry lodger up for the day, and he was easy to please for most of the morning. All Leah really had to do was the trips to the garden every hour or so, and a decent game of Fetch once Kiki was having a nap. She would feed him early in the evening, ready for Eric to take out again once he got home, and then the grateful little soul would happily curl up on the sofa. And, after the first two unsettled nights, he was now sleeping through, much to Leah's relief.

But, just like babies, having a puppy was unpredictable. He had definitely compensated for Kiki's lack of mobility, sneaking into every crevice of the house and stealing whatever he could find. And the doorbell or the phone would only have to ring at the wrong moment for Leah to miss toilet training time. The joy of using poop scoops and doggy bags was hardly a welcome addition to an already busy schedule of bottom wipes and nappy sacks.

She welcomed feeling glamorous tonight after the week she'd had. Slipping out of her bathrobe, she stepped into the smooth lines of her body-shaping underwear and zipped up her chiffon dress with its soft leaves of emerald sitting flatteringly against her complexion. Then she fixed her hair up into a glittering gold clip, with a few chestnut waves loosely dusting the jade of her earrings, and she carried her sandals downstairs to put them on in the kitchen.

As she bent over to fasten the fiddly buckles, her phone buzzed on the worktop and she paused with one shoe on, checking it in case there had been any changes of plan. But it was a group message from Rhona with the picture of the three of them that Dawn had taken in the store.

Hi girls! Looking forward to seeing you tonight. Hope you look as gorgeous as you do here!

'Look at this!' She went over to the sofa, where Eric was still sitting with Kiki, and passed the phone over while she did up the other sandal. 'Us EdenCore ladies all together.'

'With a hint of Star Trek,' he sniggered, pointing a finger at the screen.

Leah frowned. 'Why?'

'Get a load of Spock there on the left. Uncanny eyebrows!'

'Oh, Eric, stop it!' She couldn't help agreeing with his remark about Tiffany, but she snatched the phone away regardless. 'She's so nice. I get on really well with her.'

Kiki bobbed up and down on Eric's lap as he jiggled with laughter. Leah glared back until a car approached outside.

'Right, I'm off.' She pecked them both on the forehead and tickled the puppy's ears.

'I could have given you a lift, you know,' Eric grinned. 'Then again, looks like your mate has already had one!'

Leah shot him an unimpressed glance and tossed her keys into her bag.

'Love you,' he shouted after her. 'Make sure you ring if there's a problem with the taxi back.'

'Not that you'd be able to do much about it,' Leah called over her shoulder. 'That's life when you're tied up at home with a baby *and* a puppy.'

Eric nodded in the resolved way that he always did when Leah made an unarguable point. She kept triumphant eye contact until the door banged shut.

***

Tiffany was waiting outside Glovers, where the security staff were ready to lock up, and a last scattering of customers were still hovering around the beauty counters.

She was wearing a dark padded coat and her hair was loaded up in its usual mountain, but tonight, it glittered under the streetlamps with the diamante quiver of tiny pins.

'Let's go.' Her teeth gleamed white as she linked arms

with Leah and they scurried through the raindrops, skipping over the emerging puddles with their impractically high heels. 'I've been looking forward to this all day.'

Spaghetti strands of fairy lights sprawled over their heads like cobwebs, flowing out from the clock tower at all four angles of the crossroads. Icy lines of lightning flashed around the spear, like white pen strokes over the rink of darkness. As distant thunder punched the air beyond the slick of ocean, they raced through the spattering rain and reached the right road as the heavens opened.

In the nick of time, they huddled under the arched doorway of *Sundara*, the famed Indian restaurant which had just received its second Michelin star. As a waiter opened the door for them, a welcoming throb of heat and spices lashed into the downpour.

Rhona waved from a table in the corner, her lips glazed in a jammy red, which stained the glass as she sipped on something bubbly.

'Oh, you poor wee girls! It really is coming down out there.'

'It sure is,' said Leah, checking her face in the mirrored wall decor. She noticed the dryness of Rhona's hair and the dazzling eye makeup that had clearly not clashed with a drip of rain. 'I guess you were lucky and just missed it.'

'By a whisker.' Her eyelids were powdered in a graphite shadow which shimmered as she winked. 'That dress looks amazing on you!'

'It really does, babes!' Tiffany was already getting comfortable in her seat and opening a serviette into the lap of her tight neon bodycon. Her makeup, in contrast, was muted, allowing her inexplicably taut skin to do all the work.

'Thanks!' Leah replied. 'You both look lovely, too.'

'What are you glugging there, then?' Tiffany eyed Rhona's tumbler, three quarters full of a purplish concoction, a frothy trail of lilac lacing the rim where the topping was lowering with every suck. 'Is that a Star Anise?'

Rhona lifted the maroon garnish out of the foam with her fingertips.

'It's a candied one.' She smiled intriguingly and nibbled off a spike. 'I went for the *Mumbai Moonlight*. It's so good. Even had a sparkler going when it arrived!'

Leah glanced up, noting Rhona's flushed face, the natural ruddiness boldly defying the salmon swipe of her cheek tint. Her laugh was louder than usual, and the scalloped beading of her black top trickled against her elbows as she draped them casually over the table. It was clear she wasn't on her first drink.

'I think I'll go with *Delhi Bean*. What about you, hun?'

Tiffany's question snapped Leah back to the drinks menu. Her original idea of house red wine becoming more boring by the minute. She scanned the cocktails overleaf, trying to find something more exciting so she could match the others without blowing her budget.

'*Bombay Mix* for me, then,' she decided out loud.

'You're brave!' Tiffany remarked as she read the description. 'Let's hope you can still taste the rum through the chilli and coriander.'

'Coconut, pineapple...' Leah added. 'That'll do for me.'

'Let's hope you like soup.'

Glancing at her colleague in mock defiance, Leah's smile faded as she tried to read Tiffany's expression. But no frown creased with the current of her emotions. No gentle animation in the vicinity of her eyes. It was only when a giggle sailed out from between her lips that Leah realised she was speaking in jest.

On a busy shop floor, things like that weren't so obvious, with the constant attention on customers and the scrupulous counter maintenance sandwiched in between. But here, sitting side by side at the table under the saffron glow of the lights, there was an undeniable oddity in Tiffany's face that Leah couldn't quite define.

'Can I get you some drinks, ladies?' asked the waiter, his pocket tablet at the ready.

'Another one of these, thanks.' Rhona wiggled her straw.

He took the other two orders and carefully tapped them through.

'Is that everything for now?'

'Yes, I think that's all, thank y—'

'Hang on one minute!' Rhona held both hands up as she cut Tiffany off, eyes darting expectantly towards the door as she grinned from ear to ear. 'We have one more.'

Leah followed her gaze to the entrance, where someone had their back turned while they were shaking off their umbrella. She squinted across the wooden floor, channelling her focus past the lively diners and the intricate tapestries festooning the walls, using every snatched moment before the person turned to face them. The wide calves protruding from the bottom of the coat were definitely not Kehlani's, and Taeng would never wear heels outside work, so this definitely couldn't be her. Leah watched as the scarf was slowly released from her head. No blonde shock of hair that she would recognise a mile away as Dawn.

Feeling rude for staring, Leah averted her sight to Rhona, who was downing the last curdle of her previous drink to catch up for the next round.

'So, there's a bit of a surprise tonight.' She flipped her quiff with a cunning air. 'We have a special guest.'

Leah looked at the space next to Rhona and clocked the additional setting. The polished cutlery, lying in wait, and the empty water glass, primed for sharing the jug. Clonking footsteps invaded the ambient sitar and then, the scraping of the chair. The plopping down of a person, directly opposite Leah, and the puffing and panting as she caught her breath from the storm. The spiralled frizz of dark hair, springing from a ponytail, and the thick Birmingham accent as she spoke for the first time.

'Sorry, luvvie,' she nudged Rhona. 'Bloody rushed off my feet today.'

She didn't look across the table or acknowledge Leah and Tiffany.

'Drink… quick!' Rhona handed her the menu, aware the waiter was still lingering as requested.

'I'll have what you're having.'

'Make that two *Mumbai Midnights* then, thanks,' Rhona ordered. 'We'll get back to you when we've decided on food.'

The waiter nodded, then scurried away into the thrum of the kitchen, leaving silence awkwardly descending over the tealights, a decorative centrepiece that now marked a divide. Leah watched the flames as they stroked the wax until it smudged with the vintage glass shell.

'Girls, this is Jocelyn Quigley.' Rhona's voice pierced through the hush.

'Nice to meet you!' Tiffany grinned.

'Hi, I'm Leah.'

As she smiled and looked directly at Jocelyn, it all started to register. The woman in the burgundy coat, who had come into the store on that first busy Sunday. The customer checking the stock of shaving foam and sun cream, who had ridiculed marriage in front of Leah without even saying hello. Leah remembered how she had snapped at Tiffany and swanned off as fast as she had arrived.

Jocelyn nodded, a smile tightening her lips as she clicked the salt and pepper pots with a crackle of her nails.

'Jocelyn is actually a rival of ours! She is the EdenCore manager at Parlour, down the road.'

'Haven't we met you before?' asked Tiffany. 'I'm sure I've seen you in Glovers.'

'Only when our counter hasn't got what I want,' Jocelyn sniggered. 'Which isn't often. We're hot on everything over there.'

Jocelyn craned her neck to look around the room, more interested in the surroundings than conversing properly with Tiffany.

'How was it today, then?' Rhona propped her chin up on her hand, drawing Jocelyn's attention back to the table. 'Good sales?'

'Yeah, because I was there, luvvie. Different story when I'm not around to sort that bunch of losers out.'

She folded her arms and gazed smugly at Rhona, before letting out a shrill laugh, prompting the others to chuckle politely.

'They're all trailing behind me on the *T-Radish-ional* incentive.' Jocelyn continued, while checking her reflection on her phone camera. 'I've only got six more bottles to sell before I've done my fifty. That bonus cash is going to be all mine! Thing is, I talk the talk, me. No messing around, I just get down to business and they're buying it by the dozen by the time I've finished with them.'

Rhona laughed nonchalantly, taking the words as a joke. Leah glanced at Tiffany, still unable to read her smile as it froze across her face.

The hush was stubbed out by the glowing colours of the cocktails, gliding through the air towards them. Tiffany took a picture of the striped shots, layered artistically in her highball, before the kaleidoscope of jelly beans sank out of sight into her whipped kulfi topping.

'What have you got?'

Leah gulped her drink. It crashed into her mouth like a zesty wave before the creamy aftertaste ebbed as she swallowed. She could feel Jocelyn's nose almost poking at her beverage, waiting for a response.

'Mainly pineapple…' she finally answered. 'With coconut.'

'Oh, I can't *stand* coconut.'

Leah shrugged and took another sip.

'Did you know…' Jocelyn continued loudly. 'The human body is not designed to digest coconut. That's why you shouldn't consume it. I certainly wouldn't.'

'Seriously?' Tiffany asked with interest. 'But people have eaten it for ages.'

Jocelyn was already shaking her head, lacing a stray curl of hair around her plasticky French manicure.

'No, luvvie. You've got it all wrong. New studies have come out now. Coconut is a no go. Lucky for me that I just *loathe* it.'

Leah held her tongue as she nibbled on the sweets, floating in a lime leaf boat that was moored to the stirrer in the misty yellow liquid. There were red and green sugar balls and caramelised strands, all made to look like the savoury Bombay Mix snack, but that were pleasantly matched to the drink.

'Anyway, we'd better choose our food,' Rhona cut in. 'They'll be back over in a minute.'

They all opened their menus, and a hush fell over the table. One glance at the list of options and Leah just knew that things were looking up. Soon, they would be fork-deep, sampling all the wonders that had made this restaurant famous, and then there'd be far more to talk about.

As a plethora of options piled up before her eyes, Leah didn't know how she was going to choose. She was absolutely ravenous after her day of entertaining Kiki, with a peanut butter sandwich and a pot of fromage frais being the only things she'd managed to eat between hours of whinges and screams.

The words alone were a feast for the eyes, and as the theatre of each description built across the pages, it reminded Leah just how much of a rarity this was. She and Eric had eaten out twice in the year since Kiki had been born. Just a quick couple of hours, grabbing pub grub at their local, while Cheryl and Alan held the fort, trying to get madam off to sleep.

Even Friday night takeaways had become more trouble than they were worth. A perch on the edge of the sofa, where being able to gobble down the meal in peace had overtaken the goal of relaxing and enjoying it.

Just the sight of this menu was restoring her faith that decent food was still in existence, and there were chances to escape from the usual beans on toast and ready meals.

The words flowed like a river, eyes and senses trailing through the tender marinades, sumptuous sauces, succulent mains and carefully-crafted sides, topped with everything from a spice-kissed pomegranate glaze to twists of speciality lime jus.

Then the chef's signature dishes took her eye and the chicken in a creamy tamarind and chilli sauce sounded too irresistible to refuse.

'Are we ready yet?' the waiter asked. With nods all round, he glanced at Leah first.

'I'll go for the Chennai curry with pilau and naancakes, thank you.'

She sipped her cocktail as he tapped in the order and waited for the next of them to speak up.

'You might have to come back to me, luvvie.' Jocelyn frowned, the panic making her eyes dart faster over the menu. 'Can't say I'm blown away by any of this...' She held a hand up to mask her mouth and whispered into Rhona's ear. 'So many carbs.'

'Would you like some more time?'

'No, no, just...' she snapped at the waiter, 'get me one of those Kum-butcher salad things.'

'Kachumber,' he corrected her. 'And what will you have with it?'

'I don't *want* anything else.' Jocelyn curled her lip in disgust.

'But you do realise, it's a side dish. It's only...' He cupped his hands in a small bowl shape.

'I can handle it, mate. That'll do, thank you.'

'What is it?' Tiffany looked terrified. 'There's no croutons or bacon bits, are there?'

The waiter shook his head, bewilderingly. 'It's a simple mix of onion, tomato and cucumber with a squeeze of lemon and some herbs.'

'Oh, good. I'll have that too, then.'

'And for you?' he turned to Rhona.

'Can I get the dhal but without chapatis please?'

The waiter hesitated for a moment and opened his mouth to speak, but he quickly tapped out Rhona's request and told them it wouldn't be long.

A family celebration was full of life on the other side of the restaurant. The singing waiters floated across and presented the guest of honour with a candle-flickering dessert.

'I'd bloody die if anyone ever did that to me,' Jocelyn said, too loudly for Leah's liking.

'Not a fan of being the centre of attention, then?'

Rhona grinned.

'No, I mean the cake. Some birthday present that is, a load of horrible stodge. Last thing I need right now is to pile on the pounds. I've just treated myself to a whole new wardrobe for my holiday. Can't think of anything better than to lie there next to the pool. Don't have to talk to anyone, do anything… just slather myself in *EdenSun* and my lifetime supply of *this* stuff…'

She pulled out a familiar bottle from her handbag and pumped it over her chest until she glistened. The sharp wafts of radish shot into the air and choked the sultry spices that had been whetting Leah's appetite. She took slow glugs of her drink, trying to inhale the flavours in the glass.

'Of course, I've got enough of it at home to fill a suitcase. Hilary gives me a little extra when she visits because my sales figures knock everyone else's out of the park. She always tells me what the new products are well before a launch, too. She shouldn't, but she lets me into the secret because she knows that Parlour would be lost without me…'

Leah watched Jocelyn's lips move until she was no longer aware of any sound. Instead, her sight climbed up to the wallpaper behind her, escaping into the gilded arches and taking in every brushstroke of the framed golden plum trees, running in an endless frieze all the way up to the domed entrance porch.

No more than twenty minutes later, the brass crockery sailed down, over their heads and onto the table. Two small dishes for Tiffany and Jocelyn, with Rhona's only being marginally bigger. While Jocelyn immediately started digging into her salad, the others waited until Leah's food arrived.

It took two serving staff to deliver the one portion, and the aroma caressed her senses in a heady cloud of steam. The vibrant curry gleamed in the pitted centre of the plate while the rice laced fluffily around it. A separate bowl was placed to its side, stacked up with the puffy naan bread pancakes, and a fourth vessel of whipped raita, a sticky mango jam and a chunky relish, crowned Leah's placemat.

On a night out with her old college friends or an anniversary meal with Eric, she would think nothing of ordering the works when everyone else did the same. But one chunk of naancake felt out of place against the paltry salads, and the gerbil-style nibbles that hardly took up any room.

She eyed her companions. The shreds being tilted on forks and dangled in the light, just to ensure there was no trace of oil. Raisins getting scraped out of the way for fear that their sugar content would wreak havoc on the bathroom scales.

'Not bad, actually...' Jocelyn mumbled, allowing another morsel to disappear into her mouth. 'Another perk of the single life. I can eat raw onion whenever I like and I don't have to think about how much I smell. One big bed, just for me, and no one complaining about my breath.'

Leah gazed around the room, watching all the other diners, lapping up their meals and enjoying each other's company. The quicker she ate, the faster they could all go home. Back to normal life and the family from whom she was beginning to wonder why she had wanted to escape. Eric would be telling her to get it down her. He loved seeing her tucking into her food. Why was she letting such delicacies go cold when she could be devouring every morsel?

Giving her full attention to the glories sitting before her, one sensational mouthful was simply too good to stop. The flavours sailed over her palate, making her tastebuds come alive.

'Someone's having fun,' Jocelyn pointed her knife at Leah and raised her eyebrows in disapproval.

'It's absolutely gorgeous.'

'Sorry luvvie, but I don't know how you can do that.' Jocelyn smirked with embarrassment.

'Am I scoffing a bit too fast?' Leah asked with a giggle. 'It's just got to be one of the best things I've ever had.'

'Eat as fast as you like, luvvie. I've not got a problem with that.'

Jocelyn belched into a napkin and chucked it down on her nearly-empty dish. Leah piled curry onto another of her naancakes and spooned raita over the top before letting it collapse into her mouth.

'It's just all those calories…'

Everyone stared at Leah as Jocelyn continued to speak.

'Got to stay slim when you're wearing our uniform or you'll look like a sack of spuds. Just a little extra flab around the chin and people won't look twice at you when you try and sell them our products.'

Leah smiled politely and laughed off the comment.

'Yeah, I… don't do this all the time. There's hardly a chance to eat properly with my little one around.'

'Ah, so you've got a kid?' Jocelyn winked at the rest of the table. 'Better watch out for that mum tum, then!'

'Never had that with my two,' Tiffany chipped in. 'Just snapped straight back into shape.'

'Well, no surprises there, I mean, look at you? A natural beauty if ever I saw one. Does amazing hair run in your family, luvvie?'

Tiffany nodded proudly. 'That and the conditioner I use. I literally swear by it!'

Jocelyn's eyes glided over her. 'You look way too

young to have babies.'

'Not babies...' corrected Tiffany. 'They're nearly adults now.'

'Explains it. You don't exactly have that knackered thing about you like most women do when they've got youngsters. You know, all chewed up and spat out, like a cow being eaten by a vulture.' Jocelyn turned back to Leah. 'It's the early years that really show the signs. Who'd put their body through childbirth and then hope to ever fit back into their clothes? Calories and kids – the ultimate death knell on the feelgood factor. Sod that!'

She laughed into her drink and Leah let her cutlery fall on her plate, at least having finished the majority of her meal. Watching the expressions of Rhona and Tiffany, she waited for either of them to jump in and speak. Anything to defend the assault launched at Leah or lighten the atmosphere that was rapidly darkening the table.

'Anyway...' Rhona said at last, 'have we all finished, girls?'

They pushed their dishes aside, ready for collection, and Rhona gestured to the waiter. She shot him a knowing look as he piled everything up on an arm, and Leah assumed she was asking him for the bill.

With dessert clearly not an option, Leah couldn't wait to leave in the taxi. No sooner would her keys turn in the front door, but she would be kicking her shoes off and diving inside the fridge for the half block of chocolate she had saved from the night before. She intended to eat the whole lot, the TV providing far better company than what she had endured tonight. Sliding a hand inside her bag, she reached for her phone. Might as well send Eric a message now to say that she was on her way.

But clinking glasses snapped her back to the table, where four flutes were being set out in front of them and the waiter popped the cork on a chilled bottle of champagne. He poured it out between them and stowed the rest in a vat of ice on the end.

'OK, ladies…' Rhona raised her glass, eyes glinting under her spiky lashes. 'So, this is on me. There's some news I need to share with you.'

She's pregnant, Leah thought. *Or maybe engaged…*

'I'm leaving!'

There was a loud shriek from Tiffany, while Leah stayed quiet.

'Well… not exactly leaving. I've been promoted to a position in recruitment, so I'm relocating to Head Office.'

'That's amazing!'

'Brilliant, Rhona!' Leah agreed with Tiffany. 'You deserve it. Congratulations!'

Amid the excitement surrounding the revelation, Jocelyn remained surprisingly silent.

'When are you leaving?' Tiffany asked.

'It's a quick changeover, I'm afraid. Two weeks' time.'

'No way!' whimpered Leah. 'We'll miss you so much.'

They touched rims to say cheers and paused while they glugged away, Leah feeling the bubbles frothing cooly down her throat.

'Hey, Rhona…' Tiffany leaned forward. 'Who's taking your place then?'

Rhona wrinkled her nose in a smile, her freckles showing through the faded patches of foundation. Then she tilted her head to the side and directed their sight on tonight's unexpected guest.

'Surprise!' yelled Jocelyn, her nostrils flaring at either side of her prominently beaky nose.

'Oh, I can't believe it! You've known all this time?'

Tiffany grinned naively as Jocelyn nodded in response.

'Awww, I think you'll be a lot of fun.'

'Definitely.' Leah clamped her mouth into a smile. 'This is really good news.'

'Well, I'll work you hard and I'll work you good...' Jocelyn warned. 'But, you could do a lot worse. Not bad to have someone with my sales record heading your team. I'll soon get you up to scratch. No target will be left unmet with me around, let me assure you. They don't call me The Dragon for nothing.'

Rhona topped them up with the rest of the champagne and it wasn't too long before they'd finished. With the bill paid and their coats fetched from the cloakroom, they went their separate ways after saying goodbye at the clock tower.

After Tiffany had been dropped by the taxi, Leah sat in the back seat as thunder crashed and rain clattered like a car wash over the windows.

Kiki would be in bed by now, but perhaps Eric might still be awake, waiting until she was home safely. Then, she could let it all out. Tell him how she felt to lose a wonderful boss only to gain someone who'd spent the entire evening insulting her. She would get through this. Adapt to the change. But first, she needed the therapy of a rant so Eric could talk her round and bring her back to her senses.

She carefully let the door click shut and padded across to the sink, the cool floor soothing her feet, now that they were free of the stilettos. Filling a glass with water, she took a few glugs, then she turned off the lights and headed towards the stairs.

A dim lamp was still on in the living room, making her double take as she passed the doorway. She followed the red of Eric's socks, along the line of his jeans and as she squinted through the darkness, Kiki was there with him, cuddled up in the crook of his arm as he dozed flat out on the sofa.

Leah stepped closer and on Eric's other side, a black shape outlined him so perfectly. The little pup was nuzzled in, slumbering like he had probably never done before they'd found him, each one of Eric's slow breaths mirrored by this dog he adored.

These were the very things that tried Leah's patience every day, but here in this moment, there could be no deeper love for all three of them.

And as she blinked into the centre of Eric's chest, her heart bounced to see Kiki's tiny hand, wrapped around one soft, furry paw.

Taking a blanket from the pile over in the corner, she opened it out and covered all three of them. It tickled Eric's nose and he stirred.

'Shhhhh,' Leah whispered. 'You'll wake them up.'

Eric relaxed back down against the comfy arm of the sofa.

'Shall I stay here then?'

'For tonight. But this is a one-off, Eric.'

'I know,' he mouthed, eyeing his snuggling companion. 'I'll go back to the rescue centre in the morning.'

Leah shook her head. 'You'll go to the pet shop.'

He frowned, but she kept smiling.

'You'll need to get him a proper bed if we're keeping him.'

'*Seriously?*'

She nodded, her soul warmed by his sleepy grin and kind eyes shining through the dark.

'Get some rest.' She lifted his glasses away and kissed his lips. 'Before I change my mind.'

Then she tucked the blanket around her world and tiptoed upstairs to bed.

Fourteen

Leah stirred as Eric's mouth grazed her cheek. She blinked in the darkness and burrowed further into her pillow, disgruntled that he was trying his luck in the middle of the night.

'I'm off,' he said softly. 'See you later.'

The collar of his shirt pressed against her skin and she forced her eyes open to see him leaning across the bed.

'What do you mean?'

'Got to be in London for eight-thirty, remember?'

'No…' She rolled over to face him. 'That's next week, you said.'

'This *is* next week,' Eric sniggered. 'Time sure flies when you're having fun.'

'But I thought you meant…'

'Next week as in, the one after this week?'

Leah nodded blearily and turned on the bedside light.

'Anyway, you'll be OK, won't you? Just don't forget the whistle, it really helps with his recall.'

'Seriously?' She slumped against the headboard, noting the time was only just after six in the morning. 'What if he runs off or something? If I lose grip of that pushchair up a hill, Kiki's going to…'

'Can't you give her to Nana?'

'No, Eric, I can't. Mum's got a church thing on, so that leaves me stuck with the pair of them!'

'Look, I have to run. My train leaves in twenty-five minutes.' He kissed her forehead and slid guiltily into his suit jacket. 'You've got this. I'll be back in time to take him out tonight.'

He turned to give her a last encouraging glance, but she wasn't letting him walk out of there thinking she was fine. The fragility that consumed her at every new challenge was flooding back as she thought of her day ahead. While Eric would be kicking back on the train, scrolling through the news with a coffee cup keeping his hands warm, she would probably get stuck in the back of beyond, searching for a lost puppy with a toddler in tow.

She'd been feeling tense enough as it was, anticipating Rhona's last days on the counter, and the arrival of Jocelyn. Leah was less than excited about the prospect, and it didn't help that Tiffany had since heard through the grapevine about Jocelyn's reputation as a slavedriver, in stark contrast to Rhona's leadership style.

Leah pulled the duvet back over her head, clinging to the last hour of peace that would soon be snatched away. But sixty minutes felt like five when she was snapped back awake by two sets of wailing in one.

Throwing on her dressing gown, she stepped through the nursery door and lifted Kiki out of her cot. Then she hauled the thrashing child downstairs to the growing whine at the safety gate. Two longing eyes peeped out through the bars and the pup was zooming around the kitchen from the second he was set free.

Leah plonked Kiki into her highchair and sat down at the table, slowly catching her breath. A sloppy lick tickled her heel and she couldn't help smiling. The dog was sitting beside her, the bottom of her pyjamas draped over his head as he watched the slipper, half hanging off her foot, ready to grab it as soon as she let it drop.

'And just what are you up to, Mr?'

At her words, he rolled over on his back, all fours in the air while she softly stroked his chest. Kiki started to grizzle, kicking her legs against the padded chair lining.

'Oh, of course,' Leah sighed, not looking at her. 'Because you just can't stand it if anyone else gets attention.'

But as Leah glanced up at her, she saw that Kiki's hands were splayed out in a grabbing motion, trying to reach down to where Leah was patting.

'You want to say hello?'

She bundled the pup into her arms and held him towards Kiki, his tail wagging wildly as he neared her eager face. Kiki grabbed his neck and scrunched his fur between her fingers.

'No…' said Leah, releasing him. 'Gently.'

Taking her daughter's hand in her own, she smoothed it over the puppy's face until Kiki got the hang of the motion and squealed out in delight. Then she wrapped her arms around him and snuggled under his floppy ear. Something inexplicable tugged in Leah's chest as their new pet rested his chin on Kiki's shoulder, closing his eyes while she babbled away to him.

And the more Kiki hugged him, the more she tilted her body, while her two little feet pushed her upwards with all their might.

***

An hour later, in jeans, a smear of moisturiser and lips dabbed in Glovers brand petroleum jelly, Leah found her hiking boots in the garage and zipped herself into an old anorak. She wrapped Kiki up warm in her puffy all-in-one and a knitted beanie hat, covering most of her ears.

Hoisting her up, Leah glanced out at the mohair clouds as they darkened against the pewter. She watched the thickets swaying along the fence and could feel the storm brewing before she had even stepped into it.

She carried Kiki down the front steps and ensured that she was securely strapped into her pushchair. Then she fastened the puppy's harness around him, slipping the lead onto her wrist so she could push Kiki with both hands.

Just a few metres along the pavement, a footpath led the way into acres of open countryside that she had always neglected to explore. As the wheels crashed repeatedly against the flint walkway, the puppy wrenched the lead, digging the loop into Leah's skin as he cantered along beside her.

The narrow passage lapsed into an overgrown meadow where a cemetery ran along the bottom. She steered through the floundering nettles, where the track took turns in travelling flatly and edging off until it halved in width. With every halt as the pushchair hit another rut, the dog jolted onwards, slicing her arm all the more.

Kiki began to whimper and Leah clenched her teeth, wading through the grasses and weeds, and the rise and fall of gravestones in various states of disrepair. With a sudden jerk, the pup bounced over a muddy crater, flinging the pushchair over on its side. While Kiki stayed safely in her seat, Leah scraped her ankle on a rock and a furry face cowered as she screamed out loud in agony. Breathing through each throb of pain, Leah got to her knees, grappling with the pushchair frame until it was upright once again. She pulled the dog through her legs and clutched him to her chest, instinctively comforting him and trying to stop Kiki bawling.

With all her strength, she stood back up, her eyes following the trail where it disappeared beyond the bushes. It wound far more gently around the corner, through berries interspersed with clematis fluff, and as she stepped out into another open space, a park became visible at the foot of the slope. Within it was a playground and a series of dog agility equipment, both of which Leah would be unable to make use of right now.

She could hear the happy chimes as toddlers jumped up and down in their wellies on the bottom of the slide, and the overjoyed laughter of parents launching them into the air like rockets on the swings. Others played Hide and Seek, giggling through the tunnels and crawling into the wooden house in the centre of the climbing ropes.

Pressing her heels into the earth as the pup pulled her forwards, Leah skulked across the grass as the lively faces all turned around to stare at the source of the screeching. She tightened every muscle, trying to control the panting dog and the pushchair at the same time. Then she reached a concrete strip that swept uphill, further into the wilderness.

Like a husky to a sledge, the pup surged endlessly forwards, but as the wheels rolled onto the tarmac, the pressure began to ease. Together, they mounted the incline, where fields spilled outwards on either side, stripped bare after their summer harvest of toasted crops. As the gradient took hold, the tugging and tearing eased away and Leah pushed with every limb until, at last, she was standing at the summit.

She looked down at the faraway community she had just climbed away from, feeling like she had reached the very top of a mountain. The arm of sea cradled every distant roof, as if silencing the traffic noise with each swell. A train passed along it all, thin as a needle threading through cloth. Pastures of weeds and forgotten grains sprawled out in their muted bronze beneath her. Crumpled poppies laced the hillsides like muddy autumn jewels, fading away in her eyeline until they were blitzed to a pastel fog.

Every footstep she had trodden, through beaten tracks and craggy slopes, had carried her away from the stares and the people. The four walls echoing with the constant sound of crying. For the first time in forever, she could finally open her eyes. If she could dive upwards, then off she would swim into the calming lake of clouds, bathing her skin in a swan-white haze.

Kiki was beginning to nod off, snug in her blankets while the breeze nipped her nose. Leah glanced at the puppy and knelt to stroke his head. He sat next to the pushchair, his brown eyes looking longingly at the sprawling acres around him. She ran her hand along his harness and slowly gripped the clasp of his lead. Then, without another thought, she released him.

In seconds, he became nothing more than a black speck as he shot away down the path. It hit Leah like a thunderbolt, her heart flipflopping into her mouth. She squinted through the shuddering foliage where the chalk lines thinned out and collided with the woodland.

'Come back…' she whispered, her lips trembling as the terror of losing him ripped through her body like she had never imagined it could.

The seconds crept on, and still, there was no sign. Like a piece of her had snapped away as he'd left her side. That she could hardly bear to think of being without him.

'Come back!' Leah shouted with an urgency that now overcame her. 'Come on, boy. Come back here, pup…' She filled her lungs again and gave it all her might. 'Come back!'

A miniature blob caught her eye at the furthest point ahead of her, and the more she slapped her thighs, the more it grew, until two ears took shape, flapping wildly as he closed in. Tears swarmed in her eyes as he skidded to a halt at her ankles, dropping a half-chewed tennis ball on the ground and wagging his tail proudly. She scooped him into her arms, the touch of his cold nose warming her soul like she would never have believed. He nestled in, making her feel needed and adored.

Once back on his feet, Leah tossed him the ball and when he had repeatedly retrieved it enough times for her to feel confident, she took the handles of the pushchair and began to walk ahead, the pure peace of Kiki asleep, and the companionship of the little dog making her feel more alive than she had done in so long.

Her hair straggled wildly in the fingers of breeze, and the air delved over her bare skin, enriching it in a natural moisture, unrivalled by anything that humans could make. Sheets of rain turned her lashes spidery and glazed her lips in a glistening balm. She lost herself as the gentle droplets fell over her like crystal, refreshing her with their kisses of life.

She walked onwards, where the arched branches linked together like hands and the tracks wove pathways in all directions through the wooded hillside. Taking the northernmost route, she emerged into a clearing where ancient trees slumped characteristically around the edges as if morphed from wax that had dried up halfway through melting. The kind where elves and witches lived in beautifully illustrated story books.

Leah parked the pushchair under the arms of an oak, where the boughs caught the raindrops and sheltered Kiki's head. The little pup scurried here and there as Leah stepped away from the sleeping bundle. She stood in the centre of the forest, drinking in the gingery-bronze palace of seclusion. And doing nothing but breathing.

She closed her eyes, but not in the weary sense she had come to know so well. Instead, it was the irrepressible coolness of the air, mellowing its way across her lids. Lifting her face up to the skeletal treetops, it felt like her whole body was following her sight, climbing ever higher into the iced gaps of sky. The whip-crack wings of intermittent birds made her chest as light as the falling feathers, dusting her fingers like snowflakes.

The slow drip of water was no longer from her tears. Beads of leftover rain shattered through the tree bark, that was so much wiser to these secrets than she could ever be. Flavours of the breeze, spiced with freshened soil, sailed between her lips as she inhaled it all willingly, taking back more of herself with every burst.

Then, *clonk*. The pup ran past with a stick, scraping it on the pushchair where it whacked against a bar. Kiki jerked awake, and Leah froze as she waited for the whispers of the wind to drown. But there was not even a whimper.

A puff of white flower seeds danced around Kiki, painting patterns as they parachuted into her lap. She gazed inquisitively at the fuzzy specks and as each one met her nose and chin like cream on peaches, a giggle fluttered through her, with a smile like Leah had never seen.

Walking over to the pushchair, Leah placed an acorn into Kiki's tiny hands, cradling them while she held it. Then she tapped it softly against her daughter's cheek, making her laugh all the more.

The dog scampered towards them, kicking up the fallen leaves in a shower of brass and russet. He brought his stick to Leah and sat patiently next to her, wagging his tail.

'What's he got?' Leah pointed to his mouth. 'It's a

twig!'

'Tig…' Kiki stretched towards him. "Tigggg!"

Leah lifted Kiki out of her seat and sat down on a tree stump. But Kiki continued to wriggle in her mother's grasp. Then, a second later, she planted her feet firmly on the ground between Leah's knees, pulling herself higher, then higher again, until she was wrapping her arms around the pup with Leah barely supporting her.

'Kiki!' Leah praised. 'Look at you, so nearly there!'

'Tig,' she replied, looking intently at Leah while she cuddled into her furry friend.

'That's right, he's got a…' She stopped talking, then chuckled. 'Twig. You think we should call him Twig?'

Kiki toppled backwards and the dog nudged her safely onto Leah's lap. Then with one arm around Kiki and the other around Twig, the threesome huddled happily in the forest until dusk ushered them away and they headed off home, gently chased by the quickening rain.

Fifteen

Kiki was slowly getting stronger on her feet in the snatched moments when she wasn't whining. Still not quite by herself, but there was at least a glimmer of Zara's exercises paying off. There had been just a few more smiles, sleeps, and a little something extra with Twig zooming around, keeping Kiki entertained and filling the house with a new energy.

It had given Leah the chance to try again with the EdenCore makeup. At least she knew now that the concealer was compatible with her skin, and today she was debuting the new limited-edition lipstick in a deep, velvety red. It was Eric's day off, so he'd taken Kiki out bright and early to soft play at the leisure centre, giving Leah time to style some waves through her hair. Today, for a change, she was wearing it down with the front strands swept back in a clip.

'Hey, beautiful.' Taeng came in, holding the door open for Leah, who was just leaving. 'Loving the lippie. Is that the new one?'

Leah nodded and beamed back at her, knowing how white it made her teeth look.

'Might have to get one of those.'

'Well, I doubt it's going to be a match for your

Poirier *Nougat*, but it's not a bad second.'

'Let's have a look…' Kehlani appeared behind Taeng, resting a hand on her shoulder. Each nail was encrusted in white and topped off with a diamante candy cane. 'Wow! That is so good on you. Bet you sell out by the end of the day.'

'I'll do my best.' Leah craned her neck for a last glimpse at her reflection. 'Right, I should get down there before Rhona sells them all!'

There was silence in response and Leah clocked a glance between her colleagues in the background of the mirror.

'What?' She turned to face them.

'Oh, nothing it's just…' Kehlani's eyes widened under their perfect winged liner and false-effect KittyPie mascara. 'We didn't realise that you…'

'Lunch break first thing in the morning, is it?' Dawn's blancmange of hair appeared behind them, and she folded her arms as Taeng and Kelani parted ways to let her through. 'Why are you lot chatting up here? It's swamped downstairs already. The three for two gifts are flying off the shelves.'

'On my way!' Leah smiled as she squeezed through the crack in the doorway.

'Nice lips, love. *Poinsettia Pout*, right?' Dawn flashed her pretty eyes over Leah's makeup.

'That's the one.'

'Yeah, I hate to say it, but I don't think Capital G's Christmas red is that amazing this year. It's too… I don't know, pinkish.' She squinted, her eyes glued to Leah's lips as her business mind whirred into action. 'Right, you two, come with me.'

Kehlani rolled her eyes at Taeng as Dawn led them away from the door.

'I'm taking you off counter for the first half an hour.

Capital G is in need of your display skills.'

'Seriously? What about our commission?' Kehlani protested as she sloped away with Dawn.

'You're Glovers staff as well, remember that.'

Alone in the corridor, Leah straightened her jacket and took the staircase down to the shop floor. As she stepped out onto the upper level, lights and tinsel twinkled all around her and everywhere was decked in gift sets and bows. The food fridge was brimming with festive sandwiches and snacks, and across in the baby section, the new tots' partywear range lit up the hangers with crimson tutu dresses and mini tartan shirts.

Let It Snow blasted out from the speakers as she glided down the escalator, where the beauty department dazzled in an array of stunning decorations. Fragrant notes of clementine, cinnamon, and rosemary fused with the nips of cold air as customers bustled in and out.

Leah was immersed in all the classic feelings, warm and fuzzy as she wound her way through ribbons, boxes, packaging, and excitement and to top it all off, she was wearing EdenCore makeup like a pro. Today was going to be a good day and she would start by selling out the *Poinsettia Pout*.

From what she could see at the counter, Rhona had got some new shoes. Her feet peeped out from behind the testers where she was reaching down to pick something up.

'Morning!' Leah chimed, knowing her boss would love her in the lipstick.

'Alright, luvvie!' A hand slapped a jar of night cream down on the counter, and she heaved herself into full view. Dark hair straggled out of her loose ponytail and a broad smile was drawn on in a matte brick red. 'Surprise, eh?'

Leah was speechless for a moment as the vision sank

in before her.

'Oh, hi…' she stuttered. 'I didn't expect to see you…'

'So soon?' Jocelyn was already nodding. 'I know. Well, there's been a change of plan, you see. They moved Rhona's start date at the last minute so here I am!'

'I see,' Leah nodded, trying to mask the confusion. 'That was quick then.'

'Tell me about it, I had to say my goodbyes at Parlour, just like that, and they were devastated to see me go. First day here yesterday and I was all on my own.' She shrivelled her face up and pretended to wipe away tears.

'Was Tiffany not in then? She usually is…'

Jocelyn shook her head. 'Had some emergency down at the school with the kid…' She waved her hand. 'Judas or whatever his name is.'

'Junior.'

'That's it. So, anyway, I've made myself at home as you can see.'

She beamed proudly as Leah glanced at the counter. Jocelyn had rearranged some of the bottles, and the makeup brushes were all laid out flat in a row rather than in their usual place in a pot next to the customer chair. Leah could see it now, the spillages and clutter from only having half as much room on the already-small surface when multiple products were in use during makeovers.

'Looking good.'

Jocelyn snorted and eyed her up and down. 'We're not done here yet, luvvie.' She was already clomping over to the till, where she pulled out a yellow cloth and a bottle of fluid with a trigger spray. 'There.' *Bang*, they went, down on the counter. 'Get cleaning.'

Leah stared at the items and started to open her mouth.

'Don't tell me Rhona never had you doing housekeeping. It's not all slathering on lotion and topping up your lip gloss, you know.'

'No, of course not, it's just…' Leah winced at the soapy yellow contents of the cleaning fluid, 'Have we got any gloves in yet? Only, my hands come up in blotches when I use that stuff.'

Jocelyn bent over and barely looked before standing up straight again. 'Sorry, can't see any. Just slap some of the *Palm Oil* on afterwards, it'll be fine.'

Leah gave a hesitant nod as she took the cloth in her fingertips, feeling that it was already doused in the chemical-ridden spray.

'Won't take you long. I just want everything shipshape. Can't have customers complaining about dust, not with my name and reputation behind this counter.'

As Jocelyn perched on a stool near the till and tapped away on the tablet, Leah reached for a wad of tissues and wrapped them around her hand. Then she started on the top shelf, using the fluid as sparingly as possible.

'Good weekend then, luvvie? What did you get up to?'

'Oh, not much really.' Leah wracked her brains. What could possibly be worth mentioning as a highlight? Definitely not the abandoned weekly shop, when Leah had left the supermarket with a lettuce and a tube of toothpaste as Kiki had screamed down every aisle. 'Sunday was nice. My mum and I were out on the seafront. Kiki nodded off in the pushchair so…'

Her eyes shot over to Jocelyn as she shrieked out loud.

'Enough to put me off kids forever, that is.'

Leah slowed the scrubbing and glanced questioningly for a further explanation.

'Pushchairs!' Jocelyn grunted. 'I mean, who wants to be lugging those around? I see the sorry states of these parents, shunting them in doorways and having to queue up for the lift.'

Two young mothers came through the main entrance and Jocelyn kept talking as they walked past the counter.

'Stick your sprogs in a nursery, I say, and give everyone else a break. I can't stand it when I'm browsing and a wheel goes over my foot. And they're all so entitled, aren't they? Expecting you to stand aside and hold open doors that they take six hours to get through.'

'Well, you know… children only get heavier and you can't carry them everywhere.'

'And bodies are temples,' Jocelyn almost snapped. 'Better left in their original form. Not invaded by sperm, never to be in the same shape again.' She slipped her thumbs inside her waistband, beaming. 'My skirt is actually getting too big for me, you know. All that juicing means I don't even have to exercise.'

Leah managed a polite smile, her cuticles tingling as the tissue became wetter. Then a couple approached her side of the counter, and she was happy to be distracted. She held back for a second while they started looking at the serums, then seized her moment to show Jocelyn her skills.

'Good morning, how are you both today?'

'Oh, I couldn't be better,' chimed the woman, nudging her husband in his corduroy winter coat. 'He, on the other hand, would rather be down the pub playing darts, but I've dragged him out Christmas shopping instead. Only, we seem to have stopped looking at things for other people now I've got in here!'

'Perfect time for a new serum,' Leah grinned. 'Get that skin in tiptop condition for all those festive events.'

'I have a posh work do every year,' said the woman with a wink. 'And our nephew's wedding is on New Year's Eve. Fancy manor house in the Cotswolds and all that, so I definitely want to look the part.'

'That's so exciting! Well, if you're after a serum, you'll be spoilt for choice here.'

'I'm going to need a wonder product. My skin has been so dry since hitting fifty.'

Leah smiled. Always a relief when the age question was answered without asking.

'So, you'll want hydration with an extra smoothing boost.' She reached over for the *Afterlife* serum, tailored exactly for that age range.

'*SySTEM*, luvvie.' Jocelyn had swooped in from behind the counter and was already popping the lid off the tester bottle. 'This is just the magic potion you've been looking for.'

'Right…' Leah pursed her lips, feeling instantly uneasy. 'Although that's more of an all-rounder.'

She continued to hold the *Afterlife* bottle, but Jocelyn snatched if off her and put it back on the stand.

'I'll see to this customer.' Her nostrils flared as she gestured at Leah's cleaning equipment. 'As you were.'

'Yes, but I'm happy to help this lady first.'

There was a long pause and Jocelyn's stare drilled into her. 'But you haven't done the bottom shelf.'

'I do apologise if it's an awkward time,' said the woman, directly to Leah. 'I can easily come back and see you later if…'

'Absolutely not!' Jocelyn's voice drowned her out. 'Now, come over here with me and let's have a look at you.'

Leah watched the ungainly bounce as Jocelyn pumped up the seat level with her foot just a little too enthusiastically and began examining the woman's face. She stood on the spot, zoning in and out of the muffled conversation as swathes of shoppers milled around the counters.

'Quite prominent crow's feet…' she heard Jocelyn

say, and '…slack around the neck.' Leah got down on her knees, still hearing the occasional bellow over the store music. 'I'm always honest, me.'

Taking the contents off the last shelf and piling them up in a basket, she could see that there was not a speck of dirt or dust. Nevertheless, she covered the surface with spray and rubbed as best she could, gripping the last dry parts of the cloth in a vain attempt to avoid contact with the fluid.

A fallen face mask sachet was caught at the back, but she couldn't quite reach it. She leaned further forwards, feeling the hem of her skirt sliding further up her thighs, the floor ice cold through her thin nude tights and the heels of her court shoes slipping against the tiles. With a lunge, she grabbed the packet and tossed it into the basket. Then she glanced sideways to see two feet, and then a figure facing her. She traced the beige trousers, then the dark tan of his coat, finally raising her eyes to see that he was gawping up her legs.

His wife was oblivious as Jocelyn slapped lotions and potions on her face at top speed, and he had left them to it while he'd stepped away to amuse himself.

Leah slithered upright and turned her back, continuing along the lowest shelves until they ended behind the counter. She clamped her hand on her skirt, wedging it between her knees while she got the job done.

Once finished, she eased herself upright, giving her hem a good yank downwards before emerging from behind the testers. The man hadn't moved.

'Terry?' the woman called as Jocelyn buffed her cheeks. 'Come here and tell me what you think to this blusher.'

'Be there in a minute.' He locked eyes with Leah and gave her a wink. 'Just having a browse.'

'Trust me, luvvie, you don't need another opinion.

This stuff *has* to be in your life… every single bit of it.'

'I might just get the serum today after all. I do have a good foundation at home, and I really should use my old blusher first.'

'Up to you.' Jocelyn folded her arms. 'But you know that frock you were just telling me about. The one you've got lined up for the wedding.'

Leah watched as the woman nodded feebly.

'You want to look good in it, right?'

'Of course…'

'And you know, you can only do that if you take the plunge.' Jocelyn's eyes narrowed as she whispered. *'Invest.'*

'I mean… it did cost a lot of money, and I'd like to look nice.'

'Ain't going to happen. Not if your products aren't up to scratch. I mean… imagine how you'll feel on the day. Just how much you'll *regret* it when the dress looks better than you do. All those young girls swanning around in their tight-arse outfits, fillers, Botox… how are you going to compete?' Jocelyn chortled as she pulled out the hair clips and flicked them onto the makeup station. 'These little bottles are the answers to your prayers, but if you're happy with your budget brands then…'

There was silence. Jocelyn held up a mirror, allowing the woman a momentary gaze before tilting it at the blinding overhead lights.

'OK… I think I could stretch to the concealer, maybe.'

'We'll get you the primer then to go with that, and the setting powder.' Jocelyn was already rifling through the drawers. 'The mascara will set it all off and you'll want a lipstick, luvvie. What colour is the dress?'

'It's sort of a deepish dusty pink,' stuttered the woman. 'But I really don't need…'

'Have the new one. Limited Edition *Poinsettia Pout!*'

'Is it a red? I really don't wear…'

'Oh, but red lippie with pink clothes is so now! You're going to turn heads, that's for sure, being an older lady who is on trend.'

Jocelyn placed the palette on the counter along with at least six other items.

'Did you say you're going away for this wedding?' She strode back to the customer with glee.

'The… Cotswolds.' She winced as Jocelyn's fingers clicked in her face.

'So, you'll be staying in a hotel! Oh, well that's just perfect for a bit of pampering. You're getting the lipstick, so it's only right to have the rest of our Christmas range. It's not going to hang around for long! So, I'm sorting you right out with our *Hollydays* hand cream…' She reached behind the promotional stand as the woman struggled for words. 'And a *MistleToes* foot balm. Got to be done.'

Slapping both boxes on the counter, she turned to Leah.

'Grab us a *SySTEM* please, luvvie.'

'Right… which size do you w…'

Jocelyn silenced her with a glare. She dived behind the counter, seizing an extra-large box herself.

'Never, and I mean *never* even mention there's a smaller size,' she hissed under her breath.

She scanned the items at top speed, cramming them into a bag before the woman reached the till. The card reader was thrusted at the woman, who paid as quickly as possible so that her husband didn't see. He breezed back over to her, much to Leah's relief, and he led the way to the exit while his wife loitered behind him, concealing the bag in a larger carrier.

'Woo-hoo!' Jocelyn cheered. 'Just a tenner to go and I've done my target already. Mind you, it's the very least she needs with *that* face. Skin like a leather rag. Should have given it to you as a cleaning cloth!'

Leah sucked in a breath as her new manager's cackle sailed out over the store.

'How's things, my pretties?' Dawn called over to them from the Capital G stand, where Kehlani looked disgruntled to be decorating a counter of lipstick that was nothing to do with KittyPie.

'All good, luvvie, all good.' Jocelyn winked with her hands on her hips. 'Leona here is doing a top job now I've got her cleaning, and I've nearly bagged my entire day's target in one sale!'

'Actually, it's L—'

'Oh, you are just little stars,' chimed Dawn over Leah's correction. Then she gave a thumbs up to Kehlani's display work. 'And look at this one here. Capital G is not even her brand, but she's taking time out to help. This is what Glovers is all about. It doesn't matter what the department is, we should all be pitching in and helping each other. Serving every customer as if they are your own.'

Jocelyn shot a side eye at the growing crowds of shoppers and her smile seemed slightly frozen.

'Yeah right,' she said under her breath.

Leah's eyes darted over to Dawn, who was now making Taeng put up all the promotional labelling.

'Looks like I'm needed.' Kehlani eyed a group of teenage girls trying out the new KittyPie eye sets.

'Won't keep you much longer,' said Dawn firmly as Kehlani hurried to finish. 'Just another boxful to arrange at the side.'

'Excuse me, can we pay here? It's rammed over at the main checkouts.'

Dawn turned to a woman and her friend who were laden with baby products from the sale upstairs.

'We're closed over here at the moment, I'm afraid.' Dawn smiled sympathetically. 'But come with me and we'll find someone to help you.'

She led them over to EdenCore, where Jocelyn was examining her nails and Leah was busy polishing the tester rack.

'Do you mind, Joss?' asked Dawn. 'These ladies have their hands full!'

'Oh, it's a pleasure.' She grinned widely and waited for Dawn to disappear. 'Not easy with youngsters, is it?' Craning her neck, she gazed down at the two toddlers. 'Keeping your mums busy are we, little runts?'

Jocelyn's lip curled in disgust as one of them blew a bubble.

'Is it… burping?'

Leah flinched. *It?*

His mother chuckled. 'No, he's just giving you a raspberry. Seems to do it when he's happy!'

'Amazing,' Jocelyn turned away as if she had just flushed a toilet. 'Well, I bet you girls could do with a treat, eh? Something to make you feel special while they're sucking the life out of you like a vacuum cleaner.'

The women glanced at each other in silence.

'*SySTEM* is going to do that for you. Just one slick of it and all those tired eye bags and knackered lines will be off to beddie bye-byes faster than you can say…'

'For *that* price?' spluttered the friend, spying the label behind Jocelyn. 'I could get a year's supply of baby wipes and still have change!'

'Or at least five nights in my trackies with a takeaway,' said the other. 'No contest!'

They both laughed.

'So, it's just that lot, is it?' Jocelyn waved a hand at the baskets of socks, bibs, dummies and milk.

'Thanks.'

The first load was lifted onto the counter, and she stared as if it would bite her.

'Leona, can I borrow you, please?'

'Sure, just a second,' Leah replied, balancing a stack of jars as she dusted their spaces on the tester stand.

'No, I said now. Customers first, luvvie.'

Leah stiffened, trying not to drop anything and smash it on the hard floor.

'Chop, chop. They haven't got all day.'

She gained control of the toppling tower and one by one, placed each pot on safer ground. Then Jocelyn whacked the till scanner straight into her hand.

'Leona will get you sorted. Time to go on my lunch break.'

Off she strode, leaving Leah to bag up the nappies, toys and other items that the mothers then heaped over their arms.

'Here, I'll bring this one round for you.' Leah lifted the heaviest carrier and hung it on the pushchair, as they'd instructed. 'Will you be OK with all that?' She smiled knowingly.

'We'll do just fine stumbling to the car!' said the one with the fuzzy auburn plaits. 'It's our way of life now.'

'As long as we happen to fall into a coffee bar on the way!' agreed her friend.

'Have a nice day,' said Leah, beaming at the tots. 'And the baby sale is on for another week if you need anything else.'

'Good to know. Thanks for that and sorry to cramp your counter style!'

'Seriously, not at all!'

The two mothers headed out of the store and, for just a few moments afterwards, she wished she had gone with them.

Sixteen

Through the glass of her windscreen, the river lapped wildly around Ropeshore Community Hub, where its prominent oblongs were stacked above the waves. She had driven over the bridge into a corner of the car park, not sure if she was relieved or disappointed that there were less people than expected.

She glanced between the front seats at Kiki, who frowned stroppily under the pretty bow of her headband.

Gulls sang as they swirled around in the dark pools of sky, and the occasional clap of boat sails punctuated the wind. It was not making Leah feel inclined to get out of the car.

More tyres churned against the gravel and car doors clicked open, then banged shut. Some arrived in pairs, yanking out babies and bags over shoulders. Leah eyed them without wanting to stare. Not a fancy leotard in sight. Just the same casual t-shirts and leggings like she was wearing.

The flurry began to subside, and Leah knew it was now or never.

'Please…' she whispered, reaching into the back seat for her bag. 'Just be good today.'

Catching up with the last couple of people just in

time for them to hold open the door, Leah squeezed through. She sighed inwardly as she followed them along the hallway, at least not having to walk into the room by herself.

The lights were on a low setting to create a relaxing atmosphere as tots were plonked in doughnut-shaped baby seats or sitting up on blankets for those who looked Kiki's age. Water bottles emerged and exercise mats were unrolled in lines, swiping the floor with colour. Spotting a gap nicely hidden at the back, Leah headed over, flattening the strip of foam that Eric used for his press-ups.

She placed Kiki on her back with a toy, trying to ignore the thrashing legs as the chatter drowned out her grizzles. Leah slid her trainers and socks off and sat cross-legged on the mat beside her.

'Come on, Kiki Koo. Are we going to do some stretches?' She gripped Kiki's calves and playfully pulled them up in the air. 'It will be fun!'

She had promised herself that she wouldn't compare. No looking around at how the others were behaving. But every happy gurgle and jiggly crawl collided with Kiki's scrunched face and her mouth, agape in discontentment.

It had been a whole week with barely a cry, every reach of Kiki to Twig resulting in another second longer pulling upwards. Zara had been full of praise at their appointment earlier in the week. Kiki had actually smiled at her, and Leah had felt so happy as she'd held her close knowing that progress had been made.

That was when Zara had caught Leah's stare at a poster on the wall behind her.

'Oh, you should definitely try it out,' she'd said. 'Something fun you can do together.'

Leah hadn't been sure. A double whammy of lean bodies and well-behaved babies to remind her just how much catching up she had to do.

'And did you know that it's clinically proven to help with mobility milestones?'

So, here they were now. Just as Kiki's spell of happier moods appeared to be coming to a halt again. One session, Leah had decided. And if Kiki started bawling, they were never coming back.

'Ah, some newbies, I see!' The cheery instructor waved from the front and hopped between the mats like they were stepping stones. 'Welcome to Yoga Bears! I'm Cassie, and who have we got here?'

'I'm Leah, and this is Kiki.'

'Hello!' She grinned downwards. 'You're a beauty, aren't you? Look at all that hair!'

'Sorry if she makes a racket. She gets a bit grouchy.'

Cassie smirked playfully and adjusted the red band that was pushing back her short spiral curls.

'Well, we can't be having that,' she said in mock disapproval, before returning to her wide smile. 'Don't you worry, we're used to whingey ones here. Now, there's a couple of other first-timers today so you're not on your own. Just give me a shout if you need me.'

She skipped back over to her place and called out the instructions for the warm-up positions. Calming music swarmed over the room but Leah kept her limbs tense, waiting for the moment when screaming would attack the panpipes.

They began with a few simple stretches to warm up and then Cassie instructed everyone to sit with their backs as straight as possible.

'That's it…' She mirrored them with a glazed expression of peace melting over her face. 'As if you are being pulled upwards by an imaginary thread.'

Leah gazed at a spot on the ceiling, focusing on nothing but the light and shade of the empty space.

Cassie's voice crept to a whisper, each pause giving time to reflect and escape. The moments lingered and Leah felt lightheaded in the best possible way. It sank down through her veins like a weight being lifted, warmth flushing back into her body after the bursts of outdoor air.

But a thud jerked her back into the room as Kiki booted both heels into the side of her thigh. Leah suppressed an indignant snarl of pain, the imaginary cotton string slicing her spine like a metal wire.

Then, another whack, before more kicks walloped her side. The octaves of music swirled and echoed, covering the wails from Kiki's open mouth, but she threw her arms and feet in the air, jabbing at Leah again and again.

'Shhhh! Stop it, please,' she snapped through gritted teeth, sliding Kiki further to the side so the bashing feet couldn't reach her.

This was no noisy swimming pool or busy supermarket where Kiki might not be noticed. People were trying to relax here, and in fact, so was Leah. She tilted her head back and let her neck go limp, determined to stay in the zone. Kiki was not going to ruin this, for her or anyone else.

Slowly, the music changed. Now was the time for full immersion, when everyone started to take on positions that required a deeper state of mind and the physical strength to hold them in place.

With an almighty lunge, Kiki hurled herself back towards Leah, and a knee smacked into her hip like a stone.

'I've had it with you!' Leah hissed, taking Kiki's feet in one hand and holding them firmly in place on the floor as she tried to continue. But Kiki began to howl, and the soft windchimes chinking through the speakers were not enough to mask the sound. 'Don't do this.' Leah boiled over with anger, staring defeatedly at the blank spot on the ceiling which no longer lapsed into serenity with her vision. Why was she even here? She should never have listened to Zara.

'Okey-dokes everyone, have a quick breather.' Cassie paused the music. 'Five-minute loo break and rehydrate. Then it's time to get the little ones in on the fun.'

Brilliant, Leah thought. *Then she'll really bring the house down.*

Digging into her bag, she passed Kiki a drink and savoured the seconds of sipping that were a break from her grizzly cries. Leah slumped backwards, swigging from her water bottle, amazed at how a yoga class was making her tenser the more it went on. As the cool liquid seeped down her throat, she sat there exhausted and motionless, trying to stay completely numb to the waves of howling that were pulsing around her ears. And it took a few moments to realise that Kiki was no longer the source.

A dad bounced his daughter up and down which made her even more crotchety and a younger baby with bright red cheeks was apparently midway through teething. A flustered mother was trying different chewy rings, but nothing seemed to be doing the job.

'Yes, I know, I know, you're tired…' said a woman in the corner, patting her son's back as he whimpered on her shoulder. 'Should have gone down for your nap then, when you had the chance.' She grinned wearily at her nearest neighbours and Leah squinted across at her as recognition pinged.

It was the mum she had served in Glovers. The one who had been at the baby sale with her friend, stacking their pushchairs with what had seemed like the whole baby department. That little boy had been angelic in his pushchair, but now he was behaving like a totally different creature. Kiki banged her cup on the ground, but for once, her cries were not the loudest in the room.

She couldn't have explained the sensation. It was like the pressure piling over her in suffocating clouds was finally pouring out in release, washing the weight from her shoulders. This feeling was alien to Leah, just being out in public with Kiki, and for once, feeling like she merged right in. Normal had never felt so incredible.

Leah gave the woman a knowing look, unsure if she'd even recognise someone who she'd met in a shop for a fleeting couple of minutes.

'Oh, we're all getting a bit grumpy, are we?' Cassie entered the room again, unfazed by the chorus of bawling babies. She bent over to rearrange the floor cushions, her multicoloured leggings stretching over her ample thighs. 'Well, we've done the boring bit now. So, it's time for the Mini Moves!'

A shower of musical notes whooshed around the walls, but this time it was less intense, instead playful, delicate and making Leah's heart flutter slightly as she took Kiki's arms and lifted her into a sitting position, raising her hands to the sky and grinning at the confusion on her face, the pouty lower lip and damp eyelashes poking out through her two raised arms.

Next, the tots were laid down on their backs and the adults craned their bodies over the top of them from a cat to a dog pose, bringing their faces up close. Kiki was mesmerised, looking up at Leah as she dangled above her, pulling big smiles and goofy looks at her daughter. She babbled in curiosity, reaching up and touching Leah's face with her hands.

Then Leah rolled gently over until she was lying down, tucking her knees under her chin, and slowly, she placed Kiki frontways onto the flat level of her shins, gazing up at the cherubic face which was now elevated above her own. And Kiki was experiencing a freedom that she had never known before. Not stumbling or balancing for split seconds before falling, but floating and bobbing higher than ever, supported yet using a strength that was new and exhilarating. The green and hazel marbles of her eyes shone as she scoured the room, and then she was laughing. Blissful, trickling giggles that sailed out over the mirrored rows and poured into every part of Leah.

It was time for the final cool down. Leah lowered Kiki onto her chest and together, they breathed with the echoes of the tones, wispy like a breeze being dusted through a seashell. Leah rested her jaw into the warm nest of Kiki's hair, feeling her soft cheek pressed to her collarbone, and remembered those few golden moments at the birth. How it had felt, after all the hours of earth-shattering pain, the sudden rush of doctors and the intervention of knives, needles, suction cups, and forceps, when at last her tiny body and head of dark fuzz was passed from their latex hands and pressed onto Leah's flushed skin. How the little cries eased away as she met her mother's heartbeat.

As her chest rose and fell taking Kiki with the motions, she was back there now, remembering how she'd thought it was going to be. The stillness of the room once the medics had vacated it, leaving the brushstrokes of morning light to beam around the walls. Relief pouring into Eric's face as he took the first pictures of his daughter. And the comfort of Cheryl sliding a pair of pink booties onto Kiki's feet as they'd peeped from the swaddled hospital towel. A mother's proud and knowing smile, reliving the same memory she'd once experienced herself.

And at the centre of it all, Leah had felt heady and ecstatic, because she'd been enough. The simplicity of contact and pure patterns of breath had given Kiki all she had needed. Never could Leah have imagined how drastically this would change.

But despite Kiki's silence here and now, ticking away like a time bomb, Leah stayed on the gym mat, blinking the intermittent colours of the lights as they faded to pastels, then neutrals like sand on a beach, until nothing remained but the pair of them entwined. Restful and more perfect than they'd ever been.

'OK… that's lovely.' Cassie's voice trickled back into her ears. 'And you can all open your eyes when you're ready.'

The clatter of tidying up brought a deadened end to the vibe, and the magical gleam of candlelight was replaced by dull grey wall tiles. Kiki moodily rubbed her eyes against the string of Leah's hoodie, disgruntled to be stirred away from the hush.

Leah hurried to fill her bag, watching the telltale crumpling face and knowing all eyes would be on them both when Kiki started up again.

'Come on then, Kiki Koo, let's get you home.'

She lifted the tot on her shoulder and nodded her thanks to Cassie.

'Did you enjoy it?' Cassie called after her.

Leah turned around. 'It was really good. I definitely feel more… relaxed now.'

'So, back next week?'

'I'm sure we will be. As long as she behaves herself.' Leah managed a forced laugh and twisted her body towards the door.

'You don't have to worry if she's grotty, you know. We're used to it here. Should have seen what mine were like at this age!'

'Thanks, that's nice to know.' Leah's feet tensed in her trainers. 'I just hate being the only one who…'

'Is that what you think?' Cassie shook her head, then gestured subtly behind them to the loud cries of another child. 'Like I said, it's normal. Especially here.' She stashed her cushions under her elbows and gave Leah a reassuring wink. 'Hope to see you again.'

Kiki's whinging turned to shrill squeals but somehow, Leah didn't leave. Instead, she jiggled her on the spot, trying to observe the woman from Glovers who was struggling to silence the howling boy while simultaneously packing away. And in seconds, Leah was over by her side.

'Hi, do you want some help?'

The woman's shushing muffled Leah's voice and her back was turned as she knelt over her son. Leah leaned forwards and spoke again.

'Is everything OK?'

She glanced up with reddened cheeks, framed by the tangled strands coming free from her auburn braid.

'Oh, I'm fine, thanks. He's just having an off day, I guess.'

Leah gazed closer, detecting the giveaway glassy eyes. An onset of tears that was usually her own.

'Only a day?' She unpeeled Kiki from her shoulder for just long enough to expose the frown. 'Am I allowed to say I'm jealous? This one is literally non-stop!'

The woman shrugged and looked at her child. 'I don't know, maybe he's teething or something. I've just reached my limit today.'

Leah reached down as best she could and gathered all the belongings until the floor was clear. Then she passed them to the woman while she took hold of her son.

'Sorry, I didn't even say who I was! I'm Leah… and this is Kiki.'

'Tess.' She motioned her head at her son. 'And Henry.'

'I think we've met before,' Leah said. 'You were with a friend in Glovers at the baby sale?'

Tess nodded but looked confused. 'I was.'

'Remember when you paid at EdenCore? I served you.'

Her eyes widened with sudden realisation. 'Oh, I see! Sorry, it's just…'

'Yeah, I have to wear a lot of makeup at work.' Leah smirked. 'Unrecognisable, right?'

'No, I didn't mean it like that.'

'It's fine. I kind of prefer it when I'm not caked in the stuff anyway.' Leah paused for a moment, realising she'd never have felt like this a few months ago. 'Not that I get the time with this little madam around.'

'Well, I always feel like I'm winning at life if I can actually have a shower!'

'Exactly. Or eat breakfast.'

'Step out of bed and put your dressing gown on in peace?'

'More like open my eyes without being woken up!'

They both laughed out loud. Then Tess fell silent, her eyes starting to water.

'It's so hard.' She looked straight at Leah. 'He just cries his eyes out no matter what I try and do. I've lost so many friends who haven't got kids. His dad is out all the time and I just wonder if things will ever get back to normal.'

Leah absorbed every word as she stared back at another mother who was wrung out and disillusioned. At another child who was a handful. Another life that was not the opposite of hers.

'And everyone you meet is having an amazing time of it, right? Got their figures back as well as their lives?'

'Yes!' Tess nodded in complete affinity. 'Their kids just sitting there gurgling happily. Actually enjoying it when you play with them!'

'Is that even a thing?' Leah smirked and rolled her eyes. 'Because I wouldn't know.'

'So it's… really not just me?'

'It's not just you.'

Rocking Henry up and down in her arms, Tess continued to listen with interest.

'She cries, literally all the time. I mean, yes, I work a couple of day a week and I get a break, but I have to go back and face it again every time I finish there. I creep around the house just doing everything I can to avoid her starting up. I mean, even going out for a loaf of bread is an effort.'

'Wow, we need to compare notes! Maybe grab a coffee sometime?'

'I'd really like that,' Leah smiled. 'Are you back here for yoga next week?'

'Sure am. It's the only thing that keeps me sane these days.'

Henry drowned her out and she winced as he shrieked into her ear.

'Anyway, best be off and get this one some dinner.'

'See you next time then.' Leah backed away to the car. 'Nice meeting you.'

Once Kiki was strapped into her seat, Leah gazed out beyond the steering wheel, watching the kayaks breaking gently through the water, the paddles making diamond shapes as they swiped along the surface. She was not alone in her plight, and something about that felt empowering. No matter how unbearable Kiki might become, someone else was going through the same. And not just Tess, but so many more people. More than Leah had ever realised.

Drizzling rain touched her cheek through the window and a calmness filtered through her that she hadn't felt for months. A gentle reassurance of normality.

***

Later that evening, the plates were stacked in the dishwasher and Eric was out taking Twig for his final walk of the day. Kiki had long gone to sleep, tired from the afternoon's activities.

For the last hour, Leah had been soaking in a warm bath and there had even been time to spare for painting her nails in the last glimmers of a winter sky. She was fresh and energized from the yoga, and relieved to have found a friend with a similar outlook on life.

She checked the clock. Eric would be back soon and she was looking forward to some time with him as he'd spent the last few days flat out with a work project. It had been a while since they'd sat down together with a drink to unwind, so as it was Friday night, Leah filled two glasses with ice and retrieved his best bottle of whisky from the cupboard. Pouring them both a generous measure, she topped it up with some cold lemonade.

The back door soon sounded and Twig zoomed through to the kitchen, wagging his tail when he saw her.

'Hey there!' She crouched down to stroke him. 'Were you a good boy?'

'Until he stole a kid's ball,' said Eric, as he followed. 'Cleared off into the bushes and wouldn't come out!'

'Did you give it back to them?'

He nodded, rolling his eyes. 'Of course, he had to leave it in a heap of brambles. I managed to get it out with a stick.'

'Sounds like we're going to need some training classes and work on that recall.' Leah smiled, taking a sip of her drink and the crackling ice got Eric's attention.

'Well, that makes a change to a cup of tea! What's

brought this on?'

'I don't know, just fancied it really.' Leah gestured at the ceiling. 'She's nice and tired, cooking's all done and I'm actually not exhausted for once.' Leah passed Eric the other glass. 'And I even made one for you.'

'Perfect. I need cooling down after *his* disappearing act,' Eric tutted and the liquid swished as he waved in mock anger at the pup.

'You can't be too cross. Kiki literally lifted herself up for a whole thirty seconds tonight, just reaching out to hug him.'

He smirked into his drink, the glass patterns piercing his eyes and marbling the hazel with pale olive green.

Leah studied him. 'What?'

'Listen to you.'

She frowned. 'Well, she's really turning a corner, and…'

'Oh, we can't have a puppy!' He stepped over to her with his *I told you so* face. It usually wound her up, but tonight, his grin ate into her. The same one he often pulled when Kiki was having a meltdown and he was making light of her tantrums. The one where he would step through the door after work and dive in to lift her out of Leah's weary arms after a whole day of screaming. 'It's going to make everything so much worse.'

Leah sighed defeatedly, unable to control her smile. 'Shut up.'

He pulled her into his arms. 'Big mistake, right?'

'No, it wasn't.'

For the first time in what seemed like forever, she didn't look the other way or stiffen at his touch as he enveloped her waist.

'I know it now. Kiki just adores him and I'd never take that away.' She gazed gratefully into his eyes. 'You just knew he'd be good for her from the start. I shouldn't have been so against it.'

'Wow.' Eric raised his eyebrows, holding her sight in his own. 'I think the yoga is suiting you. First Mr Twig gets praise and now me.'

The words nudged at her heart. Reminded her just how much she had let life get in between them. How this person who had been nothing but supportive - encouraging through her darkest days, and patient every time she had rejected his hands - was still standing beside her, thinking the world of her and looking almost surprised just to have her pressed against him and not brushing him off.

'I'll definitely keep going.' She smiled again, the glow flushing over her skin. 'I feel really good for it.'

'You look good.' He rested his forehead on hers, then pulled away, staring more intently into her eyes. 'You always look good.'

Leah said nothing. Instead, she let her fingers glide above his shirt collar, into the waves of auburn hair, stroking the nape of his neck.

'I'm sorry,' she whispered.

Eric nodded and started to back away. 'It's OK. I get it that you don't want to…'

'No, I mean, I'm sorry that things haven't been, you know, like they used to be.'

His eyes looked as if they were glazing over. 'Well, you've not had the easiest time. You can't feel anything if all you ever get to be is exhausted and…'

'It's just taking a while to accept that I'm not the same anymore.' She blinked down at herself. 'I'm no Barbie doll.'

Eric's hand flew to his forehead, pressing down hard over clenched brows.

'Oh my God.' He paced over to the sink and leaned on the edge, back turned away from her as he stared at the dripping tap. She swallowed another mouthful from the bottom of her glass, insipid ice that had drowned the peat of the whisky. 'Is that what you think?' He twisted to face her again with glossy eyes, fighting their way across to hers. 'You think I want some *doll*?'

Leah shrugged, watching the power of so many unspoken words ignite something in Eric that she didn't usually see.

He closed in on her again, eyes fiery with the shock of her thoughts. 'How could you even imagine that?'

In seconds, she was encased once more in his arms, still not making a sound.

'It's my fault.' His words nuzzled their way into her head. 'I don't tell you enough.'

He brushed a hand through her hair, skimming her dressing gown. The knot around her waist slipped open and he pulled away, eyes descending the narrow strip of bareness from the top of the neckline to just above her knees.

'You don't understand, Leah…' His fingertips melted like butter on her shoulders as he dipped inside the satin and took her face in his palms. 'Before was one thing, but now…' Her eyelids fluttered closed at the warmth of his mouth on her forehead. 'Now, you're something else altogether.'

'Yeah, you can say that again.'

Eric shook his head dismissively. 'Our girl is up there right now because of every part of you. Do you hear me? *You* did this. All of you. So, please…' he urged, almost breathlessly, 'Don't you ever for a minute feel like you're less than amazing to me.'

He grazed her lips with the gentlest touch.

'Can I make it any clearer?'

He intended to continue talking, but she pulled him back in, lingering on his mouth and losing herself in the taste of him like they were still twenty and pulling into alleyways on their way home in the nightlife of Ropeshore.

With Twig outstretched for the night in his bed, they clicked off the lights and crept away up the stairs, the two separate shadows rushing back into one.

Seventeen

Leah groaned silently as a woman approached the till, reaching into a bag.

'Morning,' she smiled at the customer, already knowing exactly what it would be.

'I need to bring this back. It's brought me out in a terrible rash.'

Yet another tube of *SySTEM* was promptly placed on the counter for a refund.

'I'm so sorry about this.' Leah scanned it in as Tiffany watched open-mouthed. 'We can always replace it with something different that might be a better match for your skin.

But the woman was already shaking her head, her chunky necklace jangling loudly. 'No, thank you, I'd rather not risk it. My sisters have tried it and the same happened to them. And it's not the first time with your products, either.'

'Give her something else!' mouthed Tiffany anxiously.

'We'll happily replace it with an alternative free of charge,' Leah offered.

'That's kind of you but I wouldn't touch EdenCore now.'

'Of course.' Leah wasted no more time putting the full amount back on her credit card just as Jocelyn approached, listening to the end of the conversation. 'I do apologise once again and please don't hesitate to come and see us if you change your mind.'

'What's going on?' Jocelyn asked as the woman took off out of the store.

Leah lifted the bottle in the air. 'Another one of these coming back.' She tapped on the *SySTEM* icon on the tablet screen to remove it from the overall sales total of the day.

'Wait a second! Have I told you about my new rule with refunds?'

Leah shook her head, confused.

'I'm changing the way we do things.' Jocelyn folded her arms. 'From now on, whoever does a refund has to take the price of that item off their own personal sales total and you don't get the commission.'

In the background, Tiffany's eyes widened all the more. '*What the actual f…*' Leah could just about read her lips.

'Right. No problem.'

Leah opened her sales chart on the tablet and watched the amount dwindle as she keyed the *SySTEM* in.

'Blistering again, was it?' Jocelyn put on her best patronising laugh. 'She's probably just got bad skin, luvvie. I saw the cheap crap her face was covered in. Looked like cement from the builder's yard.'

'I don't think so… how many is that now, Tiff?'

'Fifteen in less than two weeks.'

'That is not good.' Leah examined the ingredients on the bottle. 'I think this needs reporting to Head Office.'

'No!' Jocelyn snatched it away. 'We're not doing that. It's only going to make us look worse. There's no way

I'm putting my reputation on the line.'

'What happens if the customers contact HQ themselves?'

'And what if they don't? Let's not be the first to show ourselves up,' she snapped. 'They're only going to say we haven't done a good enough job in convincing customers to keep hold of it. I mean, really, luvvie, you need to be insisting that it's something else they've used and nothing to do with our stuff. The minute you apologise, you're letting the side down.'

'Fair enough.' Leah tossed the *SySTEM* into the growing box of returned products.

'And another thing. Hilary is coming down from London soon for her quarterly Area Manager visit. Do *not* under any circumstances, let her see that.'

'So where should we put it?'

Jocelyn flailed her arms around, annoyed to be asked for a suggestion. 'Bury the bloody thing. I don't care, just get it out of my sight.' She slathered on a well-used lipstick tester and pouted in the mirror. 'Right, I'm going on break. Let's get some decent sales in today, please. You'll find yourself in a deficit with all those refunds.'

Tiffany watched her storm away. 'You OK, babes?'

'I guess.'

'Hey, let's make it a deal that every time someone wants a refund from now on, we duck out of the way and let Jocelyn deal with it.'

'Yeah, I think we'd be out of a job!' Leah managed a smile.

'Missing Rhona, are we?' Kehlani asked in a hushed voice from the KittyPie counter, where she was loading the stand with a fresh batch of powder foundations in new cookie-shaped cases.

Their facial expressions said it all, so she sidled over.

'What is her problem? Like, why is she having such a

go at you all the time?'

'Who knows…' Tiffany clacked her nails against the box she was holding. 'It's because people are bringing everything back. She doesn't want word getting out.'

'But that's not fair on you,' Kehlani frowned. 'Unless they get discontinued or changed in some way, it's only going to keep happening. Hiding it won't solve the problem.'

'Tell *her* that.' She motioned in the direction where Jocelyn had walked off. 'And yes, I do miss Rhona.'

'You never know, she might decide she hates it in recruitment and ends up back here in her old job.'

'I doubt it somehow,' replied Tiffany, adjusting her bra strap through the neckline of her uniform top.

'Had them done, have we?' Kehlani winked.

Tiffany pretended to slap her. 'No way, I'd be terrified of the anaesthetic!' she grimaced. 'Not my style at all, babes. Everyone's like this in my family.'

'So lucky. We're all straight up and down in ours and flat as ironing boards.'

'Oh, don't be daft, you're gorgeous,' Tiffany cooed. 'Now go and grab me a sample of your *Micellar Milkshake* before Jocelyn gets back.'

She followed Kehlani over to KittyPie while a man caught Leah's eye. He had arrived at the tester stand and was spraying aftershave into his salt-and-pepper hair.

'Hello there, are you looking for something in particular or just browsing?'

'It's my son's thirtieth next weekend,' he explained. 'Just looking for some shower bits and bobs. Thinking of putting together a hamper.'

'Brilliant idea!' Leah enthused. 'It's three for two on the Men's range right now, and we've got these sets in for Christmas.'

'Yep, I did see those. Thing is, I'm not sure what

scent he'd like.'

'Do you know what he usually uses?'

'Well, he's often got *Silverback* on the bathroom shelf. The Midnight Mace one.'

'So, that's most similar to this.' Leah flicked open the lid off some bath oil. 'It's got cardamom and kaffir leaves.'

The large man bent over and took a sniff.

'I love that, it's my favourite.' Tiffany beamed as she stood to the side, observing. The man turned to look at her and his face broke out in a smile.

'Do you now?'

'Oh yeah…' she nodded. 'I even wear it myself sometimes!'

'Well, maybe you can show me where you put it, love.'

Tiffany giggled and batted her lashes.

'No, I mean it,' he continued. 'I'm sure your friend won't mind if you take over…' he glanced back at Leah, 'will you, darlin'?'

Leah paused with the tester, waiting for Tiffany to brush him off and allow her to make the sale she had started.

'I'll happily show you everything you need to know.' She sashayed over and began spraying more aftershave, this time on herself for the man to sample. 'So, what are you after then? Something fruity?'

She shot him a gleaming smile with her unimaginably white teeth and led him away from where Leah was still standing.

As they perused the shelves and explored the different options, Leah thought of her near-empty sales sheet. Picking up a pile of leaflets featuring the Christmas specials, she made her way across to the pharmacy area where she hoped to bring interest from elsewhere in the store. At least it would make Dawn happy that the Glovers customers had extra staff around to help them.

'Good morning!' she said to the first person she saw. 'We've got some amazing offers on our gifts right now. Would you like to see them?'

'I'm in the dental section here,' replied the woman. 'That means I'm buying a toothbrush?'

'OK, well EdenCore is right near the front doors if you're passing.'

The woman waved a hand in Leah's face and headed away down the aisle.

'Do you work here?' An elderly man grabbed her attention.

'I do, yes,' Leah smiled. ''How can I help?'

He led her past some bandages and dressings, stopping at a shelf of creams and ointments.

'I'm wondering which of these would be best for some sort of bunion on my foot.' He held out his thumb and forefinger. 'It's about this big and I must have had it for about a month now.'

'The thing is, I do work here but I'm not...' Leah looked around for a healthcare assistant just as Dawn marched into view, surveying the shop floor with piercing eyes framed in a swathe of green kohl. If she got wind of Leah refusing to help a Glovers customer, she would be livid. Scanning the wording on the boxes, Leah turned back to the man. 'Can you... describe it at all?'

'Yellowish, cracked and quite sharp to put weight on.'

'So, have you tried any of these yet?' Leah picked up some corn plasters as the man talked her through the creams he already had at home.

Through the bustling beauty hall, she noticed Jocelyn back at the EdenCore counter. Tiffany was still busy flirting with the man, but Jocelyn was standing at the front, eyes scanning the shop, no doubt trying to see where Leah had got to.

Wary that Jocelyn would catch sight of her helping a Glovers customer while armed with a thick wadge of undistributed EdenCore leaflets, Leah was glued to the spot, unable to move without finding herself facing the wrath of either Jocelyn or Dawn.

'I'd say you might be best with the *Corn Blast* cream,' she suggested while several other treatments flew across her vision. 'Then again, it might be a verruca.'

'Perhaps we could nip over here and I'll show you,' suggested the man. 'If I could just sit down to take my sock off.'

'No, I don't think that would be…' Leah knew she had sounded snappy, so she swallowed hard and tried again. 'I'm sorry, look, the best thing you can do is see the pharmacist. They know all about this. You'll have it sorted in no time.'

The man squinted. 'I'll do that then. Where should I go?'

'Follow me.' She lifted his walking stick from where it was resting against a shelf and accompanied him over to the small queue. 'It's Shabbir today. He really does know his stuff. Used to be a top surgeon in London.'

'You are kind, dear.' The man placed a hand on her wrist. 'Sorry to have troubled you when you're busy.'

'Not at all,' she beamed back. 'I just wanted to make sure you get the right thing. They're not cheap, these creams!'

Handing him over to the pharmacist, Leah slunk away from Jocelyn's view where some tall display posters and a video screen advertised the new viral *Latte Love* spray tan, as seen on TikTok.

She shuffled the leaflets like a pack of cards. Why had she not just taken four or five, rather than the whole pile?

A couple of young twenty-something women purred

with excitement as they followed the signage to the array of different shades and the free tanning mitts that currently came with every purchase.

'They look good, don't they?' Leah joined them as they browsed.

'Can't wait to try it!' the blonde said. 'Not sure what shade I'd be, though.'

'Looking at you, possibly the *Caramel Creme* if you're building it up.' Leah examined the colour chart. 'Or *Chai Tea* if you just want one quick coat of something stronger.'

'Have you tried it then?'

'Well, I was going to until I read the comments on the ads.'

'Oh?' The darker-haired friend turned to face Leah.

'It loses its colour once you open it.' She checked that Dawn was out of earshot and leaned in closer, speaking truthfully from what she'd seen online. 'People are finding that it goes grey.'

The women looked at each other and frowned.

'Maybe I won't bother, then,' said the blonde. 'Come on Kel, we're better off sticking to the usual.'

'You could always try this.' Leah handed them a leaflet each with the back page facing upwards. 'EdenCore's *Butternut Drops* use all-natural ingredients, known for their staying power. You mix them with any face or body moisturiser and there is only one shade because they work with your natural colouring.'

The customers studied the picture. Then the friend spoke again. 'It's tempting but… not for that price.'

'That's for the gift set,' Leah explained. 'Limited Edition for the season. It comes with your choice of skin creams to use with the drops. They're full size.'

'We'll think about it,' replied the blonde. 'Thanks for letting us know.'

'Just come and see me at the counter. I'm Leah.'

They nodded and disappeared down an aisle full of bubble bath.

With half an hour to go until breaktime, Leah continued to rid herself of the leaflets.

'Excuse me, would you like to check out our festive range?'

'No thanks, I've done my Christmas shopping.'

'Hi there, can I interest you in these amazing offers? Once they're gone, they're gone.'

'Sorry, I'm in a hurry.'

'I see you're looking at fragrances. Our *Peach to Their Own* is flying off the shelves for Christmas... You're not a fan of peach. OK, well you could always sample *T-Radish-ional*... No?' She watched the last customer walk away dismissively, then turned in the direction of the counter, where a clear pathway swept up to Jocelyn, ready to pounce on any passers-by. 'I don't blame you.'

Leah chose her moment to slip back to the counter, placing the leaflets to the side of the till while Jocelyn was distracted.

'You know what? I'm going to need our extra-large carrier bags for all this.' Tiffany giggled as she eyed the huge pile of boxes and tubes that the same man was about to purchase.

'Bag it up, beautiful!' he boomed like a game show host. 'Are you seeing this, boss? Give the girl a promotion, eh?'

Jocelyn looked annoyed to be disturbed. She craned her neck at the basket of goods and managed a quick thumbs up.

'Are you sure you'll be OK getting all this to the car?' Tiffany asked as she scanned it all through.

'I'll take full advantage of that,' the man winked. 'Not every day I get a stunner like you offering to lighten my load.' He kept full eye contact with Tiffany until she blushed. 'Nothing like an extra pair of hands.'

Leah caught sight of the total on the till which had leapt well up into the thousand figures.

'You don't mind me helping him, do you?' Tiffany's eyes darted between the man and Jocelyn, fluttering her lashes at him while urging her manager not to refuse and risk losing the hefty sale.

'Ten minutes luvvie, and that's it.' Jocelyn warned.

'I'm only parked around the corner. Lucky, I bought the Bentley though, it's got the biggest boot space of the lot.'

'Maybe I'll just squeeze in there then.' Tiffany swept to the door as the man followed at close range, with armfuls of shopping.

'No chance, love.' He smacked her on the rump with a carrier bag, making her laugh out loud. 'The only place you're going is the back seat.'

They walked away past the window as if they could have been stapled together, Tiffany's back touching his chest as his lips moved in her ear.

'Oi, you!' Jocelyn's voice snapped Leah back to the counter. 'Break time and be quick. I need you back here in half an hour to go through the rotas.'

'No problem. Won't be long.' Leah headed off past the Poirier testers and smiled at Taeng on the way.

'And remember…' yelled Jocelyn across the beauty hall, casting her eyes on Leah's waist as she ascended the escalator, 'go easy on the sandwiches, luvvie. Turkeys are the only thing that should be stuffed at Christmas, and you're looking like a dead ringer for one.'

Taeng's mascara wand clattered to the floor as heads turned across the departments. She bent down open-mouthed to pick it up and see to the stain.

'What the hell?' she mouthed, still crouching. 'You

OK?'

Leah nodded and sucked in her middle until she reached the next floor. Over at the chiller she perused the salads, uninspired by the thought of raw spinach and barely a cube of feta. Instead, her eyes drifted to the limited-edition festive range of filled rolls, pastries, and pies. Opting for a brie and cranberry wrap, she hurried up to the staffroom, retrieving her phone from her locker on the way.

The creamy cheese and tangy sauce felt like revenge as she cosied up in a chair by the radiator, scrolling through her messages.

Zara had left a voicemail asking Leah to call her back, so she dialled the number for the Terrapin Ward and waited to be put through.

'Hello, Zara speaking, how can I help?'

'Hi there, it's Leah Frost, Kiki's mum, just returning your call?'

'Ah, that's right. It was just a quick buzz to let you know that Kiki's boots are ready, so I can now book you in for the all-important fitting!'

'That's lovely news.' Leah clenched her teeth. *Please don't be a Tuesday. Please don't be a...*

'So, we're a bit packed for the next few weeks, I'm afraid. The only time we've got free before Christmas is Tuesday the twelfth at four-thirty.'

Leah's heart sank. She would be here, on the evening shift.

'Is there absolutely no way it could be another day?'

'You'd be looking at the New Year. The first one we can do is the eighteenth of January.'

It was no good. Kiki couldn't wait another month for this. The sooner she got the boots, the quicker her ankles might stabilise and maybe, just maybe, she might start learning to walk.

'We'll go with the earlier one, then.'

'I would definitely recommend it,' agreed Zara. 'No sense in waiting longer than necessary.'

She tapped away on her keyboard and it echoed down the phone.

'All done. And don't worry about any crying as it's not the usual boring appointment,' Zara enthused. 'We make it a real celebration when a little one has a boot fitting. They get a special certificate and a little toy to take home. I promise you, it will be a moment to remember, so if you want to bring Daddy and any other family, they're more than welcome to come along.'

'I'm sure we will,' replied Leah, knowing that Eric, Cheryl, and Alan wouldn't miss it for the world, and she would just have to change her shift. 'Thanks Zara, and see you on the twelfth.'

She ended the call and checked her watch. Only ten minutes left to gobble down her lunch before she had to be back at the counter. Polishing it off with a few swigs of water, she jogged along the corridor, stopping in the toilets on the way.

Washing her hands, she waited until the room was clear before stepping back from the mirror and examining herself from a sideways view. Yes, she had just gobbled down her food, but shame clouded over at her rounded waist, failing to be disguised by the unforgiving skirt. After Jocelyn's words, she felt slightly sick at having to walk through the beauty hall with all eyes searching her body to find confirmation of her manager's critique.

From the top of the escalator, she caught sight of Tiffany dropping a bulging bag inside her mother's long coat. Dawn was only metres away at the Capital G counter. If she hadn't been turning away, she would surely have seen everything.

Diane kissed Tiffany goodbye and waved at Leah as

she passed her, unaware she knew about the stash of samples being snuck out of the store.

'Oh, my God, babes, are you OK?' Tiffany flew up to her as she reached the EdenCore tester stand. 'Taeng told me what Jocelyn said.'

'What's that?' Leah shrugged, pretending that she'd forgotten.

'Telling you not to eat too much. Shouting stuff out about your figure? There's just no need for it!'

'Oh, that. It doesn't get to me, honestly. I hardly even heard her.'

'Well, you can't help it. You've just had a kid.'

Leah felt her cheeks flush as the words sank in. There was nothing she wanted more right now than to get out in the fresh air, where she would no longer be the subject of everyone's scrutiny.

'Anyway...' She stepped behind the counter and quickly changed the subject. 'Well done on the sale earlier. Looked like he spent a fortune!'

'I know, right?' Tiffany squealed. 'Sorry, I don't want to blow my own trumpet, but yeah, I didn't think he was going to stop.'

'You sure turned on the charm. Nice moves, Tiff!'

'I did at first, but then, something clicked.'

'Oh...' Leah lowered her voice. 'So, you fancied him?'

'He's got it all.' Tiffany's eyes momentarily fluttered to a close. 'He's sexy, funny, kind. Yeah, he's rolling in it, but that's just a bonus. We only walked to his car – which is amazing, by the way – and it was like we'd known each other for ages! His name's Phil.'

'Sounds promising,' giggled Leah, locking Tiffany in her intrigued gaze. 'So, do you think you'll see him again?'

Tiffany smiled coquettishly and pulled out a business

card from somewhere under her waistband. 'I've got his number and he wants me to ring him. *So* excited! Now all I need is for Jocelyn to do one so I can go and get my phone.'

'At least you're off in an hour. Perks of doing the early morning shift, right?'

'I'm going to ring him the minute I'm out of here.'

'Where is Jocelyn anyway?'

'Stockroom, luvvie.' The voice rang out before Jocelyn could be seen. Then she plonked a half-filled basket of eye sets down next to the till. 'Actually working, unlike you two. I don't suppose you've sold anything since I've been up there.' She gestured at Tiffany. 'Well, I'll let you off after your little triumph today. However, *you…*' she grunted, drilling her glare into Leah, 'have got some serious catching up to do.'

'I'm on it! Sorry, I've not long been back from break.'

Jocelyn rolled her eyes and clomped around the other side of the counter.

'And actually,' Leah followed her. 'There's something I need to ask you.'

'Fire away.'

'It's just that I'm wondering if I could change my shift on the twelfth. Kiki's got a physio appointment and…'

But Jocelyn was already shaking her head.

'I'd rather you didn't. It takes a long time to work out these schedules, you know. The last thing we need is to balls it all up with changes. You can't not be here, luvvie. Someone needs to be on this counter constantly in December.'

'But it's just the evening, our quietest time. Even if I could just come in later. I can be here by five-thirty.'

Jocelyn raised her eyebrows, but didn't look up. 'Not possible. So, let's have a bit more notice next time.'

'Of course, but… I've only just had the phone call from the hospital, or I would have let you know much earlier than now.'

'Not really my problem. Head Office are really hot on this.'

Leah thought of Kiki. Of seeing the little boots on her for the first time. The cheers and the certificate. Something urgent tugged away at the thought of everyone being all around her. Everyone but Leah.

'But couldn't I swap the shift? I'll do whichever other one you want me to cover.'

Tiffany stepped forward with remorse on her face. 'I'm sorry, Leah. It's mum's birthday and we're away that week until the Wednesday.'

'No, that's fine, I understand.'

Leah's heart felt like it was grinding to a halt as she glanced up at Jocelyn with a last shred of hope.

'That's settled, then.' Jocelyn twitched her lips into the flicker of a smile. 'Because Tuesday nights are off limits for me. Buddha bowl, face pack, leg wax and a cheeky chardonnay all to myself.'

Leah fought the jabbing tears, pushing their way into the corners of her eyes.

'It's just that she's… she's getting these new boots, you know, to help her walk. They said it would be special and…'

'Hospitals, eh? Those admins want sacking, always messing things up with their late appointments. Lucky she's only a youngster, then, as she won't remember a thing,' said Jocelyn, unmoved. 'So, I'm afraid that's a no for the twelfth.' She patted the counter in front of Leah. '*Be here.*'

The sting was almost physical. Like Leah had been slapped across her face. It was a tingling heat that didn't leave her for the rest of the time she was still on the shift.

Once Tiffany had gone for the day, it was unbearable. Trying to remain upbeat and jumping to Jocelyn's every command each time one was barked in her ears. Smiling at customers and trying to dissuade them from buying *SySTEM* when they were instantly drawn to the mesmerising bottle. Looking Jocelyn in the eye and cooperating in discussions when this person was preventing her from being with Kiki on her special day.

When her shift finally finished, Leah stepped into the stairwell and breathed away the tension from the minute she was out of sight. She wanted nothing more than to get away from the shop, yet her footsteps were heavy and slow all the way to the locker room, weighed down with the pressures of the day. Flinging her EdenCore jacket on the peg, she slipped her arms into her warm winter coat, feeling it soothe her like a hug. She couldn't wait to be home with Eric, when she would rest her head on his shoulder and finally let it all out.

'She can't get away with this!'

Kehlani burst through the door with Dawn following closely behind her.

'That's two pots of *Ganache Flash* bronzer, five *Sugarslick* highlighting pens and nine *Marmalade Melt* evening oils that have been returned, all in one day.' She turned around and glared at Dawn. 'Nine!'

'And you're sure it's because of Jocelyn?'

Leah saw Kehlani nod from the corner of her eye as she deliberately loitered at the mirror, dabbing on lip balm, then tapping the blank screen of her phone.

'She's been telling all my customers that KittyPie tests on animals… that our stuff is full of hidden parabens, which is just not true. Every time they buy something, she's been pouncing on them when they walk away and now I know why.'

'Maybe she's just trying to encourage them to visit

EdenCore, too. There's no harm in her approaching your customers once they've finished at KittyPie. It's not as if she is stealing them from you.'

'No, Dawn. This is different.'

Dawn folded her arms defeatedly. 'How do you know for sure?'

'Because they've been telling me! They're coming back for refunds and pointing her out, then all saying that she's told them the same thing.'

'And I assume you put them straight.'

'Obviously!' screeched Kehlani, yanking off her promotional apron and slamming it inside a locker. 'But it's too late by then. They want their money back because they've been brainwashed. Poisoned by her lies!'

'Look, darling, I'm not being funny but you're just going to have to try and sell a bit harder. Mention the quality of your ingredients and warn them against believing silly rumours.'

'OK…' Kehlani fluttered her eyelashes and sniggered sarcastically. 'I mean, if I was doing what she's done, I'd probably lose my job.'

'I can't get involved in things like this,' said Dawn. 'Not with disputes between counter staff. It's customer complaints I deal with… and anything to do with Capital G, of course. So, if you want to take this further, I'm afraid it's a job for KittyPie HQ.'

'But it's happening in a Glovers store.' Kehlani dug her gem-encrusted nails into the waistband of her skinny jeans. 'What's the difference?'

'She's a shrewd businesswoman, Kehlani, and she knows how to flog shedloads of stuff. I really don't want to be getting on the wrong side of her. Especially not so near to Christmas.'

'That doesn't give her the right to…'

'Kehlani!' Dawn raised her voice, making Leah

stiffen. 'If it keeps happening, I'll see what I can do.'

There was silence. Then the phone rang on the corridor wall outside.

'Tomorrow is a new day,' said Dawn in a more hushed tone. 'So, have a nice, relaxing evening now and start afresh in the morning.' She stepped out of the room and grabbed the receiver from its holder. 'Dawn speaking… yes, I'm on my way down. Just grabbing those boxes for Shabbir.'

The door slammed shut, making the words a distant mumble.

'What an absolute joke!' Kehlani joined Leah at the mirror. 'Did you hear that?'

'Sure did. I'm speechless. Then again, I guess it's no surprise.'

Kehlani's eyes widened with realisation. 'Oh, yeah. I've heard all about the whole body-shaming thing. Literally cannot believe she said that to you.'

'That's nothing.' Leah waved a dismissive hand.

'You mean, there's something *else*?'

'Just that I asked to change my shift because Kiki's being fitted with these special walking boots and…'

'You're not going to tell me she said no.'

'She's… staying in that night, so she won't swap with me.'

'What the hell?'

'It doesn't matter.'

'Oh, give me strength!' Kehlani's lip gloss shimmered as she looked up at the ceiling. 'You can't put up with this, Leah. It's gone too far. She's your baby girl. You only get one chance to be at these things, but Jocelyn Quigley won't let you?'

'Eric will take her, it's not a problem'

'This is bullshit.'

'I can't do anything about it, Keh. If I fall out with

her, I'm only going to make things worse for myself.'

'Why is everyone so scared of her?'

'I'm not, I'm just…'

'Intimidated.'

Leah shook her head. 'I don't know. It's just not worth getting on my high horse about.'

'But you're upset.' Kehlani looked into Leah's eyes and a watery sting began to threaten. 'And you've got every right to be.'

'I should go,' said Leah, trying to smile. 'There's nothing we can do.'

She picked up her bag and walked over to the door.

'Well, something's got to be done.' Kehlani's face was fierce like thunder as Leah left the room. 'And I'll be making sure of it.'

Eighteen

Eric climbed into the car and gave Leah a reassuring smile.

'It's all fine. He's got chews and snacks, and I've left the TV on low.' Turning on the ignition, he reversed slowly out of the driveway. 'It's only a few hours, don't worry.'

'No whining when you left him, then?'

'Not a hint. He's flat out, snoring. That long walk did the job.'

'Good.' Leah turned in the passenger seat and glanced at Kiki, who was strapped in at the back. 'As for her, let's hope she's as calm as he is tonight. Although, for once, not so chilled out that she sleeps through the whole thing!'

'At least we can keep an eye on her,' Eric chuckled. 'Unlike any mischief that Twig gets up to. Mind you, we've got the camera on him. All we need to do is look at our phones.'

'Well, I knocked next door earlier and reminded them to check up on him. Dora's going round at six-thirty, that's about halfway through.'

'Let's just focus on the fun stuff, OK? He'll be absolutely fine.'

Leah took in Eric's words as they turned onto the seafront road and the promenade streetlamps blurred along in a xylophone of light. As purple dusk leaked across the glass, her mind clicked back to the day when they'd first found Twig at the side of the road. How she'd been so consumed by coping with Kiki that a puppy was the last thing she could think about. But her reluctance to adopt him was unimaginable now, and she could hardly bear to leave him home alone for the first time ever.

On snaked the line of the sea, blanching at the hem as it teased the shoreline and lashed its moonlit grey against the solitary structure of the pier. People bustled over the pedestrian crossings leading the way into the centre of town.

As the main arcade of shops dimmed down for the night, across on Chatsworth seafront the Pavilion Auditorium painted a different picture. Its arched rooftops were bedecked in coloured lights and families were piling out of the cold, straight into the busy foyer. Eric slowed at the posters that adorned each side of the building, stretching from the ground and up the entire length of its walls. *Cinderella* in glittery lettering, swirled into shape from the Fairy Godmother's wand. In the centre, reality TV star, Naomi Lynch, beamed in a princess dress that was nearly as dazzling as her mouthful of veneers.

Over each of her shoulders, the ugly sisters pulled comedic sneers in their matching dayglo wigs and garish face paint that made them unrecognisable from their TV alter-egos. Jake Ripley and Ollie Spears, aka Bumble and Buzz, hosts of the messy kids' gameshow, The Gunge Garden. It was a staple of Saturday mornings and Kiki always recognised the catchy theme tune, transfixed by the title colours as they painted crazy gnomes, grasshoppers, and plant pots across the screen. Each week, two teams of daring kids tried their luck climbing giant trellises, and dashing past wobbling watering cans, collecting Petal Points that would be totalled at the end of the game. But if they accidentally stood on a Slimy Slug, off they would go down the giant wellie boot slide where they would have to start all over again.

Kiki probably wouldn't recognise Bumble and Buzz tonight, but Leah was hoping they would have her giggling with their usual noisy antics and sloppy surprises. The prince was going to be played by Wesley Finch, a heartthrob pop star from Leah's early teens. Eric had rolled his eyes when she'd told him about the casting and had sung his biggest hit in an admittedly good mocking impression, but Leah was looking forward to a treat and this would be just what was needed.

'There they are!' Cheryl chimed as the three of them met her and Alan under the neon lights of the bowling alley. 'Managed to park OK?'

'Just about,' replied Eric. 'I think it's going to be packed at the show tonight.'

Cheryl squeezed Kiki's feet. 'Isn't it exciting? Your first panto!'

Kiki wriggled in Eric's arms and reached out for Cheryl.

'Go to Nana, then.' He passed her over and took Leah's hand as they waited at the crossing.

'Can you see the funny green man?' Cheryl asked Kiki.

'Oh, that's charming!' boomed Alan. 'Anyway, this coat is more grey than green.'

'Not *you*. I'm talking about the traffic lights.'

Leah sniggered behind them and glanced at Eric who smiled back. She threaded her fingers through his, feeling safe and happy under the glinting beachside lamplight.

They followed the crowds through the two ancient

doors and a wave of warmth welcomed them inside. Cheryl had managed to book second row seats, right in the middle, with a guaranteed optimum view. The venue was draped in a mixture of old rags and sequinned fabric with more posters covering the walls.

Taking their seats, Kiki was handed to Leah, but she started to whimper and fixed her eyes back to her grandparents.

'Alan will have her,' Cheryl said, patting his knee.

'Come on then, Little Miss. Let's look out for those ugly sisters!' He placed Kiki on his lap and let her look through the pictures on the programme.'

Seeing Leah's disappointment that Kiki couldn't wait to get out of her grip, Eric slid an arm around her shoulder. She turned to him and his gentle kiss blitzed away her sadness. She cuddled into him and decided to enjoy the performance, taking advantage of the help on hand.

Magical music swirled around the room and she turned her attention to the icy blue stage and twinkling curtains, setting the scene for the story to unfold.

A few minutes later, Cinderella's midnight clock chimed to announce the start of the show. Everything fell to a hush as the backdrop of a kitchen came to life and action lit up the room. Cinderella's prettiness was instantly evident, even with soot on her face and her dusty work clothes as she sat at the table peeling an endless pile of vegetables. The shrill sound of the wicked stepmother's voice echoed down the stairs to bark an order, rendering her momentarily sad, but the little children dancing on in mouse costumes brought a ray of sunshine, and she was soon joining them for their chirpy musical number.

Then on came Bumble and Buzz, looking hilarious as the two ugly sisters. They started to bully Cinderella, chasing the mice away with bottles of squirty cream, and Kiki was on the edge of Alan's knees, mesmerised at the slapdash craziness before her. Leah watched her daughter delightedly and was sure Kiki could recognise their usual catchphrases from The Gunge Garden.

But suddenly, there was a loud bang and crackle, followed by a puff of purple smoke as the wicked stepmother arrived. Local cabaret singer, Nadia Banks, looked every inch the villain in her demonic robes, menacing makeup, and hair piled up with black crystals. Letting out a devilish laugh, she launched into her first song inciting a sea of cheers from the audience as her incredible voice reached the back of the rafters.

More smoke clouded the stage and as the mood changed from the happy jaunt around the kitchen, Leah glanced at Kiki. Alan was bouncing her around to the song in an effort to keep her spirits up, but the telltale lip began to emerge, and her face creased up in horror. It was too loud to hear the screams that would be piercing everyone's eardrums if the room had been silent, but tears started spilling down her cheeks and dripping into her wide-open mouth.

Cheryl plucked Kiki into her arms, turning her head away from the stage and trying her best to distract her. Then the wicked stepmother made her exit, bringing the darkened atmosphere to a halt.

The scenery changed. Birds singing in a perfect blue sky as a striking palace took centre stage. The lighting softened, and the richness of the throne room made everyone gasp before the King seated himself and began talking to his advisors about what a hopeless case his son was because he couldn't find a suitable bride. Deciding that an event would be the best way to attract one, the king stood up and called out to the prince.

Kiki's crying had started to die down, but with no

music to wash away the sound, Leah tensed in her seat as the tot continued to grizzle. There was a fanfare, and screams of adoration trilled into the air as Wesley Finch took to the stage, looking dapper in his royal suit. Leah felt a rush of nostalgia at the face she'd had on her bedroom posters there in real life, just metres away. Kiki let out an indignant squeal and Leah rifled through the changing bag, lobbing a toy in Cheryl's direction without letting her eyes leave the stage.

'Check out the cheese ball,' Eric whispered in her ear. 'Fresh from the charity shop bargain bin.'

'Shut it!' whispered Leah through gritted teeth, slapping Eric's thigh as he guffawed under his breath.

She was willing Wesley to stay where he was. Not only because of the sight of him, but something in the way he spoke was keeping Kiki from kicking off. She nuzzled into her teddy toy and cooed as Cheryl jiggled her about.

As the invitations arrived through the door and the ugly sisters tried to snatch them from Cinderella, their squabble provoked another intervention from the wicked stepmother and, once again, everything turned loud, dark, and purple. This time, Kiki arched her back, yelling and howling at the top of her lungs. Then Leah was mortified as the wicked stepmother noticed, and strode forward, talking directly to Kiki and trying to lighten the mood. Cheryl raised her in full view, and Leah wanted to curl up in humiliation as the crying hit a new level.

Helplessly, Leah reached for her and tried to offer her a drink. With Kiki plonked on her lap, Leah wiggled and danced, then soothed and calmed, but there was no chance of pacifying Kiki. From the glowing introduction of the Fairy Godmother, the transformation of the pumpkin coach, and all the way through the ball itself, Kiki would not sit still, look at the characters, or stop crying.

It was a relief when the interval came and at last, they could all stretch their legs.

'Who's for ice cream?' Cheryl asked as everyone nodded in response. 'Alan will get it.'

'Let's all go,' said Eric. 'I think we need a little walk around.'

While Cheryl and Alan headed to the kiosk, Eric and Leah joined the long queue for the bar. Five minutes later, they had barely moved.

'Yes, I know. I know…' Leah tried to restrain Kiki, who thrashed in her grip and continued to shriek straight into her ears. People were staring now, and it was all too clear to see that Kiki was ruining their evening.

'That baby is so loud!' shouted an older girl, pointing Kiki out to her parents as they wrestled with a bag of popcorn.

'Honestly,' a woman whispered from behind Leah in the queue. 'I don't know why people bring such little ones to something like this. They're *far* too young to understand. Ridiculous… she should be in bed.'

Eric turned around to face Leah. He'd been too far ahead to hear, but his face changed when he clocked hers.

'Are you OK?'

She looked at the carpet and shrugged gloomily.

'It's only because of the whole stepmother thing. All those loud bangs are a bit full on.'

'My fault,' Leah snapped. 'Sorry I even suggested this.'

'I don't mean that. All I'm saying is…'

'Eric…' Leah gestured towards the bar where at last, someone was waiting to take his order.

'Pint of Guiness please and a…' He glanced behind him at Leah. 'Lemonade?'

She shot him a look and he got it in one.

'White wine, thanks,' he said to the barman.

The two-minute countdown was announced over the speaker, but Eric's pint was taking forever to settle perfectly in the glass.

'We're going to miss it, Eric!' Leah wailed, just as Kiki flew into another meltdown.

Trying to bob her up and down on the spot, Leah leaned in to kiss Kiki's hair and was met with a headbutt, straight to her teeth. Holding a hand over her bruised mouth, Leah grappled with Kiki in her other arm, trying to pin her down.

'Here!' she shouted, plunging her into Eric's hands as the music started up. 'You bloody have her.'

Leah picked up her wine and headed back to her seat, ignoring the tears in a bid to stop them trickling. She gulped half the glass of wine and sank defeatedly down in her chair.

The curtains opened and there was the prince. But it wasn't just the usual fairytale character. Here was Wesley Finch, guitar strapped to his body as the intro to his biggest hit, *Everything and More,* sounded out across the auditorium. And for a few precious moments, as the wine simmered in her head, Leah was not the despairing mother of a screaming child at a pantomime. Instead, she was a teenager at the concert of her idol.

Wesley's voice echoed out like velvet, still sounding as glorious as it had when Leah was fourteen. She beamed in her seat, cheering when he gazed straight at her as she sat there alone, relishing each drop from her glass.

'Didn't miss much then!'

It was like a vinyl record being scratched away from the needle as Eric hovered over her, balancing Kiki on his hip while trying not to let his drink overflow. Leah stared blankly back and made no attempt to take her off him.

'There's no point giving her to me, is there?' she hissed. 'It'll only start her up again.'

'Pass her here,' said Cheryl, already pulling her from under Eric's elbow. 'Alan will share his ice cream.'

With the last dregs of wine turning warm at the stem, Leah let it fall down her throat, watching exhaustedly as the prince travelled from house to house, trying a dainty glass stiletto on every foot possible until it fitted like a glove on Cinderella's, causing the ugly sisters to slip over and cover themselves in the gunk that they had planned to throw over her.

As Cinderella stood proud and transformed, looking the picture of radiance and happiness now she was wearing both of her lifechanging slippers, Leah thought of Kiki in her little pink boots. Would she ever be able to glide around in a pair of stunning shoes that would make her feel like a million dollars? Would she stride with confidence down a street, or even know how to put her two feet on the ground? Leah's eyes wandered over to Kiki, shrivelled and scrunched in a crotchety ball of tiredness, and felt an inevitable pull in her chest as Cinderella skipped away, on top of the world.

The wedding was spectacular, and Kiki stayed awake just long enough to see the scenery change to a stunning archway of opulent flowers with a red carpet running down the stairway of the palace. When the supporting cast members had taken their bows, the theatre roared as Wesley appeared in regal white wedding attire and held out a hand to lead the way for Cinderella.

She stepped through the doors wearing every little girl's dream princess dress – a cascading mass of golden glitter, tumbling over folds of champagne silk and studded with thousands of shimmering amber beads. He lifted the reams of netting off her face to reveal a sensational tiara nestling in her crown of blonde hair. Then he planted a kiss on her lips before bringing her to the front of the stage and taking a final bow.

As the curtains closed and the crowds began to leave, Leah turned to Kiki drifting off in Cheryl's arms and could hardly believe they'd made it to the end. Cheryl carried her back to the car while Leah followed behind under the crook of Eric's arm, warming her cold hands in his pockets to protect them from the harsh winds rolling off the beach.

Twig was at the door as soon as Eric turned the key, zooming around the house and pleased to have them home. His long-lasting dog chew had kept him occupied and they'd checked him on the camera, feeling reassured to know he'd spent most of the time asleep.

Once Kiki was in bed, Eric made them cocoa and brought it upstairs to drink. The electric blanket felt heavenly as Leah sank back against the pillows and turned on her phone for a late-night social media browse.

'So, I guess we can cross that off our list of things to try,' she mused, clicking on her recent messages.

'What?' Eric asked, pulling on his pyjama shorts.

'Taking her to a pantomime.'

'I wouldn't say that. You know, it's a lot to handle when she doesn't really understand what's going on.'

'Yeah, I get it. I just thought she'd at least like all the fun and the pretty dresses.'

'And she did. It's just going to take a few more years until she isn't scared of the villains and all that loud music.'

Leah was only half listening as a notification took her straight into the *Beauty Picks and Hacks (Starlingford)* group that she had been a member of for the last few years.

The post in her feed was from a Zoe Newton, with a

black background and bold white lettering.

What's the best serum for anti-ageing and sensitive skin? Would love everyone's recommendations!

Leah scrolled down to the comments and read the first few.

Kim Gallagher
Deffo try the Auclair Rose Concentrate. On my third bottle now.

Jada Louise White
I get the Tea Tree + Vit C from Poundland and honestly, it's better than more expensive ones I've tried.

Shannon Gosling
Serums are not always the best thing, as they can be too rich and clog the pores. I just use a good moisturiser after toning.

As usual, this was the typical response anyone would get when asking for recommendations in a post. Leah continued reading, purely to see if any products had been suggested more than once by several people. There were at least thirty different types, with people giving helpful tips on how to use them best.

But it was a comment near the bottom that made Leah do a double take.

Krissi Resnik
Whatever you do, just don't go near that SySTEM stuff (EdenCore). I couldn't move half my face for a week after I'd tried it. Had to go on antibiotics as the doc at A&E thought I had sinus problems. Turns out it was an allergic

reaction to the serum!

The replies were hidden, so she clicked on 'Show All' and revealed a whole chain of responses.

Ana Raymond-Smith
Same here. Treated myself a couple of weeks ago and the blisters have just about gone down.

Paige G Tavares
Literally dabbed some of my mum's on my forehead and was flaking by the morning. I mean, WTF?!

Rox Piper
Glad it's not just me then. I had to take mine back but at least I got a refund.

Casey Berill
*Yes, please don't touch this stuff. My friend tried a free sample and it nearly scarred her for life. They must put some really toxic sh*t in there.*

So, there it was. The proof, from the people who had all used *SySTEM* with horrifying results.

'Eric, you're never going to believe this!' Leah exclaimed, then lowered her voice in case she disturbed Kiki. 'They're all saying…'

She unpeeled her eyes from the screen and glanced over to her left. But Eric was already fast asleep and snuffling away under the duvet.

Leah acted quickly, screenshotting every comment before a group admin could remove them. Then she burrowed down under the covers, her eyes wide open in the darkness of the bedroom as she pondered the reaction of her colleagues once they knew.

Nineteen

'Jocelyn, I need a word.'

Leah rushed to the counter, having stopped on the way to help an elderly woman who had dropped her basket on the floor. Jocelyn didn't look up, despite the urgency in Leah's voice.

'You do realise you're three minutes late.' She tossed the pen down and folded her arms. 'I needed you here for four on the dot.'

'Sorry, I got held up,' said Leah breathlessly. 'There was a lady near the escalator who spilled her shopping everywhere. I stopped to pick it up and make sure she was alright.'

'Wrong, luvvie. You call one of the Glovers staff to sort it out and you get yourself down here as a priority.'

Leah shook her head. 'But Dawn always says…'

'Dawn can do one. *She* doesn't have a counter to run.'

'Well, I couldn't just have left her lying there like that.'

'Did she need an ambulance?'

'No.'

'There you go, then. She'd have been fine.' Jocelyn smirked as she wiped the seat of the consultation chair. 'I've got someone booked for a facial in approximately three minutes' time. What would I have done if there were customers queuing up and you'd not been here to serve them?'

'Understood,' said Leah despondently. 'I apologise.'

'Anyway… didn't you say you had something to tell me? Better be quick then, before Mrs Kirk arrives.'

'Yes, I do.' She pulled her phone from a pocket and opened the screenshots in her gallery, handing them over for Jocelyn to see. 'I came across these last night. They're all comments about *SySTEM* from people who have had bad reactions.'

Jocelyn skimmed through them, faster than Leah would have liked.

'What a load of tosh. They haven't got a clue what they're talking about!'

'They've all used it!' Leah insisted. 'Every single one of them has had adverse affects and somebody even ended up in hospital.'

'Come down a peg or two, luvvie. This doesn't mean a thing. Who knows what other low-grade crap they've used for a start?'

'But we've got a whole box of it that's been returned. I'd say it's more than obvious. We can't keep selling this stuff.'

'Unfortunately, we don't get to make that decision.'

'Right.' Leah was nodding resolutely. 'We need to tell Head Office now.'

'Are you insane? Do you know how much commission I… we get from *SySTEM* alone?'

Leah suppressed a gasp, trying not to choke. 'Isn't people's skin more important than that? Their health, even?'

Jocelyn paused, but not uncomfortably.

'You go ahead and ring them, then.' A smug smile spread itself across her face. 'But I can already tell you what Hilary will say. You'll be ridiculed, luvvie. Pitied! Don't you think they've had customer complaints before? That doesn't mean they've needed to stop making a product. EdenCore has been at the top of its game for decades and you've been here for… what… a couple of months?' She sauntered over to the landline and held it out for Leah. 'But feel free to give it a go, Missy. It's your reputation at stake, not mine.'

Mrs Kirk arrived at the counter for her appointment, but Jocelyn ignored her, instead continuing to hold the handset out, welcoming Leah to make a fool of herself at HQ while badmouthing EdenCore in earshot of a customer.

'OK…' Leah waved a dismissive hand. 'I'll take your word for it, then.'

'Good.' Jocelyn slammed the receiver back into the dock. 'And speaking of phones…' She held out Leah's mobile, which she was still clutching after viewing the screenshots, 'you are *not* allowed yours on the shop floor, and you are well aware of that.'

'But I was only showing you the—'

'Get it gone.' Jocelyn clicked her fingers in the air to the shock of Mrs Kirk, who frowned in observation from her place next to the till.

Crestfallen, Leah made her way upstairs to the locker room. She was used to being spoken to like that by now, but it was hard to keep the frustration at bay when even reading the screenshots had not worried Jocelyn in any way. Instead, Leah had ended up being seen as the one with the problem.

Stashing her phone away, she examined her face in the mirror. It had been a while since she had stopped using the *SySTEM* and the evidence had faded now, leaving only a few subtle signs of dryness. But as long as Jocelyn was in denial, there was nothing she could do.

Leah would have to keep promoting the serum, along with all the unknown entities of the other products that could easily be just as harmful.

She returned to the counter just in time to see Jocelyn slathering *SySTEM* over Mrs Kirk's face.

'Natural…' she was saying as she vigorously rubbed it in. 'Hypoallergenic… organic… one hundred percent pure.'

'Is it supposed to tingle?' asked Mrs Kirk, and Leah listened with alarm.

'That's the ingredients getting to work,' explained Jocelyn, blotting it with a tissue to quicken the absorption process so she could load up the next product. 'In just days, all those lines will be smoothed out and you'll look half your age.'

Leah had to turn her back and pretended to dust the shelves of stock, cringing at Jocelyn's words and feeling dread for the fate of Mrs Kirk's skin.

'Let's go a few shades darker with your foundation,' Jocelyn said loudly. 'Get some decent coverage on those liver spots.'

Feeling every muscle tense, Leah glanced at Mrs Kirk, trapped in the chair and looking totally bewildered. She had come here for a relaxing skin treatment to give herself a boost, and instead she was being humiliated and doused in chemicals that would do the exact opposite. Powerless to intervene, Leah offered a sympathetic smile at a brief second when Jocelyn was distracted.

'Right, I think that will do for today, thank you,' she heard Mrs Kirk say.

Jocelyn let out a shrill laugh. 'Oh, no luvvie, I can't let you go off looking like that. What about your eyebrows?'

Mrs Kirk looked like she wanted the ground to swallow her up. 'I'm not sure what you mean.'

'Righto, how can I put this politely? Let's just say,

they're a little overplucked.'

'Maybe another time.'

'This is what you need,' said Jocelyn, ignoring her. She took a large grey pencil from a pot and leaned in towards Mrs Kirk, pointing the combed end over her eyes.

'Well, I appreciate your opinion, but I've never been one for fluffing them up.' Mrs Kirk shifted away and started to make a move.

'That's the whole point of being here, isn't it?' Jocelyn replied brashly. 'To get my opinion. My *expertise*.'

Mrs Kirk pursed her lips and nodded sharply back at her. 'And I have had quite enough.'

'No problem, we'll leave the eyebrow pencil off then,' said Jocelyn, scurrying over to the shelves. 'I'll just bag up the rest of your products.'

She filled her arms with boxes and bottles, then grappled with the scanner to take the payment as fast as possible.

'I hope you're not putting those through for me,' said Mrs Kirk.

Jocelyn held an extra-large *SySTEM* awkwardly in mid-air. 'It's everything I've used on you today. No one ever has a facial without buying, luvvie. It's part of the deal.'

Leah bit her lip, thinking of the countless experiences that regularly contradicted Jocelyn's statement.

'There's a first time for everything.' Mrs Kirk's face was reddening by the minute, but whether it was anger or the serum taking hold, Leah couldn't tell.

'Fine.' Jocelyn visibly gritted her teeth. 'I'll keep it here for now. You never know, you might change your mind.'

She skulked over to a cupboard and placed the items inside.

'No chance of *that*,' Mrs Kirk mumbled to herself.

'Are you OK?' Leah whispered while Jocelyn was out of earshot. 'I'm sorry.'

'That's kind of you,' Mrs Kirk blinked at Leah, her eyes sad and mortified. 'Not as sorry as I am, though.'

Before Jocelyn could come back, she picked up her handbag and disappeared into the busy throngs of the main store, lit up for another evening of late-night Christmas shopping.

'Now, I've got a job for you, luvvie.' Jocelyn clapped her hands together, not even bothered that Mrs Kirk had already left.

Leah stood up straight, ready to take her orders.

'Head Office have asked us to put on a special event for all our customers just before Christmas. So, we need to go through our contact list and invite them here, preferably on a Saturday. We can hold it upstairs in the boardroom, with refreshments, freebies, and plenty on offer to tempt them. We'll talk them through the products, do some demos, and hopefully by the end of it, they'll pile down here and buy everything in sight.'

'Sounds good,' said Leah, ideas of décor and offers already swirling around her head.

'I'll get Tiffany to order the free gifts, when she actually decides to show up here again,' Jocelyn continued. 'So, can I ask you to go through and make a list of all our big spenders and frequent customers who'll get a VIP place?'

'No problem. I'll try and make a start later.'

'But whatever you do, don't bother with Mrs Kirk!' Clattering around the consultation table, Jocelyn threw the lids back on the testers and scooped up the used cotton pads in her hands. 'That was one monumental waste of my time!'

Leah said nothing and instead commenced the stock

take she had already been tasked with for her evening shift.

'I mean, why bother coming here if she didn't like my advice?'

There were a million things Leah could respond with, but each one would get her fired.

'If I told every customer they were perfect, they wouldn't feel the need to bloody buy anything!' Jocelyn continued to rant. 'Not that *she* was an oil painting.'

'She sure won't be one tomorrow.'

'What was that?'

Leah closed her eyes. The sentence had slipped from her mouth beyond all control, and she could no longer hold back.

'Do you want to repeat that, luvvie? You'd better remember who you're talking to.'

'I just meant… I feel sorry for her, that's all. She doesn't know about the *SySTEM* and…'

'Oh, I see.' Jocelyn squinted with spite in her eyes. 'Because I still used it on her after seeing those silly screenshots, you've got a problem with that.'

'We shouldn't be doing it,' Leah said softly. 'Promoting something that is causing so much damage. The evidence is all there, Jocelyn. How can it be safe to keep putting on the customers? If this gets out, who is going to be in the firing line?'

Jocelyn gave a stunned chuckle. 'Are you trying to suggest I'm guilty of some kind of foul play here?'

'No, I haven't said that. I'm just concerned.'

'Hang on a minute…' She folded her arms and eyed Leah up and down. 'Of course, tonight's the night, isn't it? Kizzy's going to the shoe shop.'

'It's Kiki.' Leah corrected her for the hundredth time. 'And it's a hospital appointment.'

'Well, like I said, I'm sorry you have to work,' said

Jocelyn, signing out of the tablet for the day. 'But it won't help to hold grudges or try and start rumours about the serum just because you're not happy with my decision.'

'What?' Leah could hardly contain herself. 'That has nothing to do with any of this!'

'Righto…' Jocelyn winked, unconvinced. 'Anyway, I'll love you and leave you now. Good luck with the sales…' She walked away without looking back. 'Oh, and you'd better keep flogging that *SySTEM* or Hilary's going to know about it. Got that?'

Leah stared at the ground until Jocelyn had vacated the top of the escalator. An uncomfortably bitter breeze was surging through the store and Leah felt chilled to the bone. Not even five yet, and she would have to stand there until Glovers closed at eight, by the floor-to-ceiling window and the sliding doors of the main entrance.

Half an hour later, her teeth were chattering as she tried to press on with the stock take, her bare wrists stone cold from the cropped sleeves of her uniform blazer. Soon she would have to find a tissue to wipe her sniffly nose and it was getting hard to grip the stylus each time she entered information on the tablet.

'Excuse me,' said a familiar voice behind her and she turned to see Mrs Kirk again. 'I've decided to come back. I'd like to see the supervisor please.'

'Unfortunately, Jocelyn's gone home for the day now, but I can give her a message for you.'

Mrs Kirk shook her head. 'Not her, dear. I mean, I want a word with the Glovers manager.'

'No problem, that's Dawn' Leah looked around the vicinity of the beauty hall. 'She was here about ten minutes ago.'

'How do you work with that woman?'

Leah looked into her eyes and knew she was now talking about Jocelyn.

'I mean, for goodness' sake…' Mrs Kirk's emotions came pouring out. 'I've never been so insulted.'

'Honestly, I'm so sorry.' Leah put a hand on her forearm. 'I felt terrible for you. There was no need…'

'I could go on Facebook. Name and shame…' Her lips trembled. 'But no, I should really take this up with the store. So, it's Dawn?'

'Yes, I think I can see her now,' Leah craned her neck and waited until Dawn was clearly in view. 'See the blonde lady there by the fragrance counter? Green blouse and clipboard.'

'Lovely, I'll go over straight away.' Mrs Kirk patted Leah's arm. 'Nothing against you, though, dear. You've been so helpful.'

Leah watched as she walked purposefully to the perfumes, keeping Dawn firmly in her sight. As soon as she started speaking, Dawn led her away to a quiet area and Leah knelt back down at the shelves, the frozen floor tiles like sheets of ice through her thin tights, as she wondered what Mrs Kirk was saying right now, and wished that she could be a fly on the wall.

Outside, the streets were lit up with flashing colours and carrier bags as people flitted backwards and forwards, out to grab the bargains and get stocked up for the festive season. The dusk set the backdrop to a candy land of boiled-sweet lights and signs in snowy calligraphy that looked as if they'd been piped with an icing bag. There was laughter and jagged movements as passing shoppers joked and hugged. Wafts of caramelised heat seeping in from the street stalls. Lovers kissing in alleyways, and families huddled in each other's warmth as they scampered around exploring. Little children at the centre of it all as they toddled along with their parents.

Leah turned away from the window and blinked in the stark contrast of the store. There had not been one customer all evening. Even Glovers itself was dead, not helped by the broken radiators and arctic blasts of air shooting from the vents.

And right about now, Kiki would be on the way to her appointment with everyone special all around her. Everyone but her own mother. For the sake of this empty shop, and the necessity to be present on a dormant evening counter, Leah would not see Kiki's tiny feet being placed into her new boots or witness her standing up in them for the very first time.

When the clock chimed nine, security locked the doors and Leah walked through the darkness up the steps, no longer caring that her tears were blinding the way. Standing in silence at the locker room mirror, she held her hands to her face and spread them with the salty moisture, desperate to rid her skin from every trace of EdenCore.

Twenty

Breakfast the next day felt much better. Chunky socks hugging her feet after being stretched for hours the night before in her high court shoes. Warmth circulating around the house and the comfort of soft dressing gown sleeves reaching all the way to her hands instead of the exposure from her three-quarter-length jacket.

There was sugar in her tea, syrup on her porridge, and extra helpings of both. Music hummed from the radio in the background and Eric had taken a few days off work, so was toasting bagels ready for his plate of poached eggs, monitored by Twig who was following his every move around the kitchen in the hope of a crumb dropping off the worktop.

Kiki had eaten most of her French toast soldiers and was now nibbling blueberries from a small bowl in her highchair.

'That's a good girl!' praised Leah. 'Are you liking your purple peas?'

She spilled one on the table, so Leah plucked it between her fingers and passed it back to Kiki, who held Leah's gaze as she took it from her.

'Careful,' warned Eric. 'If you drop any food, you know who'll have it.' He eyed the dog, who was sitting at his feet, still waiting for morsels to fall into his mouth.

'Oh yes, he'll think it's chips.'

At Leah's words, Twig raced over and jumped up at the table, sniffing for a snack.

'You've done it now!' said Eric.

'I forgot he knew the word *chips!*' Leah giggled. Twig got into his best sitting position and looked longingly at her. 'No,' she said, smiling at his eagerness. 'I didn't mean…'

'Chissss!' Kiki repeated, squealing as Twig then skidded to a halt in front of her, placing his muzzle in her lap.

'Oh, we shouldn't tease him like this. Give him a biscuit.'

Eric delved into the jar and called Twig who obeyed immediately.

'Let's get outside today,' he suggested, bringing his food over to the table. 'Go for a walk on the beach or something.'

'Could do.' Leah followed a bird with her eyes as it laced a path from the apple tree into the hedges. The sun was slowly rising in a bright tangerine sphere, yet was still dark and treacly in the winter sky. 'We should bring the boots.'

'She's not about to start walking just because she's tried them on.'

'I do know that,' Leah tutted. 'She might be more likely to make a move if she's somewhere different maybe.'

'Well, don't be surprised if it takes her a while. She wasn't too keen at the appointment. You only missed a whole load of crying!'

Leah glared across the table. 'That doesn't make me feel any better, Eric. I should have been there no matter what.'

'Alan took some brilliant pictures though, and that's what we've got to treasure and look back on.'

'Well, it's never going to make up for the real thing.'

'I know,' Eric nodded. 'I get it.' He cut into his second egg and piled it on the bagel with a swipe of avocado. 'Just remember there's so much more to look forward to, and a thousand memories you'll see for yourself.'

Kiki reached down to hug Twig, calling out in garbled vowels and patting his chest with her feet. He closed his eyes and moved in nearer, enjoying the attention while Leah and Eric were distracted.

'Anyway, we're going to have a fashion show in a minute, aren't we?' Eric beamed at Kiki as he came to the end of his food. 'Are you going to show Mummy how you look in your new shoes?'

'I'd love to see that!' Leah rubbed Kiki's cheek. 'No doubt they're comfier than the ones I was wearing last night.'

'No high heels for you today,' Eric ordered. 'You've got to make way for the model of the moment!'

***

All was quiet as they opened the car doors and got Kiki strapped into the buggy. The bracing breeze enveloped them as they made their way across the green, past the playground and the gulls squawking over a food wrapper that had blown out of the café bin.

Twig tugged Leah along as she clutched hold of his lead, while Eric walked behind them pushing Kiki. Up on the promenade Leah halted, waiting for him to catch up. Twig jostled around her body, weaving in and out of her legs, and she bounced around comfortably in her trainers, pulling her furry parka around her like a giant embrace.

There was no mascara streaming down her cheeks. Instead, her eyes glistened in peace, without any makeup to cage them in. No customers around her, expecting some kind of perfection. She smiled as Eric approached, and his face lit up seeing something unleash in hers.

Pebbles swooped to dust at the shoreline, where the waves took them under their wings. She traced the textures in her view. The seaweed's olive fringes and slippery brown ribbons that the water had pressed into the stones. Chalky cuttlefish bones, every so often sticking out from the rocks, and the intermittently placid pinks of shells and crab claws.

Leah unclicked Twig's lead and he tore off over the swathes of it all, chasing a flock of birds off the groynes and digging around for sticks. With Kiki babbling in her seat, they strolled along the path, past beach huts padlocked up for the winter and the sailing clubhouse which also appeared to be closed.

The further they walked, the more of Dankton was left behind and they entered the quieter outskirts of beach that sat between there and Ropeshore. The hillside down to the grass flattened out into an uncluttered stretch of green, with sparse weeds and leftover flower heads quivering pale purple into the distant foamy water.

Placing a hand on Eric's, she stopped the pushchair and flipped on the brake before opening the bag on the back and smiling.

'Right, let's have a go, shall we?' she said, bringing out Kiki's tiny pair of solid pink ankle boots.

Taking one each, Leah and Eric slipped them onto her feet securely, ensuring she had good support.

'Don't they look lovely on you?' Leah stood back and beamed, her vision turning watery over the lower half of her eyes. 'Such a grown-up girl!'

Slowly, she lifted Kiki and placed her in an upright

position, gently bolstering her until she was secure. Kiki looked down at herself and was silent for a few moments, eyes widening at this unsteady new feeling. Her brows knotted and she let out a yelp, then another until the little screams began to build in a crescendo.

'That's it, you're standing.' Leah glanced sideways at Eric, who nodded back. 'She's never done this before!'

'Come on,' said Eric. 'Shall we try and walk?'

They took Kiki's hands in theirs and slowly edged forwards. As expected, she stayed glued to the spot, her lower lip trembling and her face full of trepidation.

Leah squatted beside her, brushing back her windswept hair from her eyes. 'It's OK. Just one step. Like this…' She lifted Kiki's calf into her palm and set down her foot, just slightly forward on the grass, while Eric helped her to bear weight.

Kiki's face reddened and Leah was thankful that no one else was around to witness the piercing cries which were building from her lungs and echoing into the blustery air.

'She's getting tired. We shouldn't push her too hard all at once.'

Leah nodded at Eric's words but couldn't stop the feeling of defeat. It was only the first day of Kiki wearing the boots, she knew that. But if this was the reaction to even having them put on, it was highly unlikely she would adapt. And when Eric was at work, Leah would struggle to do this on her own. She could imagine the way it would be, with each boot slamming into different corners of the room when Kiki kicked them off in a rage.

'Let's just get them off, then,' Leah agreed resignedly.

But Kiki pulled down on her parents' hands, bending her knees as the tantrum took hold. And in an instant, she howled out in protest, stamping her foot straight ahead and taking a full step forward.

The gasps of both her parents brought the screaming to a halt. Kiki glanced up at them, her eyes full of wonder.

'That's my princess!' Eric grinned proudly.

'You took a big girl step,' said Leah, squeezing Kiki's fingers. 'So there *is* magic in those special shoes!'

They both cheered and Kiki responded, staring up at them and sticking out a dribbly tongue. There was no more crying. Instead, her mouth stretched into a yawn.

'Bless her, she's definitely getting sleepy. That must have taken a lot of energy for her to do.'

'I can go and grab us a coffee if you fancy it,' Eric offered. 'Get her back in the pushchair and I'll bring it over to that table.'

'Sounds good to me.' Leah crouched beside Kiki and kissed her cheek. 'Let's get you nice and cosy in your blanket.'

She hoisted her into the seat and started undoing the bootlaces as Eric made his way to the beach bar, back in the direction they had come from. Tucking the boots inside the bag, she unfolded a blanket and wrapped it around Kiki, who cooed at her in response. Leah's heart felt full, but empty all at once, and a tear scurried down her face as she took Kiki's own in her hands.

'I'm sorry I wasn't there for you yesterday,' she whispered. 'I'm so sorry.'

Wiping her eyes, she blinked until the landscape solidified, and the murky ocean line led the way towards Starlingford. Where Jocelyn would be there at the counter, fresh from her pampering session at home last night, and the heating problem would no doubt have been fixed, just in time for her return.

Leah turned the pushchair and walked the other way. To Eric and the steaming coffee, and then to the warmth of the fireplace at home.

Twenty-One

'You're back!' Leah exclaimed as Tiffany turned up at the counter for the first time in weeks.

'I know, I know.' She blushed with a face full of passion. 'What's a girl to do when her man keeps surprising her with posh afternoon teas and unexpected dates?'

'It's just... no one's had a clue where you've got to!' Leah tried her best to sound casual.

'To be honest, I haven't known half the time. But oh, my days, he is just the *best*. He takes me shopping, dining out, spas, you name it. I am so happy right now.'

'I'm really pleased you've found each other.' Leah smiled to see her friend on cloud nine. 'And I've missed you.'

'It's his fault I've not been turning up for work, though. He springs these things on me and then tells me not to bother ringing in. I mean, to be fair, he's loaded so it's not like I need the money anymore.'

Leah nodded, pretending to agree with her reasoning.

'But it's been OK here without me... hasn't it?' Tiffany strained to raise her eyebrows, but there was no movement in their arches and her impossibly smooth forehead did not crease in the slightest.

'Oh, you know…'

It took a few seconds for Tiffany to remember, and then her hands flew up over her face. 'Kiki's appointment! The one you had to miss. Oh, I felt so sorry for you. Did Jocelyn let you change shifts in the end?'

Leah shook her head.

'That's just awful, and all for what? A night in with a face pack? Rhona would never have done that.' Tiffany kept eye contact. 'Anyway, I know it's probably no consolation, but hopefully you had a busy night and made masses of sales.'

'Unfortunately not,' said Leah, pursing her lips into an annoyed smile. 'I stood in the freezing cold all evening with no customers whatsoever.'

'I actually have no words. I mean, I can remember my boys being little like it was yesterday. This just makes me furious.'

'Well, I was gutted to miss the fitting. But she did take a step the other day, and I was there for that.'

Tiffany's eyes widened as much as she could manage. 'So, she's walking?'

'No, no… not yet. She put her weight down in her boots with me and Eric holding her hands. But it was something at least.'

'Oh, bless her. That's amazing, though.'

Leah glanced at the people walking past outside, none of whom were coming into Glovers.

'I guess we should get back to the grind.' She logged into the tablet and opened the day's sales sheets. 'We've got ridiculous targets today and no one's even coming our way.'

'Unless they're wanting a *SySTEM* refund.'

'Exactly. And it doesn't help that Parlour has a sale on. It's three for two at EdenCore over there, with the free winter gift thrown in.'

'No wonder it's so quiet in here!' Tiffany looked cunningly around the store. 'But we could use that to our advantage. Why don't we sneak off for lunch together today?'

'We can't. Jocelyn would go crazy.'

'She's not even in until tonight.'

'I don't know… what if we get caught out by someone else?'

'We'll get Kehlani to cover. Sod it, Leah. You've had to stand around here when you should have been with Kiki. Jocelyn speaks to you like you're dirt on the ground. It's about time you stopped being such a slave to this place. And anyway, you need to let it all out. I'm buying you lunch and that's the end of it.'

Leah registered Tiffany's words and double checked the emptiness of the store. Dawn had already said she'd be in meetings with reps most of the day, so it was highly unlikely anyone would notice, and Kehlani would be only too happy to cover for their whereabouts if Jocelyn happened to find out.

'Oh, go on then. But just this once!'

'Brilliant. We'll make ourselves scarce at twelve and back here for one. If there's a lunchtime rush here, it won't be before then.'

'OK, but only if it stays as empty as this.'

'Does it look like it's going to get busy?' Tiffany asked, pointing at the threatening rainclouds and the sliding doors which were not even partially opening.

'I guess not,' Leah agreed. 'Let's get as much stuff done as we can in the next two hours then.'

'We've had a delivery, so I'll go and get that for a start.'

'Thanks Tiff,' said Leah gratefully.

'No worries. I'm only eager because I want to check

out the new nail sets they've got upstairs.' She winked slyly and glided up to the next floor on her way to the stockroom.

Leah grinned to herself, thankful that Tifffany was back to make her working days brighter. She was secretly looking forward to lunch and catching up with her friend. There was so much to update her on since she'd been away.

Preparing for the new delivery, Leah made a start on the testers. She began to go through the jars, checking for old or empty pots and throwing each one in the bin.

'Hello… Leah, isn't it?'

She turned to see Mrs Kirk walking towards her.

'That's right. How are you today?' she asked warmly.

'I'm very well, thank you.'

'That's good to hear. Can I help with anything?'

'You already did. I just wanted to come along and say how kind you were to me when that manager of yours behaved in the way she did.'

'Oh, that's OK,' Leah smiled. 'I saw you talking to Dawn, so I knew you'd found her.'

'I told her everything and she was just wonderful. She has registered it as a formal complaint and she says she'll be taking it seriously. And I'll tell you what else…' Mrs Kirk leaned closer to Leah, lowering her voice. 'She told me that this wasn't the first time a customer had complained about Miss Quigley.'

Leah stiffened with anticipation but kept her cool in the hope of getting more out of Mrs Kirk.

'I'm sorry to hear that.'

'Yes! She said several other people had sent messages to the store, and someone else phoned up the other day. It seems that her manner isn't going down well with the customers.'

Leah didn't know how to respond. She couldn't

reveal any kind of opinion in case she was quoted or overheard. But inside, she was prickling with the realisation that she hadn't been imagining her suspicions about Jocelyn.

'As long as you're alright, that's all that matters,' Leah said. 'It was horrible to see you so sad after your facial.'

'Not to mention itchy! Thank goodness I didn't buy what she put on me.'

Again, Leah held back on revealing the truth. That Jocelyn had ignored Leah's warning about the *SySTEM*.

'How is your skin feeling now?'

'Nearly back to normal. The rash under my eyes seems to have gone down at least.'

'I know I shouldn't say this, but those products probably aren't the best thing to use.'

Mrs Kirk tutted and gave Leah a slow nod. 'If only I'd known before.'

'But I can show you something that I know will be better. I've tried it, and I'm sure you'll love it too.'

'That's nice of you to offer dear, but I really don't feel I want to try anything else from your…'

'It's not EdenCore,' Leah cut in. 'This is totally different. It's so gentle, all natural. And about half the price.'

'Well, I'm intrigued. I never did get a new moisturiser.'

'Let's do it! You take a seat right here,' Leah's face lit up, leading Mrs Kirk over to the EdenCore consultation table. Then she went across to Spa-esque a brand she had used on and off for years and never had any issues with. It was over in the main skincare area of the store with the more budget-friendly ranges.

She picked up a cleanser and combined serum-moisturiser, feeling hidden empowerment after what she had heard about Jocelyn. Defiantly, she returned to the counter and in moments, Mrs Kirk was in raptures with the feel of the lotions on her face.

'Now, this is more like it!' she said, looking radiant.

'Just a couple more things and you're done.'

Leah swept a perfect light skin tint over Mrs Kirk's cheeks and finished with a brush of natural lip balm in Honeydew which was the most recent addition to the Spa-esque collection.

'Look at that!' Leah beamed, twisting the mirror to face her. Mrs Kirk glowed with pride at her reflection. 'Less is so much more.'

'I love it. Oh, thank you, Leah, for showing this to me. What an honest girl you are, recommending something else and not just out there to make a sale.'

'Well, I just wanted you to feel like you should have done when you were last here.'

'I'll be buying the lot!' said Mrs Kirk, getting down from the chair. 'And I really do appreciate your help the other day, too.'

'It's good that you've spoken up. Dawn is really nice and I'm sure she'll be looking into it.'

Leah walked her to the edge of the counter and Mrs Kirk took her hands and lowered her tone.

'The way she scribbled everything down furiously on that clipboard, I have no doubt she will!'

Waving her goodbye as she hurried off towards the Spa-esque section, Leah stood thoughtfully, taking in Mrs Kirk's words until a clattering trolley stole her attention and Tiffany returned with the delivery.

For the following hour, they worked hard, scrubbing down the tester stand and unwrapping all the replacements. They filled up the shelves with the products that had been getting low, and then created a new display for the till area.

'Another forty-five minutes and we're out of here,'

Tiffany flashed her new diamond-studded Rolex to check the time. 'What are we going to do with no one to serve?'

'Plan for the big EdenCore beauty event, I guess. Did you see Jocelyn's note?'

'Yep. Sounds like a blast.'

Leah smirked at Tiffany's sarcasm. 'I haven't even started on the invite list yet. But while we're both here, we could put our heads together about the order of everything. What the presentation is going to be about and which products we want to push.'

Together, they made some sketchy notes, but they knew full well that Jocelyn would have reservations. There was no chance they'd get away with not even a mention of *SySTEM*.

'We can only hope she overlooks it,' Leah suggested, with vague optimism. 'Maybe she'll be too absorbed with other stuff to notice.'

'That would be about right.' Tiffany raised her lip in disgust. 'Not putting in any legwork then turning up on the day like she's done it all herself.'

'And taking all the sales… not that there'll be any at this rate.'

'Come on, babes, that's enough work for now. It's nearly twelve, so go and get your coat and I'll meet you outside. Where shall we go, do you think?'

'Anywhere close really,' Leah smiled excitedly. 'Then we'll have more time to chat and…'

Tiffany looked confused as her voice trailed off. She followed Leah's eyes to the window and twisted around to see Phil getting out of an impeccably shiny sports car, gleamingly black with cream leather seats and a convertible roof, fresh from a showroom. He had pulled up on the pavement, in full view of the window and as close as he could get to the store entrance. Tiffany could hardly contain her surprise as he strode through the doors, dangling the keys between his fingertips.

'Oh, my word,' said Tiffany under her breath. 'He's only gone and bought himself another car. He'll need a fifth garage after this.'

Leah watched, dumbfounded as he grinned from ear to ear.

'Phil, what are you doing?' Tiffany's words were stifled as he planted a huge kiss on her lips. 'You can't park there! You're not even supposed to drive down that road, it's a bus lane!'

'Nah love, you mean *you* can't park there.'

'Alright cheeky!' she laughed. 'You think just because you've got good wheels, that gives you the right to plonk them where you like.'

He shook his head, waving the keys right in her face. 'Like I said, darling. You're the one who's parked there. So, *you'd* better move *your* car!'

'What?' Tiffany looked dazed for a few more moments. Then it finally dawned on her. 'WHAT?' she screamed, so loud that the beauty hall almost fell to silence.

'Bloody hell,' Phil roared with laughter. 'Took you a while.'

'You… bought that… for me?' Her hand fell onto her chest and she visibly heaved like she was getting palpitations.

'We can't have you driving around in that clapped out old banger of yours, can we?'

'Oh, Phil!' Tiffany flew into his arms and started to cry. 'I love you.' She pulled away, tears sliding down to her pillowy lips as she yelled loudly in an overwhelming outpour. 'I'm in love with you, Phil. I've never loved anyone like this!'

'Calm down, sweetheart, it's OK.' Phil pulled her back into his arms, patting her shoulders as if slightly embarrassed by her reaction. 'Now, what do you say about taking it for a test drive?'

'Are you kidding? I'd love to!'

Clinging to his waist, Tiffany could hardly walk straight as Phil put an arm around her and they shuffled over to the door.

'Hang on a minute, though, what about my stuff?' They halted next to the basket stack and Tiffany tottered back over to the counter. 'Leah, hun, you know you were just going up to get your coat, well, you wouldn't mind grabbing mine too, would you?'

Leah nodded, wondering how on earth both she and Tiffany would leave discreetly for lunch, now they'd be making such a public exit, accompanied by Phil and a car that was turning heads both inside and outside the building. She quickly ran to the locker room, bundling coats and their handbags in her arms.

'Thanks for that,' said Tiffany when she returned. 'Let's do this, Loverboy!'

She slid her arms into the sleeves of her coat and as soon as she had gripped her bag, Phil lifted her up and carried her out of the store. He helped her into the driving seat and in the next few seconds, the car was gone.

Twenty-Two

Leah stood there on the spot, her coat and bag draped over her arm, and feeling immediately awkward. She slowly walked back to the counter and hid them away out of sight. How stupid of her to have even thought that she was still invited to lunch.

Alone again, she busied herself as much as possible, rearranging the concealers back in order of their shades where customers had jumbled them up. She made a few random sales and at least managed to shift a hefty sum of aromatherapy oils and body lotions for one woman's expensive gift hamper.

With two and a half hours until Jocelyn would arrive to relieve her, she decided to take her lunch break, much later than originally planned. There were still some dregs in the Meal Deal chiller, so she picked up a cheese and chutney bap and a seasonal iced coffee before heading upstairs to the canteen.

She chose one of the comfier seats where she could sit next to the radiator and look out of the window at the sprawling view of the city streets below. Sea birds were balancing on the multicoloured lights that were threaded from the clock tower, all the way out to the corners of each shop that sat at the edges of the crossroads.

Her sandwich was tasteless and too cold from the fridge. She picked off the crusty lid and ate the piece that was softer in the middle, staring out at the cafes and the people tucking into their meals, freshly made to order. The promise of escaping with Tiffany to do the same had lifted her spirits earlier in the day, and she couldn't stop the nagging pain of feeling abandoned all over again.

It was a sensitivity she had suffered since the alienation of motherhood. Losing touch with her journalism colleagues and missing the mark when it had come to making new friends. She was genuinely delighted that Tiffany had found love, but the rejection stung so much inside. Her eyes were becoming two balls of liquid, swelling up to sabotage her vision. All she had to do was blink and out they would flow. And maybe she should just let it go right now. The canteen was just as empty as the shop floor, and no one would see her in the midst of her misery.

Then the door creaked open and she took a breath.

'Look at you in here all by yourself.' Dawn's voice echoed across the vacant tables and chairs. 'Are you OK, lovely?'

'Hi, Dawn, yes I'm fine.'

Leah didn't look up, instead slurping her coffee. Taking every second to compose herself and force her eyes not to look too damp.

'Well done you, by the way.'

'Really… what for?'

'I saw your sales this afternoon. All that body stuff! I don't know how you've managed it with hardly any people even coming into the store. All the other counters are lagging well behind you today.'

'It was quite easy to be fair,' Leah smiled faintly. 'The woman wanted to fill a hamper, so she was up for a big spend.'

'And another thing. I've had feedback from one of your customers who has told me how kind and helpful you've been to her. A lady called Mrs Kirk?'

'Of course, I remember her.' she said, expecting Dawn to mention the complaint about Jocelyn and that she was aware Leah knew.

'She had nothing but compliments for you, so congratulations on that. You're a credit to Glovers.'

'Thanks, Dawn, it means a lot.'

'I know not everyone shows you the appreciation you deserve…' She hovered closer to Leah, her mascara-clad eyelashes batting with sincerity, and using a tone that implied she was talking about Jocelyn while refraining from spelling it out. 'But I just thought you should know what a fab job you're doing.'

Leah felt a hopeful glow and was lifted for a moment by Dawn's words. She was about to thank her again when the canteen door nearly swung off its hinges.

'You're needed downstairs, pronto!' Sebastian from the security team called across the room.

Dawn jerked around in annoyance. 'I've just got up here, Seb. What is it now?'

'A massive theft, boss. Big gang with sacks stuffed up their jackets. They've raided the gift section. We've pinned two of them down, but the others got away. Kev's going through the footage right now, but the lines are down and we can't call the police.'

'How much have they nicked?' Dawn put a hand down to steady herself on the kitchen island.

'We don't know yet, but Shana left the fragrance keys out and they've ransacked the cabinets on their way through.'

The colour drained instantly from Dawn's face. 'Are they armed?'

'No, nothing on them. We just need backup.'

'I'm on my way.' Dawn ran as fast as she could, side-stepping through the furniture to get out of the room.

'Can I do anything?' Leah stood up.

'No, you stay here, lovely. Finish your lunch and we'll handle it. We get this kind of thing all the time at Christmas. Don't you worry.'

Dawn shot away, calling out ahead to Sebastian. Something about getting the admin staff to come and join them as extra witnesses.

As the door banged shut again, Leah glanced out at the surrounding roads below the windows. No sign of any police cars or scuffles overspilling that were making people stare. She sat back down and started to relax, scanning all the parts of the room she didn't usually notice when it was thronging with people on their lunchbreaks. The curvy buttons on the microwave and the set of green Glovers mugs everyone used for their tea. The swirly pattern on the tiles near the sink. And the chunky wooden worktop where Dawn had left her clipboard.

Leah's eyes fell on it and stopped in their tracks. There in the dusky light, the plastic cover could hardly be seen. She squinted at the wad of papers pinched together by the silver grip.

No. She wasn't going to do this. Instead, she tapped her fingers and looked around for something to read, trying to resist the echoes of Mrs Kirk's words on repeat.

She scribbled everything down… furiously. On that clipboard.

It felt like something was taking over her body. Up she got, and slowly, she crept across the room. She checked all around her and even at the ceiling. Definitely not a soul around, and no cameras recording her every move.

She stood next to the worktop and rested the cover over her thumb. Then, with her heart drumming up into her throat, she flipped it open and all at once, she was rifling frantically through the pages, leafing past stock updates, meeting notes, and layout plans until she saw it there, scrawled in Dawn's handwriting: *Kirk. Mrs Delilah Kirk.*

Without reading the details, she knew it was the complaint. The words were jumping out at her from the lines of jotted biro. *Rude. Inappropriate.* And *completely out of line.*

Leah jumped to the bottom of the paper, where capital letters were underlined in red.

NEW COMPLAINTS LOG (Location – Desktop – Glovers1101 – Procedures – Complaints – Staff Complaints).

There were some spare till rolls in a box under a nearby coffee table. She ripped off the end of one and took a pen from the stationery drawer, just managing to copy down the instructions before sirens sounded outside.

Leaving the clipboard as she'd found it, Leah binned her food wrappers and stepped into the darkness of the corridor. She took a left turn to the office and rested her fingers on the door handle, pressing down cautiously and gently releasing the latch. Inside, she could see the whole space was clear. Computers still left on from when the admin staff had been summoned downstairs with no time to log off, and not yet enough inactivity for the systems to go on automatic standby.

She grabbed hold of the computer mouse and clicked through the folder locations she'd written down on the till roll paper. And in no time, there it was, under *Jocelyn Quigley.* Not just Mrs Kirk's complaint, but several others, just like she had said.

One by one, Leah opened every record, printing them out in fast motion as the sweat built up in the neckline of her uniform, her hand shaking as the minutes sped by and she hastened to get through every single one. There were footsteps pounding on the hallway floor and she grappled with the printer, seizing the last of the copies and shoving them into the waistband of her skirt before exiting from the computer folders, back to the home screen, until she had covered her tracks.

The last stop was the changing rooms. She flung her locker open and rammed the printouts deep inside her bag, ensuring that everything was well out of sight. Securing it all behind the closed door, she zoomed over to the mirror and was fixing her makeup by the time someone else walked in.

When she arrived back at the beauty hall, it seemed the earlier commotion had subsided as Dawn was talking to the only police officer still present while a few of the security staff were on hand to assist. And according to Kehlani, Leah hadn't missed any sales, so her slightly extended lunch hour seemed to have gone unnoticed. Although, as she'd expected, there had been no sign of Tiffany returning to finish the rest of her shift.

She was more than ready to go home when a blob of EdenCore pink flickered among the shelves and Jocelyn bustled through them, already out of breath when she reached Leah.

'What's with all the chaos?' she asked, nostrils flaring as she looked out over the store. 'Has PC Plod just stopped by for a cuppa?'

'It was theft. Quite a big group of them, apparently.'

'Have they taken anything from here?' Jocelyn shoved her way into the narrow space between Leah's back and the fully-stocked displays.

'No, it was all fragrance and the gift sets on the first

floor.'

'That's alright then.' She perched haphazardly on a high stool and tapped to log in to the tablet. 'How's it been?'

'Not bad, considering Parlour has a sale on.' Leah waited for Jocelyn to see her figures, boosted by the items bought for the customer's hamper. 'Especially with the customer I had earlier.'

Jocelyn glanced over the screen and nodded. Then she eyed Leah, looking at her up and down. 'You still haven't reached your target, though.'

Leah stayed silent and didn't react. Despite being dumped by Tiffany and struggling to sell products in an empty shop, she held it together, refusing to crumble at Jocelyn's response. She just looked straight at her, knowing the reality on the files in the office. The truth that was stashed away upstairs right now in her handbag.

'Oh, well…' Leah shrugged. 'Hopefully better luck next time.' Then, walking away from the counter, she turned around and observed the desolate shop floor with a smile. 'I'm sure you'll make up for it tonight, though.'

With a wave goodbye, she headed off to the top of the escalator, looking the picture of calmness on the outside, while her chest banged within. She seized her bag from the locker and clutched it to her body as she made it down the stairs without tripping in her heels.

As the bite of evening air lunged at her on the pavement, she sucked it in readily and held it there until she had passed both sides of Glovers and was heading into the backstreets that led downhill to the car park.

Desperate to get home, yet too wired up to move, she held onto the steering wheel motionlessly in the darkness. Then she took off along the beach and the blurring stretch of crystal lights, every so often glancing down at the handbag on her passenger seat.

Twenty-Three

'I can't believe this...' Eric called up the stairs. 'Now she's lost her other sock!'

'OK, well, have you looked under the cushions?' asked Leah from the bedroom as she waited for him to leave the house with Kiki.

'The dog's probably had it. Haven't you?' she heard him say to Twig. 'No, don't start doing your paw. You're not having a...'

Twig barked with excitement.

'Just one biscuit then, boy.'

Leah started to pace at the sound of Eric, rustling around finding dog treats in the kitchen.

'So, do you want another pair of socks or what?' she yelled.

'Might as well.'

She took a pair from Kiki's drawer and lobbed them down the stairs where Eric caught them at the bottom.

'Right, you...' he said, going back into the living room. 'No more kicking them off this time!'

Leaning against the landing wall, she knew she should feel grateful that it was Saturday, and Eric was around to get Kiki ready, but her patience was wearing thin, on top of being drained from yesterday. Tonight, she and Eric would be having a rare dinner out, and Kiki was due to be dropped off with Cheryl and Alan from the start of the day. But it was late morning already and Eric seemed to be in no hurry to get her there.

'Everything else is packed,' said Leah, pulling a face of exasperation that Eric couldn't see. 'So, you're good to go.'

'Nearly ready,' he said, fumbling around with zips and poppers. 'By the way, have we got any stamps? I could post that birthday card for Maddie.'

'Bit early isn't it? There's another two weeks to go.'

'Really?'

'She's our niece, Eric. You should know!'

'Well, you can never predict what the Christmas post is going to be like. Better to be safe than sorry.'

'Fair enough.'

'So… where are the stamps?'

Gritting her teeth, Leah ran down to the kitchen and found the booklet under a pile of junk mail. She slapped a stamp on the envelope and handed it over to Eric.

'Are you OK?' he asked, noticing her tension.

'Of course, I just… thought you'd want to make the most of the day, seeing as Mum's having her.'

'I'm out of here.' He smiled, pecking her on the lips. 'Come on Kiki Koo, let's get you to Nana's!'

As his hands were full, Leah opened the front door and watched them drive away. Then she raced upstairs again, following the trail of Eric's car until it could no longer be seen.

Wasting no time, she pounced on her handbag and tipped out the contents on the carpet until the folded papers emerged from further down. There had been no chance to read them after getting home last night, with the dog walk to do, meals to cook, and another round of coaxing Kiki to take some steps in her boots. Even now,

Eric wouldn't be long, so she only had fifteen minutes at the most.

She sat back against the wardrobe door, separating the pages and counting a total of six complaints.

DATE: 21 November
CUSTOMER NAME: Mae Cole
I bought the SySTEM serum three days ago, but I broke out in blotches. When I asked for a refund, the woman on the counter refused, saying I should try it for longer.

I got quite upset and she laughed, then ignored me to serve someone else. Her name badge said Jocelyn Quigley. I now can't get my money back.

DATE: 28 November
CUSTOMER NAME: Mrs Petula Hicks
Thank you in advance for registering my complaint regarding a Jocelyn Quigley who cornered me when I was shopping for body lotion and pointed to my legs, saying that I needed help for my varicose veins. She ridiculed me and also swore several times. I expected more from your staff and this has put me off coming into Glovers in the future.

DATE: 30 November
CUSTOMER NAME: Mr F Atherton
Please get rid of this vile member of staff. The surname is Quigley and she works in your beauty section. We came in to buy paracetamol as my partner was getting a headache, and we accidentally knocked her display. She shouted her mouth off and told us to look where we were going, then we heard her call us idiots. We're thoroughly dismayed by this.

DATE: 2 December
CUSTOMER NAME: Katia Jopek

Today I was given the worst makeover ever. I booked it at EdenCore to look nice for a christening and left in tears.

I made it clear from the start I couldn't afford to buy much, and that's when the assistant was very aggressive, combing my eyebrows like I'd had an electric shock. I said I didn't want bright lipstick, but she insisted on using a violent orange. My outfit was lemon yellow!

This was witnessed by the lovely lady working at KittyPie, called Kehlani, who told me the woman's name was Jocelyn. I've been in bits all day and felt such a state at the christening. She even slapped my thigh when she was done and told me to get on my way. I just wanted to make you aware of what happened.

DATE: 8 December
CUSTOMER NAME: H Orbach
I am contacting you because my 16-year-old daughter came into your store today with birthday money to spend in the beauty department. She tried to buy a concealer from EdenCore and the person serving her (surname was Quigley and first name apparently started with a J) asked if she realised how much it was.

This Quigley person then followed her around the counter, sneering and giving her dirty looks. My daughter felt like she was being stalked and when she said that she wasn't going to steal anything, the reply was, 'How do I know that?'

So, before I involve your Head Office, I would like to know how you will be dealing with this matter.

The sixth complaint was the most recent and contained the full details of Mrs Kirk's experience, which

Leah knew all too well.

She read each entry in disbelief that all this had gone on since Jocelyn had arrived at Glovers. Dawn must have been incensed when Mrs Kirk had approached her, knowing Jocelyn's growing track record. Surely, there was enough evidence gathered by now for her to proceed with disciplinary action and it would only be a matter of time before Jocelyn got it in the neck.

'I'm back!' Eric chimed.

Leah jumped to her feet, looking for somewhere to hide the papers. She picked up her handbag, but threw it down again, not wanting to risk leaving them in there for the next time she went to work.

A slow thudding ascended the stairs, so she shoved everything into the ottoman between the fresh sheets and duvet covers.

'Hi!' she said merrily, springing out of the bedroom before he reached the doorway.

'Oh…' He smiled but frowned at the same time. 'You seem happier than you were a minute ago.'

'Do I?'

Eric nodded. 'I was just coming up to see if you were OK. You looked hacked off about something, but now suddenly you're…'

'What?'

'Something's going on.'

Leah feigned ignorance. 'Not at all, no, I was…'

'Yes,' he replied firmly. 'You definitely weren't fine twenty minutes ago. Come on, I know you better than this.'

'I told you!' Leah took his hands. 'It was just I was hoping you'd get a move on so we could make the most of the day and you were messing around with Kiki and Twig so…'

'Yeah, and you got a nice lie in!'

'I did. And I appreciated it, but I just wanted to have you to myself.' Leah burrowed into his arms. 'And that's why I've cheered up, because now you're here.'

Eric prised her away slightly so he could look into her eyes. 'You'd tell me, wouldn't you, if there was something on your mind?'

'Yes,' she replied assertively, feeling a flicker of guilt. 'You'd be the first to know.' She polished a smudge on his glasses with her sleeve and tenderly kissed his lips. 'Now, let's get on with our day.'

She snuggled back into his sweatshirt and rested her chin on his shoulder, staring at the wallpaper and hating herself for the dishonesty. But Eric had high morals and was the kind of person who would tell Leah quite bluntly when she was wrong about something. The last thing she needed right now was to be faced with his disapproval that she had trespassed onto a staff computer system and copied strictly confidential information. It was for the best he didn't know what she'd been up to. At least, for now.

***

After tea and cake at the garden centre followed by a look around at the plants and gifts, they came home in the late afternoon and took Twig for his walk. They circled the frosty meadows and meandered around the ancient chalkpit that was overgrown by centuries of foliage and newly garnished with the seasonal flush of berries.

With their gloved hands cosily clamped together, it was a welcome break not to be carrying a wriggling toddler or wrestling with the pushchair over the constant bumpy ground. They just brushed their toes through the coppery fallen leaves, watching the rose-gold chinks of light rippling to platinum as the clouds rolled over them.

Twig dived straight into the dew pond, galloping all around them head to toe in mud, so they hosed him down once back in the garden and headed inside to get ready for the evening.

Fresh out of the shower, Leah went through her clothes and picked out a monochrome jumpsuit she'd never had the chance to wear. She reached even further back into the closet, pulling out a black cardigan dotted with sequins. Clipping back her blow-dried hair, she stared into the mirror at the pile of dramatic makeup that she had laid out on her dressing table, ready for the evening look she hadn't sported for years.

Inching backwards, she stared at her face. Her skin was still glowing from the wintery walk, and her eyes had a brightness that she didn't usually see. She remembered what she had done for Mrs Kirk when she'd last seen her in Glovers. The advice she had sent her away with. *Less is more.*

It was about time she practised what she preached.

Away went the bottle of foundation that caked like cement. The thin tinted moisturiser created a sheer base that gave enough life to her complexion without anything else. She gently shaped her brows, then opted for a wash of neutral eyeshadow with a subtle shimmer instead of her trio of dark metallics. Flicks of mascara framed her eyes, defying the need to glue heavy lashes to her lids. A creamy kiss of blusher worked better than a contour kit, and a smear of nude gloss gave her lips plenty of definition.

She put her jewellery on and gazed back at the magic. All done in half the time and making her feel more youthful than layers of crusty cosmetics ever could.

Eric was waiting downstairs in the living room, lowering the lights and finding a decent TV show to keep

Twig company while they were out.

'I'm ready,' she said, stepping into the room.

'That was quick.' He turned to face her and lit up at the sight. 'And you look… amazing!'

'OK, don't sound so surprised!' she laughed. 'I know you're more used to my mum face these days, but…'

'No, it's not that.'

'Right…' Leah got his meaning. 'It's a bit less than the usual amount of slap I have to wear for work.'

'Exactly, it is. And it's perfect.'

'Good…' She grinned, almost bashfully. 'Love you in that shirt, by the way.' Taking her coat from the stand in the hall, she glanced at the clock. 'Look at that, eh? We've even got an extra half an hour for cocktails. The perks of a quicker makeup routine!'

Flamers Bar & Grill was only a short walking distance from home. It was just after six when they were seated in a booth by the window, with festive white lights dotted all around them and a view across the car park to the desolate recreation ground beyond.

Eric chose a Velvet Elvis cocktail with whisky and raspberry liqueur, while Leah tried a Fluffy Duck, with gin, orange juice, and advocaat.

They ordered the bread platter starter to share, with a selection of olives and dipping oils. As the table flowers flickered in the candlelight, they sipped their drinks and scrolled through the pictures Cheryl had sent them, of everything she and Alan had been doing with Kiki.

First, they'd gone out for a walk in the countryside and stopped for a photo by the stream. There was a teddies' tea party for Kiki and her toys, and in another shot, Alan was holding her up while she stood in the boots with her customary pout. Next was bathtime with her squeezy starfish in a mound of bubbles, and finally the tired tot was all tucked up in bed.

Thoroughly amused, and safe in the knowledge that all was fine, Eric and Leah opted for a wine that would complement his fish and chips, as well as her chilli and ricotta linguine. She sipped the grape-green liquid from the glass, feeling so much lighter and more blissful than she could remember. Knowing how much the two of them had neglected themselves as a couple. How important it was to have time out together in order to cope better with the day to day demands of their lives. She felt lucky to have him, like the rock that he was. Gazing at her now in her new, simple state and still making her feel so precious.

'I haven't been straight with you.'

'Sorry?' Eric chuckled with confusion.

'There's something I haven't said.'

His face clouded over. 'Is this about earlier on?'

Leah nodded.

'I *knew* it. Why didn't you say something before?'

'Because I didn't want you to…'

'Worry?' he asked, tensely rotating the wine glass stem between his finger and thumb.

She let out an audible breath. 'Judge me.'

'Oh, Leah… what's going on?'

'It's work. I'm not in trouble or anything. Well… not yet.'

Eric opened his mouth to speak but Leah cut in again, eager to explain.

'Basically, Jocelyn was rude to one of our customers and I saw the whole thing, so I helped her complain to Dawn on the quiet. Then I heard it wasn't the first incident, and I managed to access the office files where the rest of them were logged. I didn't have time to look at them so… I printed them out.'

'Leah!'

'I know, Eric. I know…' She rested her hand on his

and urged him to stay calm. 'But no one saw anything and I brought them home in my bag.' Looking into his eyes, she bit her lip. 'That's what I was doing this morning. Why I was agitated when you were getting ready. It was because I was trying to read them when I had the chance.'

'But why would you do something like this, Leah? I don't get it. Just… why?'

'Because I needed to know. For my own sanity.'

Eric shook his head, still flummoxed about Leah's motives. 'You have to let it go. This doesn't even concern you.'

'Yes, it does…'

'You care about the customers and that's understandable, but at the end of the day, their grievances aren't your problem. I mean, it's not as if these things are happening to you.'

'They are.'

Dessert arrived as his eyes searched her face, but the waiter splashed the cream which accompanied Leah's warm chocolate brownie. For a few agonising moments, the conversation hung in mid air while cloths and spray were fetched from the kitchen, and a replacement mini jug was placed by the side of her dish.

'Right,' said Eric, once they were alone again. 'Now you can tell me exactly what's going on.'

'She's a total bully,' Leah blurted. 'I can't do anything right. She puts me down, pushes me around and just generally makes life a misery.'

He sat back in his chair, perplexity taking over his expression. 'How long has this been going on?'

'Since she started.'

'And have you confronted her? Told anyone else?'

Leah shook her head. 'I've just been putting up with it, not wanting to make stuff worse. Hoping things would just blow over.' She dragged the cream lazily with her fork in an outline around the square of molten cake. 'But then she started making comments about my weight…'

She glanced tearfully across the table and Eric sat up in his seat, reddening at the collar of his shirt, his eyes sparking in fury.

'What the *hell*?'

'And then…' Leah felt her lower lip quiver beyond control. 'You know when I missed Kiki's boot fitting appointment?'

He nodded slowly, maintaining full eye contact.

'When I just told you I had to work, like I hadn't even tried to change my hours? Well, she refused to swap shifts. And I told her all about it, why I needed to be there. But she still wouldn't let me go. You know why?'

The tears finally escaped, sliding down to her chin. Eric reached for her hand.

'Because she was busy having a bath and laying on her sofa with a face mask.' Leah sniffed, wiping her cheeks with her serviette. 'So, I missed that moment, just to stand in an empty store. I nearly caught my death of cold that night, remember?'

'I sure do,' Eric replied solemnly. 'I just wish you'd said something before. Better still, gone over her head and raised this at HQ.'

'Yes, and can you imagine trying to work with her after doing that? It would only make things worse.' Her eyes met Eric's again. 'And I started there in the first place to pick myself up after everything got so hard with Kiki. I hated the idea of you seeing me fail at something else.'

'Do you not listen to anything I say?' He looked around and lowered his voice. 'You are not a failure.' The last heap of pannacotta was about to topple off his spoon, so he shovelled it into his mouth before the strawberry sauce seeped over the table. 'And you do *not* have to put up with this.'

With pudding finished, the plates were cleared and Eric asked for the bill. Then they set off together in the cold night wind, making their way up the hill towards home. They crossed over the road at the top, where a horizontal avenue took the pressure off their feet and the wispy moon beckoned in the rolling sky.

As they passed under the shadows of an aged tree that hung over the kerb, Eric stopped walking and took her in his arms.

'No more secrets, OK?'

Leah nodded against his lips as they grazed her forehead.

'And promise me that when you're ready, you'll make a formal complaint.'

'I will,' she whispered. 'When the time is right.'

'And if I were you, I'd shred those printouts,' he gazed into her eyes as they glistened in the dark. 'But I totally get why you did it. And until you actually take this thing further, just remember every single word of them, Leah. Just look at her next time she starts on you and think of all those incidents that she doesn't even know you're aware of. That right there is power, even if you don't realise it.'

She walked the rest of the way, sheltered in the warmth of Eric's coat and his reassurance wrapping itself around her. And she hoped she would still feel this strong the next time she set foot on the Glovers shop floor.

Twenty-Four

Jocelyn had already left when Leah started her afternoon shift on Thursday the following week. To her relief, no one had confronted her about being caught on camera in the admin office, so it seemed she was safe in all the knowledge without anything falling back on her.

She had taken Eric's advice and got rid of the printed complaints, throwing them into the garden bonfire they'd lit after cutting the hedges. From now on, she would keep it all at the forefront of her mind, like an undercover armour if ever Jocelyn behaved out of line or made her feel small when they were working together.

Attempting not to dwell on the low points of her job, she put all her energy into planning the big EdenCore event, narrowing down the guestlist and coming up with wording for the invitations. With Jocelyn loading the responsibility on her shoulders and Tiffany hardly ever around to do her share of the duties, Leah relinquished the expectation of help and instead took on the task by herself.

EdenCore Presents: Skin Secrets was scheduled to take place on the Saturday before Christmas. She had already booked the boardroom upstairs and Jocelyn had told her to expect representatives from Head Office to be attending. Jocelyn was apparently too busy to do any of the hard graft, so she had largely left everything up to Leah without being interested in the developments, but her one compulsory demand was that *SySTEM* was promoted to the absolute maximum. Grudgingly, Leah had tried her best to abide by this in her outline of the proceedings, although she had drawn the line at using it on any of the customers.

'Le-Le!' Kehlani sidled over to her affectionately. 'How are you doing, babe? Still putting up with the psycho witch?'

Leah looked up from her sketchy notes, grinning. 'She was in earlier. I haven't seen her today.'

'Luckily!'

She shrugged in agreement, unable to deny the truth in that statement.

'You've got the patience of an angel,' said Kehlani in admiration. 'I'd last about five minutes on the counter with her in my face.'

Leah noted her white plimsolls and the new black and pink uniform fleece. If only EdenCore could take note from KittyPie when it came to keeping their staff warm in winter.

'Well, you know, I just try and ignore it.'

As she smiled back, holding in her thoughts, she remembered that Kehlani's name had been mentioned for helping an offended customer, as detailed in one of the complaints. She could let it all out right now and tell her everything she had discovered in the files, but she knew it wouldn't be wise. Kehlani meant well, but she would soon be blabbing to everyone in sight.

'She's still going after my fan club over here.' She struck an irritated pose and looked instantly like a model, her luscious hair tumbling from the wide pink headband and the matte red of her lips making a striking contrast with her warm skin tone. 'Her days are numbered if she thinks she's keeping that up.'

'Not helped by the fact that something's off about *SySTEM*.' Leah kept her voice down, surveying the beauty hall as she spoke. 'You wouldn't believe the amount of people who have brought it back.'

'So I've heard. What's it even doing, still there on your stand?'

'I have tried so hard to tell her, but she's not interested.'

'What is *wrong* with her?' Kehlani's brows made a pretty shape, even when she frowned. 'She's clearly in some kind of denial.'

'See, this is what I don't get, Keh.' Empowered by her empathy for the customers, Leah began to let her guard down. 'There's people coming in covered in burns and blisters, and she's totally unbothered by it all. I just don't know why she won't let us report it.'

'Oh, I do,' Kehlani said decisively, rubbing her fingers together to indicate money.

Dawn's heels clickety-clacked around the corner as she appeared at the Capital G counter and started talking to the two new assistants.

Leah nodded. 'We should get back to work.'

'Catch you later,' Kehlani started to tiptoe away. 'Don't take any crap, OK?'

Smiling with thanks, Leah retreated behind the counter and tried to look busy. She watched Dawn, unsuspectingly chatting away with her clipboard under her elbow. Guilt flushed through her veins as she thought back to the way she had flipped through it, unlocking secret codes and venturing into unchartered territory on the computer system, and still wondering how she had got away with it.

Dawn soon finished her discussion and headed Leah's way, beaming as she passed by the counter.

Keeping her cool, Leah swallowed, feeling the heat rise in her cheeks and wondering when she would stop feeling so awkward in Dawn's presence.

The phone rang from upstairs with a message that the new Christmas EdenCore posters had just been delivered. Relieved to be stepping away from the limelight of the beauty hall, Leah exited the shop floor and took her time getting all the way to the stockroom. The posters were of various sizes, each contained in cylinder postal tubes. She put them all in a trolley and wheeled them along the corridor, taking a glimpse through the doorway of the office where the cheery waves from the admin staff reassured her that she was in the clear.

Back at the counter, Leah took a stepladder and got herself up on the giant window ledge. It was the only time she was allowed to take her shoes off to avoid any accidents so high up off the ground. She started on the largest posters, using the specially provided adhesive to seal them to the glass.

Working her way into the corners, she unrolled the third one to complete the line and began to press it in place. The streets were busy with shoppers at all angles in their multicoloured swarm of coats, and carrier bags sporting hundreds of logos. But a high pile of distinctive dark hair caught Leah's eye near the clock tower, and then the furry orange collar of a wet-look quilted coat.

Tiffany had both arms fully stacked with shopping, and she walked away down the opposite road with Diane by her side. They were heading towards the Montgomery Quarter, the home of all the designer outlets, so they didn't see Leah in the window and she wondered if Tiffany would even acknowledge her if she did. She wasn't due at work today anyway, but Leah had no doubt that she wouldn't have shown up regardless.

As they disappeared from view, Leah moved on to the smaller posters which were easier to mount at their stations around the counter, and before she had even finished the last one, two ladies approached her to ask about the pictured products.

'Sorry to disturb,' said the one in the paisley scarf. 'I'm just checking out the hand cream you've got advertised here. Is it good?'

'It's actually incredible.' Leah looked at them both as she spoke. 'I've got some here to try if you'd like to.'

'Lovely, thanks.'

Leah took the large tube off the tester stand behind her and flicked open the lid.

'Hang on a minute…' the other woman gasped. '*Palm Oil?*'

'Yes, I know how it sounds.' Leah smiled as they listened intently. 'But there's not actually any palm oil in this.'

'Then why…?'

'Palm, because it's a hand cream.'

Both ladies were amused once they understood the meaning.

'And also, its main ingredient is dates. They're really nourishing for the skin on our hands, especially with all the wear and tear they go through on a daily basis. May I?' she asked, gesturing for them to try an application.

'I'm intrigued,' said the first lady as Leah massaged a smear into her hand and did the same for her companion.

'Doesn't it feel so soothing?'

'Oh, I do like this, Val,' she said, glancing approvingly at her friend. 'And you're doing it in sets, did you say?'

'We are,' Leah replied. 'So you get a large *Palm Oil* with travel size foot scrub and lotion, starting from today.'

'We'll have one each.' Val opened her handbag. 'I'll

treat you, Shirl.'

'Oh, bless you!'

'In fact, I'll get another three for my cousins.'

Leah took the gift sets to the till and put them into a large bag. 'I'll throw in samples for all of them, too,' she said. 'Mini nail polish, cuticle cream, and toner.'

'Perfect,' said Val as she paid. 'Thank you so much for the wonderful service.'

'My pleasure.' Leah beamed and handed them their purchases. 'And do come back and see me if there's anything else I can help you with.'

Once they had gone, Leah finished off the display, stacking up the promotional sets to make the most of the fancy boxes. People were stopping to admire her work, picking up the products to see what was included, and a further five were snapped up in the space of an hour.

She added the sales to her sheet and felt a rush of pride. She did so much better with the customers when no one was around to assess her. Without the pushy sales techniques and the robotic rulebook of cheesy lines, she could do just fine in her own way when she wasn't under the pressure of being watched.

'Leah!'

She looked up from the tablet and came face to face with Tiffany, her teeth gleaming a plasticky white between her plumped terracotta lips. Her arms were laden with even more bags than before, and her face was stiffer than Leah had ever seen.

'Tiffany.' Leah responded with the ghost of a smile, but that was as much as she would give. 'And Diane,' she said, with slightly more warmth. 'It's been a while.'

'Keeping well?' Diane replied.

'Not bad.' Another smile. And no eye contact with Tiffany.

'I'm off to Barbados!' Tiffany shrieked, making

people stare as they browsed the other counters. 'Then we're only back for a week before we're jetting away to Dubai.'

Leah nodded, waiting for the inevitable apology. But it didn't seem to be on the cards.

'And how's the car?' she asked, wondering if that would that jog her memory.

'Drives like a dream!' Tiffany looked up at the ceiling. 'I literally turn heads wherever I go.'

'Good.' Leah remained straight-faced and there was an uncomfortable pause. 'Anyway, I'd better get on. Nice to see you both.'

'Just one more thing…' Diane opened a carrier bag in readiness. 'Got any samples?'

'Afraid not.' Leah folded her arms. 'We're running out, and I have to keep what's left for our promo sales.'

They eyed each other as the penny dropped at the shift in Leah's attitude.

'We'll be off then,' Tiffany said. 'I've got so much to get for the holidays.' They began to walk away, but she hesitated, patting her pockets and looking around the floor. 'Mum, what did I do with my shopping list?'

'I've got it, remember? You gave it to me.'

'Remind me what I still need to get then.'

Diane unfolded the scrap of notepaper and took a minute to read Tiffany's handwriting, before bursting into a loud cackle that almost silenced the beauty hall. 'More Botox? You've only just had a top up!'

A hush fell over the counters as one by one, her colleagues' activities ground to a sudden halt. Leah glanced at Tiffany, cowering on the spot, and turning hot pink around the jaw with instant mortification.

Tiffany stomped up to Diane and snatched the list in a rage. 'DE-tox, Mum,' she hissed. 'They're capsules from the vitamin aisle.'

Neither of them looked at Leah again or said goodbye before vanishing out of the store, not even to stop for the supplements. Tiffany kept her head down, shooting off ahead of Diane who was still sniggering obliviously as she scuttled along behind.

Leah quietly observed the stunned chatter all around her. The whispers on the fragrance counter, and Taeng snickering away with the girls at Capital G. She went to polish the testers, skimming over the *SySTEM*, still there on the throne as the star of the show. Making sure the cleansers and toners were gleaming in their hues of green and peach, she moved on to the age-defining skincare ranges, pausing as she dusted off *The Lift*, for the over-forties. The one Tiffany had sworn by as the source of her seamless skin.

All at once, a new thought overcame her. The glow of no longer feeling inferior. The truth was that nothing in a bottle or jar could ever give anyone the airbrushed skin of dreams, like all the adverts and promises.

She remembered what Eric had said about taking pride in her body. The same applied to every crease and blemish on her face. They were the evidence of her laughter and all her joyful memories. Of her tension and anguish during the times of hardship, where her one goal had only ever been to see Kiki happy – throughout which she had never given up on her. They were days in the sunshine, and cold winter walks. Concentration at college and work, launching her into her career as a journalist. Passion and sympathy, sadness and hope. They told the story of her life and who she was.

Too long had been spent feeling inadequate around people who lied to sell natural products, all while doing the exact opposite to enhance their own skin.

She had been fooled, just like the customers. And it was time to make a change.

Twenty-Five

Yoga the following week was a welcome interruption from everything that was unravelling at EdenCore. This was truly a place where women came together freely in their own skin, raw and unjudged. Where mum tums and tired eyes were almost like a membership card, and the calmness eased Leah's mind from the moment the lights dimmed and the rainforest echoes filtered through her limbs.

She and Tess had sat together since they'd met the first time after class. Kiki and Henry would stare at each other, the babbled notes of conversation going back and fourth between them. If one started crying, it would inevitably set the other off, but double the crankiness was a nightmare halved, as it only served to remind Leah that she wasn't alone.

As the session drew to a close, Leah and the other parents copied Cassie as she instructed them to support their little ones in a standing position. Every week, she was feeling a difference, with Kiki balancing stronger on her feet each time. The boots, which were being used as often as possible, didn't seem to bother Kiki like they had at first, and this barefoot exercise showed the progress she was making without their help.

'Well done!' Leah whispered. 'Not even any tears yet today.'

'Oh, I can reassure you, there's still time,' Tess said under her breath, trying to keep Henry upright without being kicked in the ribs.

They both sniggered silently, so as not to disturb the rest of the room and gave each other a look of relief when they were finally allowed to place the tots back down on the mats.

On Tess's other side was her friend, Darcie, who she'd been shopping with in Glovers when Leah had met them for the first time. She'd been coming along with her daughter, Cleo, for a couple of weeks and had hit it off equally well with Leah. Right now, she was scrabbling around trying to find a wet wipe before the spillage of Cleo's drink reached the cloth drawstring bag of the person in front of them.

Leah grabbed some from Kiki's stash and flung them across to Darcie, who contorted her body in a cumbersome pose, trying to stay in position while clutching them from her as quickly as she could.

'Lifesaver!' she whispered, feigning a dramatic sigh of relief. 'Can't take this kid anywhere!'

Next, they all transitioned into a more relaxed state, lying flat on their backs and pointing their babies' legs into the darkness, counting the stars with the movement of their toes. Cleo tried to wriggle away, wailing out in a grumpy protest and inadvertently stabbing Darcie's eye with her fingertip, while Kiki watched on in an ironically peaceful trance.

'And slowly come up into a comfortable sit now, crossing those legs with the little ones on your laps,' commanded Cassie in her stripy purple leotard and jogging bottoms. 'I know you like this bit, so stretch that left arm out at your side, arch it over your head…' her voice went up an octave as she followed through with the action, 'and paint the rainbow.'

The others did the same as if Cassie's motion was being reflected in a lake. First the adults on their own, and then repeating the action with the young ones.

'Yes, wonderful! Look at all those perfect rainbows out there. Let's keep them in place for just a few more seconds.'

'Henry's such a pro at that,' mused Tess with a dreamy look lingering across her face. 'He just does it on his own at home now, no help needed from me.'

'Aren't you such a clever boy?' Leah grinned at him and glanced back up to Tess's level. 'Doing it all by yourself!'

'Oh, yeah. Orange juice in one hand, broccoli pasta in the other and he just smears it up the wall. That's his idea of a rainbow.'

The mock serenity of her facial expression made Darcie and Leah shake with laughter, all while counting the seconds until they could complete the mirroring move on their right-hand sides.

To finish, it was time to lie down again, torsos and limbs fully rested on the mats with the babies lying beside them. The minutes surged onwards, swirls and beach waves sketching imaginary shapes in Leah's vision while her eyelids fluttered closed. This moment was always gratefully received. Respite from all the stretching, and a few precious seconds to cleanse the mind before continuing with her day. The dappled lighting had become a mere haze, and she felt as if she could levitate on the kiss of breeze that the music left in its trail.

A slightly agitated murmur warbled at Leah's side. Then a louder yowl of sheer indignation, which made her instantly cross at the disturbance. She tried to ignore Kiki, holding on to those last few snatched minutes, and refusing to let her ruin it. There'd be all the time in the world for the meltdown to resume once the class ended.

'Cleo!' Darcie shrieked under her breath. 'What are you doing?'

Leah opened her eyes to see Darcie upright, trying to unclamp Cleo's hand from around Kiki's wrist. She had slithered over and pulled her sideways, and now Henry had sprawled on top of them both, squawking energetically while the girls howled from underneath.

Tess was the last to snap back into the room, but she wasted no time in hauling Henry off the others, distracting him with Theo-saurus, his electronic wordy dinosaur toy, while starting to pack up her bags.

Cassie brought proceedings to a close and everyone shuffled around gathering their belongings and flattening the mats into tidy portable rolls. The two baby girls were still engaging in gobbledegook conversation, and their mums listened with growing intrigue.

'Do you think they're talking about the weather?' asked Leah.

'Nope,' Tess replied with a deadpan face. 'They've painted enough rainbows for one day. This definitely looks like something more in-depth.'

'I knew it.' Darcie swallowed, looking deliberately doomed. 'They're plotting our murder for bringing them to this boring yoga class.'

Leah shrugged helplessly. 'We've only got ourselves to blame, I guess. Forcing them in here and stretching them around like bits of plasticine.'

The three of them burst into laughter as they slung everything onto their backs, and each picked up their most important bundles, then headed out into the main part of Ropeshore Community Hub. As the rest of the parents left to go home, the three friends made their way to the café.

There was a central play area for babies and toddlers, where adults could relax and chat amongst themselves while staying close at hand to watch their offspring. It was completely soft-walled, accident proof and, provided it didn't get too crowded, was a totally safe place to let them explore.

Darcie put Cleo down first and she immediately started to crawl, reaching out for the crinkly bunting and enjoying a tumble, safe against the sponge. Henry wailed and stayed where he was, but with a little help from Tess, he was soon on the move.

Leah was hesitant as she brought Kiki to join them. Here was where the differences would show. Where the other two would leave her behind as they beetled around while she couldn't join them.

There was a little comfy seat in the corner with winged cushions for full support. She placed Kiki inside, not expecting she would last thirty seconds. Leah hovered, and Kiki looked up at her, the telltale frown forming as she began to kick her legs, but as her feet batted against squeaking pads and squishy blobs of fabric, her pretty eyes blinked in wonder, and she was transfixed on her buddies as they capered around in the pen.

Taking a seat at the table on the edge, Leah was in near disbelief, but she couldn't soak up the moment just yet. It was too surreal. Usually, she'd be making herself scarce and running a mile from a place like this before Kiki's hair-raising screams started shattering everyone's glasses.

'Here you are girls…' Tess returned from the coffee bar with an overladen tray. 'Three macchiatos, three snowball truffles, and three gingerbread men for the little brats.' She smiled unashamedly as she dished everything out, and the others giggled at her words.

'Thank you so much,' said Leah, feeling extra

comfort as she inhaled the milky steam.

'You're more than welcome.'

'Cheers, dear.' Darcie winked, taking a careful sip and craning her neck to keep an eye on the action in the pen.

Cleo scuffed past Henry, squashing his cheek against a cushion and his trickle of a whimper escalated rapidly, like a cacophony of musical scales. Tess went straight over to soothe him, but instead of picking him up, she persisted in encouraging him to stay there, clapping as he hitched himself back up and jiggled along on all fours again. Leah observed her unflustered face and how nonchalant she was that he'd made a scene. If that had been Kiki, she knew she'd be hunched over at the sound of the racket and feeling sorry for the people all around her, whose quiet coffee breaks Kiki would have been wrecking.

Or at least she would have reacted that way up until now.

'Hello, Kiki!' Tess said brightly while she was still down on the ground with the babies. 'Want to play with Mr Camel?' She reached for the furry toy and danced it in the air to get her attention before placing it in her lap. Kiki held it by a leg and shouted something animatedly back at Tess, which piqued Cleo's interest and led her over to sit by Kiki's side, taking another leg. Together, they seemed to start a game of pulling it to and fro, so Tess decided to leave them while occupied.

'I see Henry's OK now, bless him,' said Leah.

'He's all good.' Tess clenched her teeth as she sat back at the table and gestured over to the three baby friends. 'But now Kiki's got the hump.'

They giggled into their coffees, watching Kiki keeping a tight grip on the toy as Cleo seized the tail.

'Seriously, she's doing really well today, isn't she? Are you sure she's as troublesome as you've been making out?'

Leah clocked Tess's raised eyebrow of doubt and happily acknowledged that she was indeed behaving herself.

'Let's just say, it isn't too drastic so far. I'm not sure she'd be quite as chilled if the other two weren't here to amuse her.'

'Well just shout if you think Cleo's too full on with her,' said Darcie, pushing a strand of her strawberry-blonde hair back into her ponytail band. 'She's a control freak for someone who's only fourteen months old!'

'It's fine,' Leah waved a dismissive hand. 'Anything to keep her occupied.'

'Got to get going in about five minutes anyway, so at least Kiki can have the camel to herself soon. Just off into town to get some bath treats for my sister's Christmas present.'

'You should go to EdenCore,' Tess suggested. 'Maybe Leah could do mates' rates.'

'I really wouldn't if I were you.'

Leah could feel their surprise at her words as they both waited for more.

'I mean, the products might be harmful…. In fact, they *are* harmful.'

'What are you saying?' Tess folded her arms, not taking her eyes off Leah.

'Well, it's the customers. They're bringing stuff back left, right and centre, breaking out in rashes and blisters…' she lowered her voice. 'It's getting out of control.'

'You're kidding,' Darcie said, frowning. 'Do you know what's actually doing it?'

'I can't be sure. But it looks like it's the serum. The one in the big flower stem bottle?'

'Of course, there's always the possibility that people

are making excuses for wanting their money back. They could just be having you on.'

Leah shook her head.

'It happened to me, too. My face swelled up like a balloon.'

The two friends were open-mouthed.

'So, what's your boss doing about it?' Darcie asked. 'Obviously you can't sell it anymore.'

'Nothing.' Leah glanced away, already knowing they both looked horrified. 'I've tried to talk to her but… she won't let me tell Head Office and to make it worse, she's still using it on people.'

'Are you actually joking?' Tess shrieked under her breath. 'How can someone do that just for the sake of the money?'

'And the power.'

Leah knew she looked wounded, and by their reactions she was giving more away than she realised.

Darcie squinted suspiciously. 'Is she the one we saw when you served us that time?'

'Sure is,' replied Leah, with sadness in her voice. 'Jocelyn.'

'She was bloody rude to us,' Tess recalled. 'Wouldn't put all our shopping through the till and she called the kids runts.'

'Oh, she can't stand children. Goes out of her way to stop me being around for Kiki.'

It was hard to utter her thoughts out loud, and Leah knew she would have to stop soon, before she said too much or ended up bursting into tears.

'Leah, this is terrible. I'm fuming for you.'

'Me too,' Tess squeezed her hand. 'Hey, Darcie, let's go in there and let rip at her. Tell her what we think of her crappy attitude.'

'I'm up for it,' Darcie nodded. 'You just say the word,

girl!'

'Thanks guys,' Leah whispered, warming up inside and feeling grateful for their support. 'I might just hold you to that!'

The babies were getting irritable now, rubbing their eyes and looking at their mothers. Leah was the first to lean in, plucking Kiki up in her arms and putting her in the pushchair.

'I can hear you, Henry…' Tess swivelled around as his whinging went up a notch. 'You don't have to tell the entire café, lad.'

She and Darcie got packed up too and they all made their way to the car park.

'My shout next week,' Darcie winked. 'Because, you know… we need to make sure we refuel properly after all that exercise, don't you think?'

'Too right!' chimed Tess.

'See you then,' Leah beamed, turning away to grapple with her keys. 'And thanks, both of you, for letting me offload.'

'Anytime.'

They both smiled back, tossing baggage into their cars.

'Just remember not to put up with the bullshit,' Tess reminded her. 'Or she'll have us to deal with.'

Leah thanked them again, then stayed in her parking space, watching as the two of them drove separately off down the high street. And although the very idea was far-fetched and hilarious, she couldn't help feeling tempted to take them up on their offer.

Twenty-Six

Another morning with the counter to herself and Leah was making the most of every minute. She had stopped expecting Tiffany to show up, no longer feeling left out on a limb if there was no sign of her on the days she was scheduled to be there.

Instead, she focused on giving the best customer service possible, be it at EdenCore or anywhere else in the store. It was as if she wanted to give back to the people Jocelyn had refused to serve or who had been made to feel like outcasts for their budgets or blemishes.

She had made some decent sales by ten-thirty and the makeup gift sets were flying off the shelves, but when a woman and her teenage daughter came by to ask for acne-prone skin treatments, Leah took them into the main Glovers beauty aisles and stopped at Polkadotz, a bright green skincare range that had taken social media by storm.

EdenCore had lightweight products for oily skin, but nothing that treated the breakouts and spots. Polkadotz, in comparison, had facial tonic, a roller pen, and a tiny tube of on-the-go gel that blitzed away redness and created a base for concealer. It was a no brainer to talk them through these items, particularly as they were all on special offer.

Dawn observed her, putting the young girl at ease and showing a strong knowledge of other brands without sticking to EdenCore for the sake of her commission. She smiled admiringly as she passed Leah on her way to rearrange the deodorant shelves.

Leading the customers back to the counter while carrying everything they had selected, she put their shopping through the till, including samples of *HeartBeet* fragrance and a free tube of miniature mascara.

Just as the transaction completed, Jocelyn arrived to start her shift and Leah passed over the bag to the daughter, relieved the contents were out of sight before she got it in the neck for promoting a different brand.

'Sold much, then?' Jocelyn asked as the shoppers exited the store.

'It's actually been quite steady. Good on the giftsets.'

Jocelyn signed into the tablet and called up Leah's sales sheet, looking somewhat unamused as she scrolled down the page. Leah tried to make herself look busy, cringing inwardly through the silence of having her performance checked, but at least Jocelyn was taking a while to look through it all, which just went to show what a busy morning it had been.

'OK, I can see you've had a decent amount of customers.'

'There's only two lip duos left, thanks to the *Poinsettia Pout* working its magic. Although, one person did prefer the *Snowflake Smooch*.' Leah grinned as she neatened up the promotional stands. 'I'll go up in a minute and get some more stock.'

'The problem is...' Jocelyn cut in. 'There's no upselling, luvvie. One item per sale is just not good enough.' She banged her hand on the counter, repeatedly to emphasize the last three words. Leah felt her face flush.

'It looks like a lot of singles, I know. But most of those were the gift sets and people only wanted one.'

'And the serums,' continued Jocelyn as if she hadn't heard Leah, 'I don't see one *SySTEM* sold so far today.'

'I really can't do that,' Leah replied decisively.

Jocelyn looked up, her lower lip gaping.

'It's not right.' She took a step towards her. 'I'm sorry, Jocelyn, but I just don't feel comfortable recommending it to people when we know there's something wrong with it.'

'This again.' Jocelyn put her hands on her hips, glaring up at the ceiling.

'But all those people on that thread I showed you. The box under this till. These are all customers who have had the most awful reactions.'

'Get it into your head. It's not your problem.'

'Yes, it is!'

There was silence. Just Jocelyn waiting for an apology and Leah stunned that she'd raised her own voice.

'What I mean is… it's happened to me. My face was so swollen, I could barely see my feet and there was hardly any point in trying to cover it up with makeup…'

'Speaking of which,' Jocelyn came intimidatingly close, nostrils flaring as she inspected Leah. 'Why are you hardly wearing any?'

Leah snatched a glimpse into the mirror behind Jocelyn. There was nothing wrong with how she looked today. She had deliberately played down the eye makeup to show off the new kohl pencils, and the *Poinsettia Pout* was such a strong red that her sheer tinted moisturiser had been enough to complement it.

'Well, I just feel better without it trowelled on. I don't feel like myself if I'm wearing it like a mask.'

'You know you're supposed to have at least twenty

products on at all times.'

Leah shook her head. 'But I always make an effort. I'd never come in looking scruffy.'

Jocelyn suppressed a laugh. 'Sorry, but you look…'

'Radiant… and impeccable,' Dawn said proudly as she reached the counter and beamed at Leah. 'That's what I've just had a customer say about you.'

'Really?' Glee enlivened Leah's soul as Dawn's words sank in with genuine surprise.

'You were with a lady earlier and her daughter. You showed them the Polkadotz?'

Jocelyn's face was like thunder at the revelation that Leah had strayed from recommending EdenCore.

'I did.' Leah glanced at her. 'We didn't have what they needed here.'

'Anyway, they came up to me singing your praises. Said you did an amazing job, and they wanted to pass on their thanks.'

'That's really nice to hear. It means a lot.'

She couldn't help feeling slightly smug about the timing.

'You're an asset, darling. That's what you are,' Dawn said proudly.

'Well, I don't know about that, but…'

'And so modest too!' Dawn checked her watch. 'Sorry sweetie, I'm taking up your lunchbreak.'

'No, it's fine. Thanks for telling me!'

Leah started to walk away, past a beaming Kehlani who had overheard the conversation.

'You do look gorgeous today, by the way,' Dawn called after her. 'That smoky kohl is stunning on your eyes and those shoes make your legs go on forever!'

She shot Dawn a thankful grin and made her way up the staircase, deciding to do something different rather than sit in the draughty canteen. Having spent weeks of watching people shopping in their droves, she headed out to become one of them, at least just for an hour.

The sky promised darkness by the late afternoon and she walked briskly in her winter coat, feeling the sleet flicking against her skin. She wove her way around the wooden market stalls lined with colourful light bulbs, and mulled spices oozing from a large vat of punch. There were teddy bears in Santa suits and confectionary in traditional tins. Handmade tree ornaments and wax rounds of locally crafted cheese. Peppermint candy wrapped in retro packaging, and cones of hot chocolate mix with sprinkles and marshmallows.

A ballerina doll caught her eye, with pearls clustered in her hair, and her waist bedecked in wispy layers of glittering white. Perhaps if Kiki played with it and held it in her hands, she would want to try and stand on her feet so she could dance in a pretty dress. She paid the money, watching the vendor shroud it in paper and place it delicately in a box.

There was just time for a quick bite to eat before she walked back to Glovers and put the shopping in her locker. She combed her windswept hair and touched up her makeup before heading to the counter for the last part of her shift.

Jocelyn was stood at the front of the tester stand, arms folded and not looking busy. She didn't move or acknowledge Leah as she came towards her. But the face said it all. The irritated and dismissive glance when Leah said hello. Perhaps it was the earlier discussion about *SySTEM* or Dawn's glowing compliments when Jocelyn had been trying to criticise her.

'I need a word.'

Leah nodded, listening openly.

'Not here. Follow me.'

Jocelyn led her into a dingey room – the only space

on the shop floor where the beauty therapists could carry out body massages. There was nothing but a worktop and the treatment table which took up most of the space. No décor or music to soften the mood. It was a wonder any customers paid for it.

'You'll have to sit over there,' Jocelyn directed, so Leah perched on a tall chair, with nothing to lean on but the bed.

Leah watched her thumbing through some papers. This was probably something to do with the VIP event. Just a few checks that the plans were coming together. But why then had she needed to be taken off the counter?

'Now… I didn't want to do this.' Jocelyn pursed her lips and looked gravely down at the forms. 'But I'm going to have to start disciplinary action.'

Leah's nodding slowed as the words hit home.

'Sorry?'

'Company policy,' said Jocelyn, clicking her knuckles in Leah's face. 'You see, your absence is becoming a problem.'

Leah's chair toppled slightly and she put out a foot to steady herself. 'My absence?' She stared at Jocelyn, whose lips toyed with a smile. '*What* absence.'

'Well, let's see, shall we…' She perused the papers in front of her. 'Starting back in October when you signed in four minutes late.'

'But there was a three-lorry crash on the Ropeshore bypass. It was absolutely gridlocked.'

Jocelyn wasn't listening.

'Next, beginning of November. You were so late, you only made it in for half your shift.'

Trying to hold it together, Leah racked her brains. 'Kiki's ear infection,' she said. 'But that was when I'd phoned up to say I couldn't come in at all that day. Then

Eric managed to get out of his meeting, and I got here anyway.'

'Still an absence.'

'But I wasn't going to be in at all. My daughter was ill! You can see the prescription. I've still got a record.'

'Moving on,' Jocelyn almost shouted. 'This morning.'

Leah shook her head, confused. 'I don't understand. I've been here since nine and I…'

'Just thought you'd leave the counter to sell our customers a totally different brand of skincare!'

'Because we don't make anything that treats acne.'

'*The Hit* would have done. It's our youngest range.'

'But that isn't going to target the spots themselves.' Leah felt like her blood would overboil. 'And I was still here, working as usual. Surely that can't be classed as an absence.'

'Too late!' Jocelyn scribbled something down on the third row of the form. 'And if you're not where you should be, that's an absence as far as EdenCore is concerned.'

'But Dawn says…'

'I don't give a flying monkeys what Dawn says. You're here to work for *me*.'

'But I have been! I'm here even earlier than my start time each day, I've not been off sick once. I haven't even taken any holiday since I started.'

'Sorry, luvvie. Rules are rules.' Jocelyn pinched her mouth tight as she planted a signature at the bottom of the page. 'If an employee is absent on three different occasions, then the line manager must report the incidents to Head Office. Oh, and I just need a statement from you about how you're going to avoid this happening again in the future.'

'No…' Leah shook her head. This had to be a joke. 'Why do I need to make a statement? It was a one-off vehicle crash, and one other time when I had to look after my daughter. Is there no compassion for that? Am I not entitled to any understanding because I have a young child?'

'I'll be ringing this through to Head Office before I leave today.' Jocelyn clicked the pen nib defiantly. 'They'll be very interested to hear that you refused to make a statement.'

'And the third thing…' Leah nearly choked. 'I was here on the shop floor. Serving a customer!'

Jocelyn sneered. 'Wait until they hear what you got up to. Polkadotz indeed.'

She slapped the notebook shut, enclosing the report between the wedges of lined paper.

'You're free to go.'

Leah slid down from the chair and reached for the door handle.

'OK, hang on.' She turned around on impulse and suddenly stood up straight. 'Rules are rules, right?'

'Got it in one, luvvie.'

'So, I assume I'm not the only one being reported to Head Office for absence.'

Jocelyn met her eyes with a glare, then looked away.

'If you're registering a formal complaint about me for not being here when I should be…' Leah continued, 'then surely, I mean… *surely*… you're going to do the same for…'

'If you mean Tiffany, I don't think that's any concern of yours.'

'She's turned up once in the last month!' Leah hissed.

There was silence as Jocelyn started to turn off the lights.

'So, I'm asking you, Jocelyn…' Leah inhaled slowly, ready to blow her fuse at the wrong answer. 'Are you reporting Tiffany to Head Office?'

'That's a totally different situation,' Jocelyn mumbled. 'She's the face of our counter and I'm not having her upset.'

Leah blocked the exit with her shoulder, the injustice making her brain feel like it could burst.

'Why are you doing this to me?' she asked, struggling to breathe as her eyes clouded in watery pools.

'I've told you.' Her face couldn't have got closer to Leah's, her eyes narrowing in the mustiness of the lamplight. 'You're letting the team down, *luvvie*. And it's about time something was done about it.'

She yanked the door, whacking it deliberately into Leah's back and jolting her out of the way. Then Leah was on her own in the room, bent double over the treatment bed, her spine bruising from the blow, and her tears making wet stains on the murky white towel.

Her muffled panting must have drowned out the sound of the latch, as two hands on her arms were the first sign someone was with her.

'Leah, what the hell happened, darling?' Taeng's soft accent sounded in her ear. She pulled Leah to face her, alarm filling her eyes when she saw the tears. 'It's her, right? What's she done?'

'Where is she?' Leah couldn't look at her.

'It's OK. She's gone off upstairs.'

'She's reporting me.'

Taeng held her at arm's length and gave her a questioning look. 'Reporting… what?'

'Me. For always being absent.'

'But… what? I don't get this. Why?'

'When I got stuck in roadworks on the way here a couple of months ago. Then when Kiki was unwell. Oh, and because this morning I was off counter for a while, showing some customers a different skincare range because we didn't have what they needed.'

'No way.' Taeng shook her head. 'This is ridiculous.'

She booted the door open a crack and signalled as discreetly as she could. Within seconds, Kehlani arrived, and her smile quickly faded as Taeng shut her inside, bolting the door behind her so no one else could enter.

'Has she started on you again?'

Kehlani looked horrified to see the state of Leah, a fierceness sparking in her eyes.

'You're just never going to guess,' said Taeng. 'She's starting a disciplinary procedure at Head Office against Leah for apparently failing to turn up for work.'

'OK, just… what am I actually hearing?'

'Because of some road accident and another time when Kiki wasn't very well.' Taeng shrugged her shoulders and met Kehlani's shock knowingly.

'Oh, this is bullshit, Leah. She can't seriously do that.

'I also got praised this morning by Dawn for helping this young girl find a good range for acne.'

'Clearly Polkadotz because that's just the obvious choice.' Kehlani handed her some fresh tissues from her KittyPie apron pocket.

'So, Jocelyn's reporting me for that too, because I was away from the counter.'

Kehlani's frosted lips widened to a perfect round. Then she laughed out loud at the absurdity of it all before resuming her incensed expression.

'I take it Tiffany is far from off the hook then. Or is there some kind of warped allowance for never bothering to show up?'

Leah sobbed on Kehlani's shoulder while she embraced her in a hug.

'I mentioned all this, but she's fine about Tiffany. Said something about her being the face of the brand that no one can upset.'

'Oh… my… OK,' Kehlani released Leah and look

straight at her shrivelled face. 'You're not putting up with this shit. Enough is enough, honey. You've got to report her, and now, before she does it to you.'

'I can't,' said Leah hopelessly. 'It will make everything worse. My word against hers, you know how it goes.'

Kehlani and Taeng looked at each other and a deep hush filled the room. Slowly, Taeng nodded, and Kehlani knew she had the go ahead.

'It doesn't have to be,' Kehlani reduced her voice to a whisper. 'You see, she's been up to no good for a while now and… well, we started sneaking our phones down here a few weeks ago. Neither of us can believe the stuff she's been doing. One glimpse of our footage by a manager and it won't be you facing a disciplinary, love.'

'We can upload it all for you tonight and you can send it straight to HQ,' Taeng offered. 'Just do it, Leah. Before she makes your life even more of a misery.'

Leah took a minute to consider their suggestion, knowing it could give her the power to finish off Jocelyn for good. But what if it didn't? What if instead, Taeng and Kehlani found themselves in the firing line for filming Jocelyn when they shouldn't even have been in possession of their phones?

'Girls, it's really kind and I won't tell anyone, but no. I can't do something like this right now. I can't risk everything blowing up.'

'Fair enough.' Kehlani wasn't going to pressure her, especially while she was so distraught. 'But think about it.'

'I'm going to get out of here now,' Leah replied. 'My shift's done so I won't go back to the counter. I just want to be as far away from her as possible and if Head Office are on my case tomorrow, then I'll just have to deal with it in my own way.'

'Yes, you do that.' Taeng enfolded her once again.

'Just get yourself away while she's not around.'

'I really appreciate it,' she tried to smile. 'And I'll let you know what happens.'

A second later, she was racing upstairs, her head down so no one saw the tear stains. She stumbled into her locker and threw on her coat before picking up Kiki's ballerina doll and taking the back way out from the side of the warehouse to ensure she wasn't going to bump into Jocelyn.

She had meant what she'd said to Kehlani and Taeng, that she couldn't face sending their footage to Head Office for fear of the repercussions. But that didn't mean she was going to do nothing.

Because no sooner would HQ be putting the phone down on Jocelyn tonight, having received her complaint about Leah, they would be launching an investigation on Jocelyn Quigley herself. And there were far worse reasons than absence to report her for. Misconduct, for example.

Twenty-Seven

'Hello there, am I speaking to Leah Frost?'

'Good morning,' Leah answered politely, having recognised the number on her phone as the EdenCore Head Office in London. 'Yes, you are.'

'Leah, this is Sindy Galvin speaking. I'm calling from the HR department at EdenCore regarding your complaint against Jocelyn Quigley.'

Kiki let out a loud wail, so Leah tossed her a handful of toys and closed her securely behind the gate before leaping down the corridor and shutting herself in the bedroom.

'Hi, thank you for getting back to me.'

She turned on the baby monitor to keep her eye on Kiki, who was now occupied with a book, and safely propped up by floor cushions in the corner of the nursery.

'No problem at all,' Sindy said in a sympathetic voice. 'I'm just ringing to confirm that we are looking into your grievance, and I want to reassure you that we take complaints of misconduct very seriously.'

'Thank you. I'm sorry it has come to this.'

'There's no need for you to apologise. Indeed, we would never expect our staff to feel that they can't approach us with any issues. Our priority is to ensure that every colleague – including managers and senior members – adhere to our values and set an example to those under their care.'

'That's good, I really appreciate your time,' Leah said.

'You may not hear anything for a week or two, but please feel safe in the knowledge that we are assessing your case, and we will be back in touch as the investigation gets underway.'

'OK. Can I just ask... does she know yet?' She wriggled into her EdenCore blazer with the phone perched on her shoulder. 'That I have complained, I mean. It's just... not exactly going to be easy on the counter in the meantime if she is aware.'

'Miss Quigley has not been contacted,' Sindy replied. 'But we will obviously need to inform her in the near future.'

Leah's eyes closed in dread, just imagining how tense things would be, just going about her business in Jocelyn's company for three hours at a time, once she had received word of Leah's complaint.

'Of course. I guess I'll just have to cross that bridge when it comes to it.'

'Would you like any counselling or emotional support, Leah? Every employee is entitled to it.'

'No... no thank you, I'll just see how things go and perhaps it's something I might consider further down the line.'

Or probably never, she thought, having zero confidence in anyone trying to calm her nerves or, worse still, come up with techniques she could adopt in order to maintain an amicable relationship with someone like Jocelyn.

'And please don't hesitate to contact us again if anything else happens or if you feel there's extra information you'd like us to be aware of.'

'I will.'

Kiki was waving her arms around now, having had enough of her book. Leah needed to end the call before her voice was lost in the commotion of a tantrum.

'Thanks again for looking into this. I'll wait to hear from you.'

'Take care of yourself and we'll be in touch.'

Sindy said goodbye and Leah was relieved to hit the cancel button before the perils of her private life screeched out on loudspeaker all over HQ.

Flinging open her bedroom door, she lifted Kiki off the mat and grabbed her changing bag on the way downstairs. She turned off the TV Eric had left on at breakfast and, at last, she opened the front door with Kiki and the baggage in tow. She stopped halfway down the steps, noticing a dribble of Kiki's toothpaste blobbed across her lapel.

She put everything in the car and strapped Kiki into her seat, then hurried back into the kitchen to wipe away the stain. Then her phone buzzed with a message in her pocket and she glanced at the clock, knowing she didn't have time to check it.

Driving straight off through the busy morning traffic, she reached Cheryl's house in the nick of time, but panic overcame her at the sight of the empty driveway. She reached for her phone to ring Cheryl and clicked on the message that she'd been in too much of a rush to read.

A poor man has had a fall at the corner shop. We're waiting with him for the ambulance so won't be home when you get there. We'll be as quick as we can. x

Leah sank back into the car, knotting her hands together and counting the minutes until Cheryl and Alan returned. Of course, this couldn't be helped and anyone would do the same. But she only had twenty-five minutes to get to Starlingford, find a space in the multi-storey car park, and be there on the counter. Jocelyn wouldn't be there, but she would still have a field day if Leah signed in late, and it would only serve as more ammunition for the absence complaint.

Alan's silver SUV turned into the driveway less than five minutes later and Leah had Kiki ready to hand over before he and Cheryl were on their feet.

'So sorry about that!' Cheryl reached out for her granddaughter and her eyes met Leah's. 'Are you alright?'

Leah nodded. 'How is the man?'

'Possible fractured leg, but he's in good hands now. The ambulance staff were brilliant, and his family are on their way to meet him at A&E.'

'That's nice to hear. I hope he recovers quickly. Anyway, I've got to go.'

'What's the matter?' Cheryl asked. 'You look like you're about to cry.'

She handed Kiki to Alan and told him to take her inside.

'I just really don't need to be late,' said Leah, who was now clicking on her seatbelt with the car window down. 'You know… with everything going on.'

Cheryl's face straightened with understanding. 'No, of course you don't.' She leaned into the car and brushed a strand of hair away from Leah's cheek. 'And have you heard anything from Head Office?'

'They rang me earlier on.' Leah started the ignition. 'Nothing about the absence thing. But they said they were looking into my complaint about Jocelyn.'

'Good.' Fury ripped visibly through Cheryl, just to imagine what Leah was going through. 'Because no one hurts my girl. And if they don't take that woman down, believe me, I'll be going into Glovers to do it myself.'

'Mum, it's fine.' Leah squeezed her hand, feeling delicate and trying to keep herself together. 'She's not in today at least. And Tiffany's probably in the Maldives, so I can bet my life savings she won't turn up. I'll talk to you later when I get Kiki.'

'Hope you have a nice day, darling.' Cheryl waved her off as she reversed onto the road. 'And hold that beautiful head up!'

The luck of time was on Leah's side, and she arrived in Glovers two minutes ahead of her nine o'clock start. Full of relief for Jocelyn to see that she had logged in perfectly on schedule, she picked up the tablet, feeling happy to be there alone with the gleaming baubles and shimmering bows lighting up the beauty hall, and the seasonal scents of pine and nutmeg catching every so often in the air.

There were two new messages on the system under her profile. One was just from a promotional mailing list, and the other had been sent to her by Jocelyn.

Just a couple of things.

All the stuff you ordered for the VIP event is upstairs in the trolley with the rest of the stock, so you might want to put it in the boardroom ready for next week. Haven't opened it as I'm too busy.

I want SySTEM pushed as much as possible please, with your sales today and as the main product at the event.

Hilary is coming down from Head Office for a visit and she'll be here for the event. Let's put any issues to bed, at least while she's here.

Thanks, J

With the counter still quiet so early in the morning, she asked Kehlani to keep an eye on it while she went to check her order. Slicing through the cardboard boxes, she unrolled the magenta-trimmed posters, all featuring glorified bottles of *SySTEM*. There was pink potpourri for the tables, and champagne glasses with golden rims. Fuchsia and white balloons, and a large EdenCore banner for the front. It was all intact and perfect for the occasion, so she wheeled it through into the boardroom, storing it neatly in the walk-in cleaning cupboard to the side.

Leah felt the pressure pile up again, remembering Hilary from the training week in London. There had been something in her demeanour that Leah couldn't quite work out. She'd been excessively bubbly and to say she was passionate about the products was an understatement. Any questions from the new employees, or concerns that had been raised about the techniques they were trying out had literally been stamped on. Sealed with a smile and a flick of Hilary's wig-like bob.

Under her watchful eye and obsessive standards, Leah's presentation would have to fit the bill, and the only way to do that was to lie. She would have to turn a blind eye to everything she knew. Those comments on social media and the box of returns that was still stashed away under the counter. The slapped-on foundation she would have to wear when she stood before the audience, that hid the remnants of her own flare-ups. She would face everyone in the room, like there was a knife twisting in her back, and declare that *SySTEM* was a wonder product like nothing else that existed.

She left the room, walking down from the top floor feeling like a cloud was hanging over her head.

'There you are!' Kehlani puffed as she met her halfway up the steps to the beauty hall.

'I'm sorry,' said Leah, picking up her pace. 'Is it manic on the counter? Typical, I leave you to watch it for a second and you're rushed off your feet!'

'No, it's not busy at all.' Kehlani ran a hand through her luscious ponytail. 'There's a bloke downstairs waiting for you at the counter.' She stopped Leah and gazed at her intently. 'It's Tiffany's loverboy.'

Leah frowned. 'Waiting for me?'

'Well, he didn't actually ask for you. Just wanted to speak to anyone on your counter.'

'Strange. Is Tiffany with him?'

'No sign of her.'

'OK, thanks Keh, I'll see what he wants.'

Kehlani headed off as there were customers milling around the KittyPie counter. As Leah reached midway into the beauty hall, she could see Phil standing alone at the EdenCore till.

'Hi!' she greeted him as he caught sight of her. 'Sorry to keep you waiting. How can I help?'

'Not a problem, sweetheart.' He winked then scanned the store. 'Is the boss around?'

'Jocelyn? No, it's her day off. But I can tell her you were here.'

Phil reached inside the pocket of his long overcoat and pulled out a sealed letter.

'I'm just handing this in on behalf of Tiff.'

Leah took it from him and put it in a folder under the till where Jocelyn kept notes for work.

'It's her official resignation,' he said.

She snapped the file shut and slowly stood up to face him again.

'I'm sorry to hear that.'

'Well, let's face it, she doesn't need to work here anymore. Lady of leisure now, bless her.'

'I… haven't seen her much lately and she was… in a

hurry last time she was shopping in here,' Leah chose her words carefully. 'But let her know that we wish her all the best.'

'Oh, she'll do just fine,' Phil said confidently. 'She'd have come herself today but she's busy packing for Jamaica. We're getting married out there next week.'

'Congratulations,' Leah feigned enthusiasm. 'She must be so excited.'

Phil leaned in and lowered his voice. 'Well, she doesn't know yet.'

Apart from Leah's intake of breath, there was silence.

'So, keep shtum about it if you see her, alright?'

'Your secret is safe with me. I'll make sure Jocelyn gets the letter.'

'You're a star. Thanks a lot, sweetheart.'

Leah watched him walk away, past the security guards and out of the main entrance. As the bracing wind whooshed around him, something fluttered out of his coat and got trapped under the sliding doors as they banged shut. He hurried off briskly across the road with no idea that he had dropped anything. Leah ran to the door and unwedged the item, picking up the small card in her hand and sprinting out to catch up with Phil. But he was long gone, and there was nothing Leah could do.

She looked down at the picture in her hands. Two love hearts with a big diamond ring. Clearly this was an engagement card for Tiffany. Leah would have to keep it safe until Phil hopefully came back.

Placing it next to the till, she rummaged around in the small stationery pile and found an envelope to put it in. It was a snug fit, and as she eased the edges apart and tried to slide it inside, the card fell open and a gift voucher slipped out onto the counter. She read the logo on the small plastic token.

BODYWORX

Phil had already written inside the card and the words bounced out at Leah before she could stop herself reading them.

To my one and only,

No ring could be enough for you, my queen, so here is an extra little something. Thought you might like an upgrade on the airbags – and I don't mean for the car! Or maybe we should pump up that rump (leak-proof this time, guaranteed), so you'll fill out those bikini bottoms good and proper on the honeymoon.

The choice is yours, as always.

Love every part of you – and more when the work's done, lol!

Your king,

Phillip xxx

She slapped the card inside the envelope, ensuring the voucher was securely enclosed, and put it in Jocelyn's folder with the resignation letter, leaving her a note in case Phil returned to collect it.

Not that she had expected Tiffany to show up for the VIP event, but the confirmation that she was never coming back still had Leah feeling left out in the cold. There would be no help with the presentation and the full responsibility now lay with her alone. She gazed out across the blustery streets and felt the weight of the world falling heavily on her shoulders as she tried to consider the options. A public demonstration of dishonesty versus facing the consequences for telling the truth. The only other choice was to run as far away as possible.

Twenty-Eight

'Yes, that's right…' Hilary looked like she was salivating. 'Rub it all over, even around the eyes. Doesn't it just feel divine?'

It was the day before the VIP event and Hilary had arrived for her visit. She was pitching in on the counter to help out between meetings when she would slip away upstairs and join Head Office over Zoom. Leah was finding it excruciating, watching her obliviously slathering *SySTEM* on the customers.

All the while, the box of refunded bottles was sitting inches away under the counter, which Jocelyn had forbidden her to tell a soul about. But to make it worse, she had the feeling that even if she did come out and say it now, Hilary would only respond with denial.

'I'll take two, then,' said the woman Hilary was serving. 'You don't know how long I've been looking for something that works on my sensitive skin.'

There was no question about size. The woman was getting extra-large whether she liked it or not, and Hilary stood strategically in front of the smaller options to hide them. She lifted the card reader up in a desperate bid to connect it with the customer's phone and hear the contactless beep, sealing the deal on the transaction.

'Hilary, I need an hour upstairs to get the boardroom ready for tomorrow. I'll be back before you go to lunch.'

'Hang on a minute,' she replied, clicking her fingers. 'Are there any spaces left? Perhaps this lady would like to come along.'

'We can squeeze a couple more in,' said Leah, smiling at the woman. 'If you'd like to bring a friend.'

'Sounds lovely. I'll leave my details.'

'It's ten o'clock and the meeting point is here. We'll show you all the way when everyone arrives.'

The woman scribbled down her name and number, and Hilary waved a hand at Leah.

'Off you go then and take whatever time you need.'

Leah left Hilary in control of the counter, not even wanting to think about the customers that she would unwittingly lead astray. Who knew what state their faces would be in when they woke up tomorrow having coated themselves in lashings of the suspect serum.

For the next forty-five minutes, she put everything out of her mind to focus on the job in hand. She covered the walls in full-length posters of *SySTEM*, the *T-Radish-ional* fragrance and the *Palm Oil* hand cream, with other shots of models bathing themselves in the bestselling products.

Balloons were fastened along the coving until the ceiling spilled magenta and white from every angle of the room. A long bar stretched out at the back, ready to be filled with drinks and nibbles first thing in the morning, and two further platforms lined the sides, covered in magenta fabric and topped with fresh stacks of pristine white towels and the full EdenCore product ranges laid out in between them. She wheeled a trolley up to the front, complete with testers and samples to try, and at a separate station, there were cotton wool pads next to tissues, applicators and pink tubes of Glovers hand gel.

Her ankles could have snapped in her high heels as she dragged the round tables into the centre and positioned six chairs at each one. They were adorned in a scattering of confetti around intricate flowers making decorative displays in glowing pink vases, and she had even studded the walls with strings of matching lights, and candles at the ready to bring an ambient atmosphere.

The door creaked and Hilary's face peered around the crack.

'Oh, bravo, Leah. This looks *incredible*!'

She swept into the room with her arms outstretched.

'I had no idea you had such creative flair.'

Leah could feel a slight blush on her face. 'I suppose I do quite like that side of things. Working with colour and themes.'

'Hmmm, but how are your presentation skills, eh?' She raised an inquisitive eyebrow. 'I can't wait to find out tomorrow.'

'I'm a bit nervous, I guess. Especially with no Tiffany to do it with me.'

'Nonsense. I'm sure you'll do us proud.' She gestured her head over the empty chairs that filled the room. 'They're all going to be ordering *SySTEM* by the gallon.'

Leah swallowed and her throat felt suddenly parched. Standing there amid all the luxury and anticipation, she could no longer fight the guilt that was pounding mercilessly through her chest.

'Hilary…' Her hands were turning blue with the cold and she clutched them together, her nails digging her skin. 'There's something you should…'

Jocelyn swung the door open and marched into the room.

'Darling, darling!' Hilary sailed over and embraced her, kissing her on both cheeks. 'So lovely to see you.'

Smiling over Hilary's shoulder, Jocelyn's expression

changed when she caught sight of Leah. It was the first time they'd come face to face since Jocelyn had interrogated her over the absence claims. She wasn't supposed to be working today, and Leah was surprised to see her here, especially out of uniform.

'Long time no see,' she said to Hilary, failing to acknowledge Leah. 'And already having a cracking day on the counter from what I saw on the sales sheets down there. I hope you're not doing all the hard work.'

'Only while Leah's been getting on with this. Looks good, doesn't it?'

Jocelyn stared at the decor and nodded slowly. 'Yep…' she spoke like it was suffocating her to offer Leah a compliment. 'Not bad at all.' She walked over to a table and rearranged some of the flowers. 'Where are the drinks?'

'Everything's over there in the fridge,' replied Leah, pointing to a small kitchen area off the main room.

'Shall we check out what there is?'

Jocelyn walked towards it, eyeing Hilary and motioning at her to follow. Leah was left standing in the middle of the room while they went out of view somewhere at the back. There was whispered conversation and intermittent bursts of laughter. Then Hilary emerged with Jocelyn by her side.

'Now… shall we do this here or is there somewhere else we can go for a chat.'

Leah had no idea what Hilary was talking about, but Jocelyn seemed to be well aware.

'The office next to the stockroom should be free.'

'Perfect.' Hilary beckoned to Leah. 'If you'd like to join us, please.'

Leah lagged behind them as they all left the room. They both walked down the corridor a few steps ahead, muttering to each other in voices that were inaudible against the loud clack of their shoes.

Inside the room was a small table, with two chairs on one side and a single seat opposite. Jocelyn and Hilary sat next to each other and Leah was ordered to sit alone.

'Right, let's get started,' Hilary said, reaching into her work bag and taking out a small laptop. 'The reason we're all here, and why Jocelyn has kindly come in on her day off – thank you, Jocelyn – is that you registered a complaint of misconduct against her. Didn't you, Leah?'

As their two pairs of eyes drilled into her, Leah felt the blood pulsing up into her ears. She looked over at the door, knowing she was trapped and there was no way out.

'Yes…' she murmured eventually. 'Unfortunately, I did.'

'So, you contacted Head Office, and you were told that someone would be carrying out the investigation. Is that right?'

Leah nodded.

'Well, that person is me.'

Hilary's expression was unreadable, while the hint of a smile played on Jocelyn's lips.

'So, Jocelyn, I would like to ask you some questions based on Leah's claims. Is that OK with you?'

'Fire away,' replied Jocelyn, still staring at Leah.

'Are you Miss Jocelyn Quigley, Account Manager of EdenCore at Glovers, Starlingford?'

'That is correct.'

'And you have been in your current position since October?'

'I have.'

'That's fine…' Hilary tapped something into her laptop. 'And now I am going to ask you some questions concerning Leah's complaint. Are you happy for me to do that?'

'Go ahead.'

Leah looked at the floor because Jocelyn's constant glare was unnerving her.

'Firstly, Leah claims that the disciplinary procedure you carried out regarding her repeated absences was done completely without any prior warnings. Is that true?'

'False.'

Leah stiffened in shock.

'She states that the incidents you have cited as absences were based on completely unavoidable situations. Do you agree?'

Jocelyn chewed her lip. 'I do not.'

'Leah also claims you have been making derogatory comments about her weight and appearance. Is this true?'

'It is not.'

'Another incident Leah has raised is that you refused to allow her to change shifts on the twelfth of December, resulting in her missing an important hospital appointment for her daughter. Did this happen?'

'I *absolutely* did not.'

Hot tears swelled in Leah's eyes and she willed them not to fall. She felt strapped to her chair like she was a hostage. As if she had been mugged, despite her mouth being free.

'And Leah also says she has witnessed you belittling and insulting the customers to make sales. Have you been doing this?'

'No, I have not,' answered Jocelyn.

Leah shook her head in complete disbelief and opened her mouth to speak.

'The final complaint is that you have been made aware…' Hilary slowed down as she read out the last line, laughing as she uttered the words… 'that *SySTEM* has been causing allergic reactions in the customers, but you have continued to recommend it, and have forbidden the staff to report this to Head Office. Is this true?'

Jocelyn emphasised a shrug. 'No! Absolute rubbish.'

'But…' Leah shrieked.

'So, in conclusion,' Hilary interrupted, 'you are saying that you completely deny any of these allegations and that none of them are true?'

'That is exactly right,' Jocelyn said firmly. 'All lies.'

'Oh, this is absurd!' Leah couldn't help but raise her voice. 'Everything I've said is true. Everything.'

Jocelyn sneered. 'I'm not even going to stoop low enough to defend myself.'

'How is this even allowed to happen? I should have been told in advance, not just have it sprung on me like this. I'm entitled to have someone here with me. How can it be appropriate to just bring us both into a room and—'

'See, this is what I mean,' said Jocelyn, pointing at Leah across the table. 'She has anger issues. Every time I try and remind her of rules or give her any directions, she flies at me and bites my head off.'

'I can assure you, I am following company procedure, Leah.' Hilary looked irritated to have been challenged. 'It does seem that there's a different story here compared to the one you reported to Head Office.'

'No!' Leah lurched forwards in her chair. 'This isn't my word against hers. There's evidence. Witnesses who can confirm I'm telling the truth.'

'That's beyond inappropriate!' Jocelyn shouted. 'Dragging other people into this when it's nothing to do with anyone else.'

'Quite right, Jocelyn. I don't think that will be necessary.' Hilary put out a hand in an attempt to calm things down. 'I've heard what you both have to say. It is up to me to make a decision on how to proceed.'

'But we've hardly even—'

'That's enough, Leah. I can see Jocelyn is getting upset.'

Leah searched Jocelyn's face for any sign of distress.

'You're free to leave.' Hilary gave Jocelyn a sympathetic smile. 'Go and get yourself a tissue and an early night. Then you can come back here fresh for the big day.'

Jocelyn kept her head down as she reached for the door, but her face was stone cold with not a hint of a teardrop. She mouthed a word of thanks to Hilary, shot a final look of disgust at Leah, and then she was gone.

Hilary clicked the laptop shut and folded her arms on the table.

'Now, I'm going to say one thing.' Her eyes chiselled into Leah's through the gloomy shadows of the office. 'This is not the time to be having silly arguments. There are far bigger things to think about. Tomorrow is going to be *huge* and there is an enormous amount at stake. EdenCore will be right in the spotlight. And did I mention that we have a special guest who has just flown in from Paris? None other than Antoine Dejardins himself.'

A wave of nausea coursed through Leah at the mention of the founder and CEO of EdenCore. With the colour draining fast from her face, she stared back at Hilary in total disbelief.

'Yes, you heard me,' Hilary nodded. 'So, if you play your cards right and make enough money off the back of it, this branch could find itself with flagship status and renewed exclusivity of *SySTEM* for another two years.' She raised her eyebrows so high that they disappeared under her thick dyed fringe. 'So, do you want to let this little issue get in the way of all that?'

Leah was unable to utter another word of protest.

'Of course you don't. And with that in mind, you

should also know that I'll be presenting an EdenCore Elite award to Jocelyn tomorrow, because of all her hard work since she took over here. We only give five of these out to employees every year and no matter what happens with your complaint of misconduct, she has definitely sold enough *SySTEM* to deserve this.'

Defeated didn't even begin to cover how Leah felt inside.

'So, as her closest colleague, why don't you be the bigger person here, and find some positives that you can shout about, so everyone knows why she is getting such prestigious recognition?'

There was no response. Leah just nodded and tried to stop her trembling lip from inducing the onset of tears. It was hard enough to have been shown up in the meeting and as good as branded a liar while the real culprit walked free. But to give a presentation of praise for Jocelyn after everything she had done was like rubbing a handful of salt in an already colossal wound.

'Thank you, Leah. I think you know it's the right thing to do.' Hilary gestured for her to leave the room, so she obeyed, too stunned to say anything else. 'I will be in touch once I have come to a conclusion about your complaint, and you'll receive a full report in writing.'

Leah clicked the door shut and bolted along the corridor, almost falling inside the locker room when she reached it. She locked herself in a toilet cubicle, slamming back against the wall, head in her hands as she panted out loud, trying to gain control of herself before someone else walked in.

'Come on, you can do this,' she whispered to herself, feeling cheated, confused, and almost delirious with rage. 'Just get it over with and say something nice.' She crumpled up her face and collapsed into a flood of tears as Hilary's words reverberated in her mind and then out loud in her voice. 'Be the bigger person!'

She felt weak as she stumbled out of the building, yet again feeling that things couldn't get more abysmal. Rain drenched her as she clamoured for her car keys, the festive berries of high street décor blurring into streaks of red and white.

From the front seat of the car, she dried the spatters from the screen of her phone and thumped out a message to Eric.

Get the kettle on. Today has been one big nightmare.

Then she started the car and texted him again.

I've changed my mind. Double gin on ice.

Twenty-Nine

'Ouch…' said Eric as Leah opened the door of his study, bedraggled and soaked to the skin. 'You weren't kidding when you said you'd had a bad day.'

He turned down the volume on The Cure as they echoed around the room while he finished off some work.

'And I had to choose the coat with no hood,' Leah murmured as the colourful shelves of his superhero figures blurred into her tired vision. Twig's tail wagged wildly against the sofa bed, and in seconds he was up on his feet, nuzzling his nose into Leah's body.

Kiki was on Eric's lap in her pyjamas while he finished some work he was doing from home. She wriggled at the sight of Leah, holding her arms out and whimpering for some attention.

'Hi, Kiki Koo,' Leah bent down and kissed her. 'I know, but Mummy looks like a drowned rat. I'll make you into one too if I cuddle you.'

'There's a warm bath ready for you. Go and have that first, then I'll put this one to bed and we'll talk.'

'Thanks, I will,' Leah managed a faint smile. 'But I'll do her stories tonight once I've freshened up. Feels like I've hardly seen her recently with all the overtime.'

She lifted her head and Eric stopped clicking at the computer. He stroked her face, wiping the tears before they could trickle down her cheeks.

'It's all going to work out fine,' he soothed. 'Just get yourself warm and changed. You'll at least feel better for that.'

Leah didn't hesitate for a second longer. She peeled off her wet clothes and stepped gladly into the waves of steam, sinking like a concrete block in the depths of bubbles and rose-scented bath oil.

Never could she have imagined that something like this would have topped all the pressure of tomorrow. It had been bad enough that she was going to give a presentation and push people into buying a toxic substance. It had been doubly as bad that Tiffany had abandoned her, so she was doing it alone. Then tripled by the unexpected presence of Antoine Dejardins.

But now, it had spiralled to epic proportions of doom. And being told to compile wonderful words about Jocelyn was the last straw. Everything else was doable. Excruciatingly so, yet she would still have been able to drag herself through it all. But this extra task wasn't just going to require being a bigger person. Leah would have to be an absolute saint.

Swilling in the foamy water and ducking her shoulders down in the tub, Leah felt like her body was one giant knot. Tied up tightly by Jocelyn and then kicked to the kerb to unravel by herself. She took slow breaths, tried to visualise calm thoughts from the yoga classes, but instead resorted to silent screams until her fingertips were shrivelling and the water was turning cold.

Feeling at least half human again in her dressing gown and slipper socks, she cuddled up with Kiki on the sofa and read her four books while Twig curled around the tot and rested his head on her knees.

'Camomile tea,' said Eric, placing a mug down next to Leah. 'You don't need alcohol tonight.'

As the warm infusion soothed her with every sip, she knew it was the right decision. Downing one too many gins was never going to help her come up with twenty reasons why the world should worship Jocelyn.

Kiki guzzled her bedtime bottle and snoozed like a kitten in Leah's arms. How Leah wished it could always be this way. Wrapped up in contentment, no noise but the hushed TV and Kiki's soft breath against her chest. No writhing legs or stiffening back, just her cosy little self, tucked safely up in the cocoon of Leah's arms.

Eric got the cot ready and helped get Kiki in without a stir. Then he sat with Leah by the fireplace, Twig stretching out across them both to get his fair share of the heat. She poured her heart out to him, offloading the burdens of the day while he made her feel strong, saying he was proud of her no matter what happened tomorrow, and that if she dug right down inside her soul, she would scrape together that list of praise, even if she didn't mean a word of it.

He left her to brainstorm while he went upstairs to watch TV in bed. And there, with the backdrop of Twig's gentle snores and the intermittent crackle of the fire, something fell into place and Leah began typing.

Because none of it was important. Work, and Jocelyn, and everything she had been put through were just insignificant fragments of life compared to the heart of this home. Her pillar of a husband. Their loyal pup who had come to them in one of those meant-to-be moments. And the little girl who was doing her best in those tiny pink boots, her growing smile trusting Leah's with every step she tried to take. *This* was what really mattered in her life.

She opened a new document and the instant she

stopped caring, the words finally spilled out.

There couldn't be a better person to win this EdenCore Elite award. Jocelyn Quigley's professionalism is second to none and she is an incredible role model. She is always considerate and kind, taking time for all customers and making every single one of them feel happy with the products and confident in themselves when they have visited the counter. She always puts wellbeing at the centre of everything she does, and she recognises the importance of looking after her colleagues. She is also…

An email sounded with a ping on the bottom of her screen. She clicked into her inbox and saw it was from Hilary. It was nearly ten o'clock and late for her to still be working. Leah opened the message and frowned at the contents.

From: Hilary Mason
Sent: 21:54
To: Leah Frost
Subject: Complaint of misconduct

Dear Leah,

Complaint ref no: 0201936

Following our discussion earlier today in the presence of Jocelyn Quigley, I have now investigated the above matter, and I conclude that no misconduct has taken place.

I have undertaken an intensive assessment of your case and have formally interviewed Ms Quigley in your presence. As you witnessed, I asked her about every allegation you made against her, to which she responded that she had not done these things.

As Ms Quigley is a longstanding member of staff who has deservedly achieved the status of Account Manager at EdenCore at Glovers, Starlingford, I am inclined to believe her under these circumstances and therefore, I dismiss your complaint against her.

I am confident you will now be able to move forward in the knowledge your issues have been taken most seriously and I find no further cause for your concern.

Kind regards,
Hilary Mason

Area Manager
EdenCore
London and South East

She swallowed and stared into the flames, processing the finality of the words, despite already knowing it would come to this. That everything had been against her from the moment she'd walked into that room.

Looking back over the compliments she had just written, the sentiments, false as they were, still drained away like tepid water down a plughole. She could barely even muster up the energy to continue. Her thoughts and feelings meant nothing to the company, so why would they even care about her opinion of Jocelyn in the morning?

Belittled and dismayed, she read through Hilary's email three more times, not sure what she was hoping for. That the wording would change? Or perhaps disappear altogether.

Twig rolled over in a daze, nudging her wrist as she moved down the page until she realised it didn't end where Hilary had signed her name. Below it was another email that had inadvertently been forwarded.

'What?' she screeched, jolting the pup wide awake. She slapped a hand over her mouth so she didn't disturb Kiki and held her breath in disbelief.

From: Hilary Mason
Sent: 21:15
To: Jocelyn Quigley
Subject: Frosty knickers!

Just going to send her this. What do you think? Should hopefully do the job and shut her the hell up!

'Is this a joke?' Leah shouted. 'Is this an actual…'
'Are you OK down there?' Eric called out.
She was too dumbstruck to respond to him. Instead, she scrolled further, astonished to see that she had been sent the whole thread.

From: Jocelyn Quigley
Sent: 21:22
To: Hilary Mason
Subject: Re: Frosty knickers!

Love it. Absolutely nailed it mate. Knew I could count on you.

J x

From: Hilary Mason
Sent: 21:25
To: Jocelyn Quigley

Subject: Frosty knickers!

I just need to know one thing. Did you actually tell her she needs to lose weight? Because if you did, it hasn't had much of an effect on her. Waistband still looks like it's stretched around a tree trunk.

From: Jocelyn Quigley
Sent: 21:31
To: Hilary Mason
Subject: Re: Frosty knickers!

Just spat out my coffee, that was bloody hilarious!
Yes, I might have mentioned it to her — purely out of the kindness of my heart of course.

J x

From: Hilary Mason
Sent: 21:36
To: Jocelyn Quigley
Subject: Frosty knickers!

You're a bitch but I love ya!
This is the problem with hiring people who've got kids though. They think they're entitled to unlimited time away, and let's face it, a postnatal figure is not a good look for our uniform.

From: Jocelyn Quigley
Sent: 21:40
To: Hilary Mason
Subject: Re: Frosty knickers!

Oh, don't get me started about the whole hospital

appointment thing. You should have heard the fuss she kicked up when I wanted her to work.

You'd think she'd have thanked me for giving her an excuse to get away from baby duty. Apparently, her kid's a little brat.

J x

With tears in her eyes, Leah reached the very end of the thread.

From: Hilary Mason
Sent: 21:48
To: Jocelyn Quigley
Subject: Frosty knickers!

Just like its mother!

She tossed the laptop to the side, her back rigid against the sofa as she tried to process every unimaginable line of the messages. As they repeated in her mind, she buried her face in her dressing gown sleeve, trying to muffle the anguish as it sounded out in flurried breaths.

Embers flickered around the coal as something ignited inside her, and suddenly she was reaching for her phone and prodding the keypad in a frenzy. She did not even recognise herself in the words, but she had to reach one person before morning came. Shaking as she clutched the screen, she watched the two ticks appear and refused to look away. She counted the minutes until at last the colour changed and she knew Kehlani had finally read the message.

Thirty

They wanted immaculate, and that was exactly what they were going to get. Leah stepped out of the car in a pair of black stilettos that were far too uncomfortable to wear for a normal shift at work, but they were worth it today for the way they made her legs look. She had slept in rollers so her hair was voluminous as she wore it now, swept up and piled sleekly off her face, revealing a delicate pair of diamante earrings that glittered under the light. Her makeup was meticulous, with flawless foundation, dramatic eyes, and a dewy blusher grazing her cheekbones, topped off with two coats of striking red lipstick to match the glossy polish on her nails. Every product was worn defiantly as none of it was from EdenCore.

She smiled at the security guards as she walked through the doors and felt their eyes on her as she took the escalator down to the beauty hall. Holding her head high as she descended, she saw Taeng and Kehlani's faces lighting up in approval as she made her entrance.

Hilary and Jocelyn were chatting behind the counter, not realising she had arrived. The change in Hilary's face was undeniable as she clocked her striding through the Christmas displays, turning more heads as she moved.

Leah saw her nudge Jocelyn who twisted around in almost slow motion, clamping on a forced smile and scanning every inch of Leah from her hair all the way down to her shining patent toes.

'Good morning.' She flashed them both an icy smile.

'Leah…' Hilary nodded a greeting. 'You're looking nice.'

'Definitely,' agreed Jocelyn, as if it was paining her to say it.

Hilary's bob had been crimped like a poodle, and Jocelyn was sporting a peculiar sideways bun, with a long curl of hair deliberately falling out of the middle. Leah eyed her face. Almost definitely *Carnation Carisma* from EdenCore's *TuLIPS* palette, but the intended red was already turning into a smudgy wash of fluorescent pink.

'Thanks.' She could feel their stares following her as she walked over to one of the mirrors and needlessly checked herself. Then she faced them again, the words rolling glibly out of her mouth. 'Not that anyone can hold a candle to you two!'

Clearly flattered, yet surprised by Leah's warmth, they looked at each other and collapsed into a giggle.

'I'm so pleased to see you've had a change of heart,' Hilary said, gazing back at her. 'And have you managed to… include the last-minute updates to the presentation?'

The wink told Leah she was referring to Jocelyn's award intro.

'Oh, yes. That's all organised. In fact, I'm happy to show you now if you'd like.'

'No, no….' Hilary smiled with a warning look about Jocelyn being present. 'I have every confidence you've excelled yourself.'

'It took some doing, but I got there.'

Hilary grinned back at Leah, but a squint of perplexity gave itself away. 'And I gather you received my email?'

'I certainly did.'

By now, a swarm of guests were clustering by the counter and lining up to have their invitations checked against Leah's guest list.

'I do hope you understand,' Hilary sidled a little closer to Jocelyn as they stood in a united front.

'Loud and clear,' she whispered, leaning across the counter with a killer beam. And before they could say another word, she turned away and faced the crowd. 'Hello everyone, and a very warm welcome to *Skin Secrets!*'

Excitement rippled through the gaggle of women as she checked off each name and walked them to the staircase.

'Just follow the signs to our special VIP room and make yourselves comfortable around the tables. We'll be with you in just a minute.'

'Excuse me, Madame,' a distinctive French accent called out from behind her. She turned to face a small middle-aged man with round glasses and a sharp pinstripe suit. His giveaway magenta tie matched her EdenCore uniform. 'Today is your special event, yes?'

A shiver snaked down her spine. She had seen his face so many times on training videos, in magazines, and heading the founder page of the official website. For the first moment that morning, she felt as if she were shrinking back down to the lowly sales assistant that she was.

'Allow me to introduce myself,' he said politely. 'My name is…'

'Monsieur Dejardins!' she smiled, willing herself to hold everything together.

'That is correct.' He shook her hand and seemed glad that she recognised him. 'And you are…'

'I'm Leah. So pleased to meet you.' It felt like she was swallowing a rock, but she kept calm, instead concentrating on charming him with her smile. 'I'll be leading the proceedings today.'

'Wonderful,' he cocked his head and gave her an approving grin. 'Will you show me the way?'

'Oh, allow us to do that, Sir!' Jocelyn gripped his shoulder from behind. 'I'm the Account Manager here.'

She stood just a little too close to him and he jerked his head at the brash volume of her voice. Back at the counter, Leah had initially thought that a speck of dirt had landed on Jocelyn's cheek, but as she glanced again, she realised it was a beauty spot, dotted on her face with an eye pencil.

'And you must know me by now!' Hilary shoved her way between Antoine and Leah. 'We've met at least a couple of times before.'

He frowned, the recognition escaping him. Then he shook a finger as it started to come back into his mind.

'Ah, yes. Is it Hilary?'

She looked delighted he had remembered.

'You're one of the training staff, no?'

Her face darkened.

'Many moons ago,' she mumbled. 'I'm Area Manager now.'

'Well, thank you for offering, but I'm already being escorted by this beautiful young lady.' He turned to Leah, gesturing for her to step in front. 'Shall we?'

'Absolutely.' She led him away delightedly, speaking to him in French, and couldn't resist looking back at two aghast faces.

As she entered the room with Antoine, beholding it for the first time in all its glory, filled up with the anticipating audience, she could have passed out from the dizzy feeling that was rapidly overtaking her. Antoine went over to his place on a reserved chair at the back of the room, where Hilary and Jocelyn joined him at either side.

Leah made her way to the front, where a huge projector screen was ready for the presentation. She opened the laptop and linked up, starting a trial run of the first thirty seconds just to make sure everything was working.

All eyes were on her and it felt as if they were physically drilling into her skin.

'OK, everyone,' she attempted to speak loudly, but all that came out was a croak. 'I just… need a drink.'

She craned her neck through the chatter and scanned the food table, but she could only see several bottles of prosecco, which were already being enjoyed by the guests.

'I'll be back in a second.'

Calmly, she slipped out of sight, then her body sank weakly as she hurried along the corridor and got herself some water from the machine. Letting it slide down the sandpaper dryness of her throat, she refilled the cup and started her shaky journey back to the waiting boardroom.

'Sorry to trouble you, but is there room for one more?'

Leah spun around, a mixture of dread and joy infiltrating her being.

'Rhona!'

'Well, I had to come and see this, didn't I?'

In the shady light of the walkway, Rhona's face lit up. Her hair was longer now, and the deep brunette shade had changed to lighter toffee, tonged into waves. She wore a long navy coat with a sheer leaf print scarf and looked every inch promoted, with her effortlessly natural makeup. She stepped closer and gazed in admiration.

'You look wonderful, Leah. How are you doing?'

'Fine,' she said quickly, feeling her mouth tremble. 'Things are fine...' Tears threatened to betray her if she even blinked. 'I'm just a bit nervous.'

'Don't be.' Rhona placed a hand on her shoulder. 'You know you've got this.'

Leah just stared back. How she had missed her reassurance. Those kind words giving her confidence. Helping her grow and building her strength. She had never felt inadequate under Rhona's care. Seeing her here now just reiterated the enormous hole she had left when she'd gone.

'It's really good to see you,' she said, biting her lip before she became too overwhelmed. 'Things aren't the same without you here.'

'Hey, I'm always here for you, though. You know that don't you?'

Holding her breath until it hurt, Leah nodded.

'Now... you go and knock 'em dead.' She squeezed her elbow. 'OK?'

Leah smiled convincingly as Rhona headed to the boardroom.

'Remember, we're all rooting for you!' she chimed, stopping at the door and vanishing from view.

The locker room was only around the corner. It would take two minutes to get her things and make a quick exit through the back door. Even Dawn had come upstairs now and Leah watched as she stepped inside the boardroom, her cheery and expectant voice echoing around the walls. Antoine would probably be getting impatient, too. She imagined his earlier pleasant manner was likely to diminish if she kept him waiting for too long.

As a whirl of conversations eddied in her ears, she slowed her pace as the doorway opened ahead. She glugged her water once again, spilling a trail on the floor from her quaking hand. Her eyes fell on Jocelyn, bantering with Hilary over Antoine's rigid frame, and in another moment, she took her place at the side of the projector screen, suddenly feeling like a match had struck as she raised her eyes and smiled.

Thirty-One

'We welcome every single one of you to *EdenCore Presents: Skin Secrets*. My name is Leah, and on behalf of my colleagues, we are delighted to have you here.'

Everyone fell to a hush and the expectant smiles of the guests pushed her on to continue.

'Today, we'll be looking at the inspiration behind the brand and I'm going to be introducing you to some of our bestselling products. You'll get to try them out, learn about our ingredients, and there are even amazing free gifts for you all to take home.'

As animation sounded through the audience, Leah caught sight of Jocelyn frantically mouthing at her as if she had forgotten to say something important.

'Oh yes...' she said quickly. 'We're offering you all an exclusive VIP twenty per cent discount downstairs at the counter after this.'

Jocelyn waved her hand in desperation for Leah to drive the point home.

'And if you buy five products or more, we'll even throw in some extra treats.'

She glared back at Jocelyn, who was now giving her the thumbs up with a huge look of glee.

'So, help yourself to some bubbly if you haven't

already, and we'll get started.'

She clicked on the first slide and a giant picture of *Palm Oil* appeared on the screen.

'Firstly, I give you our staple hand cream. You have a tube of this in the middle of your tables, so go ahead and smooth this all over from your wrists to your fingertips.'

Pausing, she watched the guests hesitate as they began to apply it.

'Gorgeous, isn't it?'

'Sorry… I just have a question,' said a woman sitting near the window. Leah smiled at Tess and gestured for her friend to continue. 'Why would EdenCore use palm oil in their products? I mean, all that deforestation, climate change, and destruction of habitats for several endangered species. Isn't that a little… controversial?'

As she expected, trepidation mounted, and people started to push the tubes back into the middle of the table.

'Well, the interesting thing is…' Leah replied, 'There is no actual palm oil in our hand cream. You can be safe in the knowledge that the ingredients are all sustainable and dates are the main one you're using here. *Palm Oil* is just the name. Nothing else.'

The lids were soon flicked open again and hands everywhere were smothered in blobs of white.

'Weird move from the marketing department,' muttered Tess with a wink.

'If I had a pound for every time I've had to explain this to a customer…' Leah sniggered as a wave of laughter rang out awkwardly across the room.

Hilary coughed, eyeing Jocelyn uneasily and pursing her lips in annoyance.

'Anyway, let's carry on.' The next image appeared, and this time it was the three EdenCore fragrances, sitting on a bed of crushed ice. 'Our very distinctive scents are another highlight. I want to focus on the pink bottle here because this, everyone, is *T-Radish-ional*, our signature scent. Get stuck in and give it a spray.'

The first few wafts were not too offensive, but as more pumps of the rancid concoction multiplied in the air, Leah was relieved to see she wasn't alone in her aversion to the perfume. The repulsed faces were unmistakeable, and several women buried their noses in tissues.

'What do we all make of it?'

Some shook their heads and a smattering of wheezes heaved around the boardroom.

'I'm just trying to think what it reminds me of...' Darcie spoke up from another table, gazing wistfully into the air. 'A farmyard? No, I know... cat litter when it needs changing! Can we please open a window?'

Leah obeyed and pushed the nearest pane ajar, the cool breeze giving her relief. Hilary clenched her teeth with eyes like saucers, imploring Leah to continue.

'Now, moving on...' She clapped her hands together, bringing the attention back to the front of the room. 'We come to the pièce de resistance.'

Antoine looked bemused as she glanced across at him.

'The one and only miracle formula and all-rounder extraordinaire that is *SySTEM* serum.'

In another click, the huge bottle dominated the screen on a backdrop of gold fabric with symbolic glitter splashed over the graphic, and an arrow diagram pinpointing all the things it promised to do.

'EdenCore at Glovers, Starlingford is the only branch in the country where you can buy this groundbreaking product. So, if you're going to purchase this downstairs today, remember you won't have a chance to get it anywhere else.'

Jocelyn and Hilary sat up in their seats, renewed pleasure gleaming across their faces.

'As you can see, we've got two massive fans of this stuff at the back there,' Leah pointed and everyone turned to look at them both. 'So, perhaps my colleagues would be happy to do a demonstration on themselves?' She took two large *SySTEM* bottles from the tester trolley and held them out in front of her.

Hilary said nothing but Jocelyn reddened as she stumbled to find the words. 'No, no… you just keep going, luvvie.'

'Surprisingly reluctant,' Leah shrugged. 'Well, in that case, why don't we find out what everyone else is saying about it.'

She turned away from the waiting visitors, fingers quivering as she clicked on the slides. And one by one, every screenshot from the social media thread was stamped onto the screen.

Disbelief burst out in the sea of eyes as the words littered their vision.

"I couldn't move half my face for a week."

"The blisters have just about gone down."

"Nearly scarred my friend for life."

The music stopped as the section of slides came to an end, and Leah's chest tightened. She could only see the top of Rhona's head as her hands were covering the rest of her face.

'Apparently, we're not allowed to mention it, though. Isn't that right, Jocelyn?'

'Oh, come on now!' she cackled back at Leah. 'Are you trying to imply that I had any idea about this?'

Leah stepped away from the laptop and reached under the long tablecloth behind her, dragging out the full cardboard box of hidden refunded items that were predominantly *SySTEM*. She used her foot to slide it into the very front of her presenting space, then stood over it, hearing the sounds of perplexity ringing out before her.

'Over the last three months, we have given out refunds for a total of seventy-two bottles of *SySTEM* due to bad reactions.' Leah felt the heat rise in her face, and the release of the truth that she no longer had to conceal. 'She's been hiding this box under the counter the whole time. I've been forbidden to report this to Head Office.'

'Pathetic,' Jocelyn said dismissively. 'As if I'd do something like that.'

'I even showed you the social media post, but it didn't stop you using it on people.'

'What?' hissed Rhona, shooting a sickened look at Jocelyn.

'But you used this on me last week!' said a longstanding customer. 'No wonder I've not been able to get rid of the blotches.'

'And me!' said another. 'I didn't want it on, but she insisted.'

'Well, imagine being in *my* shoes.' Mrs Kirk looked a picture in a floral blouse and the Spa-esque makeup she'd been using since Leah had recommended it. 'My face was burning when she put it on me, but she said it was how it was supposed to feel. I'll never forget that day. The service was appalling.'

Leah took a glimpse at Dawn who responded with a knowing glance then stared helplessly back at Mrs Kirk. Antoine appeared bewildered yet seemed as if he wanted to find out more, while Jocelyn snapped back at the women, her voice drowning in the commotion.

'I think that's quite enough,' Hilary shouted, clapping

her hands until everything quietened down. 'This is a beauty event, not a witch hunt.' She shot a threatening glare at Leah, then put on her best smile for the spectators. 'Let's just leave the presentation there. Everyone has brochures with plenty of information on the products already. Now, kindly wrap it up please. I won't stand for any more negativity.'

The heads turned back to Leah, who said nothing. Everyone's scrutiny was weighing on her shoulders, and the interruption had thrown her further off course. She sat down on the stool, the faces all around her seeming to lose faith and momentum now that she was staring vacantly at the ground.

'Absolutely.' She brought her eyes back up to Hilary. 'You're right… we shouldn't be doing this.'

Hilary relaxed back into her seat, visibly sighing with relief and sharing tormented eye contact with Jocelyn.

'So, let's finish with something positive, shall we?' Leah stood up again, a glittering smile relighting her face once more. 'I am delighted to announce that we have an extremely special award for an outstanding colleague.'

Through the wave of people settling back down across the room, she watched Hilary respond to her words by reaching underneath her chair and pulling out a white glass disc with the EdenCore logo etched into the centre in metallic magenta lettering. She handed it to Antoine, who clearly hadn't been warned that he would be giving it out.

'That's right,' Leah continued. 'Because Miss Jocelyn Quigley, Account Manager at Glovers, Starlingford, is the winner of an EdenCore Elite award!'

Only just recovering from the shock of the *SySTEM* scandal, Jocelyn glanced back and forth, making sure she had heard right. Then a smug grin crept over her face as the realisation set in. She ignored the protestation sounding out from various tables, instead sitting proudly in her place and waiting for Leah to elaborate.

'You know, I was asked to come up with some thoughts for you all today about this very worthy winner, but to be honest…' she paused, resting a dramatic hand on her chest and beaming out to the crowd, 'I just couldn't put it into words!'

As all eyes followed her over to the laptop, she loaded up the screen.

'So instead, we're going to take a look at just how much she has touched everyone's lives.'

'Oh, bloody hell!' Jocelyn mouthed euphorically as she waited for the testimonials. 'I can't believe this is happening!'

With a wary glance at Dawn, Leah hovered over the button. Then, as if electricity flashed through her fingers, she clicked Play.

The customer complaint printouts were long gone on the garden bonfire, but not before she had scanned copies. Up they came relentlessly, each one unravelling another catastrophe on the screen. The one about Jocelyn swearing and pointing out someone's varicose veins. The one where she had shouted at an unwell customer when they'd accidentally knocked her display. The one where she had ruined the wedding makeup. And the one from Mrs Kirk, whose face said it all as she sipped her prosecco and read the rest in triumph.

'You're having a laugh!' Jocelyn shrieked. 'She's making all this up, I swear.'

'Leah…' Dawn was frowning. 'How on earth did you…'

'I'm sorry,' she mouthed back over the furore coming from the tables.

'You think you're so clever, eh?' said Jocelyn piercing her with a sneer. 'Couldn't stand me getting an award so you've written all this bullshit yourself.'

Dawn turned to face her. 'No, she hasn't Jocelyn.'

'Are you actually telling me…' Rhona spat out the words, emphasised all the more by her Glaswegian twang. 'These are real?'

A slow nod from Dawn confirmed it, and she ran her hands through her hair in a stupor, like she was about to knock Jocelyn out of her seat.

Kehlani and Taeng slipped into the room and their reassuring smiles were just what Leah needed.

'Want to see her in action?' Her voice recaptured the attention of the onlookers. 'Check this out.'

The secret video footage played at top volume, and it was not an easy watch. In the first clip, Jocelyn was refusing to serve a customer in a wheelchair who had come to the EdenCore counter to pay for some medical supplies.

'I take it you can at least read,' she could be heard saying to the man. 'The checkouts are over there. Sorry, but my till is reserved for beauty sales.'

Next, the filming was at a jauntier angle, but Jocelyn could clearly be seen talking to a young woman at the consultation table.

'I think you'll find you are going to buy this as soon as I've put it on your face.'

'Oh, I'd love to but I can't afford anything like that until payday. If I could just try it on, though.'

The camera zoomed into Jocelyn just as she proceeded to pound her foot down on the seat adjuster in what appeared to be a deliberate attempt to unsteady the customer.

'Please…' the woman cried out, grabbing hold of the table. 'I'm going to fall!'

Jocelyn ignored her, continuing to bounce up and down until the woman was tossed off the chair and just managed to stumble back onto her feet. She recoiled on the spot, clearly in pain, but Jocelyn strode off with a stack of baskets, only returning to the counter seconds after the woman had limped away.

Meanwhile, a riot was breaking out in the boardroom, with the guests cringing in their chairs, unable to believe what they were seeing.

Leah paused the reel before the next clip started playing, but Taeng nodded supportively, urging her to continue.

At first, the image was too grainy to see that it was Jocelyn, but the magenta blazer made it obvious and once she spoke, it was an instant giveaway. Her back was turned as she talked into the shop phone which hung on the wall just metres from where Taeng would have been standing at the Poirier counter.

'Look, Mrs… Hooker… is it? … *Hooper*, sorry. I'm not going to argue with you. This is merely a courtesy call to let you know that the *Conker It All* cream is back in stock. As I said, I'd be happy to reserve three or more for you, but not just one… I don't see that I need to give you a reason… No, luvvie, I'm not being rude… I don't do favours for single-unit customers… Pardon? Yes, I do work on commission but that's not the point…' She covered the receiver with a hand and silently mouthed an expletive. 'Yep, you just do that then, go somewhere else… Five more seconds and I'm hanging up… two… one…'

She was then filmed cancelling the call, raising her hand and waving her middle finger at the receiver before unknowingly facing the camera lens and storming off out of sight.

Leah scanned the room to gauge everyone's reactions. Rhona was trying to stop Antoine from leaving, while screaming something inaudible to Dawn.

Hilary looked utterly livid as she attempted to pacify Jocelyn. Women everywhere were rising from their seats, and Leah said nothing as she let the final scene play out.

There was Leah, standing at the counter ready and waiting to serve. Behind her, Jocelyn stared out into the beauty hall, a sudden mix of panic and eagerness taking over her face. She had caught sight of a very wealthy and longstanding customer and Leah would be the first one to greet her when she arrived.

Leah remembered the incident the day it had happened. The splash of toner that Jocelyn had accidentally spilled on the floor. Jocelyn had ordered her to go and get a cloth, and she had dashed off, not giving it a second thought.

But over at the KittyPie stand, Kehlani's phone had been propped on a shelf, recording all the action from behind the Popping Candy bath bombs. It had been perfectly centred on Jocelyn to capture the moment when she had whipped the top off the bottle and deliberately poured a pool of liquid at Leah's feet.

It had been a shock when Leah had watched it through last night, but now she was numb as she saw the replay, instead observing the effect it was having on the first-time witnesses.

'Right, thank you everybody...' Hilary sprung to her feet and snatched the award from Antoine. 'Can you all please sit back down?'

It was no good. Handbags were being shaken in the air, glasses knocked over in the frenzy and EdenCore products being chucked into the far corners of the room.

Hilary waded through it all, her face hot with rage. She grasped a bottle of wine and banged it hard on the table, finally bringing the commotion under control.

'You will stop this now!' she bellowed, the veins creeping up her neck like weeds. 'I'll take over from here, thank you.'

Silence set in as Hilary placed a hand on Leah's shoulder and pushed her down until she was sitting in a chair.

'Right,' she said, facing the guests and obscuring Leah from view. 'Before we were *rudely* interrupted, I think we had an award to give out.' She beckoned to Jocelyn, who skulked her way to the front and still managed a defiant smile, safe under Hilary's protection. 'As Area Manager, I can affirm that she is hardworking, loyal, and a credit to the company. Miss Jocelyn Quigley, it is an honour to present you with…'

Leah looked down at the prosecco-drenched carpet, the pain and exhaustion finally caving in on her. But with the last spark of energy, she stood back up.

'I haven't finished.'

'Miss Frost, you really have got some nerve!' Hilary spluttered, clutching the award in mid-air as Jocelyn's nails splayed around it. 'Now, kindly sit back down and I'll handle it from here.'

Leah shook her head in a near daze as she fixed her sight on everyone in the room. Then she dived between the two managers and grabbed hold of the laptop.

Above their heads, their entire email exchange from the previous night scrolled down the screen in slow motion.

"Her waistband still looks like it's stretched around a tree trunk."

"You're a bitch but I love ya!"

"Apparently, her kid's a little brat."

"Just like its mother."

There was no hysterical response this time. Not a murmur of objection or a stirring of unrest. The power of silence was enough.

She stood there before everyone, floppy-limbed in the magenta straitjacket, the truth now transferring from the screen into her eyes. Nakedly, she gave in and blinked away the pockets of water that she had strained to keep from falling all this time.

With an earth-shattering smash, the award slipped from their clutches, projecting fireworks of iconic magenta and white glass up to the ceiling and raining out across the room. Leah exhaled a final time, like she was blowing it all away. Then she closed the door behind her as every last shard scattered lifelessly to the ground.

Thirty-Two

Leah stepped inside the car park lift and the doors banged shut, encasing mirrors all around her. Through her haze of exhausted vision, she thought she was staring at cracks before realising they were stripes of dissolved makeup, frozen in salty lines down her face. She unclenched her fingers, unsure how long her nails had been in that state, the red lacquer scratched away at the tips.

It still felt like everyone was surrounding her. Following her like paparazzi down the corridor once they'd realised she'd been on her way out. The persuasion in their hands was still imprinted on her shoulders and she had almost forgotten the sensation of being alone. She watched the numbers change at every level, hoping she could reach the right one without another person invading her space.

Released into a heady blast of air, she slowed as she reached the car, collapsing against the curve of the windscreen and breathing everything away. The weight of it all thumping through the length of her body and down to the pinch of her toes.

As she slumped there, buried in the heap of her arms, she felt the breeze pull at her hair and rouse her face from the wreckage. Through the open square of the car park wall, the flat sea metamorphosed in the wind, arching like a creature rising from sleep. Grey movement mingling with the serenity of aquamarine and pulsing the horizon with life.

Coastal scents kissed every layer of her skin and the whooshing gusts felt joyous after the cloying smog of the boardroom. She opened her eyes, every blink soft and comfortable now that her lashes were free of the stiff mascara.

She slid behind the steering wheel, unzipping the back of her skirt and tossing her shoes away, pressing the balls of her feet into the spongy rubber mat where the blisters had sent shockwaves with every move she had made at the presentation. Reversing out of the space, she edged her way down the ramps of the car park until she reached the exit barrier.

It was all clear of traffic, so she surged south to the seafront where the rim of misted ocean continued to beckon, the westerly current spanning the entire strip and leading the way back to the only place she needed to be.

Wind rocked the car as she sped past the coffee bars and huts, where napkins and empty cups spiralled around the tables, and newspapers flapped wildly from their racks. So much hair had been teased out of her clips, that she shook it loose, letting the gale comb through it all and do whatever it wished.

The road thinned through Ropeshore's high street, where giant stars blustered on the sides of the lamps, and glittery pinecones were strung around shop windows. She crossed the bridge over Coombe River and gulls swooped overhead, heralding her arrival at Dankton Beach. She followed the rows of art deco apartments until she reached Cheryl and Alan's house, perching on its own at the end.

Standing barefoot on the driveway, she stretched and inhaled the sulphury wafts crawling in with the tide. She slipped out of her uniform jacket, screwed it up into a crinkled ball of magenta, and hurled it as far as it would go.

Breathlessly, she stepped inside the porch and pushed the doorbell with a stone-cold finger. In minutes, Cheryl was letting her in.

'You're early!' Then she took another look at the bedraggled hair, the bare feet and the glimmer in her eyes. 'Good God, are you OK?'

'I had some time to kill, so I thought I'd come and pick Kiki up.'

Cheryl frowned. 'Did everything go to plan? I mean, look at you. What's happened?'

'So much.' Leah fell into her arms for a moment. 'I'll tell you everything… I will. But I just need to get myself together.'

'Come on into the warm and have a cup of tea. Alan will do it.'

'I'd love to.' She squeezed Cheryl and shook her head. 'First I need to go home, though, have a shower and get this stuff off.'

'You know, I can keep hold of madam if you like. We can drop her off later when you've had the chance to get sorted.'

'That's lovely of you, Mum,' she said, as Alan brought Kiki into the hallway and floated her over to Leah. 'But I think me and the little one have some catching up to do.'

Cheryl glanced at Alan, and they exchanged a beam.

'Anyway, you've done so much, taking care of her all these months. It's about time I gave you a break!'

'So, you don't need us to babysit for your date night tomorrow then?' Alan asked with a wink.

'Oh, I wouldn't go that far!' Leah grinned, kissing

them both. 'I'll ring you for a chat as soon as I've had that shower, OK?'

She strapped Kiki into her car seat, then took a few seconds, just staring at her face. The two almond eyes, widening and mesmerised at Leah's smile, and the rosy blush of cool air lighting up her olive skin. Leah brushed a hand down her cheek and through her chestnut waves of hair. She touched her lips to the tiny hands and shut her safely inside.

As she turned to get into the front seat, Cheryl was there behind her. There were no words needed to understand why her expression was radiant.

'I never thanked you enough. All this time of looking after her for me…' Leah hugged her again. 'You're one amazing mother.'

Cheryl loosened her grip, holding her daughter's face in her palms.

'You are, my girl,' she said with more pride than Leah had ever seen. '*You* are.'

***

There was no better feeling than a fleecy tracksuit, comfy slippers, and nothing on her face but a slap of her trusty old moisturiser, leaving more time to cuddle up with Kiki on the sofa. They'd had a late lunch and then Leah had got more Christmas decorations out of the loft, dangling each bauble out of the box and passing it to Kiki, who laughed and gurgled at the different shapes, watching them sparkle in her hands.

Outside in the garden, Leah held Kiki in her arms as Twig raced around the lawn, kicking up sugary frost from the grass. She tucked Kiki's hat over her ears and lifted her up in the air, making her squeal every time she soared, and enfolding her back in her arms when she swooped down again.

They warmed up at the dining table with Kiki's frothy milk and Leah's whipped cappuccino while Kiki giggled as Twig nibbled the biscuits she fed him. And when Kiki got tired and started to whinge, Leah unrolled a blanket and stretched out on the sofa, letting her snooze while she watched the clouds collide in a promise of snow beyond the window, and Twig piled himself on top of them both.

As Kiki slept, Leah closed her eyes and the events of the morning replayed in her mind. The boardroom door slamming shut and alerting everyone to the fact she had fled. The footsteps clattering behind her as they tried to make her stay.

Rhona in tears, devastated at what she had left Leah to endure while she had moved on with her career. Antoine, who had been unable to even speak. Dawn, begging Leah to stay at Glovers and screaming out that she would be dealing with everything. Kehlani and Taeng, having known it all in advance, were by her side with their support and praise for Leah's courage to have revealed it all.

But all she could offer them in return was a weak smile from a mouth that had shed itself of lipstick. She had turned away and continued to walk, holding her head high until she had reached the car park. No chance of ever looking back.

Once Kiki was wide awake, they sat together on the rug, reading books and doing a jigsaw, just managing to complete it before Twig could steal any of the pieces. Then her phone rang in the kitchen, so she left Kiki to look at the finished puzzle picture while Twig rifled through the toybox with his paws.

'Hey,' said Eric. 'Wasn't sure if you'd answer or not. Is it OK to talk?'

'Fine by me.'

'Are you… still at work? How did everything go?'

'Well, I've been out of there since eleven-thirty if that answers your question.'

'Yeah, I didn't think you'd be hanging around! Did you… say everything?'

'I did,' she said, hardly believing it herself. 'Don't worry, I'm OK. And I'll tell you all about it tonight.'

'So, I guess you're just taking some time to calm down. At least Kiki's off your hands for a few more hours.'

'She's here with me at home. I picked her up early.'

There was a pause. She could just feel Eric's ripple of surprise.

'That's something I didn't think I'd hear… I hope she's behaving.'

'She's been perfect. Although I don't know how long it will last!'

'Better make the most of it, then.'

'Exactly.' Leah gripped the phone with her jaw while she reached to the top of a shelf and picked up Kiki's boots. 'In fact, we're going to put those magic shoes on in a minute.'

'That'll be the end of your peaceful afternoon!' he joked. 'Anyway, did you want me to get something for dinner on the way home?'

'Yes, please. Can we have fish and chips?'

'Tell me what you want, and I'll order ahead.'

'Well, definitely the chips!'

'I know that, obviously. But what else?'

'Mama, up… up!' she heard Kiki say.

Leah turned at her voice and stopped in her tracks, dropping a boot on the floor and flinging the other one into the corner of the living room.

There in the middle of the carpet, Kiki was standing

on her own two feet, resting her hands on Twig's back as he stayed patiently in front of her. She gazed up, sticking out her tongue, then giving Leah the biggest grin that she had ever seen.

'Eric, I'll call you back.'

'Leah?'

'She's standing!' she shouted down the phone as Eric responded with a delighted sigh. 'All on her own. She is, Eric. She's doing it!'

Leah said a quick goodbye and flew over to her little girl, spinning her around so she was still on her feet, but with Leah's hands on her waist to keep her steady.

'Oh, Kiki!' she whispered as her heart climbed up into her chest. 'You did it.'

Tears fell gently and Kiki patted a hand on her cheek, her inquisitive face starting to beam again as Leah reassured her with a smile. She cooed into Leah's arms until she was resting against her neck. The same skin pressed together. Their two bodies close again and starting a whole new story.

And as Kiki looked into her eyes, knowing what it was to see her mother glowing back at her, Leah could not have felt more beautiful.

Thirty-Three

Eighteen months later

'OK, are you ready for this?' Leah glanced at the rickety steps that led all the way up the hillside. 'I think you'd better hold my hand.'

'No, I go…' Kiki, determined as ever, held onto the wooden railings and immediately scampered up the first three slabs.

'I'm behind you!' Leah squealed, sneaking up and tickling her neck.

'Come on, girls.' Eric called out from further down the track, a picnic blanket rolled up under his arm and the bags slung around his neck. 'Look at those two, they're beating you to it.' He gestured to the top, where Cheryl and Alan were waiting.

'Yeah, one yoga session a week clearly isn't enough for me anymore, I can't keep up with them!'

Leah helped Kiki, lifting her off the ground halfway there and letting her walk up the last part herself. Reaching the highest point, they stepped out into a vast clearing of flat grass, cupped by the ancient ruins of Loganberg Castle all around it. The centre was a huge mound of earth covered in trees and wedges of roots that could be explored and climbed at all angles.

Eric let Twig off the lead and he tore around the

space, barking excitedly and wagging his tail as he wove in and out of the bushes.

'What about there in the shade?' Cheryl suggested.

'Anywhere I can put all this down will do!' said Eric, following her over and opening a button on this shirt.

They spread the blanket in a smattering of gingham and started putting out the food. Miniature pies, salads, sandwiches, and crisps. Chilled bottles of fizzy drinks, scones, and fruit flan. Cheryl's chocolate layer cake and a large flask of tea.

Leah sprawled out in her jeans and t-shirt, listening to the birds as they chattered in the leaves above her head. As Twig darted around, racing after his ball, she remembered how tiny he had been that first time she had laid eyes on him, his fuzzy little form so different to the shapely, boisterous dog he had become.

He chased something, pouncing away behind the cobbled pillars, and she followed the structure with her eyes, trailing over the flint and rubble as it rose majestically, still impressive after so many centuries. She traced the very top where it arched into the heavens, giving way to an expanse of sky broken only by the buttery sunlight.

Eric brushed her arm, and she turned to him. Kiki was on his lap, tucking into a plate of snacks Cheryl had given her.

'Looks like he's waking up,' he beamed, nodding his head at the pushchair next to Alan.

'Hello you,' said Leah, sliding over to Casper, who was just stirring. His teal eyes fluttered open and she smoothed his sandy hair. He gazed up at Leah and smiled, taking in the scenery all around him. She pulled him into her arms. 'Someone's getting heavy these days!'

'Well, he is six months now.' Cheryl waved at him from her deckchair.

'And he's going to be a handful. Did I tell you he nearly shuffled out of the front door the other day?'

'You can't complain about that,' Eric said knowingly. 'Come on!' He bounced Kiki up and down on his knee.

'I wouldn't dare!' she laughed, still marvelling over how two siblings could be so different.

Casper had come along when Kiki had just turned two, and Leah had spent her pregnancy dreading a similar birth to the first one. But when the time had arrived, it was a smooth labour, and he had been born in a fraction of the time it had taken to deliver Kiki.

He was the polar opposite of how his older sister had been, and was generally satisfied playing in his bouncy chair and watching the world go by. But Leah couldn't turn away for a minute if she left him on the floor and she knew that in no time, he'd be on his feet with Kiki and Twig.

Kiki had gone from strength to strength, both physically and as the fun and feisty character she was blossoming into. The screams and tantrums had mellowed into a gobbledegook of vocabulary, and her kindness was shining through in the way she took charge of the beloved dog and her brother.

If Leah had learned anything, it was never to compare. Just enjoy her own bubble with patience and watch the bonds grow in their own precious time. The moment she had embraced this, motherhood had bloomed into how she knew it now.

'Cake, please!'

'Well, if you want that, you'll have to come over here,' said Alan, reaching out and picking Kiki up. 'Nana will cut you a nice big piece if you're good.'

'Maybe even a bigger slice than yours!' Cheryl nudged Alan as he feigned shock and they busied themselves with the chocolatey delight.

Leah kissed Casper's head and gave him a banana. He chomped it down between glugs of milk, making her chuckle with his creamy grin. She glanced at Eric to find his gaze was already upon her, lit up in the honeyed rays and full of something inexplicable.

Her hair was in a messy braid, with strands falling effortlessly at the front, and with her skin already tanned from the fast onset of spring, a dab of tinted moisturiser was enough for a healthy shimmer, topped off with a natural smear of blush and a rosy slick of pink lip balm. Fresh as a daisy, with nature at its best.

After all, what more did she need when she was juggling two children with a relaunched career as a journalist? Once she had sold the story and it had gone viral for exposing the truth about *SySTEM*, the offers had come flooding in and she was carving out a name for herself now she was freelance. Working from home had been the answer, keeping her buoyant and distracted through the tougher times, while being around more to enjoy Kiki and Casper – and, of course, Twig.

Eric moved across to Leah, wrapping an arm around her and cradling their son. Then he touched her face with his other hand and no words were needed. He whispered that he loved her and grazed her with the proudest kiss.

'Mummy…' a voice sounded behind them. 'Mummy, walk?'

Leah swivelled to face Kiki. There stood the pretty little girl, her feet planted firmly on the luscious green ground. Her skin was drizzled with sunshine, and the ribbons in her dark hair flickered in the balmy breeze. They were the exact powder blue of her floaty dress, with its pleated bodice and tulle puffball skirt. Her adoring eyes were full of hope as she stretched out her fingers to beckon.

'Yes, please!' Leah passed Casper safely to Eric. Then

she got up and took Kiki's hand. 'There's nothing I'd love more.'

They dashed away down the gentle slope, picking up their pace as they crossed the swaying grass. Then Leah crouched deep into the dandelions, counting the footsteps that had lived inside her dreams. Watching every moment as Kiki ran, fast and steady, straight into her arms.

Acknowledgements

After surviving the rollercoaster of early motherhood and enduring a toxic work culture in the beauty industry, I felt compelled to blend those experiences in this novel and share the light at the end of both tunnels.

There are several amazing people I could not have done this without.

My two incredible children, Blake and Scarlett, who have both inspired this story. Blake, your very slow birth and the almost worrying level of contentment you had as a toddler was just you being the chilled-out, happy and intelligent young man that you are today. And Scarlett, your constant screaming and inability to be satisfied no matter what, was simply you talking shape as the strong, creative and fun-loving young woman that you have become. I could not be prouder.

Andy, you are the best husband and father out there. You work so hard and you are a rock, supporting me through the difficult times, celebrating when the good things come, and making our house of vinyl records and floor-to-ceiling comic figures a home. I love you.

Margaret, the mother of dreams. You have guided me through parenthood and everything else with kindness, compassion, laughter and selfless care. I am eternally grateful.

Derek, my stepdad, who has been the most terrific grandfather. A voice of reason through the chaos, and only you had the power to get the babies off to sleep! I'm forever thankful.

Jasper the beagle and Badger the springer spaniel. You are both Twig, rolled into one. The happiness you have brought to our lives is indescribable.

Finally, to Stuart and everyone at SRL Publishing, a huge thank you for believing in this book and bringing it out into the world.

SRL Publishing don't just publish books, we also do our best in keeping this world sustainable. In the UK alone, over 77 million books are destroyed each year, unsold and unread, due to overproduction and bigger profit margins.

Our business model is inherently sustainable by only printing what we sell. While this means our cost price is much higher, it means we have minimum waste and zero returns. We made a public promise in 2020 to never overprint our books for the sake of profit.

We give back to our planet by calculating the number of trees used for our products so we can then replace them. We also calculate our carbon emissions and support projects which reduce C02. These same projects also support the United Nations Sustainable Development Goals.

The way we operate means we knowingly waive our profit margins for the sake of the environment. Every book sold via the SRL website plants at least one tree.

To find out more, please visit
www.srlpublishing.co.uk/responsibility

9 781915 073570